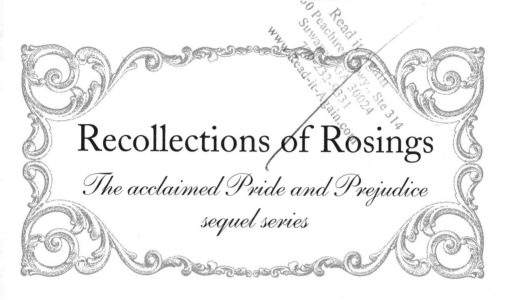

Recollections of Rosings

*The acclaimed Pride and Prejudice
sequel series*

*The Pemberley Chronicles:
Book 8*

DEVISED AND COMPILED BY
Rebecca Ann Collins

sourcebooks
landmark

Published by Sourcebooks Landmark, an imprint of Sourcebooks, Inc.
P.O. Box 4410, Naperville, Illinois 60567-4410
(630) 961-3900
FAX: (630) 961-2168
www.sourcebooks.com

Originally printed and bound in Australia by Print Plus, Sydney, NSW, September 2003. Reprinted October 2004.

Library of Congress Cataloging-in-Publication Data

Collins, Rebecca Ann.
    Recollections of Rosings / devised and compiled by Rebecca Ann Collins.
        p. cm. — (The Pemberley chronicles ; bk. 8)
    "The acclaimed Pride and Prejudice sequel series."
    1. Sisters—England—Fiction. 2. England—Social life and customs—19th century—Fiction. 3. Gentry—England—Fiction. I. Austen, Jane, 1775–1817. Pride and prejudice. II. Title.
    PR9619.4.C65R43 2010
    823'.92—dc22
                                    2009046822

Printed and bound in the United States of America
VP 10 9 8 7 6 5 4 3 2 1

To Helen,

With many thanks for affording me the opportunity in July 1996 to begin work on the Pemberley series.

An Introduction . . .

IT MIGHT APPEAR A little odd that in this modern age, with its quick and easy marriages and even quicker and easier divorces, one could be preoccupied with the marital situations of women in Victorian England.

Yet I have always been intrigued by them.

Their capacity for endurance and generosity was quite remarkable. Many women married early, bore several children, found themselves widowed by disease or war, and usually married again to escape the indignity of dependence upon the charity of relatives or the dreaded workhouse. Doubtless, some did so for convenience or simple survival, having no means of support for themselves or their children in a world without welfare. But others found genuine love—not fleeting, romantic rapture, but deeper feelings shared with mature men, whom they came to esteem and cherish and with whom they enjoyed enduring and often passionate relationships.

Many women left diaries and letters containing moving personal testimony to this phenomenon, in an age that paid little attention to the emotional needs of married women. Once she had raised a family, a woman's satisfaction was supposed to be complete. That she would yearn for the warmth of romance or passion was almost unimaginable.

In *Recollections of Rosings*, I chose to explore the lives of two sisters—Catherine and Becky Collins—their aspirations and experience of love and marriage. Because they were my own rather than Jane Austen's characters, I was less constrained and even as I retained the ambience of traditional stability implied by Rosings and Pemberley, it was possible to follow their lives down very different paths than those of, say, Elizabeth and Jane Bennet. Both sisters have had their share of the slings and arrows of life, but neither is ready to retire into comfortable middle-age or the pointless social round of gossip and match-making that was supposed to occupy the time of older women of the day.

For many of us, a sudden change in circumstances or the return of someone from the past can pose an unforeseen dilemma or throw up a new opportunity.

Both Catherine and Becky must face such situations and deal with them alone. As mature women, with the capacity to enjoy rewarding relationships, they confront the consequences of decisions made in youth and draw upon their inner resources as they search for deeper meaning and greater satisfaction in their lives.

The generous warmth of one sister and the resilient determination of the other made the telling of their stories worthwhile and particularly pleasurable for me.

I hope my readers will agree.

RAC 2003
www.geocities.com/shadesofpemberley

For the benefit of those readers who wish to be reminded of the characters and their relationships to one another, an *aide-memoire* is provided in the appendix.

Prologue

IT WAS THE MORNING after the wedding of Darcy Gardiner and Kathryn O'Hare. At Pemberley, where some of the guests had stayed the night, almost everyone had risen late and, having made very leisurely preparations, processed downstairs where breakfast was being served.

Only Mr Darcy had risen earlier than most, taken his usual ride around the park, breakfasted, and collected his mail from the footman. Taking it into the morning room, where he read his newspapers at his usual table beside a window overlooking the terrace, now bathed in warm sunlight, he opened his letters, methodically sorting out the personal from the business communications as he did so.

One in particular puzzled him.

He did not recognise the hand, nor when he turned it over to read the sender's name, did he immediately recall the face of a Mr John Adams.

But, a moment or two later, he had it.

Mr Adams was the curator at Rosings Park, the late Lady Catherine de Bourgh's estate, which was now managed by a trust for the National Estate. Mr Darcy was a member of the trust, though he did not attend every meeting. His nephew Jonathan Bingley represented him, and he did now remember that a Mr Adams had been appointed to the position of curator a year or more ago.

He was, Mr Darcy recalled, absurdly young to be so well qualified, but came very well recommended and was engaged to catalogue and document the many priceless treasures of Lady Catherine's great estate. Jonathan had had no doubt at all Mr Adams was the right man for the job.

He is better educated than most and has a fine understanding of Art, having studied in Europe. He dined with us at Netherfield last week and my dear wife, whose knowledge of these matters far exceeds my own, having had the opportunity to converse extensively with him, has pronounced him suitable. I think we need have no further concerns, Jonathan had written, and Mr Darcy had concurred. On these matters, he trusted his nephew's judgment implicitly.

Besides, Jonathan Bingley had himself been the manager of the Rosings estate for some years and would be well able to judge Mr Adams's qualifications for the tasks he was to perform.

Assuming Mr Adams's letter contained matters relating to the Rosings Park trust, Mr Darcy put it aside and returned to it only after he had finished reading an entertaining letter from a favourite correspondent—Dr Charles Bingley, Jonathan's eldest son.

He wrote to apologise for his non-attendance at Darcy Gardiner's wedding, due to urgent and unavoidable matters arising at his hospital in Hertfordshire. Written some days ago and unusually delayed in the post, the letter proceeded to give Mr Darcy a detailed and hilarious account of an incident concerning a local dignitary, who had attempted to force his way into a meeting of the hospital board, to protest their objection to his plan to extend his railroad through vacant land adjacent to the hospital.

Charles wrote:

Quite clearly, he assumed that his wealth and standing in the community gave him the right to do as he pleased with the route of his railroad. He was outraged that the Hospital Board should have objected on the grounds that a railroad running alongside Bells Field, in such close proximity to the hospital, would disrupt the work of the hospital and disturb the patients.

You will be happy to hear, Sir, that he was given short shrift by the board and urged to find some other field through which to run his trains. He left in such an explosive state of rage that we expected to see him return e'er long as a patient himself. I have not seen such infernal arrogance in all my years in this profession, nor have I witnessed it so well put down!

Mr Darcy was still chuckling when he put it away and returned to the letter from Mr John Adams.

On opening it, however, and reading the first few lines, he fell silent and his countenance altered so radically as to be quite extraordinary. As he continued reading, so shocked was he at the news it contained that he rose to his feet, scattering the rest of his unopened correspondence on the floor, and hurried out of the room and up the stairs with unusual urgency.

At the top of the stairs, he met Elizabeth, who, on seeing her husband's face, knew at once that something was very wrong. So pale and shaken was he, she was very afraid that he had been taken ill.

"Darcy, what is it? What has happened? Tell me, are you unwell?" she asked and he answered her quickly, "No, no, Elizabeth, I am perfectly well, but something quite catastrophic has occurred."

So saying, he took her arm and returned with her to their private sitting room, knowing they would not be disturbed there. Seating her down upon the sofa, he handed her the letter from Mr Adams.

Elizabeth, somewhat bewildered, read it quickly and as she did so, looked across at her husband, understanding now his extraordinary demeanour.

Mr Adams was writing to inform Mr Darcy that, on the Friday night, a fire had erupted in one of the rooms below stairs at Rosings. Undetected, it had spread through the lower floors of the building and most of the West Wing before it broke through into the main hall and was discovered by the caretaker, who had raised the alarm.

Despite the best efforts of the staff and many people on the estate who had rushed to assist, much of the impressive mansion that had been part of Lady Catherine de Bourgh's domain had been destroyed.

There was no mistaking John Adams's despondency, as he wrote:

Little remains undamaged, save for the chapel, the library, and school room, as well as the music room with its collection of manuscripts, all of which, being situated in the East Wing and separated from the path of the fire by the main courtyard, were able to be saved. So also were some of the private apartments and guest rooms on the floors above. The rest, it is my melancholy duty to report, is for the most part beyond reclamation.

There was more detail of some of the treasures lost and other valuable items fortuitously recovered from the ashes of one or other of the great rooms of her Ladyship's mansion and, in conclusion, there was a request for instructions as to how he was to proceed, but Elizabeth had stopped reading.

Going to her husband's side, as he remained still shocked, speechless, she sat beside him.

"It is impossible to imagine such a disaster at Rosings. How could it happen? Surely, it cannot have been an accident?" she asked.

Mr Darcy shook his head.

"It is entirely possible, Lizzie. My aunt had been urged often enough to have certain alterations made, especially below stairs, to improve the heating in the staff quarters and be rid of log fires and wood-burning stoves, but she would not hear of it. Rosings, despite its apparent opulence, was in reality an old-fashioned edifice, with few concessions to modern living, especially where the staff were concerned," he explained. "Since my aunt's death, when the house was no longer a family residence, the trust has been unwilling to spend money on such things, preferring instead to maintain the areas that visitors see, enhancing the grounds and reception rooms and protecting the rich accessories. Jonathan has tried to advise them, but on matters pertaining to expenditure, the lawyers are not easily persuaded."

The mention of Jonathan Bingley reminded Elizabeth that Mr and Mrs Bingley were still at Pemberley; they had planned to spend a few more days in Derbyshire before returning to Netherfield.

"Jonathan—of course, we must tell him at once, and Catherine Harrison, oh my God! Darcy, how shall we tell Catherine? Rosings was her home for most of her life!"

Elizabeth had never liked Rosings; it was far too grandiose and pretentious for her taste, but to think of it gutted and destroyed... it was just too shocking to comprehend. Besides, there were many priceless antiquities and artworks in the house that she knew from Darcy, had been collected by the de Bourghs over several generations. That most of these remarkable items may have been destroyed in the fire was difficult to contemplate. Mr Darcy's explanation of the ill-advised parsimony of Lady Catherine and, since her death, a penny-pinching attitude on the part of the trust appalled Elizabeth, who was accustomed to the meticulous maintenance undertaken at Pemberley.

Downstairs in the kitchens of Pemberley, which, thanks to the master's determination to maintain the best standards for his staff, were far more salubrious than those at Rosings, Mrs Jenny Grantham, the housekeeper, presided over the long kitchen table.

Her staff, having cleared away the last of the late breakfast, were enjoying a well-deserved cup of tea. They were still talking of the wedding: of how handsome young Mr Darcy Gardiner had looked and how fortunate he had been to have found such a charming bride as Miss Kathryn O'Hare.

What a year it had been, so many celebrations... engagements, weddings—not one but two of them in one year! And now there was Lizzie Carr's new baby! The young maids could barely contain their excitement.

But Mrs Grantham was being nostalgic, recalling the days many years ago when, as a very young girl, she had been chosen by Mrs Reynolds, her aunt, who had been housekeeper at Pemberley, to attend upon Mr Darcy's bride.

Jenny admitted she had been nervous. "I never knew if the mistress would like me. If she did not, I may well have been sent packing; but I was lucky, Mrs Darcy was ever so good to me and asked for me to be her personal maid."

She was telling them of the halcyon days when there had been an annual ball at Pemberley and several grand dinner parties every year, with many distinguished guests arriving and staying on overnight or for some days.

"There was Miss Georgiana's wedding, of course, and Miss Cassy's wedding—you would not believe how much there was to do. You would be that busy you had no time to stop and think how tired you were!"

All their lives were far quieter now, she explained to the young ones around the table.

They were all very relaxed, enjoying the tales of days past, when one of the chamber maids came rushing in with the extraordinary story that she had seen Mr and Mrs Darcy with Mrs Catherine Harrison and her daughter, Miss Lilian, and then she had heard a loud exclamation followed by sobbing.

The maid was sure it was Mrs Harrison weeping and Miss Lilian trying to comfort her mother, she said, but she had no idea what it was about.

No one said a word; then Jenny Grantham rose from her chair and was off upstairs, determined to discover what had occurred. If there had been some bad news, her mistress would need her, she was sure of it.

Even though they were all curious to know what was happening, none of the other servants followed her. She alone could go to her mistress, confident that her concern would never be misunderstood for idle curiosity. Jenny Grantham had lived through too many difficult years with the family at Pemberley and shared too many crises with Elizabeth to worry about protocol. They were more like two friends than mistress and servant.

She met Mr Darcy going downstairs, his face drawn and pale, and then found Mrs Darcy coming out of the room occupied by Mrs Harrison and her young daughter, Lilian. There was no mistaking it; Elizabeth looked shocked and disturbed.

"Jenny," she said, reaching for her arm and moving towards her private apartments, "something quite dreadful has happened."

Jenny Grantham's heart sank; "Not another sudden death, please God," she prayed silently. There had been too many of those.

"What is it, ma'am? What has happened?" she asked anxiously.

"There's been a fire at Rosings. Mr Darcy has received a letter from Mr Adams, the curator," Elizabeth explained and, seeing Jenny's expression, added, "and much of Lady Catherine's mansion has been destroyed."

Stunned, Jenny stood with a hand to her mouth, suppressing a gasp of horror, as Elizabeth continued, "That is all we know at this time, but poor Mrs Harrison and her daughter will want to leave for Kent later today, so would you ask Lucy to help them pack and tell Thomas to have the carriage ready to take them to meet the afternoon train?"

Jenny was so astonished she was unable to say much more than "Yes, ma'am, of course, ma'am," before returning downstairs to break the news to the servants. It was shocking, terrible news, yet Jenny's predominant emotion was one of relief.

At least, as far they knew, no one was dead.

Elizabeth returned to comfort Catherine and Lilian, while Mr Darcy sought out Jonathan Bingley, who'd just returned from a brisk walk in the park.

"Ah Jonathan, I am glad to have found you, I'm afraid there has been some bad news," he said and drew Jonathan into the morning room, where a footman who had found the scattered letters was collecting them into a neat pile. Waiting only until the man had left the room, Mr Darcy handed

Jonathan Bingley the curator's letter. Jonathan, a little puzzled, took it over to the window to read.

Mr Darcy sat in his chair, silently regarding his nephew, but not for long. It took Jonathan only a few minutes to read swiftly though John Adams's letter and as he did so, he exclaimed, "Good God, this cannot be true!" as he strode back to where Mr Darcy waited. "When did this arrive, sir?"

Mr Darcy was uncertain. "It must have arrived yesterday, whilst we were at Colley Dale for the wedding. It cannot have been earlier or I should have seen it. It is likely that one of the servants received it and put it aside with the rest of my letters. I opened it this morning."

"The letter is almost two days old—the news must be all over London," said Jonathan and even as he spoke, they heard the sound of a carriage on the gravel drive. Moments later Anthony Tate, owner of the *Matlock Review*, and his wife, Rebecca, were admitted.

Mr Tate had a copy of that morning's paper in his hand and held it out to Mr Darcy. The front page carried an account of the fire at Rosings Park, accompanied by a remarkable picture of the great mansion in flames.

The artist had done well.

"Mr Darcy, I did not know if you had heard yet, what with the wedding; I felt it my duty to come over, and Becky had to see Catherine."

He seemed almost apologetic at being the bearer of such bad tidings. His wife stood quietly beside him, awkward, unable to speak.

But Mr Darcy greeted them warmly and thanked them for their courtesy.

"I have received information from the curator, Mr Adams, but I am grateful for your concern, Tate. We have broken the news to Mrs Harrison a little while ago; Lizzie is with her now."

Rebecca asked if she might go to her sister and when Mr Darcy replied, "Of course," she left them to rush upstairs. She was well aware of the effect the news must have had upon Catherine, who had lived all her life on the Rosings Estate; it was the only real home she had known. Becky knew it would be a dreadful blow.

Jonathan Bingley had been standing in the centre of the room, unable to believe completely what he had read in John Adams's letter, until he saw the account in the newspaper. There were more details and some speculation as to the cause of the fire—a suggestion, quite without proof, that a servant may have been careless and left a fireplace unattended. It was a dreadful prospect.

"What do you propose to do, Mr Darcy?" Tate asked.

Mr Darcy replied, in a somewhat matter-of-fact manner, which surprised him, "Well, I was about to suggest that Jonathan, who represents me on the Trust, should go down to Rosings; there will be some kind of enquiry, I expect, and the trust will decide how to proceed," and turning to his nephew added, "that is if you had not intended to be doing something else, Jonathan."

Jonathan may have had other plans—such as fishing or visiting his sisters—and it was unlikely that he would enjoy the journey to Kent in these circumstances, but he knew it was his duty to go and agreed at once.

"I shall have to explain to Anna and the children; I assume they may remain at Pemberley until I return?"

Once again Mr Darcy said, "Of course."

Jonathan nodded, asked to be excused, and went upstairs to prepare for his departure.

Anthony Tate explained how the news had been received from London by electric telegraph.

"I am very sorry, Mr Darcy, it will be a great blow to your family to lose such a magnificent mansion."

Mr Darcy acknowledged that it would; even though Rosings had been too opulent for his personal taste, it had been in the de Bourgh family for many years, and it was difficult to accept that it was suddenly and irretrievably lost.

After the Tates had departed, Catherine Harrison and her daughter Lilian left with their maid to take the train to London and thence to Kent. With them went Jonathan Bingley and Mr Darcy's steward, Mr Grantham, who had instructions from his master to do everything possible to assist Mrs Harrison and her family.

Jonathan parted reluctantly from his family. Anna Bingley and their two sons, Nicholas and Simon, were to remain at Pemberley until he returned to report to Mr Darcy.

"You do understand, dearest, do you not, that I have to go? Someone has to represent Mr Darcy and the family and ensure that the right decisions are made. John Adams is too new and has not the authority to do so. There will be a great deal to be done in a very short time; I expect to return within the week, but cannot be certain," he said as he bade farewell to his wife.

Anna smiled, "Of course you must go, Jonathan. Do not concern yourself about us; we shall miss you, of course, but the boys will have fun with Anthony and James while Mrs Darcy and I will have plenty to talk about. Besides, it will give me time to do those sketches I have been meaning to make of the grounds and the house. Pemberley looks splendid at this time of year; I shall make the best of the opportunity. Poor Catherine will need your support, especially as I understand Dr Harrison is not in very good health."

Catherine Harrison was Anna's cousin and she felt great sympathy for her; besides, Anna knew well how dutiful and loyal to Mr Darcy her husband was, and he was grateful for her understanding and sensibility.

They had hoped to enjoy a pleasant holiday in Derbyshire with the Darcys; this was a most inauspicious interruption to their plans.

END OF PROLOGUE

RECOLLECTIONS OF ROSINGS

Part One

C ATHERINE HAD TRIED MANY times during the journey from Derbyshire to Kent, first by train and then by carriage to Rosings, to imagine what it would be like.

From the scant information in Mr Adams's letter to Mr Darcy, it had not been easy to create a picture of how Rosings would look after the fire. She could not contemplate it. The scale and grandeur of the building, set as it was in a formal park of much beauty, surrounded by hundreds of acres of orchard, woods, and farmland, had so impressed themselves upon her mind since childhood that it was well nigh impossible for her to picture its destruction.

She felt stunned, disbelieving, exactly as she recalled feeling when told that her father, Reverend Collins, had died suddenly of a heart attack, which had felled him without warning as he inspected the chapel at Rosings with Lady Catherine de Bourgh. Then she had been a mere girl, yet it was she who had had to support her mother and comfort her younger sisters, while still unable to accept it herself.

Which is probably why the shock was so severe, when the carriage turned off the road into the long drive and there, before their eyes, was revealed the terrible truth.

Nothing had prepared them for this.

It was nearly four days since the fire, yet parts of the building were still smouldering—the smoke, acrid and dark, drifting upwards—while everywhere across the once immaculate park was strewn the debris of days past. Scorched walls, crumbling masonry, and shattered windows—all those many dozens of windows that her father used to speak of in a hushed voice, whose glazing had cost Sir Lewis de Bourgh a fortune—shattered now, hung with ragged bits of rich curtains blowing in the wind.

Catherine gasped. She could hardly breathe, and beside her Lilian was weeping as Jonathan and Mr Grantham helped them alight.

The driver of the vehicle they had hired stood beside them open-mouthed, so shocked he seemed to have been paralysed, unable even to recall the agreed hire when Mr Grantham attempted to pay him.

"Jesus!" he said. "Jesus, I never seen such a sight before!" and it seemed he spoke for them all.

Standing before the blackened entrance to the mansion, they were met by Mr Adams, who came swiftly to their side, followed by the manager, Mr Benson, who had been with the estate for many years, since Jonathan had relinquished the position after Lady Catherine's death.

Jonathan, having conferred with both gentlemen, asked if the ladies wished to see inside.

"Yes," said Catherine and Lilian together.

Whilst warning them that it was far too hazardous to enter certain parts of the building, where beams and walls were in danger of collapsing and shards of glass lay everywhere, Mr Benson conducted the party through the main courtyard into the vestibule and let them see some of the devastation wrought by the fire within the house.

Many areas had been completely destroyed.

Equally, Mr Adams was at pains to show them how the entire East Wing had been preserved by being cut off from the fire.

"We were most fortunate in the weather on that night… there was very little wind and what there was blew from east to west, thereby pushing the flames away from the courtyard and fountain, protecting the East Wing. Some rain on the following day helped douse the remaining fires, but it was, alas, too late to save the main building and the West Wing, which held many of Sir Lewis de Bourgh's trophies," Mr Adams was explaining, when Lilian, no longer able to hold back her feelings, burst into tears.

Catherine, though distraught herself, remained for the most part calm and collected, understanding her daughter's distress. As a child she had explored every nook and cranny of Rosings. A particular favourite of her father's patron, Lady Catherine de Bourgh, she had been permitted certain privileges at Rosings, making it a special place.

To Lilian likewise, coming from the modest parsonage at Hunsford, where she was the youngest of three children, permission to wander at will among the treasures of Rosings had added a touch of magic to her otherwise prosaic childhood. Now, much of it was gone.

Jonathan suggested that the ladies return to Hunsford and rest awhile after the strain of their journey. He asked if Mr Benson would arrange for him to be accommodated at the house and was happy to hear that rooms had been prepared for him in the East Wing.

He did not realise, however, that there was still another shock in store for them, though of a somewhat different kind.

Catherine and Lilian had gone out into the courtyard, still in earnest conversation with the manager Mr Benson, who had been one of the first on the scene after the fire had been discovered. Following some yards behind, Mr Adams pulled Jonathan back to tell him that Dr Harrison had suffered a heart attack on the night of the fire and was confined to bed at the parsonage at Hunsford, with a nurse in charge.

Speaking in a low voice, he explained, "He worked as hard as the rest of us, never sparing himself, and no one knew he had suffered severe palpitations until one of the men found him gasping for breath and rushed to summon Dr Whitelaw, who fortuitously was also present, helping me save some of the precious books from Sir Lewis de Bourgh's study."

In a voice that betrayed his genuine fears, he added, "Mr Bingley, had he not been here, I dread to think what might have occurred."

Jonathan was anxious to discover how seriously ill Dr Harrison was. "What has Dr Whitelaw prescribed for him?" he asked.

"Complete rest and daily medication. I know he calls at the parsonage twice a day and has asked the nurse to summon him if there is any change in Dr Harrison's condition. I should perhaps explain that Dr Harrison expressly forbade me to send word of his affliction to Mr Darcy, lest Mrs Harrison be even more distressed by the news. He insisted that he would tell her himself and explain that it was only a temporary indisposition."

"And is it? What is Dr Whitelaw's prognosis?" asked Jonathan.

"While I am not privy to the detail of it, Mr Bingley, as a friend of the family and with a particular interest in Miss Lilian, I did inquire on their behalf. Dr Whitelaw revealed that Dr Harrison has been in indifferent health for several years. I believe he has carried a heavy load of work since the rector at the parish of Lower Apsley retired. The exertion and stress he was under on account of the fire may well have been the last straw, so to speak. However, Dr Whitelaw hopes that with rest and careful nursing, he may recover to live comfortably for a few more years."

Mr Adams spoke with a degree of concern and understanding that did him great credit, a fact that Jonathan Bingley did not fail to notice.

He shook his head. He could scarce believe what he was hearing. Catherine Harrison would have to cope with two profound calamities at once.

Jonathan had great respect and affection for her, having once been married to her younger sister, Amelia-Jane. Catherine had supported him through the tribulation and trauma of a failing marriage, the loss of two infant children, and finally, tragically, the death in a most horrific accident of his young wife. He knew she was a woman of strength and compassion. Jonathan had valued both qualities then and was confident of her ability to deal with and survive her family's present misfortunes.

Having first reassured Mr Adams that Mr Harrison would not learn how he had discovered the truth about his illness, Jonathan set out to join the ladies and accompany them to the parsonage at Hunsford. He was determined to do everything possible to assist Catherine and her daughter, who might now be left to cope alone.

Arriving at the parsonage, they were met by two grim-faced servants, clearly unable to conceal their concern. Catherine assumed they were still suffering from the shock of the fire at Rosings, as indeed was she. But when she saw the housekeeper in tears, she began to worry.

"Mrs Giles, what is it?" she asked and then, as Lilian ran towards the stairs, the nurse came out of the bedroom and Catherine knew without a word being said that Dr Harrison must be very ill indeed.

As Jonathan stood helpless in the hall, mother and daughter rushed up the stairs and it was only with the greatest difficulty that the nurse persuaded them not to enter the main bedroom, where she said Dr Harrison was asleep after taking his medication. Dr Whitelaw had visited his patient that morning, she said. Jonathan could not hear everything that was said, but her tone, though gentle, was firm as she urged them to return with her to the parlour where she would explain everything.

As they did so, Mrs Giles went to fetch the tea tray, and Jonathan followed them into the parlour. The arrival shortly afterwards of Dr Whitelaw for his usual afternoon visit to his patient afforded them an opportunity to discover the facts about Dr Harrison's condition.

In his letter to his wife Anna, Jonathan provided some detail of what had occurred but could in no way convey either the full extent of the ravages of the fire nor the dismay he had felt at learning of Dr Harrison's condition.

It is impossible to describe the devastation we have seen here, he wrote.

Rosings as I knew it, and we have seen it often, is no more. Only one section of the grand mansion—the East Wing—remains, spared by the merest chance from the fire. The rest, all those splendid rooms, their rich furnishings and accessories, are reduced to a smoking ruin.

Even the great park seems scorched and bereft of its beauty. Poor Catherine and Lilian are both distraught; this place has been home to them for all of their lives. But, dearest, that is not all they must bear, for since arriving here, we have learned from Mr Adams and had confirmed by Dr Whitelaw that Dr Harrison, while trying to help salvage some of the treasures from the fire, suffered a severe heart attack. He is now confined to bed.

It is surely the very worst thing that could have befallen this family at this time, for Catherine and her young daughter Lilian are alone here and must fend for themselves. Their only son is a midshipman in the Navy, sailing somewhere between Southampton and the West Indies, while their elder daughter lives in India, where her husband is chaplain to some regiment or other, keeping order in the colony! Obviously, they cannot be much comfort or help to their mother at this time.

Fortunately, they are not entirely without friends, because Mr Benson, the manager, is a kind and reliable man, and there is also the young curator, Mr Adams, who I think has formed an attachment for Lilian and seems ready to do all he can to assist them. I intend to speak with both these gentlemen and ascertain what needs be done to help Catherine and her daughter—for they will need much help and advice at least until Dr Harrison is on the way to recovery.

If he were not to recover sufficiently to carry on as incumbent at Hunsford, the family will have to move from the parsonage into other accommodation on the estate or elsewhere. Where will they go? This is not immediately clear to me, and I shall need to discuss it with Mr Darcy if and when the need arises.

I shall write to Mr Darcy and also to Becky Tate, but I doubt anyone can provide us with an answer immediately. The Rosings Park Trust will probably have to decide. It is, I am sure you will agree, dearest Anna, a most unfortunate situation, very distressing indeed for Catherine and young Lilian, who seems totally desolated by the catastrophe...

When Anna Bingley took her husband's letter to Elizabeth, she was so grieved, she could not say anything for a while. Catherine Harrison was the eldest daughter of her oldest and dearest friend, Charlotte Lucas. Elizabeth could imagine how Charlotte would feel when all these matters became known to her, as they must very soon. While it was unlikely that Charlotte, having endured the patronage of Her Ladyship for many years, would have quite the same feelings as her eldest daughter, Elizabeth was certain she would be deeply shocked by the destruction of Rosings.

Presently Elizabeth stood up and said, "I shall go to Mr Darcy at once and ask him if there is anything that can be done for them."

"Perhaps the Trust will consider letting them stay on at Hunsford for some time?" suggested Anna hopefully and Elizabeth was inclined to agree.

But, on speaking with her husband, Elizabeth was disappointed to learn this was not very likely, since the parish of Hunsford, being the largest living on the Rosings estate, would need an active incumbent.

"Particularly so, because Mr Harrison has been serving the parish of Lower Apsley as well for some months, and it would not be possible to leave both positions vacant for too long," Mr Darcy explained.

He did say, however, that he intended to urge Jonathan Bingley to persuade the Trust to let the Harrisons have one of the vacant houses on the estate, if and when a new incumbent was appointed to Hunsford.

"My aunt, Lady Catherine, would have wished it; she was exceedingly fond of Catherine, considered her one of her own family, and regarded Mr Harrison with great respect. It would not be in the spirit of her will to leave them without a place to live, especially if Dr Harrison does not make a complete recovery."

Seeing his wife's anxious expression, he sought to reassure her.

"You must not worry, my dear, let me assure you we *will* find a way to help them."

Elizabeth returned to Anna in much better spirits, confident that their husbands together would find some means to ensure that Catherine and her family were not abandoned as a result of the destruction of Rosings.

Chapter Two

JONATHAN BINGLEY TOOK THE news to Catherine that the Rosings Trust would wait a month or more, to allow time for Dr Harrison to recover, before deciding upon the appointment of another incumbent to the living at Hunsford.

Furthermore, he said, if it became necessary due to continuing ill health for Dr Harrison to retire, the family would be offered the Dower House as a residence, for whatever time they needed to make their own arrangements.

This suggestion, said Jonathan, had come directly from Mr Darcy, in view of Dr Harrison's long service to the parish and the late Lady Catherine de Bourgh's particular affection for Mrs Harrison.

The suggestion, he said, had been accepted without question by the Trust.

For Jonathan it was an especially poignant subject, because when he had been Lady Catherine's manager and lived on the Rosings estate with his wife Amelia-Jane, the Dower House had been their home too. Small in comparison with Rosings, it was an elegant and comfortable residence nonetheless, and he recalled it with a mixture of nostalgia and sadness.

He noted however that Catherine was clearly pleased and having ensured that she had thanked him sufficiently and asked that her gratitude be conveyed to Mr Darcy and the Trust, she hurried upstairs to tell her husband of the offer.

Dr Harrison, though he continued to insist that he would soon be well enough to resume his parish duties, was relieved to hear the news. Quite clearly, he too had been anxious about the future of his wife and young daughter.

Later that night, Catherine wrote to her sister, Rebecca Tate, telling her how much she appreciated the offer of the Dower House, and though she tried bravely to suggest that it may not be necessary, because Dr Harrison may yet recover fully, Becky could read between the lines.

There was not a very great chance of Dr Harrison making a complete recovery. Furthermore, she had also received that week a letter from Mr Jonathan Bingley, in which he had made it quite clear that Catherine would need both help and comfort in the days ahead.

Keen to be with her sister and share in the cares that must now fall upon her alone, and discounting Catherine's reassurances, Becky packed a trunk, caught a train, and not long afterwards, arrived at the Hunsford parsonage with her maid, Nelly. The joy with which Catherine greeted her left her in no doubt that she was very welcome indeed. As they embraced, tears filled their eyes and Becky noted how strained and tired her sister looked.

"Oh Cathy, my dear, what can I say? Tell me first, how is Dr Harrison? Is he recovering well?" she asked.

Catherine, clearly unwilling to alarm her sister yet unable to lie to her, replied cautiously, "He is much better this week than he was when we first returned from Derbyshire, but, Becky, I fear he has suffered an attack of greater severity than we suspected, and it may be a very long while before he is quite well again. Dr Whitelaw, though he fears he will distress us and so will not say it outright, seems to be hinting that Dr Harrison will not recover sufficiently to return to work in the parish."

Her voice fell as she concluded her sentence, and Rebecca put her arms around her.

"Oh my dear sister, what you must have gone through this last week! No wonder you look so pale. I am certain now that I was right to come."

Catherine's expression suggested that she agreed.

"Thank you, Becky dear, it was kind of you. I am glad you have come."

When they were seated together in the parlour, taking tea, Rebecca asked more searching questions about arrangements at the parsonage and learned that Mr Benson, the manager of the estate, had just that morning called to assure

Catherine that if the need arose for her family to move, the Dower House was being made ready for them.

"He told me Jonathan Bingley had insisted upon having the house opened up and had inspected it himself. It is some time since it was occupied permanently, and Jonathan had given orders that all the rooms should be aired and prepared in the event that we may need to move there. He has been exceedingly kind, Becky, he cannot do enough for us," said Catherine and Becky agreed.

"Indeed, it would seem that Jonathan feels no bitterness towards us at all, despite the fact our sister Amelia-Jane used him very ill. I always said he, above any of Jane Bingley's children, has inherited her sweetness of disposition and generosity of heart."

Catherine understood exactly what she meant but was disinclined to go down that path. It had been for her a particularly harrowing period, during which she had watched her young sister, self-willed and ill-advised by fickle friends, destroy her marriage and later herself through a series of events that had driven her husband, Jonathan Bingley, close to despair. The memories were too painful to recount at this time.

She chose instead to recall the many years that their family had lived at the parsonage at Hunsford, when their father Reverend Collins had been the incumbent. Later, after her marriage to Dr Harrison, she had returned to live there and had raised her family in the parish. Catherine had no other memories of a home.

"I was born here, Becky, I have known no other home but Hunsford and Rosings, of course, thanks to Lady Catherine."

Her voice sounded forlorn, as though she had already accepted the inevitable, and Becky, hoping to lift her spirits a little, spoke of earlier days when, as children of her chaplain, they had enjoyed the condescension and even the occasional benevolence of Lady Catherine de Bourgh. Their father, Reverend Collins, had always insisted that they should be grateful; it had not always been easy for Becky, a precocious little girl, to understand why this was so.

"You were always more amenable than I was, Cathy; no wonder Lady Catherine invited you to stay on at Rosings," she said with a grimace that indicated her own perception and made her sister smile at the memory.

Jonathan Bingley, arriving to say his farewells before returning to his family, who were still at Pemberley, found them thus occupied and was relieved indeed to note what a significant difference her sister's arrival had made to Catherine.

Though she was still undoubtedly in shock and anxious about her husband's health, she appeared in better spirits. Becky Tate was renowned for her natural cheerfulness, tending to optimism in the face of adversity. Combined with a genuine and strong affection for her sister, this would surely help Catherine greatly at such a difficult time, Jonathan thought. When he left them after a welcome cup of tea and taking with him their warmest wishes for a safe journey, he was feeling a good deal more hopeful than he had been all week.

∞

In reality, Rebecca Tate, having suffered in her own life some grievous misfortune, including the loss of her only daughter Josie, was far less inclined than before towards optimism. Her husband, Anthony Tate, deeply dejected following the death of their daughter, had so immersed himself in his work, leaving Becky very much to grieve alone, that they had grown apart and were now as strangers in the same house. As he found solace in expanding his commercial empire, Becky had turned to Catherine and the two sisters had found comfort in each other's company.

More recently, as Mr Tate had made preparations for a journey to the United States, where he expected to do business with a fellow publisher, Becky had found less and less to occupy her at home. With both her son Walter and her husband away for many months at a time, there were fewer functions to attend and families to visit. Since her husband preferred to meet his business friends at his club, they rarely entertained at home.

She went up to London only occasionally, usually invited by a new friend, Lady Ashton, who had decided that Becky could be useful to her, but with whom Becky shared very few interests, which meant she was often alone and bored.

Yet, Becky's generous disposition had not deserted her, and finding her sister in a nostalgic mood, she chose wisely to let her indulge herself, reminiscing about the things they had shared, hoping to draw her out of the contemplation of her present circumstances.

There was much to remember and talk about, which very soon had them both in a lighter mood. Indeed, so addictive a pastime did this become that over the days and weeks that followed, when at the end of the day they sat down to tea, inevitably their conversation would begin with one or the other saying, "Do you recall the day when…?"—so delving into their shared recollections of childhood at Rosings and Hunsford over the years, even as the debris of the recent calamity was being gathered up and cleared away.

Catherine, as the eldest daughter of Reverend Collins and Charlotte Lucas, had held a very special place in their home at Hunsford and later in the household of their patron at Rosings. She had never been certain what had engendered Lady Catherine's partiality towards her. It could not have been only her father's egregious deference and loyalty, surely, but that young Catherine Collins had been specially favoured, no one had any doubt.

Throughout the years she had spent at Rosings, many people had seen fit to inform her that never before had Lady Catherine been known to be so generous, even affectionate in her treatment of any other person outside her own immediate family, and even they were called upon to show a high degree of gratitude and respect for her Ladyship in return.

Rebecca was curious to learn if Catherine had ever discovered the secret of her popularity with the almost universally disliked Lady Catherine de Bourgh. Recalling the days when, as children, they would accompany their parents to Rosings and then be banished to the old schoolroom at the other end of the house, to take tea with the maids and perhaps Mrs Jenkinson, Becky reminded her sister of the way she would often be summoned to return downstairs afterwards and entertain Her Ladyship by playing the pianoforte or reading to her.

"You were favoured because you read so well and played so sweetly on the instrument, unlike myself. I never gained such a high degree of proficiency as you did," she declared.

"Only because I practised assiduously, as Lady Catherine said I should," Catherine explained and Rebecca retorted, "Whilst I spent all my time scribbling things on bits of paper! No wonder Lady C had such a strong prejudice against me."

Her sister was more charitable. "I do not believe it was really a matter of prejudice, Becky dear, so much as her desire to be obeyed by everyone around her. When she commanded me to practice, I did!"

"Poor Catherine, she must have had you truly terrified," said Rebecca, but her sister disagreed again.

"Indeed no, she did not. You must not think that—I was not afraid of her; but she was a most formidable person and being very young, I was in awe of Her Ladyship and found it difficult, if not impossible, to refuse her anything or to disagree with her on any significant matter."

"Did you ever?" asked her sister, amazed at this confession.

Catherine's voice was low as she replied, "No, not in anything really significant; sometimes I wish I had done so, but then it is all very well to be brave after the event, is it not?"

"If Mama is to be believed, Papa was not very different, so you need feel no shame. He was so much in awe of Lady C he went nowhere, made no decision, expressed no opinion without her prior approval!" Rebecca said, to which Catherine added quietly, "Which of course, made it easier for Her Ladyship to demand the same degree of compliance from the rest of us. You were probably fortunate, Becky—you acquired an early reputation for recalcitrance, and I do believe she gave up expecting you to do as she advised."

Becky did not hide her consternation. "Advised! Commanded, more likely. Yes, I was very much the black sheep, was I not? I recall how angry she became when I said I wanted to be a writer. I was only a little girl, but she addressed me with such seriousness—it was as though I had announced my intention to join the Revolution! She ordered me to abandon such a foolish notion forthwith. 'Women,' she declared, without fear of contradiction, 'should have better things to do than waste their time on such frippery,' and she urged Mama to have me taught to sew and knit and make pin cushions, which she said would help me get a good, respectable husband—and a boring one, no doubt! I recall telling Mr Tate about it when we became engaged and we had a good laugh about her Ladyship's notions. He was not particularly troubled by my lack of skill in sewing or making pin cushions."

Becky was enjoying herself, recounting the days of her youth, when she suddenly noticed her sister's countenance. Catherine looked deeply unhappy, as though some painful memory from the past had intruded itself upon her thoughts.

Becky was immediately solicitous. "Why, Cathy dear, what is it? Are you not well? Do forgive me for going on and on, I wasn't thinking... I do apologise..."

Catherine brushed aside her concerns. "I am quite well, Becky, it's just that recalling Lady Catherine reminded me of something she once said about her daughter. She declared to Mrs Jenkinson and myself that Miss Anne de Bourgh could well have married a knight of the realm, who had shown some interest in her, if not that her poor health would not let her live in Scotland!"

Becky exploded, "And how pray was this to happen when she scarcely let the poor creature out of her sight? Cathy, I truly believe Lady Catherine had quite lost any connection with reality. How else would she make such a preposterous prediction?"

"Ah well," said her sister, "you certainly proved her wrong, Becky; you have achieved your ambition to be a writer *and* you have married a most eligible and successful gentleman as well. Lady Catherine would have been very pleased and not a little surprised, I'm sure."

Rebecca did not respond to this statement.

Their confidences had not included the current, somewhat parlous state of her own marriage. She had been reluctant to speak of it, too mortified to reveal the truth, even to a beloved sister.

Catherine continued, "I suppose, Becky dear, there are times when every one of us must wish we had acted differently. I have often wondered how very different our lives might have been had Papa not been appointed to the living at Hunsford and we were not brought so totally under the influence of Lady Catherine de Bourgh. I do not wish you to think I am ungrateful for all she did for me; indeed, in many ways there was little difference in her treatment of myself and her daughter Anne, and being blessed with good health, I was better able to benefit from those opportunities than poor Miss de Bourgh. But one cannot help wishing we might have been a little more emancipated," said Catherine.

Puzzled by this cryptic remark, Becky wanted to pursue the matter but was thwarted by the arrival at that moment of Lilian, who on finding her mother's bed empty had come downstairs to look for her. Seeing her with Rebecca and noting that she looked weary, she asked with more than a little concern in her voice, "Mama, are you not coming to bed? It is well past midnight."

Catherine rose and, bidding her sister good night, accompanied her daughter up the stairs, leaving Rebecca to follow later.

Earlier that same evening, Dr Whitelaw had called to see his patient and declared that Reverend Harrison's condition appeared to be improving, though slowly.

"But he must not be permitted to hasten back to his parish work, Mrs Harrison," he warned, "or he will suffer a relapse. I know he will claim that he feels fit enough, but in such cases as this, it is far better to err on the side of caution."

Catherine agreed, though Rebecca noted that she seemed to do so with reluctance and sadness, promising to ensure that her husband did not overtire himself. Rebecca could not help wondering if she would succeed; she knew her brother-in-law to be a most determined man, with a tendency to declare that he intended to do something and proceed to do just that despite the advice to the contrary of all those around him.

Her own husband, Anthony Tate, had often been aggravated by the rather patronising tone Dr Harrison adopted and had warned Rebecca that he could not be expected to defer to him on every occasion simply because he was a clergyman.

"He pontificates on a variety of subjects as though they were matters of church doctrine rather than commonplace issues affecting ordinary people in society; his manner suggests that he expects everyone in the room to agree with him, while in reality few of us do," he'd said.

Dr Harrison and Catherine's marriage to him had become the subject of frequent comment in their home.

"I cannot comprehend why she married him," Mr Tate had said, "he is quite the most boring clergyman I have known. He has a number of predictable opinions from which he cannot be moved, no matter how strong the arguments may be to the contrary—yet your sister Catherine is a woman of intelligence and common sense. I cannot account for her having accepted him."

Neither could Becky, who had always respected her sister's independence and judgment. She had regarded Dr Harrison as an upright and respectable clergyman, which he undoubtedly was, but had to agree with her husband that he was far from being an interesting or dynamic one. In fact he was rather dull.

Yet, Catherine had never complained or even hinted that their union had been anything but happy. Their three children were all pleasant, well-educated young persons and seemed to love both their parents.

Becky could not make it out at all.

There was, of course, the fact that Catherine had been almost twenty-nine when the then incumbent at Hunsford, with the enthusiastic blessing of his patron Lady Catherine de Bourgh, had made an offer for her hand. Her sister had accepted him; their mother had given her consent and announced their engagement to the family.

Rebecca recalled their wedding at Rosings—it had been quite a grand affair, hosted by Lady Catherine herself. It had seemed to her at the time that the bridal couple had very little say in the matter—everything had been organised by Lady Catherine's efficient staff—and most of the guests, apart from their immediate families, had been members of Lady Catherine's favoured circle. Yet, as she recalled, none of this had seemed to impress or worry Catherine, whose calmness and singular lack of excitement on the day had amazed her sisters. Young Amelia-Jane had been quite vocal about it.

It was late and the fire had gone out behind the grate when Becky, having exhausted her review of times past, finally went to bed, still dissatisfied.

On the morrow just as they were finishing breakfast, they heard brisk footsteps in the lane, which stopped at the gate, and then a knock on the front door. Lilian went to look out of the window, and when the maid came in to announce that Mr Adams had arrived and was waiting in the parlour, she left the room immediately.

Rebecca looked across at her sister, but Catherine seemed absorbed in the application of some honey on her toast. It was some time before she finished her breakfast and went into the parlour to join the young couple, who seemed quite happily ensconced in there, Rebecca had noted.

Mr Adams, a good-looking man of perhaps twenty-six or twenty-seven years, always elegantly but never overdressed and very well mannered at all times, rose as the ladies entered. Neither he nor Lilian appeared at all put out by their entrance, a fact that caused Becky to speculate that they were either mere indifferent acquaintances or that her sister already knew of the status of their relationship and had approved of it.

Reasonably confident that it could not be the first, she assumed the latter to be true. Determined to discover if this was the case, she planned to talk to her sister when they had a moment in private to speak of such matters.

However, this did not eventuate—not that morning, nor for a few days afterwards—for that afternoon Dr Harrison suffered a relapse and his condition worsened considerably. A servant was dispatched forthwith to fetch Dr Whitelaw and a message sent to Mr Benson to request his immediate assistance.

Catherine was run off her feet trying to attend upon her husband and, while Becky tried her best to assist with household work, it was left to Lilian to comfort her mother.

Later that evening, while Dr Harrison was resting and the ladies were in the parlour, Mr Adams arrived. He had heard the news from Benson, he said.

"I came as soon as I heard. Is there anything I can do? An errand I can undertake or a message I might deliver?"

He was clearly sympathetic and eager to help, but Catherine did not wish to impose upon him. She thanked him and said, "Mr Benson has been very helpful and Dr Whitelaw will call again tomorrow morning, so we are being very well looked after."

But Rebecca did notice that Lilian rose and went to stand at the bay window, where she was joined by Mr Adams, and they stood together for a long while, looking out at the darkening scene.

Since there was little to be seen except the familiar garden and the lane beyond, it was obvious that they wished to speak privately. A few words were exchanged, too soft for Rebecca to make out; plainly he was trying to alleviate her distress with comforting words. Before he took his leave, Mr Adams came to where Catherine was seated and said good night, promising to call in again tomorrow to enquire after Dr Harrison's health and see if there was anything he could do to be of assistance to the family.

Catherine and Lilian both thanked him, and Lilian accompanied him to the door, where once again they stood talking together awhile, before he finally left the house.

This time Becky could not remain silent.

"Young Mr Adams seems a very pleasant gentleman," she remarked, adding, "He has such an open countenance, no airs and affectations at all."

Her sister answered without looking up from her needlework.

"Yes indeed, he is quite free of pretensions."

Becky pressed on, "And he seems both thoughtful and considerate."

"Hmmm, he certainly is that," was Catherine's only response.

Lilian's return to the room prevented her aunt from pursuing the subject of

Mr Adams's good nature any further, but by now she was convinced that this young man was either forming an attachment to her niece, which her mother approved of, or they had already reached an understanding but would not speak of it publicly because of Dr Harrison's indisposition.

It was quite plausible, she thought, that Mr Adams had not as yet been able, because of the fire at Rosings and Dr Harrison's seizure, to make a formal offer of marriage, but she was quite certain the couple were in love or at least on the verge of being so.

Rebecca was baffled, however, by her sister's silence on the subject.

Unwilling to press Catherine further at this time, she kept her counsel, observing the pair closely whenever she could. Ever since the unhappy end of her daughter's marriage to Julian Darcy, Becky Tate had become painfully aware of the risks attendant upon young couples entering into matrimony. Her niece and goddaughter Lilian's happiness was dear to her heart, and Becky was determined that another mistake would not be made.

This was made clear when she wrote to her friend Emily Courtney, who had recently moved from the rectory at Kympton to occupy her late parents' home at Oakleigh, and in her letter, was quite candid in her assessment of the situation—as she saw it—between Lilian and young Mr Adams.

She wrote that night:

My dear Emily,

You must forgive the long delay in responding to your last, but with the disaster at Rosings followed by the ill health of my brother-in-law Dr Harrison, I have had to hasten to my dear sister's side and have had little time to write to anyone.

I assume you have heard the worst from Lizzie and Mr Darcy, to whom no doubt Jonathan Bingley would have reported, but, Emily, no words can describe the terrible devastation we see here.

However, all is not gloom and doom, for here at Hunsford we are witnessing the beginning of what may be a new romance, I think.

My young niece Lilian, who is very pretty but also quite a sensible girl, seems to have caught the attention of a certain Mr John Adams, the curator of the Rosings estate. I could not say this for certain, because my dear sister has said not a word of the matter to me, but one would have to be blind not to see there is some understanding between them.

He visits, ostensibly to enquire after the health of her father and offer to run errands for her mother, but I am not deceived, for his eyes follow Lilian around and he agrees with almost everything she says. This is not as strange as it may seem for she is a particularly intelligent and practical young person with a wisdom beyond her tender years.

However, of Mr Adams I am able to tell you very little.

He is very personable and good looking, but we know nothing of his antecedents, or the extent of his fortune or the lack of it. This is of particular importance at this time, because were Dr Harrison to retire on account of ill health, he, his wife, and daughter would have to live on his annuity and it will be absolutely imperative that Lilian marries a man who can support her and assist her parents if need be. Whether Mr Adams can do so on his present income is uncertain, and if he has other means, we know nothing of it.

Now, I should have thought it was the sort of matter that would concern my sister, yet try as I might, I cannot get a word out of her about either of them.

It is certainly rather vexing, Emily dear, that one has to remain in ignorance, for Lilian is not just my niece—Mr Tate and I are her godparents, and I do feel responsible for her.

There was more to tell, but time was short and she concluded with the promise that she would observe the young couple carefully and perhaps if an opportunity arose, she would ask her niece directly what the situation was between herself and Mr Adams. Promising to communicate forthwith with her friend, she dispatched her letter with the usual affectionate felicitations.

On reading Rebecca's letter, Emily Courtney sighed.

She wished her friend would not intervene in the lives of her sister and her niece. Emily was well aware of Becky Tate's propensity for observing and interpreting the circumstances of other people's lives; it was never maliciously done, but it had often placed her at risk of being misunderstood and resented by both family and friends.

"But Becky will never change," said Emily as she put the letter away, hoping without much hope that something would occur to thwart her scheme.

For a variety of reasons, the opportunity to do as she had promised she would did not arise for several days. Rebecca felt greatly put upon as every member of her sister's family appeared to frustrate her intention to discover more about Mr Adams and his association with Lilian.

The gentleman himself had to go to London in order to submit a catalogue of items salvaged from the ashes of the fires at Rosings to a specialist at the British Museum. Lilian was called upon to sit with her father for most of the day, while her mother concluded the preparations for their removal to the Dower House. Dr Harrison, while a fastidious man, was not a difficult patient and was very appreciative of his daughter's kindness in reading to him, often until he was too tired to concentrate or the light was too poor for her to continue.

Lilian, being the youngest in the family, had enjoyed a closer relationship with her parents than either of her siblings and found no hardship in her present role of carer and comforter. Besides, she had noted her aunt observing her whenever Mr Adams called and was well aware that she was keen to speak with her on such matters, and was glad to be able to avoid a private inquisition.

Dr Whitelaw, on his daily visit to his patient, had finally convinced Dr Harrison that he would never be fit enough to return to all of his parish duties, and Catherine, having spoken with her husband, had obtained his reluctant consent to the move to the Dower House. Despite his sense of frustration, Dr Harrison was sufficiently practical to comprehend that his condition was unlikely to improve in the near future and it was in the best interests of himself and his family that they accept the very generous offer of accommodation from the Rosings Trust.

Catherine believed furthermore that the sooner they moved, the better would be her husband's chances of recovery.

"Once he is got away from the parsonage, which is to him a constant reminder of all the duties he cannot perform, I am confident he will make progress," she had said, and Becky, though she was not as certain of this outcome, had to agree. Whereupon Mr Benson was consulted, a date fixed in a fortnight's time, and preparations were immediately afoot.

Even as they made their plans, Rebecca could not fail to sense the feelings that assailed her sister. Although she went about the business of sorting and packing their things with an enviable degree of composure, there was no mistaking her anxiety, for it was clear that Dr Whitelaw was no longer optimistic in his hopes for his patient's return to health.

Dr Harrison himself, having accepted the inevitability of retirement, began now to take his own condition seriously. He kept to his apartments upstairs, taking all his meals there, causing Lilian or Catherine or sometimes both to be on hand when he partook of them and frequently sending instructions to the cook for some variation or improvement to the menu. There were also interminable discussions as to the efficacy or otherwise of the various medications prescribed by the doctor. Although she never complained of it, Rebecca could clearly see her sister's exasperation and weariness.

One evening, after a particularly difficult day, Rebecca found her sister close to tears in Dr Harrison's study. She had been poring over a folder filled with papers and had extracted a number of bills, which had obviously arrived some time before her husband was taken ill.

When Rebecca, standing in the doorway, asked, "Cathy, what is it? I can see you are worried and anxious. Please tell me, is there any way I can help?" Catherine had abandoned the pretence of composure and wept.

Her sobs, so violent that her shoulders shook as she laid her head upon her arms, took Becky by surprise and she rushed to her side. Not since the death of their father, when they were both young girls, had Rebecca seen her sister give vent to her feelings with such intensity. Catherine had always been calm and composed, like their mother Charlotte. Seeing her thus was for Becky a most disconcerting and painful experience.

But she was both warm-hearted and generous of spirit and putting her arms around her sister, pleaded to be allowed to help.

"Dear Cathy, please do not weep, it will only make you ill. Please, please tell me what troubles you and let me help. Is it money?" she asked, pointing to all the bills that lay upon the desk in front of them, and when Catherine nodded, she continued, "Money is no object, Cathy. Mr Tate allows me an exceedingly generous allowance of which I use very little. I am not extravagant and have most things I need already, which means much of the money is saved. I can draw some of it out for you, as much as is required to settle these accounts—you need only tell me how much you require."

Catherine did not lift her head at first, but gradually her sobs eased, and at last she took out her handkerchief and dried her eyes. She looked anxious and exhausted.

Seeing her, Becky's eyes filled with tears.

Slowly, haltingly, Catherine explained that there were many bills unpaid, some dating back a month or two, now already overdue!

"Becky, I know he would not have let things come to this; it must have been that he was not himself—perhaps he was already ill and did not know it or, if he did, did not wish to alarm us by speaking of it. Now he must retire; we shall have much less money, yet I must find the means to pay these accounts. I will not have it said that we left the parsonage with bills unpaid and in debt to shopkeepers and tradesmen," she said, her voice still shaking.

Rebecca was relieved. "If that is all that has been troubling you, why it is nothing at all. Cathy dear, we shall have these accounts settled within the week."

After protesting at first that she could not accept, Catherine was persuaded that it was by far the best way out of her difficulties. She expressed her gratitude, promising to repay every penny, if it took her ten years to do so.

"I shall only accept if it is regarded as a loan," she insisted. "I do have some money of my own—Lady Catherine was very generous to me both when I was married and in her will—but much of it is invested in bonds. As soon as I am able, I shall start to repay you; dear Becky, it is not that I am not grateful, I do appreciate your kindness, but I will not take your money outright. Furthermore, you must promise me that this will remain forever our secret; no one must ever know."

Rebecca agreed readily and over the next few days all of the outstanding accounts were settled, to the great relief of her sister, and her creditors, no doubt.

During this period, the matter of Lilian's romance slipped into the background, as the plans for their removal to the Dower House came to fruition. Dr Harrison was, at Mr Benson's suggestion, first transported in a carriage to rooms in the East Wing of Rosings, where he was spared the bustle, dust, and noise of moving house. When everything was in place, he was conveyed to the Dower House, where the best suite of rooms had been prepared for him.

The house was both more elegant than and as comfortable as the parsonage had been, and Mr Benson had ensured that everything had been satisfactorily arranged, exactly as Mr Jonathan Bingley had specified.

Dr Harrison seemed content, though he did point out that his study was not quite as commodious here, and Catherine was pleased with both the house and the garden. Even Mrs Giles the housekeeper was delighted with the kitchen and servants' accommodation, which was far less Spartan than it had been at the parsonage.

As for Lilian, she wandered in and out of her pretty new room, her eyes shining with pleasure, unable to believe that what had begun as a piece of dire misfortune should have ended so agreeably.

Writing in her diary, she noted:

How very strange that what seemed at first a terrible tragedy for everyone, and especially for poor Papa, has resulted in such a satisfactory conclusion for us all.

I do believe Papa means to enjoy his enforced retirement; he says he plans to read more and perhaps write as well—though I do not know if there will be anyone who will wish to publish his sermons.

For my part, I have no regrets at all—indeed, if I were to regard it in purely practical terms, I have a larger and more pleasing room, a prettier view of the grounds and, since the Dower House is situated within the boundaries of Rosings Park, it will be a shorter distance to travel, should someone wish to visit!

Even in the privacy of her own diary, she would not name who it was that might visit!

Chapter Three

THE ARRIVAL AT ROSINGS of two gentlemen from London was to keep Mr Adams so busy over the next few days that the family at the Dower House saw him but rarely.

Rebecca remarked upon it to Lilian and Catherine as they sat reading in the parlour.

"We have not seen Mr Adams in some days; his visitors must be very important persons," she said. "I was walking alongside the lane that goes down to the village this morning, and I thought I saw Mr Adams drive past in a curricle with another gentleman—a very tall, distinguished-looking man, much taller than Mr Adams; but they were gone so quickly I could not get more than a glimpse of him," she said, adding curiously, "I wonder who it could be."

Catherine could provide no answer to her question. She knew of no gentleman, tall or otherwise, who might be riding in a curricle with Mr Adams, she said. And if Lilian knew anything about it, she was keeping her own counsel, concentrating her attention wholly upon her book.

Rebecca persisted. "Has Mr Adams not mentioned his name to you in conversation, Lilian?"

Lilian, cognisant of her aunt's curiosity, replied quietly, "No, he has not, Aunt. Indeed I know only that two gentlemen were arriving to look over the Rosings estate and Mr Adams expected he would be very busy answering all their questions. That, I am afraid, Aunt Becky, is all I know of the matter," she concluded, before returning to her book.

Though unsatisfied, Rebecca could proceed no further along that track.

A day or two later, while taking a walk in the woods that surrounded the Rosings estate, she saw in the distance two people she thought she recognised. They were, she was almost certain, Mr Adams and Lilian, strolling together through the trees. She recognised him by his coat, which she had seen often when he visited the parsonage, and knew she could not be mistaken in his companion, for the lady was wearing the pretty new bonnet her niece had worn to church on Sunday.

They appeared to be deep in conversation, quite oblivious of her presence, and Rebecca thought it best to avoid meeting them face to face. Turning down another path, she made her way back to the house. Once there, she decided it was prudent not to tell her sister what she had seen, lest it should cause her to worry. She had no way of knowing if Catherine had any knowledge of her daughter's friendship with the gentleman and wished not to add to her sister's present concerns.

She did, however, write again to Emily Courtney, describing in some detail her recent observations.

My dear Emily,

Now we have moved from the parsonage to the Dower House, which is far more commodious and has much better accommodation for visitors, we are all a good deal more comfortable. We are also somewhat closer to Rosings—or what is left of it—and I have been better able to observe my niece Lilian and Mr Adams.

The gentleman has been rather busy of late with visitors from London, looking at ways to save some of the treasures of Rosings, I believe, but not so busy as to be unable to find time to walk in the woods with a certain young lady.

I do not know if you will agree with me on this, Emily, but I do think my dear sister is indulging young Lilian a little too far. It is not seemly that she should be walking in the woods with a young gentleman unless some firm understanding has been reached between them. Do you not agree?

She put the unfinished letter aside, expecting she would have more news to impart in a day or two, when Mr Adams, free of his interlocutors, would return to visiting them regularly as before.

It was on the Sunday following their removal to the Dower House that they were returning from church, with Rebecca, Lilian, and Catherine all engaged in animated conversation about the dramatic sermon preached by the visiting chaplain who had conducted the service at Hunsford.

Taking for his text the parable of the woman taken in adultery, he had railed against those who would cast the first stone, while their own lives were far from exemplary.

"I cannot think why he chose such a text," said Rebecca.

"I believe he means to astonish us all," said Lilian. "He must think the people of this parish need waking up."

Catherine agreed, "Well, he certainly did that. I saw at least two people who had dozed off start and sit bolt upright again!"

She did not add that it was quite likely many of them had been accustomed to taking a little sleep during Dr Harrison's sermons, long and erudite as they always were. Catherine was far too loyal to say that.

They had almost reached their gate when Mr Adams and another man appeared, coming towards them from the direction of Rosings.

"It's him!" whispered Rebecca quickly, "it's the tall man I saw in the curricle with Mr Adams last week."

The stranger was certainly tall and had a short, thick beard in the popular style affected by Mr Dickens, but it was the clean-shaven Mr Adams who came forward to greet them with a cheerful smile.

"Good morning, ladies, what a very fortuitous meeting this is; we were just coming to call on you. Mrs Harrison, Mrs Tate, and Miss Lilian Harrison, may I introduce Mr Frank Burnett, who is here to advise us on restoring and conserving what is left of the Rosings heritage."

Rebecca noticed a degree of gallantry in the manner in which Mr Burnett greeted each of them in turn, claiming he was delighted to meet them. She decided, from observing his general demeanour and dress, that he must have spent some time in Europe, a fact that was soon attested to by Mr Adams, who explained to the ladies that Mr Burnett was a very experienced authority on antiquities, who'd spent many years of study in France and Italy. So interested was Rebecca in this information that she did not notice the look of absolute astonishment that crossed her sister's countenance as Mr Burnett greeted her and took her extended hand.

As they walked up the path, Lilian, assuming they would all come into the house, hurried ahead to alert Mrs Giles and order tea for the visitors, while Mr Adams chatted on to her aunt. As for Mr Burnett, apart from his first courteous greeting, he said little as he walked beside the ladies, hands clasped behind his back, appearing rather to observe and listen, while John Adams talked enthusiastically of the prodigious task that lay ahead.

Once within, Catherine excused herself and left them to hurry upstairs to Dr Harrison. The regular nurse did not come in on Sundays and Catherine was anxious to ensure he was comfortable. Finding him asleep, she returned to the parlour just as the tea was brought in. Grateful for something to do, she sat down to dispense it and as she was pouring out tea for Mr Adams, she heard him say to her sister, "I learned only yesterday that Mr Burnett had once, quite some years ago, been employed as the librarian at Rosings."

This extraordinary piece of information was met with incredulity, as both Lilian and Rebecca looked at one another and turned to Catherine.

"Did you hear that, Mama? Do you not remember Mr Burnett from when you used to live at Rosings?" asked Lilian. Catherine's face was instantly covered in a deep blush, and she looked distinctly ill at ease. Unable to answer immediately, Catherine appeared to suffer some embarrassment until the gentleman himself came to her rescue.

Coming over to pick up his cup of tea, he looked at her and then said, "It was so very long ago—some twenty years or more. I am not at all surprised that Mrs Harrison does not remember me."

"But do you recall her?" asked Rebecca.

Mr Burnett was unequivocal in his response. "I certainly do; she was then a very young lady—a Miss Collins, I believe, and what is more important, she was a great favourite of the late Lady Catherine de Bourgh, I think. Am I not right, Mrs Harrison?"

Catherine was completely confused; she felt awkward and silly, like some young ingénue who had made a *faux pas* and been caught out.

Grateful for his intervention, however, she gathered her thoughts together quickly and apologised.

"Mr Burnett! Yes, I do remember. I am sorry, I have been much distracted lately with the fire and Dr Harrison's illness, as well as the move from the parsonage at Hunsford to this house... I cannot have been thinking clearly and my memory failed me... I did not mean to be rude... I do apologise..." She was clearly ill at ease and mortified by her lapse.

He was very gracious indeed. "Please do not apologise, Mrs Harrison. I did not expect you to remember me at all—it has been so long and, while you are not changed a great deal, my friends who knew me then tell me I am quite unrecognisable!"

When the others laughed, Catherine smiled too, as if recalling how he had looked those many years ago; he had not sported a beard, she thought, as he continued, "When Mr Adams mentioned that you and Dr Harrison had lately moved to the Dower House and suggested that we call on you, I was not at all hopeful that you would remember me." He paused and said lightly, to the entire party, "Librarians are not the most memorable of people—the books and artifacts they preserve are often far more worthy of recollection."

At this, Catherine smiled, more easily this time, and Rebecca noted that Mr Burnett smiled with her; it was as if they had known one another quite well and were sharing a familiar memory after all those years.

When she spoke again, Catherine's voice was more natural. "Be that as it may, I am truly sorry that I did not recall you at first. But let me make amends by saying here and now, that when I lived at Rosings, I found the library to be one of the most magical places in the house and spent many happy and improving hours there. I owed that experience almost entirely to your encouragement and the generosity of Her Ladyship, of course. As to being a favourite with her, I was her goddaughter and she took her responsibilities *in loco parentis* very seriously. In permitting me to remain at Rosings, my mother had clearly accepted that."

This time it was his turn to bow and thank her for her kind words, adding that he had been exceedingly relieved to discover that the fire had not in any way damaged any part of the excellent collection of books and manuscripts in the Rosings library.

"I think we might all say Amen to that Mr Burnett," said Mr Adams and the ladies were in complete agreement, of course.

Before the two gentlemen departed, they were invited to dine on the following Sunday, which invitation was accepted with alacrity by both men. They claimed that they worked assiduously through the week because there was so much to do, but Sunday was different and the prospect of dining at the Dower House was too good to turn down.

Besides, said Mr Adams cheerfully, he was sure Mr Burnett would look forward to another opportunity to exchange with Mrs Harrison their mutual recollections of Rosings Park.

"I have heard so much about those days, when Her Ladyship held court at Rosings, I know you will have a great deal to talk about together."

He was hoping, no doubt, thought Becky, that in being so occupied, they would allow him to spend more time with Lilian. Catherine said nothing and while Mr Burnett smiled and nodded as if in agreement with his young friend, he made no comment.

Becky did notice that he kissed the hands of all the ladies as he took his leave. Very charming indeed, she thought, very European.

That night, Rebecca continued her letter to Emily Courtney, detailing for her friend this most extraordinary encounter:

> *Thereafter, more tea and shortbread arrived and soon they were talking so amiably together that it seemed as though they were old friends. Indeed, we now discover that Mr Frank Burnett was Lady Catherine's archivist and librarian for some years before leaving to pursue further studies in Europe.*
>
> *During that time, my father had passed away and Mama had left Hunsford, taking Amelia-Jane and me with her, while Cathy had accepted Lady Catherine's invitation to live at Rosings.*

It was all the information she had been able to glean from the brief conversation she had had with her sister after the gentlemen had left. She had not been able to understand how it was that Catherine had so completely forgotten Mr Burnett and yet was able to recall in a moment his fine work in the library at Rosings those many years ago.

It was a puzzle; one Becky was determined to solve.

※

That night, Catherine slept but little.

Not only was Dr Harrison restless, his condition causing her some concern, but lying on the narrow day-bed in his room was not conducive to restful sleep. Awake, with her mind in some turmoil, she could not begin to concentrate her thoughts upon the here and now alone. Inevitably, after the morning's encounter, they kept returning to the time some twenty-odd years ago when she had first made the acquaintance of Mr Frank Burnett.

She had not been entirely honest in claiming that her memory had failed her and she had no recollection at all of him when they had been introduced that morning. Catherine had not immediately recognised the tall stranger with a well-trimmed beard and thick, greying hair as the man she had known at Rosings those many years ago, yet the moment she had heard the name she had known who he was. At first, she had thought he had not appeared keen to renew the acquaintance and in her response, had sought to accommodate what she assumed were his wishes. When, however, Mr Adams had revealed his knowledge of Mr Burnett's past employment in the library, it had become clear that he had not intended to conceal his past association with Rosings at all.

Catherine's own knowledge of Frank Burnett had begun when, after the sudden death of her father, Reverend Collins, Lady Catherine had invited her first to spend Christmas at Rosings and afterwards to accept a position as companion to her daughter, Miss Anne de Bourgh.

Encouraged by her mother, she had accepted both invitations and had thus been drawn into the circle of Her Ladyship's household. It had not been an unpleasant or uncomfortable circle; indeed, it had often been for her a most beneficial one, for Lady Catherine could be both generous and kind to those she regarded with particular interest and from whom she expected and received respect and due deference. There had been however an ever-present sense of obligation, which had from time to time proved irksome and occasionally downright disagreeable.

But Catherine had, in general, succeeded in coping with these minor inconveniences, thanks mainly to her equable temper and amenable disposition. If there had been times when it had all become too much to bear, they were few and far between.

Undaunted by the grandeur of the mansion and the domineering presence of its owner, Catherine had set out to make the most of her time at Rosings. She had not anticipated ever having such an opportunity, and when it had presented itself, she had used it to observe and learn and in general improve considerably her knowledge and understanding of such diverse subjects as literature, history, and art not ordinarily open to a young girl in her situation.

With Miss de Bourgh never in the best of health, frequently troubled by colds and chills, Catherine had often found herself on her own, when not required to keep Her Ladyship company, looking for ways to occupy her time. The substantial collection of paintings, trophies, and *objets d'Art* that were liberally scattered around the house was not of very great interest to her. The music room, however, was and she spent much of her time playing upon the very superior instrument there. Lady Catherine had urged her continually to practice and Catherine had been happy to comply.

She had also visited the library, being an avid reader herself, but had found its collection and aspect rather intimidating. Its valuable and extensive collection was locked away in ornate, dark mahogany cabinets, and there had been no librarian since the death of the man who had been hired by the late Sir Lewis de Bourgh many years ago, which only increased its inaccessibility.

However, all this had changed when, on a visit to Rosings, Lady Catherine's nephew Mr Fitzwilliam Darcy had recommended that a librarian be employed to catalogue and restore the collection, and in the course of that year a certain gentleman had been appointed to the position.

Lately returned from Italy, Mr Frank Burnett had arrived at Rosings full of enthusiasm for his task and had proceeded to work very hard, indeed; so much so that he was rarely seen unless one visited the library.

When Catherine had accompanied Her Ladyship on one of her visits to the library, she had been astonished to discover that Mr Burnett had transformed it from a somewhat forbidding place into a veritable treasure house of books, maps, manuscripts, and other items of interest.

The dark cabinets had been opened up to reveal their remarkable contents and the striped blinds at the windows removed to let in more light, while reading desks and chairs had been procured from other parts of the house and placed around the spacious reading area for the benefit of anyone who might wish to read there in comfort.

Catherine had been delighted by the change Mr Burnett had wrought, and even Lady Catherine, who had never been a frequent visitor to the library, had been impressed.

"You have accomplished a great deal, Mr Burnett—do go on as you have begun, I am sure there is much to be done," she had said, but she did not stay long to sample the pleasures provided.

Catherine, on the other hand, had returned later to borrow a book and found Mr Burnett helpful, if a little patronising. When asked if he would recommend a good book, he had asked, to her chagrin, how long it was since she had graduated from the schoolroom.

Too modest to boast of her scholarly achievements, Catherine had hastily borrowed a copy of one of Mr Dickens's early works and left, feeling somewhat slighted.

She had written to her sister Rebecca at the time, expressing her annoyance.

Insufferable man, to think I am unable to read and understand a grown-up book! Perhaps the young ladies who inhabit the circles in which he moves are all silly and ill-educated. I intend to show him that I am not like them at all. On my next visit to the library I shall ask for a novel by Mr Fielding and see how he responds!

No doubt he will be shocked and may even advise that it is not the sort of material young persons, lately out of the schoolroom, should be reading!

Dear Becky, I wish you were here, for you would surely tell him how widely and well read we are. He cannot be much more than twenty-five or six, I do not think, yet he does conduct himself with the greatest degree of decorum and speaks as though his words are so precious they should be measured out in little portions!

I must give him credit though for the transformation he has wrought in the library, which was once so gloomy it resembled more a museum, yet is now become a most welcoming, pleasing place. If only the librarian were less awesome!…

Her next meeting with Mr Burnett had taken place not in the library, nor in one of the splendid reception rooms of Rosings, but in the garden in the midst of a downpour that had drenched them both.

She had been sent by Lady Catherine to pick some roses for the rose bowl in the music room, which Her Ladyship insisted must always be filled with fresh blooms from the rose garden.

"I absolutely insist upon it," she had said, handing Catherine a pair of seca-teurs. "I cannot abide wilting blooms in the house," and Catherine had picked up a basket and gone out to the rose garden to do her bidding.

Having collected a number of excellent blooms in the colours she knew Lady Catherine favoured, she had been on her way back to the house when she had missed the pair of secateurs. Afraid that this would seriously displease Lady Catherine, she had set down her basket in the vestibule and raced back into the rose garden, taking a shortcut through the shrubbery, ignoring the heavy, dark clouds gathering overhead.

It was then, as the rain began to fall, that she had almost collided with Mr Burnett, who had the protection of a large umbrella. Catherine had said nothing at first, when he had asked what she was doing racing around in the rain and did she want to catch her death of cold? Then, not wishing to appear foolish, she had confessed to losing the pair of secateurs.

"Oh good God! we certainly cannot have that!" he had said in mock despair as the rain fell. "Poor Lady Catherine, why, that must have cost all of two shillings!"

"I have no time for frivolity, Mr Burnett, clearly I have dropped it some-where and I must find it... I really must," she had cried and then, seeing her distress was genuine, he had relented and offered to go back and retrieve it for her, while she stayed out of the rain. Which was exactly what he had done, returning within five minutes with the wretched instrument, which he had found on the steps leading to the rose garden.

"There you are, now, you need fear Her Ladyship's wrath no more—but a word of advice, Miss Collins: I should go directly to your room and change out of those clothes and shoes, unless you want to be sniffling all evening," he had said in a rather stern voice before disappearing up the back stairs. She heard him striding across the landing and running up the second flight of stairs leading to his apartment, as she gathered up her basket and took it into the music room. She was already beginning to feel the chill of her damp clothes and shoes, and despite her resentment of his tone, she was sensible enough to heed his advice and retired to her room to change and partake of a hot lemon drink provided by her maid.

To Catherine's surprise, when she came down to dinner later that evening, Mr Burnett had joined them, at the invitation of Lady Catherine.

Since this had never happened before, Catherine had wondered at the reason, until she discovered that a distinguished friend of the late Sir Lewis de Bourgh, a man with a reputation as an eminent Oxford don, was expected to dinner. Mr Burnett had obviously been invited to make intelligent conversation with their guest during the meal. Catherine was well aware that while Her Ladyship knew the monetary value of most of the treasures in her mansion, she was less well informed of their significance as works of art or literature.

Mr Burnett, on the other hand, proved he knew a good deal about the provenance and age of most of the pieces in the collection and was able to carry on a creditable conversation with their distinguished visitor for most of the evening. After dinner, the two men visited the library and returned still engaged in erudite discourse.

Later, Catherine was invited to play the pianoforte and when she did, Mr Burnett came over to the instrument and complimented her upon her performance.

"A quite delightful interpretation of a very complex piece, Miss Collins; may one ask if Schubert is a favourite of yours?"

"Not especially, but I have always enjoyed playing that particular composition, since my days in the schoolroom, when I first mastered it," she had replied with a wry smile.

He had had the grace to laugh.

"Oh dear, I fear I have annoyed you; believe me, I did not mean to belittle your knowledge on that occasion, Miss Collins, it was my complete ignorance of your degree of achievement that was to blame. I know better now and I apologise," he'd said and Catherine had smiled and accepted her victory with grace.

There were calls from Lady Catherine and her guest for more music.

Mr Burnett had returned to his seat to listen, while Catherine had proceeded to play and sing, choosing this time a completely different piece, a pretty English air, so as to confuse him a little in his estimation of her, she thought. But it seemed he was equally well pleased with it, too.

Lady Catherine was clearly impressed with Mr Burnett's contribution to the evening; in future, he would be invited to dinner whenever there was a visitor Her Ladyship wished particularly to impress.

When, on another occasion, Catherine had remarked that he was becoming a regular guest at Her Ladyship's table, he had made light of it.

"Yes, I do believe Lady Catherine sees some benefit in having me perform a professional role as well as a social function. I conserve and maintain her library by day and divert and entertain her guests at dinner! A sort of court official and court jester in one, so to speak, if you get my meaning, Miss Collins," he'd said.

Catherine had protested that he was devaluing his function in the household.

"I am not sure that you do not misconstrue Her Ladyship's intentions, Mr Burnett. I know she values your work in the library very highly; she has said as much. Yet, I am also certain that the invitation to dinner when she has distinguished guests is as much a compliment to your knowledge and ability to converse with them at a level that none of us can achieve."

At this Frank Burnett had smiled, quite a pleasant, acceptable little smile, not at all arrogant or patronising, and said, "You are always able to put the most benign construction upon a person's actions, Miss Collins; it is indeed a most charming quality."

"I say only what I believe to be true," she had protested and he had replied, "Of course you do, I would not for one moment suggest otherwise, but if I may offer just one little word of advice, Miss Collins, do remember that not every other person's motives are as pure and as transparent as your own."

Which remark had puzzled Catherine somewhat, but unwilling to demonstrate her naiveté by asking for an explanation, she had nodded sagely and said nothing.

There had been many more such meetings, during which Catherine had grown to respect and trust Frank Burnett's character and judgment.

Gradually, she had come to accept that it was not a lack of modesty that had made him seem arrogant at first, but a confidence in his knowledge of certain specific subjects, of which he had made a study. On other matters, of which he confessed to know little or nothing, he was happy to concede his ignorance.

He had surprised her by his admission that, despite his love of European music, which he had enjoyed greatly during his time in Italy, he had never mastered a single instrument.

"I would have given anything to learn to play and be as proficient as you are, but sadly, I had neither the time nor, I must confess, the discipline to apply myself to the task, as you clearly have done with such excellent results," he had confessed.

Catherine, at first a little embarrassed by his praise, had soon realised that his was quite sincere appreciation, and indeed he seemed to like nothing better than to hear her play whenever he was asked to dine at Rosings.

Occasionally, when Lady Catherine became more involved in conversation with her guests or on occasions when she retired early, he could be persuaded to join Catherine in a duet, revealing a pleasing though not highly trained voice. For Catherine, it had been a welcome change from performing for Her Ladyship alone, from whom she received some little praise, but mostly advice to practice even more assiduously. Frank Burnett openly expressed his pleasure and encouraged her to attempt more difficult works. In return, she had acknowledged his knowledge of art and literature, which went well beyond her level of under-standing, and was content to be guided by him in her appreciation of both, keenly reading the books he recommended, thereby unlocking the door to a whole new range of material of which she had known little and providing them with a number of subjects on which they could agreeably and profitably converse.

With his encouragement, she had entered a world of knowledge that opened up horizons such as she could never have imagined during her days at the parsonage at Hunsford.

For years, as children, they had heard their father Reverend Collins extol with obsequious enthusiasm the expensive furniture, fireplaces, staircases, and trophies that graced the rooms at Rosings, but at no time had he or anyone else opened her eyes to the treasures in its library.

For this, she would always be indebted to Frank Burnett.

While all these recollections had crowded into her mind as she lay awake, Dr Harrison had slept, fitfully, but without causing her any anxiety.

Towards morning, Catherine had dozed off and was suddenly awakened by a most alarming sound. She found her husband struggling to breathe, gasping, and trying to sit up in bed. Rushing to his side, she tried to help him but was uncertain what she should do. Afraid, she called to Lilian and Rebecca in their rooms across the corridor. Lilian was at her side in seconds, and finding her father very distressed, she hurried downstairs to send a servant for the doctor. Rebecca, rushing in, found her sister in tears, unable to help her husband, whose breathing had grown more laboured. Together they struggled to alleviate his distress, but with little success. His breathing eased a little, but he was clearly very unwell and they waited impatiently for the doctor.

By the time Dr Whitelaw arrived, the first streaks of dawn light were colouring the sky and a small chorus of birds had begun to greet the new day. But Dr Harrison, though somewhat less distressed now and breathing more easily, had lapsed into unconsciousness.

Dr Whitelaw began to fear that his patient had slipped beyond his help. He tried to reassure the ladies, but his concern was difficult to hide and though Dr Harrison lived through the day, he remained unconscious throughout, while all around him, the household was in turmoil.

The visiting chaplain from Apsley was sent for, and having prayed with them and administered the sacraments, he left. It seemed there was nothing more they could do for Dr Harrison but pray.

This, they took in turns to do, reading his favourite passages from the gospels and the psalms and sitting by his bedside, all through that long day and into the following night.

End of Part One

RECOLLECTIONS OF ROSINGS

Part Two

Chapter Four

I T WAS NOT THAT Catherine was entirely unprepared for the death of
Dr Harrison; she had been very concerned, despite the assurances of Dr
Whitelaw at the onset of his illness, that he was not making much progress
at all.

Lilian, too, had seemed unwilling to speak of her father's condition, as if
afraid to contemplate the inevitable. Other friends and family had consistently
and confidently declared that he would soon be well again and about his parish
business, and Dr Harrison himself had confidently proclaimed his belief that it
would indeed be so.

But now he was dead.

Only Rebecca, understanding her sister's anxiety, had not attempted to
belittle her concern. She had sat with Catherine at his bedside, throughout the
long night and into the morning, until it had become clear he was gone.

Dry-eyed and tight-lipped, Catherine had been unable to respond to the
sympathy expressed by those who called at the house, feeling alone and cold, as
she sought to comfort Lilian, while worrying that she had felt no great shock
or sorrow herself.

Mr Benson attended to everything that needed doing in preparation
for the funeral, and Mr Adams was always available to lend his support.
Members of the family and friends of the Harrisons came from many parts

of England: the Darcys, the Bingleys, the Wilsons, and of course her dear mother Charlotte Collins, who was in some pain with her rheumatism and yet had insisted on accompanying Jonathan Bingley and his wife, Anna, who travelled from Hertfordshire.

It was a melancholy occasion, made considerably worse for Mr Darcy by the sight of Rosings after the fire. His reaction, one of shock, almost of disbelief, was natural; nothing anyone had said could have prepared him for the sickening vision that met his eyes.

Darcy had been back and forth from Rosings Park since childhood; his mother and Lady Catherine were sisters. In adult life, he had been frequently called upon by his aunt to advise and assist her on matters of managing her estate after the death of Sir Lewis de Bourgh. Though they had often disagreed on many matters, there had ultimately been a grudging respect between them. Rosings had been everything to Lady Catherine; now she was gone and so was most of her heritage. Both Darcy and Elizabeth were quite unable to absorb the shock of it all.

The funeral service was a simple one. Catherine had insisted that her husband be laid to rest in the churchyard at Hunsford among the parishioners he had served with great dedication and not at Rosings, where lay the more distinguished graves of several generations of faithful servants, including her own father, Mr Collins.

Supported only by Lilian and Rebecca—for her two elder children were many thousands of miles away overseas—Catherine appeared remarkably calm, and afterwards, as they gathered at the Dower House, she was gracious to everyone who had attended.

She had noticed that John Adams had been at the funeral, standing with a group of people from the Rosings Estate, but there had been no sign of Frank Burnett. It did cross her mind that he may have returned to London, but thought no more about it at the time. After all, she thought, he had never known Dr Harrison personally.

On the day following, Mr Hanson the attorney came to read the will, and both Mr Darcy and Jonathan Bingley attended at Catherine's invitation. Dr Harrison did not have a very great deal to leave, but what he had was carefully and prudently invested and the whole of it willed to his wife. There was sufficient to support her in a modest way and little else, save for a collection of

Bibles, many theological books, and writings, all of which were destined for the library at Rosings!

A letter addressed to his children was handed to Lilian, but that was all.

When it was over, Mr Darcy assured Catherine that she could continue to live at the Dower House for as long as she needed.

"The lease has been paid for a complete year and you need have no concern at all should you wish to stay on," he had said.

Catherine thanked him for his generosity and replied that she would like to stay on for a while until she had made some plans for herself and Lilian.

Jonathan Bingley offered his assistance and his wife Anna invited her to spend some time at Netherfield Park in the future, if she wished to get away from Rosings for a while. Catherine thanked them all sincerely.

Rebecca had already offered her and Lilian a home with her in Matlock, but Catherine had made it clear that she had no wish to move to Derbyshire.

"Becky, I have lived all my life in Kent, I would be a complete stranger in Derbyshire... even if I could get accustomed to your weather!" she had said, protesting even as she thanked her for her offer. "I should be quite lost. It is very kind of you to ask me and I am not ungrateful, but how would I feel knowing no one in the community? I have grown up here, there is hardly a person in the parish who does not know me, every tenant and farmer's wife on the estate is familiar to me. How shall I leave them all?"

"But what do you propose to do? Where will you and Lilian live?" Becky asked, concerned at the vagueness of her sister's response. A practical sort of person herself, Becky worried that Catherine had no real plans.

She answered just as vaguely, saying something about needing to discuss it with Lilian because Lilian had never known any home but the parsonage at Hunsford. "Besides," she added, "she is unlikely to wish to leave at this time; she is just seventeen with all her life ahead of her. The friends of her childhood are all here, and I am not inclined to remove her from this place just when she has lost her father and needs the comfort of her friends."

Rebecca agreed. "I can see that Lilian's interests lie here. Indeed, I had hoped to speak with her about them..." she said and was astonished at the speed and sharpness of her sister's riposte.

"Becky, I would rather you did not. Although Lilian is young, she is exceedingly sensible and would never do anything untoward or stupid. I am confident of that. Pray, do not intervene to query or quiz her about matters that are surely for her alone to decide; she may well be resentful and I would not wish such a circumstance to come between you two. Believe me, Becky dear, it is for the best."

Seeing she was being quite serious, Rebecca said no more about it, but could not help wondering at the liberality of her sister's views.

Writing once more to Emily Courtney, she complained:

> *I cannot understand Catherine at all; she seems prepared to let young Lilian continue an association with Mr Adams without having ascertained if his antecedents, his background, and income are entirely suitable. I am convinced that they are in love or very close to it, but Catherine shows little concern, which is very unlike her usual meticulous nature.*
>
> *I am afraid I cannot comprehend it at all.*

A week later, Rebecca returned home to Matlock, promising to be back at a day's notice if her sister needed her.

"Promise me, Cathy," she pleaded, "you will send word if you need my help. There is little to occupy me in Derbyshire now and I will come at once, should you send for me."

Catherine promised. She knew her sister was not happy to be going, while some matters remained unresolved, but clearly there was nothing more she could achieve by remaining at the Dower House at this time.

Some days later, Catherine and Lilian together had been upstairs in Dr Harrison's room, looking askance at the piles of books and papers that seemed to fill every available space. They were wondering how they would sort out the material to be sent to the library at Rosings and what they might do with the rest.

"We could take them all down to Papa's book room, but I cannot begin to pack them up, until I know which are those considered suitable to be preserved and which might not suit. Papa appears to have kept copious notes on everything," grumbled Lilian.

"He certainly did that," said her mother. "There are more boxes in the attic, filled with his sermons and notes of all the reports he did for the bishop. I do not believe I know enough to decide upon their value."

The sound of footsteps outside alerted them to the arrival of visitors.

Looking out of the window, Lilian whispered, "It's Mr Adams, Mama, and look, there's Mr Burnett with him, too. We have not seen him in several days; I have wondered where he had gone."

Catherine did not rise immediately from her chair; instead, she sent Lilian down to greet the gentlemen and settle them in the parlour.

"I shall be down very soon; do ask Mrs Giles to send in some tea and cake," she said.

Both men rose when Catherine entered the room, and Frank Burnett's face was grave as he took her outstretched hand.

"Mrs Harrison, please accept my heartfelt condolences and forgive me for not calling on you earlier... I was summoned to London... on the very day before..." he appeared to become tongue-tied and awkward until Catherine intervened.

"Thank you, Mr Burnett, there is no need to apologise, I was aware that you had left Rosings for London. Had you been here, I know you would have come, of course."

Mr Adams looked puzzled, wondering how Catherine had known of Mr Burnett's journey to London. Burnett had declared he had received an express summoning him to an important meeting at the British Museum and left to catch a train to London, but John Adams had not spoken of it to anyone. His time had been spent comforting Lilian, who had suffered both shock and grief at the sudden deterioration and death of her father. Mr Adams had believed that neither Lilian nor her mother could have known of Burnett's departure for London.

He had subsequently returned as suddenly as he had departed and almost immediately asked if they could call on Mrs Harrison and her daughter.

"I feel I have been remiss in not calling on them before I left for London; it was most unfortunate but unavoidable. I wish to offer my condolences..." he had said and had appeared so determined that Mr Adams had not tried to dissuade him.

What he did not know was that prior to his departure for London, Frank Burnett had written an informal note of condolence to Mrs Harrison, expressing his sympathy and his own distress at having been called away to London. Catherine had opened it two days after the funeral and had told no one, putting it away with the rest of her correspondence, intending to respond to it later.

After they had taken tea, Lilian and Mr Adams walked out into the garden, where they claimed they wished to admire the newly blooming roses, which grew in a secluded area to the east of the house, leaving Catherine and Mr Burnett together in the parlour.

After a brief silence, Catherine took the opportunity to thank him for his note, and he sincerely reiterated his regrets at not being present at the funeral.

"It was the least I could do; I had hoped to call on you, but there was no opportunity. Mr Adams had informed me that many members of your family had arrived already, and I did not wish to intrude upon you at the time. I hoped you would forgive my presumption in writing to you as I did; I was loathe to leave for London without a word to you," he said.

He seemed genuinely concerned and Catherine was at pains to reassure him. " There is nothing to forgive; there was certainly no presumption on your part. Indeed, I appreciated your thoughtfulness in writing to me."

He smiled then, clearly pleased to be reassured.

After a few more minutes of silence, Mr Burnett asked if Catherine wished to walk in the garden too, but she declined.

"I have been out to see the roses already; it is a habit of mine to go out directly after breakfast. One I cultivated in the days when I lived at Rosings and had to ensure that Lady Catherine had fresh blooms on her table when she sat down to read her letters each morning," she said quietly.

Frank Burnett recalled with some amusement that indeed it had been one of Her Ladyship's many requirements.

"I do remember seeing you often in the rose garden, gathering the best blooms for Lady Catherine, no doubt," he said and she smiled too, nodding and thinking to herself, "He remembers the roses but has clearly forgotten the silly incident with the secateurs."

She was not about to remind him, and it seemed their conversation had reached an end, when he asked in a very matter-of-fact way about the collection of books and papers that Dr Harrison had wished to be lodged in the library at Rosings.

"I understand there is a considerable amount of material; Mr Adams has told me that Miss Lilian and you intend to sort through it yourselves."

Catherine, rather glad of an opportunity to embark upon a new, less personal topic of conversation, said with some degree of eagerness, "Yes indeed, there is a great deal—books, papers, notes, manuscripts, besides a quite valuable collection of rare Bibles, which Dr Harrison acquired over many years. According to his will, they are all to be sent to the library at Rosings, except his personal family Bible and prayer book, which we are to keep. Lilian and I have been trying to sort the papers and books, but I am afraid we have not got very far. Neither of us is conversant with the material to the extent that we feel qualified to decide what is and what is not worth keeping. I should hate to discard, through ignorance, something that is of value, but there is so much, it cannot all be preserved, surely?"

"Indeed no, it is a task that requires both time and special knowledge," said Mr Burnett, acknowledging her concern. "John Adams told me of it last night and I wondered whether you would let me help. I should be more than happy to assist, if you wished it. I could sort and collate the papers here and have them removed to the library, which has been mercifully spared the ravages of the fire, where they could, at a later date, be catalogued and stored appropriately. As for the books and the collection of rare Bibles, they should be stored safely as soon as possible, to avoid any damage."

At first, Catherine had been taken aback by his offer, more by the directness of his approach than by the offer itself; but she did genuinely appreciate his kindness in suggesting it. There would be so much to do to reorder her life that the additional responsibility of organising her husband's bequest of books and papers had loomed as an enormous task, which would probably take weeks to complete. Yet, she knew that a practised librarian, with an eye for the important details, would no doubt have it done in half the time. Quite clearly, Mr Burnett understood this too.

She looked and sounded relieved as she said, "If you are quite certain you could spare the time, Mr Burnett, it would assist me very much indeed. I am unfamiliar with the processes of such a task and…"

Frank Burnett was quick to reassure her. "Please do not concern yourself on that score, Mrs Harrison; if the material is to be lodged in the library at Rosings as part of a bequest, I shall need to see it and assess it myself for cataloguing and storage. The responsibility is mine, and I would be honoured to undertake the task."

She thanked him and they arranged that he would call on the morrow around mid-morning to begin work.

Returning from their sojourn among the roses, Lilian and John Adams found Frank Burnett and Mrs Harrison in the midst of a discussion on how many boxes would be required and by what means they might be transported to Rosings. The question was soon resolved when Mr Adams suggested that perhaps Mr Benson could be pressed into service and would organise it all.

The gentlemen were preparing to leave when Catherine surprised them by reminding them of a previous, unfulfilled engagement, which had sadly been foregone due to the sudden deterioration of Dr Harrison's health. She wondered if the gentlemen would care to dine with them on the following Sunday.

"There will only be Lilian and myself, and it will be a simple meal, but if you have nothing else to occupy you, you will be most welcome to join us," she said and both men accepted with pleasure.

Lilian looked pleased too, but was, it must be admitted, more than a little surprised. She had not supposed that her mother would be ready for company at this time, yet for herself, she was exceedingly glad of the opportunity that it would afford her and Mr Adams to meet again soon. It was the first time that Mr Adams had been invited to dine with them.

Between then and Sunday, Mr Burnett called thrice at the house and, having been shown into Dr Harrison's study and provided with the keys to his desk and cabinets, had worked all through the day, quietly and assiduously, disturbing no one and emerging only to ask Mrs Giles for some string. The housekeeper had taken him some tea and biscuits, which were gratefully accepted as he continued on with his task.

On the Friday, he indicated that all of the preliminary work was complete and he would return on the morrow with Mr Benson and a vehicle to remove the boxes, and Catherine was amazed at the speed with which he had completed the task.

However, there was one thing that he wanted Mrs Harrison to see, he said, inviting her into the room. Catherine followed him in, curious to discover what it was he had found.

He picked up a rather worn, tooled leather wallet, which appeared to contain several quarto-sized sheets of drawing paper.

"Mrs Harrison, I found this in one of the drawers of Dr Harrison's desk;

it had probably been put away and forgotten," he said. "You can tell from the discolouration on the paper, it has lain undisturbed for many years. On opening it and seeing its contents were of a purely private nature, I put it aside. I do not believe it should be sent to Rosings with the rest of Dr Harrison's papers. I think you should have it."

Surprised, Catherine took the case and it fell open, revealing a number of pencil sketches of herself and the children; work done a long time ago, when she was a young woman and they were very little.

They were, some of them, rather faded, but many of the drawings retained a remarkable degree of freshness and spirit. Catherine could recall quite clearly when they had been done, over a long Summer, when Lady Catherine and her entourage had travelled to Bath, leaving the family at the Hunsford parsonage to entertain themselves. It had been a particularly happy time.

As she extracted the drawings from the case and laid them on the desk in front of her, her eyes filled with tears. Sketching, making pen-portraits, had been her husband's only diversion from his work for the church and parish, and she had enjoyed sharing it with him.

But, so wholehearted had been his dedication to his calling, even that innocent pastime had fallen by the wayside some years ago and she had never seen him take it up again. Nor had she seen again the delightful sketches, which he had made that Summer, until this day.

She sighed; so concentrated was her mind upon the drawings in front of her, drawings that brought back happy memories from many Summers ago, she almost forgot Frank Burnett was in the room, until he, looking over her shoulder, said, "They are very good; Dr Harrison must have had a real gift; he has captured the expressions and attitudes of his subjects to perfection."

Wrenched back to the present, Catherine looked up at him and said, "He had indeed; it was a pity he hid it all away, almost as though he was ashamed of it. It was just a little fun, nothing serious, yet it brought all of us a lot of pleasure at the time. I had quite forgotten about them after all these years; I must thank you very much for finding them for me."

"Shall you have any of them framed for hanging, do you think?" he asked, adding, "They are certainly good enough."

She thought for a while and hesitated before replying, "Yes, why not? I dare say Lilian would like one for her room, and Mama, too. Perhaps when

Lilian returns from the village, we could select some of the best and have them framed."

Mr Burnett spoke quickly. "When you do decide, I should be happy to take them into town for you and have them framed by a man who often does similar work for me. He is a fine craftsman and will do them justice, I promise you."

Catherine thanked him again and left the study, taking the wallet and its contents with her. Before returning upstairs, she took a moment to remind him of their dinner engagement on the Sunday and received his assurance that he would be there.

"I am looking forward to it, very much," he said.

If success may be judged by the satisfaction and pleasure of the participants, then the dinner party might have been judged to be completely successful.

It was the first time they had entertained anyone at all, however simply, since moving to the Dower House. Dr Harrison's illness had precluded the possibility. Catherine was careful not to make too much of it, though.

Lilian, conscious of the fact that Mr Adams was dining with them for the first time, paid special attention to the table linen and silverware, ensuring that everything was exactly as it should be. She had slipped out into the garden and picked a small bunch of cream roses to adorn the table and set candles at either end.

Catherine had discussed the menu with Mrs Giles and decided upon fish and a terrine of veal and ham rather than a roast, with plenty of vegetables from the garden. She was satisfied that it provided a variety of tastes without being extravagant. She surveyed the room before going upstairs to dress for dinner and was well pleased.

When the gentlemen arrived, both ladies had been down and waiting in the parlour for almost half an hour. Catherine, though in formal mourning, appeared remarkably well, if a little pale, while Lilian, who had taken great care with her preparations, looked very pretty indeed. Her golden hair and fresh complexion, enhanced by the glow of candlelight, were quite exceptional. Indeed, Mr Adams seemed so completely captivated, he could not leave her side even for a moment, a fact that both her mother and Mr Burnett noted, separately, but upon which neither made comment.

At dinner, when they could drag their attention away from the excellent fare, the conversation was all about Rosings and what was planned for the estate after the fire. The accountant engaged by the Trust to ascertain the extent of the losses and recommend the best course of action for the future was still working on his figures, Mr Burnett informed them.

"I understand that he believes there is so much damage to the West Wing, it does not warrant restoration. I think he intends to recommend that the main body of the house be restored and refurbished, and the West Wing be demolished."

Catherine was curious. "And do you suppose the Rosings Trust will be willing to accept such a recommendation?" she asked.

Frank Burnett was cautious. "While I am not privy to the attitudes and opinions prevailing among members of the Trust, I am inclined to think that they would see it as a practical solution. To restore the entire property would cost many thousands of pounds and to what end?" he continued, as the others listened. "I recall that much of the West Wing was devoted to displays of trophies and memorabilia of wars, collected by Sir Lewis de Bourgh and his father. Now, except for some miscellaneous pieces of armour and a few medieval artifacts that have survived the fire, that original collection has been totally lost, together with the furniture and accessories. What good would it do to restore the West Wing without any of its contents?"

"Could not similar items be found and purchased?" asked Lilian, but Mr Adams explained that not only would that be very costly and probably impossible to do, since many of the items were exotic pieces, collected in foreign parts, but the value of the original collection could never be replicated.

As Lilian nodded, understanding the point of the argument, Catherine said, "I do not think it would be either sensible or wise to attempt such a thing. I cannot predict what the Trust will decide, but if I were to be asked, I should tell them that what money is available should be spent not in restoration of the West Wing, or the purchase of expensive items to replace those destroyed by the fire, but in establishing a school for the children of the parish, in particular the girls of this district, who get no schooling at all. It would be a far more fitting memorial to the family of Sir Lewis and Lady Catherine de Bourgh. I might even be so bold as to predict that both Jonathan Bingley and Mr Darcy, if consulted, would agree with me."

There was a silence after she had spoken.

Clearly, her ideas had surprised the rest of the diners, but her words and
her voice had left no doubt in the minds of her companions that Catherine felt
passionately about the matter. Unlike the children of the parishes of Kympton
and Pemberley and, more recently, Netherfield and Longbourn, whose schools
had benefitted from the generosity of Mr Darcy and Jonathan Bingley, those
children on the Rosings estate had only the charity of the church to rely on
for their education. Consequently, many of them received no teaching at all,
except at Sunday school. It was a circumstance that Catherine and the late Dr
Harrison had long regretted. Their efforts to remedy the situation had not met
with success because of the intransigence of Lady Catherine de Bourgh; now,
Catherine could see a way to set it right.

Mr Burnett made the point clearly.

"I believe I am not wrong in thinking that the de Bourghs and in particular
Lady Catherine never grasped the principle that a community that is educated
and enlightened makes for a better society; rather, they feared such notions
would only serve to give the children of the poor ideas above their station."

Catherine concurred. "Indeed, and while she would gladly encourage young
women from the villages on the estate to enter into domestic service at Rosings
as a means of improving their lives, Lady Catherine would not contribute to their
education, lest they sought to rise above the status of servants. Similarly, young
men could be apprenticed to artisans or employed as labourers on the estate, or
be trained as footmen and butlers, but would then forfeit the right to attend a
school! There is an illogicality about it which offends me deeply," she said.

Mr Burnett declared he had seen a lot of that all over England.

Mr Adams said he thought that was very unfair and Lilian, her eyes
flashing, added that it was surely more than unfair, it was also un-Christian, for
were we not taught that all children were equal in the eyes of God?

At this, her mother smiled and said, "Ah, but there are many similar things
done, which might have been considered un-Christian, such as the taking of
tithes from tenants, at times when harvests were so poor they had little enough for
themselves, and disallowing the taking of game, even to feed starving families.

"Too many children went hungry while there was more than enough food
around, which they were forbidden to take. I used to wonder at the heartless-
ness of men and women who would enjoy sumptuous meals while their tenants
survived on meagre rations."

By the time this discussion had run its course, no one wanted any more food and as the servants cleared away the dishes, Catherine rose to leave the room. They repaired to the parlour for tea and coffee, and the younger couple seemed determined to enjoy as much of each other's company as possible, leaving Mr Burnett and Mrs Harrison to entertain one another.

Seating himself in a chair beside Catherine's, Frank Burnett asked if she had decided which of Dr Harrison's sketches were to be framed.

"I have to be in London next week and can take them for you, if you so wish," he said.

Catherine went to fetch the wallet of sketches, which she then laid out on a card table between them. After some discussion and upon his advice, she chose three sketches of the children. "There, I think I should like those framed—they would look well on the wall behind the landing, do you not think?" she asked.

Mr Burnett agreed, but added, "Will you not choose one of yourself as well?" and he turned over several as he spoke. They were all well drawn, some of her alone, capturing a quality of youthful energy and freshness, that he remembered well, and others with one or all of her children, which had a different but undeniable charm of a contented and serene woman and her family.

Catherine shook her head. "No, I do not think I should care to be framed and hung," she said with a crooked little smile. "Now, it would be different if I were dead!"

He looked rather shocked, but persisted.

"Would not your mother, Mrs Collins, wish to have a framed likeness of her daughter and her children? Or your sister?"

She thought about it and hesitated, then relenting, said, "Yes, perhaps Mama would like one, and maybe Becky. All right, Mr Burnett, I shall let you choose a couple; I am not particular which; pick any that you consider might suit," she said, and went away to ask for a fresh pot of tea.

Frank Burnett did as she asked and by the time she returned, he had set aside the sketches to be framed and replaced the rest in the wallet. When she returned, Catherine treated the subject as closed and proceeded to pour out more tea for everyone.

Changing the subject, Frank Burnett asked, "Mrs Harrison, I do recall that you used to perform exceedingly well upon the pianoforte at Rosings. May one ask if you still play?"

She replied without hesitation, "Not often and certainly not as well as I used to. I have had little time and no inclination recently, and without Lady Catherine to prompt me, I am probably badly out of practice."

He looked genuinely disappointed.

"Do you not mean to take it up again? It would be a pity to waste such a fine talent. I remember even Her Ladyship being silenced by your rendition of Mozart, one evening when we were privileged to have the company of the bishop at dinner. I cannot believe that you have lost your love of music?"

Catherine laughed, surprised by the accuracy of his recollection.

"Mr Burnett, you *do* have a good memory. I had quite forgotten that occasion. Well, I do still deeply love music and perhaps I shall play again—sometime in the future," she mused.

"Please do," he said, encouraging her. "I am sure it will afford you both pleasure and comfort. I can vouch for my own enjoyment and would entreat you to practice and play again."

Catherine bit her lip, discomposed a little by the directness of his remarks.

"Perhaps I shall and I will tell you if I succeed. Meanwhile, may one ask, Mr Burnett, if you still sing as well as you used to do?"

This time it was his turn to look confused and embarrassed that she had remembered. It was clearly unexpected and he took a moment to frame an answer. "I have to confess that I have not had occasion to sing of late, Mrs Harrison, and unlike the skill involved in playing an instrument, which may be regained by practice, it is unlikely that the voice can be similarly restored if left unused for many years," he replied, rather self-consciously.

Catherine looked very censorious.

"For shame, Mr Burnett, that is a poor excuse. I am quite certain that a good singing voice can and will, with some practice, be restored. When you are next here, Lilian could play for you. Mr Adams has a very pleasing tenor voice and sings in the church choir; perhaps you and he might attempt a duet. Will you at least try?"

He was genuinely disconcerted, not ever having anticipated that the tables would be turned on him. Unable to refuse, he agreed to try when he returned from London and was immediately rewarded with some encouragement. "Excellent; I shall ask Lilian to learn some of the songs you used to favour and we shall see how well you do. I have no doubt you will do very well," she said, and seeing his rather crestfallen demeanour, she regretted her initial reproving manner and smiled warmly, which appeared to have an immediate effect upon his spirits.

The evening had passed so pleasantly that when it was time to go, both gentlemen seemed reluctant to leave such congenial company. Likewise, the ladies, who for the first time in many months had been able to enjoy an evening of good food and interesting conversation.

Neither Catherine nor her daughter had ever before entertained two gentlemen without either Dr Harrison or another male family member in the party. Each had been privately concerned that awkwardness or plain ineptitude would spoil the occasion.

But no such thing had eventuated.

As Messrs Adams and Burnett took their leave, they thanked Mrs Harrison for inviting them, and John Adams especially expressed his particular appreciation.

"It has been a very great pleasure, ma'am," he said, and though he was addressing her mother, it was upon Lilian's lovely face that his eyes were fixed, leaving Catherine in no doubt that the time was fast approaching when she would have to speak seriously to her daughter about Mr Adams.

She may even have to speak to Mr Adams himself, she thought, feeling somewhat daunted at the prospect.

But for tonight, she decided, it was sufficient that the evening had been a most satisfactory one. In truth, thinking over the past six months, which had been more than usually melancholy, she could not recall a happier occasion.

Chapter Five

MRS DARCY WAS VISITING her cousin Emily Courtney at Oakleigh. Mr Darcy had promised Emily he would advise her on some of the work that was being done on the manor and had come over with his steward to take a look. While they were out inspecting the work, Elizabeth and Emily took tea together in the parlour.

"I understand Rebecca is back from Kent; has she brought you word of Catherine?" asked Elizabeth. "Cassy met her in the village a few days ago and said she looked well, if a little anxious."

Emily laughed. "Anxious is certainly right," she said. "Lizzie, I do not understand why Becky allows herself to be so distracted by matters over which she cannot possibly have any influence. I have advised her that it is of no use to worry endlessly about the way other people lead their lives, even if they are your nearest and dearest."

Elizabeth was curious, but careful about asking too many questions.

"You are quite right, Emily," she said and asked casually, "I suppose she worries about Catherine's future, now she is widowed and with Lilian to support? But in truth, she need not at all. Mr Darcy tells me that the generous endowment left to Mrs Harrison by Lady Catherine, as well as her portion of Dr Harrison's annuity, should see Catherine quite comfortably settled. Rebecca need have no fears for her on that score."

Emily waited until Elizabeth had finished speaking.

"Lizzie, it is not Catherine's future that exercises Becky's mind; she is far more concerned about Lilian's prospects."

"Lilian? Why, she is only seventeen and I am informed as sensible as she is pretty. What can there possibly be about Lilian to cause Rebecca any concern?" she asked and it was clear to Emily that her cousin Lizzie knew nothing of the matter of Mr John Adams.

Reluctant to gossip, yet keen to obtain the advice of her cousin, whom she both trusted and admired, Emily showed Elizabeth some of Rebecca's recent letters, in which she had voiced her disquiet about Lilian and Mr Adams. Furthermore, upon her return to Derbyshire, Rebecca Tate had gone directly to see her friend, Emily Courtney, and much of her visit had been taken up with a recital of her observations and reservations about her goddaughter and Mr Adams, as well as what Rebecca assumed was Mrs Harrison's unwillingness to take an active interest in her daughter's affairs.

Becky had been both puzzled and somewhat censorious on that score.

These matters Emily related to Elizabeth, making every effort not to exaggerate Rebecca's fears, but hoping that Elizabeth would help her provide her friend with some reasonable information that may allay her concerns.

"I cannot believe, Lizzie, that Catherine would neglect to advise her daughter, if there were reason to do so; she is both a loving and conscientious mother. I feel Becky is being unduly anxious. Do you not agree?"

Elizabeth did agree, but could not hide her confusion as to why Rebecca Tate should harbour such fears.

"I think, Emily, that it is far more likely that Rebecca has misconstrued Catherine's attitude—for she is by nature a remarkably serene and imperturbable woman, who will not, unlike her sister, permit a situation or person to cause her to panic. Cathy is very like her mother, Charlotte; unless she judges that there is something quite seriously wrong with Lilian's friendship with Mr Adams, she is unlikely to interfere. I do not think for one moment that one could ever suggest that Catherine would be derelict in her duty as a mother."

Emily shook her head, still bewildered, "I do hope you are right, Lizzie. Becky seems to fear that Catherine has made no enquiries about the gentleman's family or background. She claims they know little or nothing about him or his family."

Elizabeth laughed, "Is that all? If it is, it should not be difficult to remedy. It was Jonathan Bingley who appointed Mr Adams to his position as curator of the Rosings estate; I shall write to him forthwith and discover how much he knows about young John Adams, and you will be able to set Rebecca's mind at rest. It is not possible that Jonathan would have recommended him to the Rosings Trust unless he had very good references."

The entrance of Mr Darcy and Emily's wish to get a fresh pot of tea interrupted their conversation, and there was no other opportunity to return to it before it was time for the Darcys to leave.

Back at Pemberley, Elizabeth could not help turning it all over in her mind.

She remembered well enough Rebecca Tate's distraught state when her own daughter Josie had been deceived and cruelly used by a man whose smooth charm had hidden a multitude of misdeeds. Indeed, his iniquity had destroyed not just Josie, but had very nearly ruined the life of her husband, Julian Darcy. It was not a matter his mother was likely to forget.

Elizabeth, having watched the disintegration of Julian and Josie's unhappy marriage and all of the subsequent sorrow their families had endured, was not therefore entirely unsympathetic to Rebecca's concerns and decided she would make a serious effort to ascertain the facts about Mr John Adams. Deciding not to trouble her husband about it just yet, she wrote that night to their nephew Jonathan Bingley, confident that he would be able to give her the information necessary to set all their minds at rest.

The occasion of the birthday of one of the Bingleys' children afforded her the opportunity she needed.

She wrote, *My dear Jonathan,* and following the customary greetings and enquiries about the health of all the members of the families at Netherfield and Longbourn, continued thus:

We have recently been hearing a great deal, mainly from Mrs Tate, about the work being done at Rosings by the new curator, Mr John Adams. It would appear he is a very gifted and pleasing young man and has been paying quite a lot of attention to Rebecca's young niece, Lilian Harrison.

Now, while I do not wish to jump to any conclusions, in view of the fact that Lilian and her mother no longer have the benefit of Dr Harrison's counsel and support, I wondered if you would help us with some information about Mr Adams.

I have no doubt, and Mr Darcy assures me of this, that he came to you highly recommended for his work, but what more do we know of him? Who exactly are his family? Where is his home? I ask, Jonathan dear, not in order to interfere or make trouble for Mr Adams, but rather to reassure ourselves and particularly Lilian's mother Catherine, if need be, that there is no cause for concern in his friendship with her daughter. Your assistance in this delicate matter would be greatly appreciated.

Jonathan Bingley's response reached Elizabeth some ten days later.

He apologised for the delay in writing, blaming it upon business and his desire to obtain as complete an answer as possible to her query about John Adams.

He had searched through his papers, he said, to discover if he held any personal information about the gentleman concerned, but had found none. He wrote:

Mr Adams, in his letter to me applying for the position of curator at Rosings, made no mention of his family, except to say they had lived in Europe for several years, during which time he studied art. He was also briefly at Cambridge but did not complete his studies there, owing to the death of his father.

His previous employer, Sir ___, spoke very highly of young Adams in relation to both work and character, but again there was no reference to any other members of his family.

Dearest Aunt Lizzie, it does seem as though that is all the information I am able to provide at the moment. However, if you wish me to continue my enquiries, I shall do so discreetly and keep you informed of my success.

I might mention, for what it is worth, that since his appointment to Rosings there has never been a single complaint, nor even the slightest aspersion cast upon him. He appears to perform his often difficult duties well and conduct himself in an exemplary fashion.

Elizabeth was greatly relieved, though not entirely satisfied with her nephew's response.

She sent a further short note to Jonathan Bingley, thanking him for his efforts on her behalf, and suggesting that he make some enquiries in confidence about the sojourn of the Adams family in Europe.

I have no desire at all to be prying into his life, but it would be good to know who his parents were exactly and why they were living in Europe. Was his father a diplomat, perhaps? Some definite information would be invaluable.

No more was heard on the subject for some weeks, and with the onset of a busy Summer at Pemberley, Elizabeth almost forgot about Mr John Adams and Lilian.

~❧~

As the Summer wore on, it had become clear to Mrs Harrison that Mr Adams was paying a very great deal of attention to her daughter.

He called at the house two or three times a week, often on some pretext or other, but occasionally without any reason at all, except to drink lemonade and walk with Lilian in the garden. Sometimes, when Lilian went for a ramble in the woods or down to the village, she would meet him there and he would accompany her home.

So frequent had these visits become and so much did the couple have to say to one another that Catherine began to wonder whether it was time to ask Lilian if Mr Adams and she had reached some understanding. It was a question that was beginning to tease her mind day and night.

Then one afternoon, returning from the village, she found them sitting in the parlour, inexplicably indoors on a perfect Summer's afternoon; it was most unusual.

Mr Adams, who rose as Catherine entered the room, looked rather dejected, while Lilian clearly had tears in her eyes—of that her mother had no doubt.

Having greeted her with much less than his usual cheerful manner, Mr Adams proceeded to inform her, in an apologetic tone, that this very evening he was to leave Rosings and travel to London and thence to Paris, to be at the bedside of his mother, who was gravely ill.

"To Paris?" Catherine said, uncomprehending. "Your mother lives in France?" to which he said, "Indeed, Mrs Harrison, my mother has lived in France for most of her life. She has, unfortunately, been unwell recently and since the death of my father, I am her only male relative and must attend her at once. I received yesterday an urgent message by electric telegraph from my younger sister, who begs me to come directly, else I may not see my dear mother alive again," he explained as Lilian stood by, clearly distressed. "I have already spoken with Mr Burnett and sent a message by telegraph to Mr Jonathan Bingley explaining my circumstances. Mr Burnett and Mr Benson have very kindly agreed to make good my work whilst I am away and will assist you and Miss Lilian in any way possible. I came over particularly to reassure you and Miss Lilian on that point and to say my good-byes."

Catherine, having offered her sympathy and expressed her hopes for an improvement in his mother's condition, asked, "Are you travelling alone? And how long do you expect to be away?"

He answered unequivocally, "Indeed I am, I have no other family in England and only two sisters and a brother-in-law in France. As for my return, I confess it is not in my power to predict, for it will depend upon my mother's health. Were it to improve, as we earnestly hope it will, I should be back within a fortnight. On the other hand, if it were to decline, I may well be delayed longer."

Both ladies nodded, understanding the difficulty of his situation, and when he finally parted from them, they sent him on his way with every good wish for his journey.

Afterwards, Lilian went upstairs to her room and that evening seemed not to want food or company until dinnertime and even then, she was very quiet and said little except in answer to her mother's questions.

Despite Catherine's desire to comfort her daughter, who was quite clearly distressed, no opportunity arose for her to do so, mainly because Lilian chose not to seek it.

Catherine wrote that night to her sister.

Dearest Becky,

I write to give you some unhappy news—at least it is unhappy for Mr Adams and in consequence has made us, Lilian and me, somewhat despondent too.

Having related the gist of the story, she told of her surprise at discovering that Mr Adams had no family in England and his mother had lived all her life in France, where it appeared his sisters also were settled.

I did not feel comfortable asking too many questions—one does not have the right to pry—especially at such a time as this, which is why I was unable to ascertain if his mother was French. Perhaps she is from an émigré family? Which would explain a lot of his own qualities of gentleness and charm, I think. Do you not agree, Becky?

Rebecca did not entirely agree. She had always found Mr Adams to be somewhat different—in his manners, which were certainly impeccable, but also in his bearing, which Becky had thought rather superior.

"It must be the French in him," she said, putting her sister's letter away.

It was the first clue she had had.

Determined to discover more if it were possible, Becky decided it was time to visit her friend and recent mentor, Lady Isabel Ashton. There was very little Lady Isabel did not know and if she did not, she would find out, since she had an astonishingly large circle of friends and acquaintances.

Rebecca summoned her maid and asked that her trunks be packed. They were going to London, she said, and went upstairs to write a little note.

❧

Lady Ashton lived in a very desirable part of town, in a terrace house she had received as a wedding gift from her doting husband. There she entertained her many and varied friends, of whom Mrs Tate had recently become one. In fact, she had become quite a favourite with her.

Sir William Ashton, many years her senior, was a diplomat and businessman whose title had been a reward for services to the Tory party, rather than his country. Some few years ago, through a fortuitous coalescence of their business and private interests, he had become an associate of Mr Anthony Tate, and consequently, their wives, being thrown together on many social occasions, had also discovered a mutuality of interests.

Rebecca had admired Lady Ashton's style and envied her endless capacity for social manipulation, while Lady Ashton, who had few pretensions to education or culture, enjoyed having Rebecca around to answer her queries. It was useful to have an obliging and educated friend who could interpret from the French and Italian when one went to the opera or remind one which of Mr Dickens's characters appeared in a particular novel, when attending a book reading.

Best of all, Rebecca was herself a writer albeit of slight reputation, and Lady Ashton could use her modest achievements to stimulate conversation at her soirées and coffee parties. Many of her guests had never heard of Marianne Lawrence, the pen-name Rebecca had adopted when she first began to write for her husband's newspapers and journals, but were prepared to be impressed by a real live author in their midst.

It was therefore a mutually advantageous association in which neither woman made demands that were too onerous upon the other and each was tolerant of the other's foibles.

Preceded by her note, Rebecca and her maid arrived in London and took up residence at the town house that Mr Tate leased in a fashionable street, not far from Lady Ashton's somewhat grander establishment. The servants, though a little surprised at her sudden arrival, coped well with her requirements. The absence in America of Mr Anthony Tate meant that Rebecca was free to come and go as she pleased, beholden to no one and having to give no explanations for her activities.

Upon arriving, she sent a little note and a bouquet of flowers round to her friend Lady Ashton, and within the hour an invitation to afternoon tea was delivered to the door.

Rebecca took great care in her preparations for the visit. She was still a very handsome woman, and with the generous allowance her husband allowed her, she was well able to dress to impress anyone she pleased. She had fine gowns and jewellery in sufficient quantities to outshine any society lady, but Mrs Tate was also sensible enough to realise that it would do her no good at all to appear to compete with Lady Ashton. Which was why, when they were seen together, Rebecca chose quite deliberately to dress with a degree of modesty, ensuring that Lady Ashton was always the centre of attention and the cynosure of all eyes.

Moreover, despite Her Ladyship's constant urging, when they were together, Rebecca never took the liberty of using her first name in the presence of the servants or indeed any other person. Whether Lady Ashton understood the reason behind this behaviour or not is unknown, but she certainly approved of it, seeing it as a mark of the respect accorded her by her new friend.

Rebecca arrived at Lady Ashton's house to find that there were only two other ladies invited, neither of whom could be considered particular friends of Her Ladyship.

"I was sure you wanted to talk to me about something in particular, dearest Becky, or you would not have written in such urgent terms. The others will be gone within the hour, and we can then retire to my boudoir and you can tell me everything! There, is that not a good scheme?"

Rebecca agreed that it was an excellent scheme and could not wait for the other guests to depart. She was quite sure that when Lady Ashton had heard her story, she would understand her concerns and almost certainly she would suggest the means by which they might be best addressed. She knew no one who had such influence, nor such access to information in society, as Lady Isabel Ashton.

Thus, unbeknownst to Catherine, Lilian, and Mr Adams, Rebecca prepared to lay before her friend her apprehensions concerning her niece and the young man who was courting her. These concerns were such that, when communicated to Lady Ashton, they were likely to coincide with her own views exactly. Had Rebecca known what might be uncovered and how it would affect Lilian and her mother, it is possible she may have had some misgivings about the course of action upon which she had embarked.

As it happened, so convinced was she of the correctness of her motives, she never gave another thought to the possible consequences.

After the two ladies had left, Lady Ashton led the way upstairs to her private boudoir, where, over hot chocolate and truffles, Rebecca related the circumstances of her sister Catherine Harrison and her daughter Lilian.

Lady Ashton had once shown some interest in young Lilian Harrison. Lilian and her mother had been in London, before Christmas, and Rebecca had succeeded in introducing them to Lady Ashton at a soirée, after which she had remarked that it was good to see a young girl "who was both pretty and accomplished, yet apparently uninterested in flirting with every man she met."

"I am quite vexed by these 'modern' young women, who seem to think it is their prerogative, simply because they are single, to monopolise every eligible male in the room. I noted that your niece Miss Harrison is happily not afflicted with a similar condition."

"Indeed she is not, Lady Isabel," Rebecca had responded, realising the import of her words, "my niece Lilian is a very good girl, well brought up and God fearing. She has absolutely no interest in flirting."

This time, Lady Ashton listened as Rebecca reminded her of Lilian's virtues and proceeded to tell the tale.

"You will recall my niece Lilian, Lady Isabel, who is such a good girl. Well, she is being courted by a young man, a certain Mr John Adams, and I must confess I am very anxious about her."

"Why?" asked Lady Ashton, "is this John Adams a man of ill repute?"

"Oh no indeed, there is no evidence of that, Lady Isabel, in fact the problem is no one knows anything at all about Mr Adams, his parents or his family... where they lived and what they did... it is all a mystery."

Lady Ashton frowned and seemed puzzled. "Has not her mother made some enquiries about his background?"

Rebecca explained that her sister Catherine, recently widowed, seemed averse to doing so.

"Which is why I feel I must do what I can to assist, young Lilian is my goddaughter, I feel responsible..."

"I am sure you do and it is to your credit, Becky dear, and I shall do whatever I can to help," said Lady Isabel. "In cases such as this, where the mother is incapable or unwilling to play her part, it is essential that friends intervene if necessary to prevent what may be an unfortunate mis-match. Later, they will thank you for it, Becky, mark my words."

Rebecca was immediately encouraged to continue, "My feelings exactly, dear Lady Isabel, and I had hoped you would agree with me. In addition to my earlier misgivings, I have heard just this week that Mr Adams has gone to France to attend his mother, who is very ill. My sister is uncertain whether his mother is French or merely lives in France for some unaccountable reason."

Lady Ashton had many English friends who lived in France and did not see this of itself as a serious drawback and said so.

"And do we know where in France his mother lives?" she asked.

Rebecca persisted. "I do not have an address, but it is possible Catherine will be able to obtain one from Mr Burnett. Shall I write to her tonight?"

Lady Ashton was quick to respond. "No, it would be unwise to do so at this point. If you wish to discover something about this young man, it would not do to alert your niece to your intentions. She may resent them and work actively to prevent you achieving them. She may even attempt to turn your sister against you by arguing that you are interfering in her life."

"What then must I do?" asked Rebecca, getting rather desperate.

"Nothing for the moment; let things lie while I have some enquiries made about this Mr Adams and his French connections. I have friends, as you know, who travel regularly between Paris and London; we shall see what they can discover. Once we know for certain what his antecedents are and whether or not he is a suitable young man to be courting your niece, we can decide how to proceed."

Rebecca nodded her agreement, waiting for further advice, which was soon forthcoming.

"Meanwhile, Becky, why do you not write to your niece and invite her to come to London and spend a few weeks with you? Make no mention of Mr Adams—now he is away in France, she will have time on her hands—let her believe you are in need of a companion; better still, write to her mother and ask her as a favour to send the girl to London to keep you company. There can be no objection, surely? Mrs Harrison will know the girl will be quite safe in your care," she argued, then went on. "Once she is here, we can arrange for her to meet so many more eligible and clever young men that Mr Adams's attractions will soon pale into insignificance by comparison. Do you not think, Becky, that this is a good scheme?" she asked.

Rebecca was so completely taken with the prospect that she agreed wholeheartedly.

"Dear Lady Isabel, it is an excellent scheme indeed. I shall write to my sister Catherine tonight and invite Rebecca to stay with me in London. You are quite right, I *am* in need of company and *would* appreciate having a young person who can accompany me to the shops and read to me in the evenings."

"And drive with us in Hyde Park or go to the theatre? The possibilities are endless," added Lady Ashton, with a light laugh. "Poor Mr Adams, especially if he stays too long in France, may be entirely forgotten—supplanted by a clutch of young men whose savoir-faire and chic may far exceed his own."

"We shall have to get her some fashionable new gowns first," Rebecca warned, "my niece is inclined to dress rather plainly. It is something she has learned from her mother; my sister Catherine abhors many of the latest fashions and so does Lilian. Her clothes may not be suitable for being seen in London society."

Lady Ashton brushed aside her reservations. "Dear Becky, that is no problem at all; once she is here, we can have my dressmaker fit her out in a few days. A couple of day dresses, a ball gown, and a few other accessories—she must have a fashionable hat to drive in the park—that is absolutely *de rigeur*, my milliner will advise you... Oh my dear Becky, I think I shall enjoy this very much, to take a simple young country girl and introduce her into London society should be lots of fun... I am quite looking forward to it."

She rose and indicated that she had to rest before going out, and Becky, grateful for the time she had been allowed, left feeling quite satisfied.

~🦇~

That night Rebecca, well pleased with her friend's plan, wrote to her sister Catherine, but in so doing revealed little of her intentions.

Dearest Cathy, she wrote:

> *You are going to be surprised to receive this from me in London, but I have had to come up to town for several reasons and with Mr Tate away, I am very much at a loss for company. It is particularly awkward when one is invited to attend soirées and dinner parties and such to have to go on one's own.*
>
> *I was wondering, dear Cathy, whether you would be so kind as to send my dear niece to stay with me for a few weeks.*
>
> *Seeing as Mr Adams is in France, she may have some time on her hands and it would do her good to have a change of scene. London is usually at its best in late Summer and I am sure Lilian will enjoy it very much.*
>
> *I promise I shall take good care of her, as if she were my own daughter.*
>
> *Please send word if you are agreeable and I will make all the arrangements for her journey.*
>
> *Tell Lilian there is to be a performance of Mr Sheridan's School for Scandal at Drury Lane—I know it is one of her favourite plays. I hope to obtain good seats for us.*

As she concluded with affectionate greetings to her sister and niece, Rebecca, knowing Lilian's love of the theatre, hoped that last piece of information would be sufficient to entice her niece into coming to London, if nothing else would.

Chapter Six

CATHERINE AND LILIAN WERE seated in the parlour when Rebecca's letter was delivered.

On opening it and scanning its contents, Catherine looked at her daughter and smiled, clearly pleased at what she saw.

Then, she read it again, more carefully, before handing it to Lilian.

"Look, dear, your aunt Becky invites you to come up to London and spend a few weeks with her. Would you not like that?"

Catherine had noticed that since the departure of Mr Adams for France, Lilian had seemed somewhat distracted. She completed all her usual tasks and went about her work without complaint, but her mother could see she was not herself. Clearly she was missing him, Catherine thought, and Rebecca's invitation could be just what she needed.

Lilian's initial response was not promising. "I do not wish to go up to London, Mama," she said. "I never enjoy it; it's too busy and crowded. Whenever we travelled there with Papa, I was cold and bored and could not wait to come home."

Catherine was not so easily discouraged.

"But, my dear, that was because your papa was usually too busy to escort us around to all the interesting places there are to visit and we always stayed at the same small hotel. If you go to your aunt, you will be staying at her home in one of the best streets in town, and Becky will see that you are never bored or cold. Besides, do you not wish to see a performance of *School for Scandal* ?"

Lilian appeared to relent. "I will admit it is the one thing that makes me consider accepting the invitation—I have so enjoyed reading it, I should love to see it performed."

"Well then? Let me write to Becky and say you will come," said Catherine but Lilian was not yet ready to capitulate.

"No, Mama, let us wait a day or two—there is no hurry, is there? Let me think it over and perhaps by Wednesday, we will send Aunt Becky an answer."

Catherine agreed; she had sensed that Lilian was keen to delay her decision in order to learn what had happened with Mr Adams's mother. If, as he told them, she was seriously ill, even in danger of dying, it was possible his return would be delayed by some weeks. As the only male relative, perhaps it would be his responsibility to attend to a number of matters affecting the family.

Catherine understood her daughter's restlessness and decided to wait a day or two before writing to Rebecca. It would do no harm to let Lilian make up her mind without any persuasion from her, she thought.

On the following day, the warmth of the weather encouraged them to take a walk in the woods, which were beginning to reflect the onset of Autumn with the first cool nights of the waning Summer. The bright greens and golds that had clothed the trees were beginning to give way to patches of russet and red, while drifts of fallen leaves crunched crisply underfoot.

"I love the woods like this," said Lilian. "Mama, if we must leave the Dower House next year, where shall we go? I should hate to be too far from this beautiful place."

Catherine was taken aback at her question; it was not something she had anticipated at all and she did not know how she should answer. Even as she struggled to think of something comforting to say—for in truth she had no firm answer to the question—a familiar figure appeared at the end of the path.

It was Mr Burnett and he had in his hand a letter.

He greeted them cheerfully enough, but there was no doubting the gravity of his countenance as he said, "I was coming over to call on you; a letter has just reached me this morning, from Mr Adams."

"What does he say? Is his mother's condition improved?" asked Catherine quickly, while Lilian looked at Mr Burnett earnestly, hoping he did not have bad news for them.

"I am very sorry to have to tell you that the news is not good; his mother Mrs Adams died three days ago, very peacefully, I understand, but it does mean that John Adams will have to extend his stay in France. He writes that it falls to him to arrange the funeral and attend to all the family matters, including the settlement of his mother's estate. Being the only male relative, his two sisters depend on him to be there until the conclusion of these questions. He send his regards and apologies."

"Does he say when he may return?" asked Lilian in a soft voice.

"Not in so many words, I rather think his return may be delayed by at least a few weeks, perhaps even a month. I am not entirely familiar with the processes of the laws of inheritance in France, but I imagine it will take some while to settle all the matters that are likely to arise," he replied.

"Do you know if his mother's estate was a large one?" asked Catherine and almost immediately regretted her question; she had not meant to pry. "What I meant was, is the disposition of it likely to be complicated?"

Mr Burnett said he had no specific knowledge of Mrs Adams's estate but he had understood from John Adams that his father had no estate as such, only a successful wine business in the Bordeaux region, but his mother's family owned a farm and a vineyard.

"I am not privy to the extent or value of it, Mrs Harrison, but I gather it was sufficient to support the family quite comfortably. I expect it will be divided among her three children."

While no more was said on that subject, Mr Burnett walked with them as they returned to the Dower House and was invited to come in and take tea with them, which he gladly agreed to do. Whilst her mother went upstairs to change her shoes, Lilian asked Mr Burnett if he would let her have Mr Adams's address in France.

"I should like, and I am sure Mama would also wish, to write to him and convey our condolences. It is the least we can do. After Papa's death, Mr Adams was exceedingly helpful to us, as indeed you were, Mr Burnett. I should not like him to think that we were unappreciative of his kindness," she said and Frank Burnett was quick to respond. "I am quite certain that he would never think such a thing, Miss Lilian, but of course you can have the address, it is at the bottom of the last page of the letter, if you wish to write it down…" and so saying he handed her the letter.

Lilian went directly to a bureau by the window and, taking out a sheet of note paper, wrote down the direction, perusing the letter swiftly before returning it to Mr Burnett.

"I intend to write myself, and when I do so, I shall let him know that Mrs Harrison and you are both aware of his present situation. It will put his mind at ease; he appears concerned that you may be inconvenienced by his delayed return."

Lilian hastened to assure him that no such thing had even crossed their minds and urged him to reassure Mr Adams that he should not think so at all.

"It is his duty to attend to the needs of his sisters, and he must not think even for one moment that we would wish him to do otherwise. I am quite confident Mama would agree with me," Lilian said.

Despite her confidence, the return of her mother and the entrance of the maid with the tea tray ended their conversation, which now turned upon the work in progress at Rosings.

On this subject, Frank Burnett had some good news. "Mr Jonathan Bingley is coming down to Rosings next week," he said, "and in the absence of Mr Adams, I am to see him and discuss the consequences flowing from the decision of the trust to accept the proposition to demolish that part of the building that was too badly damaged to restore. I understand Mr Darcy and the other trustees have agreed this is the best course of action."

Catherine was delighted to hear that Jonathan Bingley was expected and had a plan of her own, which she intended to put to him when he arrived. "Do you know if Mrs Bingley is coming too?" she asked, to which Mr Burnett replied that he believed this to be the case, as the couple were to attend a dinner party in London later that week and had planned only to stay overnight at Rosings.

"Anna, Mrs Bingley, is my cousin and I should be very happy to accommodate them here," said Catherine, smiling. "Indeed, I should like to write at once and invite them to dine with us at least. Perhaps you would care to join us, Mr Burnett?"

Frank Burnett thanked Catherine and accepted her invitation; he did not stay long after he had finished his tea and left, having thanked the ladies for their kind hospitality.

Once he had left them, Catherine turned to Lilian and asked if she did not think it was a good thing Jonathan Bingley was coming to Rosings.

"Now, if he brings Anna with him, that would be doubly delightful, do you not agree, my dear?" asked Catherine.

Anna, who was Jonathan Bingley's second wife, was an accomplished artist with a penchant for interior décor. She had spent many years in Europe studying art and music and had been responsible for much of the elegant refurbishment of Netherfield House. Lilian, who admired Anna Bingley greatly, agreed that it certainly was. Her mother's next question afforded Lilian an unexpected opportunity.

"Now, Lilian dear, I have had a thought; if Jonathan and Anna are returning to London, would it not be convenient for you to travel with them to your aunt Becky's place?"

Since learning that Mr Adams would not return for some weeks and obtaining his address in France, Lilian had begun to think more positively of the prospect of spending a few weeks with her aunt in London. She had thought it would give her the chance to write to John Adams, something she had not been able to do without explaining her actions to her mother.

This time, therefore, it was Catherine's turn to be surprised when Lilian replied, "You are quite right, Mama, it would be much more fun than travelling alone or with a maid for company. You know how much I like Anna. I believe I should enjoy travelling to London with her and Mr Bingley very much."

Catherine beamed. "I hoped you would say that. Anna is a remarkable woman and I was sure you would find the prospect of travelling with them enjoyable. Now, shall I write to your aunt Becky and say you will come?" she asked.

Lilian nodded, smiling with pleasure.

"Yes, Mama, I think that would be a very good idea," she replied.

~⋎~

Jonathan and Anna Bingley arrived late on the afternoon of the following Thursday, having accepted Catherine's invitation to stay at the Dower House. They were made most welcome and Catherine's pleasure was increased when they revealed that they would be staying not one night but two, because they had to be in London on Saturday afternoon.

"We are due to attend a Parliamentary dinner at the invitation of my son-in-law Colin Elliott, who is to join Mr Gladstone's ministry. Anne-Marie and Mr Elliott are already in London and we shall be joining them," said Jonathan and Catherine expressed her pleasure at the news.

"Indeed? I always knew Mr Elliott would do well; he is such a conscientious member of Parliament. Please do convey our sincerest congratulations."

Later, after they had rested and changed for dinner, they were joined by Mr Burnett, who appeared to be very much at ease with the Bingleys. He was interested, he said to Jonathan, in the forthcoming election.

"Would you say the discontent with Mr Gladstone is widespread?" he asked and Jonathan replied that he could not be certain because he was no longer in the Parliament.

"But I do hear from my son-in-law that the working people, who had very high expectations of the man they used to call 'the people's William,' are somewhat disillusioned. I am not intimately aware of the issues, though. Are you familiar with their grievances?" he asked.

Frank Burnett revealed then the rather surprising information that he had a cousin involved in the Trade Union movement among the engineering workers of the North East. As all eyes were turned upon him, he said, "He is working actively to get the men at the engineering works a nine-hour day."

"And what is his success?" asked Jonathan.

"Only one or two of the major employers have agreed—the others are digging their heels in. My cousin believes that the only way they will succeed is by getting working-class candidates elected to the Commons. And of course, the Liberals have not agreed to support them. They are very disappointed."

"Why is it not possible for a working man to be worthy of a decent wage?" asked Catherine plaintively, and Jonathan Bingley explained that it was not a simple matter.

"Because the employers hold all the cards, Catherine. Strikes are costly to workers because they must have wages to feed their families and pay the rent. Impecunious tradesmen and labourers have no bargaining power, they do not fight on equal terms," Jonathan explained.

"Especially not when their opponents are unprincipled men with entrenched power," added Mr Burnett and Lilian applauded. "Spoken like a true radical!" she cried and he said as if in jest, "You will get me into deep trouble, Miss

Lilian, calling me a radical. I am not a radical, I promise, but I am very aware of the grievances of the poor. My late father was an attorney and he was forever going to court to plead for some poor man who had been arraigned for taking trout or game and once boasted he had saved two of the men arrested for rick burning and machine breaking from the gallows."

"And where did your father practice, Mr Burnett?" asked Anna Bingley, to which he replied, "In the Midlands, ma'am, where much of the troubles occurred."

Catherine listened, fascinated; she had had no inkling of this aspect of Mr Burnett's family. No one had told her, when he had worked at Rosings as a librarian all those years ago, who his parents were and where he came from. Nor had it ever occurred to her to ask, being so little aware of events in the wider world outside of Rosings.

The ladies withdrew, leaving Jonathan and Mr Burnett to continue their discussion and enjoy the port. Lilian, who knew how well Anna Bingley played, opened up the pianoforte and Anna was happy to oblige. By the time the gentlemen joined them for coffee, the mood had changed to one of genteel pleasure. Jonathan joined Catherine as she sat on the sofa, and they listened to the very superior playing of his wife and the rather less perfect but very acceptable performances of both Lilian and Mr Burnett, who had been persuaded to contribute their voices to entertain the company.

"I did not know Burnett could sing," said Jonathan, and Catherine smiled as she said, "Oh yes, I do believe he used to have a very fine voice, but is a little out of practice these days. We, Lilian and I, intend to work on him and persuade him to practice more often when Mr Adams is back. He sings too, you know."

Jonathan nodded. "He does indeed have a fine voice; we have heard him sing. It has a most mellow tone and excellent pitch. My wife was very impressed."

～❦～

Two days later, Lilian left home in the company of Mr and Mrs Bingley to travel to London, where she was delivered into the welcoming arms of her aunt, Becky Tate.

Mrs Tate gathered her into an embrace.

"Oh my dear Lilian, how glad I was to receive your mama's letter saying you would come. Now, let's go upstairs and take a good look at your things; we may need to visit my dressmaker tomorrow to get you a couple of new gowns and we must shop for a hat and some gloves."

Lilian protested. "My dear aunt, I have plenty of perfectly good gowns; Mama made me bring a ball gown even though I said I did not think I would need it, and I have two very good bonnets."

Rebecca smiled as if she had not heard a word.

"Of course you are going to need a ball gown—your mama was quite right to make you bring one. But your bonnets, now, they are quite out of the question. I know them well, and while they are quite fine for walking in the woods around Rosings or trotting down to the village, you cannot be seen driving in Hyde Park wearing one of them. No matter, my love, we shall get you a more suitable hat tomorrow. Now, you must be tired after your journey; when you have rested and had some tea, we shall talk again."

Lilian could neither argue nor demur. Her aunt Becky carried all before her and later that afternoon, they were making lists of the sorts of things they were going to have to purchase on the morrow.

"Ah well," thought Lilian, "at least I shall be able to write a letter while my aunt is busy buying me all these new clothes!"

Sitting alone in her room, which overlooked a quiet street, Lilian's thoughts were all of Mr Adams and how she might contrive to send him a letter. It had been her primary purpose in accepting the invitation to come to London. She turned it over in her mind, pondering how she should write; she must suggest warmth and friendliness without appearing too eager and yet she wanted more than anything to know his feelings.

"How shall I discover them if I do not, at the very least, let him see that my own are open to engagement?" she wondered.

It was a conundrum she would take awhile to resolve.

Chapter Seven

Back at the Dower House, Catherine faced the prospect of spending several lonely evenings without her daughter.

For the first time since the death of her husband, she understood how much she had come to depend upon Lilian for company and friendship. Lilian had promised, when she said good-bye, to write regularly and tell her mother how they spent their time in London, but Catherine knew this would not be very often. Once Rebecca drew Lilian into all the varied activities she had planned for them in town, there would not be a great deal of time for letter-writing, Catherine thought.

She was usually kept quite busy through the day, but did not look forward to those long Autumn afternoons.

On the first evening, she decided to dine early and retire to her room. As night fell and the servants completed their work and retired to their rooms, the silence in the house was unsettling. She came downstairs again and went into the study to get a book, which she hoped would help occupy her thoughts. It did not and she turned to the Bible, which lay on her bedside table; that helped, but not for long.

Finally, determined she would not allow herself to be driven into a panic by loneliness, she opened the bottom drawer of her bureau and took out a pile of old notebooks, which had lain undisturbed in a cupboard under the stairs at Hunsford for many years. They had come to light again when they were disposing of the books in Mr Harrison's study and she, reluctant to consign them to the attic, had hastily gathered them up and carried them upstairs to her room. Here, she thought, was something to engage her mind.

Dating back to the days when Catherine had lived at Rosings, the old notebooks were her own diaries, which, though rather worn and faded, were filled with memories that transported her back through the years. Opening first one and then another at random, she perused quickly the entries—written at first in the round, girlish hand of a fourteen-year-old, they traced the many events of her early days at Rosings Park.

They ranged from very short sentences and scraps of information, such as:

Very cold this morning. Not even the birds are about.

The service at Hunsford church was well attended. Lady Catherine, Mrs Jenkinson, and I went in the carriage. Miss de Bourgh did not feel well enough to go out today, and Mrs J was late. Lady C was seriously displeased and said so.

It is six months since Papa's death and I do miss him, even though he did used to say quite a lot of things I did not agree with… at least he would answer my questions. I do not think I would like to ask Lady C too many questions. She may be "seriously displeased" with me, too!

Then some months later a brief note:

Wrote again to Mama today… she seems quite happily settled at Mansfield… I should very much like to visit the school there… Becky likes it too, she says she wants to write for the newspapers. Poor Amelia-Jane is not yet herself, Mama says. She misses Papa very much, which is no surprise, she was his favourite after all and always seemed to get her own way with him…

Then longer, discursive passages describing various events and important personages within the social circle of Lady Catherine de Bourgh. Recollections of life at Rosings came rushing back as she read on, picking up an entry here and there from later diaries.

Lady C is not in a good mood today, even though God is in his Heaven and all seems right with the rest of the world, she had written rather irreverently.

There was a letter from Bath this morning, which must have contained some vexing news, for she has been quite grumpy all day.

Tomorrow, we are to have the honour of entertaining her cousin Lord someone or another, who is visiting from Hampshire. Cook has been warned many times that he does not enjoy fish, so she must search her repertoire for a suitable alternative for the first course!

I have been told I must practice long and hard until my playing of Mr Handel's Harmonious Blacksmith, which Lady C loves, is quite perfect! I shall try my best, of course, though there is no knowing how much of it Lord so-and-so will hear… if Lady C keeps up her usual practice of talking all through the performance!

Then, that night, a surprising entry:

Miracles do happen! Lady C spoke not a word through the entire time that I played and His Lordship applauded heartily and said, "Well done, Miss Collins!"

Phew!

A couple of years later, she chanced upon an interesting entry that made her smile:

We now have a librarian again at Rosings—a rather severe-looking gentleman, named Frank Burnett. He seems not in the least afraid of Lady C, whom he addresses without any of the usual fuss as "ma'am" and she, surprisingly, does not appear to mind!

The library is open again, which means we can take books out to read, which we could not do when there was not a librarian to look after it. I am astonished at the wealth of reading available, yet Lady C hardly reads at all! Perhaps Sir Lewis de Bourgh was an avid reader—he certainly was a dedicated collector for there must be thousands of volumes here, as well as maps and charts and things!

Lady C knows very little of what is in the library. Lately she has come upon me reading and has made me read a page or two to her. But no more… I believe she is just curious to know what I read so earnestly, but is not really interested enough to read it herself.

Her Ladyship clearly approves of Mr Burnett—and not just of the work he has done to improve the library, which is quite considerable. She has asked him to join us at dinner, because we are expecting an important visitor—a Dr Halliday from Cambridge. I think she wants him to keep the great man company. I was to practice and play a piece by Schubert—Lady C does not like it much, she said, but no matter, she thinks Dr Halliday will. He did, and said so, too.

Mr Burnett also liked my playing of the Schubert composition. He seemed very much at ease in the company, and their conversation hardly ceased all evening. Lady C, who had a little snooze while the gentlemen enjoyed their port and cheese, seems very appreciative of Mr Burnett's contribution to the conversation. Perhaps his knowledge of art and literature has impressed her.

Some weeks later she had written:

Mr Burnett came again to dinner today. Lady C must approve of him. They never run out of matters to talk about when he is present. Lord Denham was here for a few days—he is Lady C's cousin.

After dinner, Lord Denham asked for the pretty song by Ben Jonson, "Drink to me only with thine eyes…" which I had learned to sing last Summer and I did not think Mr Burnett would know it. However, he joined me at the piano and we sang it as a duet, though I was a little nervous about singing and playing the accompaniment at once. I think I fudged a chord or two, but no one noticed.

Mr Burnett said it was very good and Lord Denham clapped and called out "encore," which Mr Burnett says is Italian for "once more"—but we did not oblige, because Lady C looked like she was tired and called for her maid Sarah, which is a sign that she would soon be retiring upstairs.

Mr Burnett stayed on to keep Lord Denham company, while he drank more port, no doubt. He is a great storyteller and they were talking late into the night. Sarah says Her Ladyship is somewhat displeased about the amount of port the gentlemen consume when they come to dinner!

Catherine giggled, recalling the occasion; it had been rather funny seeing both Lord Denham and Mr Burnett laughing together at matters Lady Catherine neither knew nor understood, but wanted so much to know.

As she read on into the night, Catherine was drawn deeper into the time when her life at Rosings had introduced her to people and ideas she had never dreamt of whilst at the Hunsford parsonage. From the pages of her old diaries, there emerged long-forgotten pictures of persons and occasions that had been a part of the life she had lived then, a style of life that had seen her grow from a quiet little girl in a country parsonage into an intelligent young woman, able to move in society with confidence.

Lady Catherine de Bourgh had been directly instrumental in this; her patronage had provided the scope for Catherine to discover and pursue her interests and, being a resourceful and intelligent young person, she had set out to make the best of every opportunity that Rosings and its social circle afforded her.

Keen to improve her mind, as much as to entertain herself, Catherine had been attracted to the library at Rosings. She had written enthusiastically of its collection in the Summer of 1833.

There is such a treasure store of wonderful books and things here, such as I never believed existed in England, much less in this very house.

Mr Burnett has recently found me a copy of the poems of John Keats, the fine young poet who died of a dreadful disease when only twenty-six years of age—a terrible, tragic loss for England, surely.

I had read some of the poetry of Wordsworth and thought it very pretty, but Mr Burnett says Keats far surpasses him in intensity and having read his lovely Odes, "To Autumn" and "To a Nightingale," I must agree. I could not have imagined such beauty; the words seem to flow with such felicity and grace. It is perfection itself.

Later, Mr Burnett asked if I had enjoyed them. I had to confess that I had, to such an extent that I had copied them out into my notebook, so I could enjoy them again and again. He laughed and said, "I thought you would."

And in her room that night, standing by her open window, Catherine read them again and the mellifluous Odes of Keats still evoked a response in her, no less intense than they had done those many years ago.

Some of the entries were speculative...

I wonder how old Mr Burnett is. He cannot be much older than Jonathan Bingley, perhaps three or four years older at the very most... yet he seems a good deal more knowledgeable than Jonathan on several subjects but most of all about books and learning. To hear him talk with Lady Catherine's visitors, you would have to be forgiven for thinking he was a professor or something...

Later that Summer, there was much excitement.

Mr and Mrs Darcy are visiting this week and what a surprise—they have brought Mama with them. Amelia-Jane and Becky are spending the Summer at Ashford Park with the Bingleys, and Mrs Darcy thought Mama would enjoy the change.

It seems Mr Darcy arranged it all with his aunt Lady C but they kept it a secret—so as to surprise me! Which was kind indeed!

Dear Lizzie and Mr Darcy seem very happy, and their two children Cassandra and William are great favourites of Lady Catherine, especially William, who she says reminds her of her sister, Lady Anne Darcy, Mr Darcy's mother. He is a beautiful child—fair and gentle and already quite remarkably proficient at playing the pianoforte, which greatly impresses Lady C, of course.

I said I thought he will go very far if he chooses to be a musician, but Mama says it is unlikely, for William will need to prepare himself to be the Master of Pemberley one day. Cassy Darcy is very beautiful. Next year, when she is seventeen, there will be a great ball at Pemberley and Cassy will be engaged, Mama says, although she will not say to whom. I wonder who it is?

Then, in the Autumn of 1834, Catherine had recorded a terrible event.

I can hardly write... It has been such a dreadful day.

News came this morning by express from Pemberley of the death of William Darcy and his young cousin Edward Fitzwilliam in a horrific riding accident on the very day that Cassy Darcy and Richard Gardiner announced their engagement! What can be more heart-breaking?

Lady Catherine is desolated—she has not eaten all day and keeps to her room. Her maid says she will take only tea. No one knows what to do.

The funerals are to be next week—I wonder, will Her Ladyship attend?

And on the morrow:

Worse news for me today! Miss Anne de Bourgh is ill and Lady C says I am to go to Pemberley and represent her at the two funerals. Oh dear God! how shall I bear it? Am I to travel alone? How shall I know where to stay?

This evening Lady C said I should be ready to leave tomorrow. I will be accompanied by her personal maid Sarah, and Mr Burnett will travel with us to ensure that we get there and back in safety. We are to have the big carriage, the one with the de Bourgh crest, and we are to stay at Pemberley.

I shall need mourning clothes. The gowns I had made when Papa died are all too short for me now. Besides, Lady C will insist that I wear something fine in silk, no doubt. The dressmaker has been sent for—she will have to hurry...!

On returning from Derbyshire, her words had seemed to rush out on to the page, as though eager to escape from the pain she was feeling.

It was dreadful being at Pemberley... all that beauty and so much sorrow...

I do not know how I coped with the funeral; I did stay calm, but I wept all through the journey home. Each time I remembered William and Edward, I could not erase the memory of the agony on the faces of everyone around me—Lizzie and Mr Darcy most of all, but also poor dear Caroline, who could hardly support herself for weeping, and Colonel

Fitzwilliam of course, very brave, holding her throughout as she sobbed. Their Edward was only twelve years old!

Sarah was very helpful and Mr Burnett was kind and patient. On the journey home, he talked to me about the deaths of Keats and Shelley, both young—not as young as William and Edward, but gone before they could fulfil the promise of their youth, he said. Of course, he did not know either William or Edward at all, but he seemed to understand the sorrow of their families. I do believe Mr Burnett is a very kind man.

Back at Rosings, some days later, she had written:

Mr Burnett has found me a copy of "Adonais," the poem Shelley wrote for Keats. It was very kind of Mr Burnett and it is indeed a most moving piece.

Catherine paused, trying to remember, after all those years, how she had felt about the two boys and found herself remembering also her changing impressions of Frank Burnett. As the memories returned, she recalled how it had been... he had always been kind and gentlemanly towards her, friendly and concerned, but never presuming upon the acquaintance. There had been, however, at some point in their friendship, a subtle change in her own feelings about him. She tried to recall when she had started to regard him as more than the friend and mentor he had been over many years. Catherine's diaries did record some alterations in her attitude to him, even as she documented his changing role in Lady Catherine's household.

From being the librarian, who confined himself and his activities to the East Wing of the house, he had gradually become increasingly involved in advising Lady Catherine on other matters: where certain artworks should be hung to be shown to best advantage, how best to have a picture framed or a valuable object mounted for display... Her Ladyship clearly valued his advice on all of these questions. She regarded Mr Burnett as an expert for whose services she was paying and whose advice she was entitled to use.

To Catherine, however, it appeared that there was rather more involved—she thought she detected some respect in Lady Catherine's attitude to Mr Burnett for his knowledge and skill and she'd had no difficulty following Her Ladyship's lead.

He comes more often to dinner now and not only when he is invited to help with entertaining a distinguished guest. In truth, it seems he always dines with us on Sundays. Lady C likes to have company on Sunday evening, and Mr Burnett obliges her, I think.

Sometimes, he will call with a couple of books, which he believes I might enjoy, and then he stays to tea. If Her Ladyship is feeling tired and has not come downstairs, we take tea in the small sitting room overlooking the park and read from the books he has brought. Yesterday, we read from my favourite, Keats's "Endymion." Such beauty and such sadness.

As well as his generosity and kindness, Catherine had obviously appreciated also Mr Burnett's well-informed and discerning mind.

I must confess I owe a great deal of my enjoyment and knowledge of literature to Mr B. because without his excellent judgment and discriminating taste, I should be floundering in a sea of words, unable to tell greatness from mediocrity, not knowing which composition was best.

He is so well read and has such a good understanding of all matters pertaining to books and writing it is quite amazing—but then I suppose it is only to be expected—he is after all a librarian, whose livelihood is made from his knowledge of books and their writers. So, in truth, I ought not be surprised.

Yet I am, having met not one other person with such clear comprehension and passionate appreciation of so many wonderful books in my small circle of acquaintances. He is so knowledgeable—talking to him about a book or a poem is like entering a closed, darkened room and throwing open the shutters to let the light into every nook and corner of it and seeing it all illuminated.

So absorbed was she in reliving her impressions and remembering the days that had been, that sleep eluded her completely and she read on until the small hours of the morning and then fell into a deep sleep, from which she was awakened only when her maid came in with her tea and drew back the curtains to reveal the day.

A few days later, Mr Burnett called at the Dower House.

He had returned from town and brought with him the framed sketches, he said. Catherine was delighted. She invited him to stay to tea and they spent some time looking at and admiring the work of the craftsman as well as the sketches, which, now being mounted and framed, showed to best advantage.

Then he had to leave but promised to return with a workman from Rosings who would hang the framed pictures for her in the places she had chosen.

Before leaving, he asked if she was missing Lilian.

"I am indeed," she replied and told him of the disconcerting silence in the house and how she had been driven to read half the night in order to fall asleep.

"I fear I shall soon run right out of books and then I shall not sleep at all," she said with a light laugh. She did not mention the notebooks and their contents at all.

On the morrow, he arrived with a workman and an armful of books, which he thought she would enjoy.

"I cannot promise you that they will cure insomnia, but I am quite sure they will occupy your mind until you are ready to sleep. Two of them are by a young woman—Charlotte Brontë—who would have been about your age, had she lived. Sadly, she, like her two sisters, died too early."

"Like Keats and Shelley?" she asked on an impulse.

"Indeed, exactly like the poets, but sadly with less recognition of their talent," he replied and she wondered if he had remembered their earlier discussions of the two poets, but he said nothing more.

Catherine could not wait to look at the books he had brought. They included Miss Brontë's first novel, *The Professor*, and her most famous, *Jane Eyre*.

That evening, she dined early and went upstairs determined to read them; they should have held her interest, yet they did not engross her as had the diaries, which night after night had taken her on a long journey into her past, into the days when she had been as carefree as it was possible for a young woman in her early twenties to be—before her life became serious again.

She had recorded, too, many of the important occasions in the life of her extended family. Early in 1835, she had written:

Two big surprises, one sad: Emily Gardiner's husband, Paul Antoine, who
was afflicted with tuberculosis, has died in Italy, just like the poet Keats.

The other—well, it must be happy, because our Amelia-Jane is to marry Jonathan Bingley! She is only sixteen but he must love her very much and I hope they will be very happy. Jonathan is such a fine gentleman and soon to be a member of Parliament, too!

Becky is also toying with the idea of becoming engaged—she writes that the publisher of the Matlock Review, Mr Anthony Tate, has made her an offer, but she has not made up her mind whether to accept him. Is that not just like Becky? But then, I do not know Mr Tate at all. I confess I had thought that Becky liked Jonathan very much, but I was probably mistaken. If she weds Mr Tate, that leaves just me.

In the course of that same year, Catherine's feelings towards Mr Burnett had changed imperceptibly, in subtle ways even she had not recognised.

It had begun with their journey to Derbyshire for the funerals of Edward Fitzwilliam and William Darcy. His sincere desire to comfort and console her, without in any way taking advantage of her vulnerability, had created between them a bond of trust and confidence, which had greatly increased her feelings of esteem for him.

Afterwards, she had begun to notice certain changes in tone and exchanges of looks between them, of unexpected laughter and inexplicable silences, when there had been no need for words. Gradually, these impressions and the deeper feelings that flowed from them had begun to engross her thoughts and occupy most of her waking hours.

Still, she had not allowed herself to slide into fantasy, refusing to believe and even less to put into words what most other young women of her age would have rushed to embrace—that a personable gentleman some years her senior was falling in love with her.

Early in the Spring of 1836, her words were clear:

I seem to be thinking of Mr Burnett a lot of the time I am alone. I cannot explain it. When I ought to be reading the books he has brought me or practising my music with greater perseverance, my mind returns to him.

I have no sensible explanation for this phenomenon unless, I wonder—is it possible that I am falling in love with him?

Oh dear, this is difficult—whatever would Lady C say? And Mama?

Should I write to her and tell her of it? But what is there to say? How shall I describe what I feel? He has said nothing to me that I can relate—there has been no offer of marriage... no profession of love... so what will I tell Mama? A look... a smile... a kindness? Are all these part of falling in love, or are they mere manifestations of friendship?

Never having been in love before, I cannot rightly say what this means. But I do know that I have not thought so often or so well of any other gentleman of my acquaintance, as I do of him. His gentle goodness as well as his remarkable learning set him apart from every other man I know.

Many years later, Catherine's cheeks burned as she read her words and recalled with startling clarity how she had felt at the time.

She remembered also what had followed thereafter.

She put away the notebooks and dowsing the light, retired to bed. This time sleep came swiftly.

The following day was wet and cold and not conducive to walking out or any other occupation which required leaving the warmth and comfort of one's home. Sitting by the fire in the parlour, Catherine determined to complete her reading of Charlotte Brontë's *The Professor*.

She had begun to read it several nights ago and found the inclusion of so many French words and phrases into the dialogues vexing. (Catherine's French had never been as good as Becky's—at her father's urging, she had studied Latin more earnestly instead.) Yet, she was determined to press on, knowing Mr Burnett would surely ask for her opinion of the novel.

As the tale progressed, however, she was drawn into the story of the Englishman in Belgium and his young Swiss wife, Frances Henri, and she was glad she had persevered, for the passionate young heroine was a teacher, whose love for her beloved professor was matched equally by her burning desire to teach and educate the young. With his help, she sets up a school, at which point Catherine cheered up considerably.

If Miss Brontë's heroine could start a school and run it successfully, so could she. She decided then and there that she would write to Mr Darcy and Jonathan Bingley and ask for their support.

She wondered what Mr Burnett would say to that!

So taken was she with the idea, she set aside her book and brought out her writing desk; inspired by the enthusiasm of Miss Brontë's heroine, she began to draft her appeal, looking for the most persuasive words she could think of to put her plan to Mr Darcy.

The arrival of the post interrupted her thoughts.

Two letters were delivered, one from Lilian and the other from Mr Adams, who, it appeared from the postmark, was still in France. Curiosity on this occasion overcame even maternal affection and she opened the latter first. What could Mr Adams have to say to her?

His letter consisted of two finely written pages. Catherine was struck by the elegance of his composition and language, as well as the modesty of his manner. It contained a simple offer of marriage for her daughter Lilian.

He was requesting Catherine's permission to propose to Lilian, for whom he professed a deep and sincere love. He claimed that he had not felt able to speak earlier, although his affection for the young lady had been increasing over the past year, because his prospects, despite his title of curator, were not much above those of a clerk in terms of income.

Now, however, following the disposition of his late mother's estate, he was to inherit one third of her property and the whole of his father's wine business, which was a very successful enterprise, bringing him a regular income.

He therefore felt able, he said, to ask for Miss Lilian's hand in marriage, knowing he could provide for her a life of reasonable comfort, while yet continuing his work at Rosings, which he greatly enjoyed. It would mean also that Lilian would live in close proximity to her mother, which he assumed would be a matter of satisfaction to both ladies.

Catherine was still sitting in the parlour, with Lilian's letter lying unopened in her lap, when the door bell rang, and soon afterwards, the maid admitted Mr Burnett. Catherine was a little flustered at his arrival and wondered if she should confide in him and let him see Mr Adams's letter. After all, she thought, he must know the gentleman quite well, having worked together for several months.

But she decided against it and proceeded instead to tell him she had almost finished reading *The Professor* and related with some degree of excitement her decision to write to Mr Darcy and Jonathan Bingley, asking for their support for the school she wished to establish at Hunsford.

Seeing a degree of bewilderment upon his countenance, she explained.

"There is a great need here for education, Mr Burnett, especially for young girls, who on this estate and the adjacent villages have no encouragement to do other than enter domestic service or work on the hop fields and orchards as casual labourers. Both Mr Darcy and Jonathan Bingley have, on their own estates, promoted the extension of parish schools to provide some education for the children of the district. I propose to ask for their assistance to start a similar school here at Rosings. My late husband Dr Harrison was keen for us to open such a school, but Lady Catherine would not allow it. I feel the time is right to try again. You seem astonished, Mr Burnett, what do you think of my plan?" she asked.

Frank Burnett admitted to being surprised.

"I confess I did not think, when I brought you Miss Brontë's book to read, that it would lead you so firmly in this direction, but I am not unsympathetic to your plan. I value learning more than anything; my life would have been very different had I not received a sound and comprehensive education, and I am well aware that any man or woman who wishes to improve his or her station in life must seek to learn."

Catherine smiled. "Then you do not think it is some silly scheme of mine, which will not stand up to scrutiny?" She looked at him, willing him to say no, and when he said, "Indeed I do not, Mrs Harrison. There is nothing silly about the idea of a school," she was delighted.

"Thank you, I am so very pleased to hear you say that. May I convey your opinion to Mr Darcy? I was just composing a letter to him when you arrived."

He smiled and said he did not know if his opinion would count for much with Mr Darcy, but did not discourage her from submitting it.

"I would have no objection at all, if you wished to do so," he said.

"I do, I am sure it would carry much weight with him," she replied, adding, "Indeed, I would be grateful if you would help me complete my letter. I intend to lose no time—it shall be in the post tomorrow."

Though a little surprised to be asked, he agreed and together they composed the letter to Mr Darcy, which she hoped would help fulfil her dearest wish.

Frank Burnett could see that Catherine would benefit considerably from her involvement in such a project. It would take her right out of her domestic environment and give her solid responsibilities and specific duties, which would absorb and extend her mind as well as occupy her time. He had sensed her frustration at having no particular role to play in the community, now she was no longer the parson's wife.

While he had little knowledge of the details of running a school, he was confident Catherine's project was worth supporting and not only because it would surely bring her great satisfaction. His own life experience had instilled in him an unshakable belief in the value of learning, which where he grew up had not been easy to acquire. Mrs Harrison's plan for a school, he had no doubt, would make a material difference to the lives of young women in the community around Rosings Park.

Later, after he had left, taking with him the letters, which he promised to take to the post on the morrow, Catherine went upstairs. Once in the privacy of her room, she read again the carefully worded proposition of Mr Adams. Then setting it aside, she opened up Lilian's note.

It was brief and written on highly perfumed notepaper, which quite took her breath away. No doubt, she thought, this is another of Becky's little extravagances, hoping Lilian would not become too attached to her aunt's style of living.

Lilian wrote:

Dearest Mama,

This must be only a short note, because Aunt Becky says we must hurry out to the dressmaker's. I am to have a fitting for a new gown, which I am to wear on Saturday night to a supper party at the home of Lady Ashton. (Apparently none of my gowns will do!)

Lady Ashton is a friend of my aunt and since we have been in London, this is the third occasion upon which we have been invited to her residence—that is if you do not count the first time, when we called on her in the middle of the day. (Lady Ashton does not rise and come downstairs until half past ten or thereabouts, Aunt Becky says).

Catherine, an early riser, raised her eyebrows at this piece of information and read on.

I am not so sure that I shall enjoy this supper party on Saturday; the last time we were invited, there was something of a fuss, because I really did not wish to go at all. I had been with Aunt Becky the previous night to a soirée at which they were quite determined to make me sing and I refused, because I had not brought any music with me and did not like to make some silly mistake that would make me look stupid.

Aunt Becky was displeased; she said I had been disobliging and should have done it anyway because Lady Ashton had been kind enough to introduce us, which made me feel guilty, but I still did not think I wanted to sing before all those strange people.

Oh Mama dear, it is such a bore. I am sorry to sound ungrateful, but many of the people I have met are very dull indeed. They have little to say that is of any interest to me, and if I were never to see them again in my life, I should not miss them at all! I do wish I could be back at Rosings!

I must rush or we shall be late for the dressmaker and Aunt Becky will be cross. This is a very special gown for a special occasion, and Aunt Becky says it must be just right!

I shall write again soon,
Your loving daughter,
Lilian.

Catherine smiled as she folded the note and put it away.

At least, she thought, she need have no anxiety at all that her daughter was becoming too attached to Becky's London friends and their expensive style of life. Lilian didn't sound as if she was enjoying it very much at all.

Catherine wondered how much her young daughter knew of Mr Adams's intentions. She was sure Lilian must have some knowledge of it—a woman always knows, she thought, and as her mind played over it, she could not help recalling her own feelings as she had come gradually to an awareness of Mr Burnett's interest in her, all those years ago.

END OF PART TWO

RECOLLECTIONS OF ROSINGS

Part Three

Chapter Eight

L ILIAN'S INTRODUCTION TO LADY Isabel Ashton's social circle had not been entirely propitious.

Not long after her arrival in London, her aunt Mrs Tate had arranged that they would call on her friend Lady Ashton, but had omitted to mention that Lady Ashton rarely rose before ten and never admitted callers until eleven or thereabouts.

Which meant that Lilian had been dressed and ready since breakfast and, becoming somewhat impatient, had wandered back upstairs. There, in a little box room below the attic, she had discovered a veritable treasure trove of newspapers and journals from all over the globe, part of a hoard gathered by her aunt's husband, Mr Anthony Tate, on his travels. So numerous and varied were they, she had become completely immersed in them and had lost all sense of time.

Mrs Tate, having searched everywhere for her niece, had finally sent a maid to look for her, and when she was located in the box room, Rebecca had made her displeasure quite clear.

"Oh look, Lilian, not only are we going to be late for Lady Ashton, your morning gown is creased as well," she had complained and her mood was not improved by Lilian's offer to change her clothes.

"I could wear the one I travelled in—it has been washed and pressed."

"No, you could not, it would not do for you to be presented to Lady Ashton wearing an old travelling gown. Besides there is no time to change, never mind, the creases will probably fall out if you are careful not to crush it some more in the hansom cab."

Lilian had made matters worse by suggesting that Lady Ashton would probably not even notice her gown, much less the creases in it, especially since she had only risen at ten and it was just gone eleven. This suggestion had further outraged her aunt.

"Lady Ashton notices everything! And remember, you must not allude to her habit of rising late, it will be considered very rude to do so, since it is a purely private matter. And do speak up when she addresses you."

Lilian, having promised to say very little and to speak very clearly, if at all, had thereafter maintained a stony silence, broken only when she was presented to Lady Ashton and they exchanged the most perfunctory of formal greetings.

When Lady Ashton had barely looked at her and then proceeded to talk entirely to her aunt, Lilian had begun to wonder whether she would be expected to say anything at all. Sitting quietly with a cup of tea in one hand and a plate of cake on her lap, she had been surprised to hear Lady Ashton address a question to her from across the room.

In fact, it was more in the nature of a declaration than a question.

"Miss Harrison, I understand you play the pianoforte."

Remembering her aunt's instructions, Lilian spoke up at once, clearly.

"I do, ma'am," she replied, adding modestly, "but not particularly well."

Lady Ashton ignored the latter part of her remark and asked again.

"And you do sing, I suppose?" which prompted her aunt to say quickly, "Oh yes, Lady Ashton, she certainly does."

"And have you learned to dance as well?" she persisted.

To which Lilian replied, "I have, ma'am, but since the fire at Rosings and the death of my father, we have not attended..." She got no further with her explanation; clearly Lady Ashton had heard sufficient for her purposes.

Turning to Mrs Tate, she said, "Then you can bring her along to my supper party on Thursday, Rebecca. There will be music and dancing afterwards, and we shall need all the young women we can muster—there are far too many men coming and they will all be looking for partners. If your niece can play, she will be useful, too. We could do with a second pair of hands at the pianoforte; my dear friend Miss Higgins gets rather tired keeping up with the dancers."

Lady Ashton then proceeded to ignore Lilian again and began to discuss the guest list with Rebecca. She was pleased to declare that all of the gentlemen she had invited had accepted.

"Of course, they all know my supper parties and are assured of an entertaining evening. My cousin Mr Armstrong is here for the season and has promised to bring along a couple of his friends, who are eager, he says, to be introduced into my circle of acquaintances. I am delighted of course, dear Becky, but it does mean we will be short of ladies to partner them. So young Miss Harrison is very welcome, if she can dance."

After that, Lady Ashton had declared that she had an appointment with her French masseuse and swept up the stairs, leaving Rebecca and Lilian stranded amidst the debris of morning tea. When the servants came to clear the things away, they left and walked back through the park.

All this had left Lilian feeling somewhat *outré*, like a visitor whom no one knows what to do with, she said in the letter she wrote to Mr Adams that afternoon.

I am very confused by my aunt's friend, Lady Isabel Ashton. She is not a very young person and yet in her manner and clothes she affects the style of a woman in her twenties. Though she is quite a handsome woman, I am yet to decide whether she is really a "lady" in the polite sense of the term—I have seen no sign of it in our first encounter. She speaks with so much emphasis upon herself that it puts one in mind of an actress in a play. Mama has always said that ladies do not deliberately draw attention to themselves in company...

For my part, I am nervous about being asked if I could play and sing. I do hope she does not expect me to perform for her visitors. I would not like that at all.

The letter, written in the friendliest terms, proceeded to make polite enquiries about his family and when he expected to return to England, but made no mention of any special friendship that may or may not have existed between them. In that, Lilian was totally discreet, not wishing to embarrass Mr Adams in any way. Indeed, a casual reader who may have chanced upon the document may well have thought them no more than acquaintances.

Using the services of a footman, while her aunt was resting upstairs, Lilian succeeded in getting the letter away to the post without Mrs Tate knowing about it. In that, at least, she had been successful.

As for Lady Isabel Ashton's plans, they were quite another matter.

Arriving at the house on the appointed day for Lady Ashton's supper party, it seemed to Lilian that not many of the ladies who had been invited had accepted with the same alacrity as the men, for there were but four other women in the room, apart from themselves and their hostess. At a glance, she thought there appeared to be at least double the number of men around.

One of them, surveying the company from the vantage point of a small raised stage, clearly a place prepared for the musicians, seemed to be a rather superior sort of person—dressed as he was in the very latest fashion. On catching sight of Lilian and her aunt, he appeared to survey them, too, before coming down from his elevated position and approaching Lady Ashton, who happened to be engaged in conversation at the centre of the room. Lilian noticed the said gentleman draw Lady Ashton's attention to them as they stood just inside the doors of the large room, and then both he and Lady Ashton came forward to meet them.

Lady Ashton greeted Rebecca effusively and then, turning to the gentleman, said, "Josh, this is my dear friend Mrs Tate—her husband is in newspapers and things," then waving a hand in Lilian's direction, added almost as an after-thought, "and this is her niece—what was your name, dear? I did not quite hear it when we last met."

"Lilian," said Lilian, more than a little piqued at this discourtesy. "Lilian Harrison," she declared again, more clearly than before, lest the gentleman happened to be hard of hearing, too.

The superior-looking gentleman, who turned out to be Lady Ashton's cousin, Joshua Armstrong, said, "Lilian," and said it again, in a manner that suggested he had never heard such a name before, but then went on to say in a pleasant sort of voice, "May I say, Miss Lilian, how very pleased I am to meet you."

At this both Lady Ashton and Mrs Tate beamed at one another, as though it was exactly what they had hoped to hear.

"There you are, Josh will look after you," said Lady Ashton as she turned away, leaving Lilian to take the gentleman's arm and accompany him across the room, which had clearly been made ready for dancing.

"You must meet my friends," he said and made for a corner of the room where several young men stood around drinking wine and talking volubly about nothing in particular. Two of them detached themselves from the group and were introduced to her as Mr Nigel Vanstone and Mr Percival St John.

"Miss Harrison, these gentlemen are my very good friends," said Mr Armstrong. "They are delighted to meet you, I'm sure."

His friends turned out to be even more superior in dress and manner than Josh—and sporting luxuriant moustaches, they made Lilian giggle when they bowed exaggeratedly low over her hand to kiss it and declared that they were "charmed" and "delighted," indeed. She could not imagine what she would say to either of them and prayed she would not have to enter into conversation with them.

As it happened, the musicians came out soon afterwards, and she found herself almost constantly engaged to dance with either Josh or one of his friends, who were all very superior dancers. While Lilian quite liked dancing, so tired was she with being engaged for almost every dance, that when supper was served, she sat down with relief beside a kindly looking middle-aged woman, who smiled at her.

The lady was French, a Madame du Valle, visiting from Paris. Her English was not much more than passable, which meant she preferred to concentrate upon her food, and Lilian was pleased to have a genuine reason for not entering into too much conversation. After they had commented upon the weather and the music, Madame returned to her supper, for which relief Lilian was grateful indeed.

At the end of the evening, everyone stood in line to tell Lady Ashton how very enjoyable the party had been. Her Ladyship, flattered by their praise, was clearly convinced that the occasion had been a huge success, yet Lilian could take very little satisfaction from it.

When they returned home, her aunt was keen to discover if she had enjoyed herself.

"Well, Lilian my dear, was that not a great evening's entertainment? And so many personable young gentlemen, too!" she remarked and Lilian, not wishing to appear ungrateful, agreed that it had been an entertaining evening.

But not even Rebecca's best efforts could coax her into acknowledging that any of the young men she had met at the party had made a favourable impression upon her. She had spoken very little to anyone, and though her partners had danced with vigour, none of them had appeared to have anything to say that was in the least interesting.

Her aunt was more enthusiastic. "But, Lilian dear, were they not most attentive? You danced almost every dance; you were never left sitting out alone. Most young women I know would have been honoured by such attention."

Lilian tried hard not to give offence. "Aunt Becky, of course I was pleased to be asked to dance—it would have been unbearable to have had nothing to do all evening. But none of the gentlemen who danced with me had anything at all to say, unless it was about the races or some other party they had attended. Since I knew nothing of either matter, we had little that was worthwhile to speak of."

"My goodness, Lilian, you must not expect to have intellectual discussions with everyone you meet. You will soon become known as a blue stocking if you do," warned her aunt, and Lilian had to bite back the riposte that was on the tip of her tongue, that she would rather be known as a blue stocking than a simpleton. Conscious of her aunt's feelings and not wishing to hurt them, she said nothing.

Begging to be excused on account of being tired, Lilian went up to her room. She had no wish to distress her aunt, who was clearly trying to persuade her that London society, and especially the circle of her friend Lady Ashton, was worth cultivating. Lilian was unconvinced.

Writing to her mother, she could not have made her opinion clearer.

I think you would have found them dull, too, Mama, because apart from the races and clubs, they have very little conversation. They neither read nor play any instrument and have little interest in anything or anyone who is not part of their own circle of county gentlemen and their families.

Nor did they seem at all keen to discover anything at all about me, except to ask if I was Lady Ashton's niece or cousin. When I said, No, I was only an acquaintance visiting from the country, they lost interest and talked about the weather or the races again.

I think I must have told at least half a dozen of them that if one was to speak of the weather, then Kent was far pleasanter than London in the Spring and a good deal prettier. Needless to say, this was considered absolute heresy!

Poor Aunt Becky, I cannot imagine what she sees in them. I know she is so much cleverer than any of them—she must understand how silly and ignorant they are—yet she makes out that she enjoys their company and praises them to me. I cannot make it out, Mama.

Clearly, Lilian was unimpressed.

It was therefore not surprising that she prepared to attend the next function at Lady Ashton's house with little enthusiasm. Her aunt had insisted on having her fitted out with a new, more fashionable gown and persuaded her to let her own personal maid style her hair, making her look somewhat more grown-up than on previous occasions.

Looking at herself in the mirror, Lilian was not altogether unhappy with what she saw. She rather wished Mr Adams could have seen her and wondered idly what he might think of her in her elegant new gown.

Mrs Tate felt a sense of responsibility for her niece but seemed blind to her sensibilities and wishes. So determined was she to wean Lilian away from what she deemed to be an inappropriate attachment to Mr John Adams, she seemed not to realise that Lilian had gained little pleasure from the company of the suave but feckless young men of Lady Ashton's circle. She put her discomfort down to her lack of experience of society functions, where small talk rather than sensible conversation was the key to amusement. Lilian, Becky knew, was deficient in these social skills, but she was certain her niece would soon learn to enjoy herself, just as she had done.

On this occasion, the party turned out to be much larger and the guests more diverse than they had expected. In addition to Lady Ashton's usual circle of friends, there were several young and some rather older men in regimental uniform, adding a splash of colour and quite a lot of gaiety to the proceedings.

Lilian, who had had very little knowledge of the military, was not in a position to be impressed by any of them, since she could scarcely distinguish between a captain and a colonel. When introduced to one or two of them, she smiled and tried to be agreeable, preparing herself to be bored by their usual line of conversation.

She was, however, completely unprepared for their boldness, which she found disconcerting and occasionally bordering upon effrontery. Her unfamiliarity with such behaviour made her somewhat uncomfortable.

Seeing Mr Joshua Armstrong on the far side of the room, she smiled and wished he would come over and speak with her; at least she knew him a little better than these military gentlemen. But he appeared to be otherwise engaged. Sitting in a small circle with one or two ladies, observed closely by several of the officers, Lilian's discomposure increased as she became conscious of their looks.

The dress her aunt had had made for her was cut lower and fitted more closely than anything she had worn before, and Lilian, feeling their eyes upon her, pulled her silk shawl around her shoulders. She was on the point of rising from her chair and making her way across to where she could see her aunt in conversation with some ladies, when a very tall man, who had been introduced to her as Captain Hastings, appeared in front of her, bowed low, and asked if he might have the honour of the next dance. So relieved was she, she accepted his invitation without a second thought, and ignoring the undercurrent of laughter from the knot of officers around the circle, she let him lead her to the floor. When the music began, she realised she had been asked to dance the European waltz. Although she knew the dance, it was not one she had danced often; there were not many gentlemen at country dances who had mastered the Viennese waltz.

But Captain Hastings certainly had. Almost instantly, she found herself clasped very close at the waist and whirled away around the floor at such speed as to render her dizzy. Determined not to make a fool of herself, Lilian clung to her partner and let him lead her through the steps of the dance, her feet scarcely touching the floor as they flew around the room.

So close was she held, she could barely see over his shoulder; she never knew how she got through it without a mishap. When, to her great relief, the music stopped, she pleaded to be excused, claiming she was feeling unwell. She could feel her head spin and her heart race as her face was flushed with the exertion and not a little embarrassment at being in such close proximity to a man she knew not at all.

Her partner became immediately solicitous and, begging her pardon for having exhausted her by such vigorous dancing, led her away from the crowd of dancers and ushered her into an adjacent room. It appeared to be a study or reading room and he led her to a chaise longue beside a window. While she sat down, he hastened to procure a glass of water from a goblet that stood on a table and, when she accepted it gratefully, seated himself beside her.

The warmth of the room and her own state of unease had resulted in some degree of confusion, and Lilian did not immediately notice that Captain Hastings had closed the curtains behind them and placed his arm along the back of the chaise longue, against which she was resting.

He said nothing for a while, except to ask if she was feeling better. When she said, "Yes, a little better, thank you," and tried to rise to return the glass to the table, he took it from her hand, leaning across her and moving even closer as he did so.

Lilian, who had taken his concern for her to be genuine, leaned back and found he was now disconcertingly close; so much so, she could feel his breath upon her, with the reek of wine upon it. When she tried to move and make some space between them, his arm tightened around her shoulders, from which her shawl had slipped, leaving her feeling uncomfortably bare. She began to doubt his intentions when he took her hand in his, but when he made to draw her closer, she had no doubts whatsoever. Captain Hastings was no Sir Galahad, ministering to her in her moment of need; he was a scheming seducer, who had seen an opportunity and decided to take advantage of her. Never having dealt with such a crude approach before, Lilian was at first confused and then somewhat panic-stricken. How could she ward off his advances without creating a scene?

Pushing him away with both hands, Lilian got to her feet and when he rose and stood in front of her, blocking her exit, she threatened to scream unless he moved out of her way.

"Don't be silly, that will do you no good at all. All I want is a little reward for my kindness. If you say I attacked you, no one will believe you—certainly not Lady Ashton. You will only be making a scene," he said and his voice had changed from the smooth, urbane tones of a few minutes ago into something quite unpleasant and threatening.

Undaunted and desperate enough not to care, Lilian retorted, "And I intend to do just that. If you do not let me leave immediately, I *shall* scream and I do not care whether they believe me or not, I shall tell them what you tried to do. It matters little to me what they think, for I shall be returning to Kent tomorrow, but you, sir, will have a lot of explaining to do."

He stepped towards her and for a moment she thought he intended to call her bluff, but then, surprising her greatly, he said, "And if I open that door and let you leave?"

"I will say nothing, but I wish never to see you or speak with you again," she said.

To her immense relief, he appeared to have second thoughts; with a somewhat forced laugh, he stepped to the door and, opening it with an exaggerated bow, let her pass through, still keeping himself well concealed behind it.

The first person she saw as she came out of the room was Josh Armstrong and he, noticing how ill she looked, asked, "Miss Lilian, you look unwell, is anything the matter? Can I be of some assistance? Get you a drink, perhaps?"

Lilian shook her head; thankful he had been at hand and grateful for his concern, she appealed to him.

"Mr Armstrong, please, could you find my aunt? I am feeling unwell and I wish to go home."

So distressed and exhausted was she by her ordeal, she held on to his arm as he led her to a sofa in a small alcove at the end of the room. When he returned with her aunt, Lilian could scarcely hold back tears as she asked to be allowed to leave at once. Mrs Tate was concerned not to upset Lady Ashton, but Lilian insisted.

"I am most dreadfully sorry, Aunt Becky, it must be the heat, but I am truly feeling very ill and I beg you to let me leave."

At this point, Josh intervened to say that it was plain Miss Lilian was unwell and could not continue to remain at the party. Even Becky could see that something was very wrong; her niece was pale and looked as if she might faint at any moment. Asking Josh Armstrong to make their apologies to Lady Ashton, she appealed for a servant to call them a hansom cab and they left the house soon afterwards. Mr Armstrong, clearly troubled by Lilian's distress, stayed with them and escorted them to the vehicle.

In the cab, her aunt tried to discover what it was that had caused her sudden indisposition, but Lilian was too distressed and still too much in shock from her encounter with Captain Hastings to speak.

She had not decided whether she was going to confide in her aunt. It was a situation of great delicacy and could cause her much embarrassment. Lilian did not wish to regale her aunt with a narration of events nor even to complain about his behaviour, since Captain Hastings was clearly a friend of Lady Ashton and it was more than likely she would not be believed.

In any event, she thought, if he is Lady Ashton's friend, she will not think him capable of such conduct, and were I to complain, he will deny it and they will both accuse me of lying. She decided, therefore, to remain silent on the subject.

On reaching the Tates' house, Lilian, claiming that she was exceedingly weary, retired to her room, leaving her aunt thoroughly bewildered.

Becky had expected her niece to enjoy the company and admiration of the numerous young men present at Lady Ashton's party. She had thought Lilian looked exceptionally well. Certainly one of the prettiest girls present, she was dressed and coiffured more fashionably than she had ever been before, ensuring the attention of quite a few of the gentlemen, all of whom would have far better antecedents and social prospects than Mr Adams, Becky thought. It had promised to be a singularly successful evening; she could scarcely endure the disappointment at the way things had turned out.

꘎

When Lilian came down to breakfast on the morrow, her aunt could not help returning to the matter of the night before.

"Lilian dear, I cannot think why you were so out of sorts last evening," she said, noting that her niece was still a little pale. "I thought you were enjoying yourself—I did notice that several of the officers present paid you some attention, especially young Josh Armstrong, and Captain Hastings asked you to dance, too, I noticed. Now he is a real favourite of Lady Ashton's and very popular at balls and parties. Did you know he is the younger son of Lord ___, who is married to Lady Ashton's cousin and connected also to Mr Armstrong, who is such a fine gentleman? They are both men of property and substance, with excellent prospects, and I was pleased they had shown you some special attention."

Lilian looked up from buttering her toast. She had been silent hitherto, but could take no more.

"Aunt Becky, they may be friends or relations of Lady Ashton and have excellent prospects, but neither of them appeals to me at all, nor, I am sure, have they the slightest interest in me. I wish to ask, please, that you arrange to send me home to Kent as soon as possible."

Becky Tate looked stunned. She put down her cup of tea and gazed at her niece as if she could not comprehend a word of what she had said. And in truth, she could not.

"Lilian dear," she said in a disbelieving voice, "whatever do you mean, you wish to return home to Kent? Why, you have hardly been here a fortnight!"

"Indeed, and it has been quite long enough for me to understand that I shall never be happy in London, I miss Mama, I miss my home and all the things I used to enjoy there." Her voice broke and she stopped awhile, but bit her lip and continued, quite adamant in her demand that she be allowed to return home.

"Please, dear Aunt Becky, do not think me ungrateful, I know you have wanted to do everything for the best; but unfortunately, I am not the sort of person who can be happy here. I am ill at ease with all these fine ladies and gentlemen. *Please* let me return home."

At this, Rebecca laughed lightly, as though she had understood at last what ailed her niece.

"You poor child, so that is what troubles you? You are not accustomed to the ways of all these smart, fashionable people, they make you feel shy and uncomfortable... you are afraid that they will not accept you... is that what it is?" she asked.

But Lilian shook her head and said in a determined voice, "No indeed, aunt, I am not afraid of them nor do I wish to be accepted by them. I just do not wish to spend any more time with them; all their silly town talk and county gossip bores me and I have no desire to become accustomed to their ways. They seem to have a fear of thinking for themselves; instead they simply say and do what everyone else says and does and never question it, however odious it may be. It seems that to have an original thought is an unforgivable sin! They flirt and gossip endlessly of matters that are of no consequence at all. I am truly tired of them, Aunt Becky, and wish to return home. I do miss Mama," and this time she could not hold back the tears.

Her aunt was so shocked by this unexpected tirade, she said not a word in reply. She had not expected this. She had no idea what to do and hoped that when she'd had a good cry, Lilian would feel better and perhaps change her mind.

Some minutes later, the doorbell rang and the maid announced that Mr Joshua Armstrong had called to see Miss Lilian and was waiting in the parlour.

Rebecca was even more astonished. Why, she wondered, was Josh calling on Lilian? She could not explain it and jumped heedlessly to all the wrong conclusions. Recalling his real concern for her niece the previous evening, she turned to her with a gleam in her eye.

"Lilian," she said archly, "am I about to learn that you have been flirting with Mr Josh Armstrong? Is that what brings him here?"

Lilian was speechless at this as Becky went on.

"And could this be why you wish to return to your mama so suddenly, have you got cold feet?"

Becky was teasing, smiling in anticipation, but Lilian's answer wiped the smile off her face.

"Aunt Becky, I beg you, please do not take me for an idiot as well. I most certainly have not been flirting with Mr Armstrong or anyone else. I confess I was very grateful for his assistance last evening—he was very kind and understanding—but I have no idea at all why he is here today."

Rebecca was not convinced. "Are you quite sure? He was certainly very concerned about you when you were taken ill so suddenly."

Lilian's eyes flashed. "I am absolutely certain, Aunt Becky. I do not know why he is here; perhaps he wishes to discover if I am sufficiently recovered to go for a drive in the park! He did suggest that it might be something we could do. You are quite welcome to ask him yourself."

"I shall and we shall soon find out what he means by calling on you at this early hour, without an appointment," said Rebecca, as she rose and marched out of the breakfast room and into the parlour, where Mr Armstrong waited with a large basket of flowers.

The rather bashful look on his face did nothing to change Rebecca's mind, which was by now running along a very specific track. It was made worse when, after some initial greetings, he asked in the politest terms, and with an unusual degree of diffidence, if he could see Miss Lilian in private.

Rebecca was unsure if she should agree without enquiring what it was for, but he was Lady Isabel's cousin and she could not refuse him. As she left the room, she threw one last look at Lilian, which conveyed only her complete confusion.

Lilian too was embarrassed. She had no way of knowing why Josh Armstrong was there that morning. She had found him pleasant and amiable, far more so than the rest of the company assembled at Lady Ashton's, but she could not account for his visit that morning. As for the flowers, perhaps, she thought, he had expected she would still be unwell and wished to improve her spirits.

But, in truth, Josh Armstrong was on a very different mission, which he was finding equally difficult to carry out. He had come, he said, to apologise on behalf of his cousin Captain Hastings. Lilian was so taken aback at his words, she had to sit down at once. Her face reflected the dismay she felt, as she thought that somehow, the contretemps of last evening had become known to Mr Armstrong and the rest of the company. She was filled with mortification and was very near tears.

But as he spoke, she listened and was soon reassured on that score, at least.

"Miss Lilian, I am here because I have become aware that you were most shamefully importuned by Captain Hastings last evening. My excellent friend Percy St John has informed me that Captain Hastings, before he asked you to dance, had entered into a wager with a couple of his fellow officers that he would invite you to dance with him and, if you accepted, would entice you into letting him kiss you. It was a stupid, tasteless prank, no more—but having seen you so distressed before you left last night, Percy, concerned that it had all gone too far, approached me and spilt the beans, as it were. I am here to present my humblest apologies; that such a thing should even have been contemplated by a gentleman in our company is utterly obnoxious and I wish to assure you he will not go unpunished."

Lilian, though reassured on one count, was still too disturbed to speak except to say, "I am astonished that you, Mr Armstrong, would still consider him a gentleman—his conduct was so odious. I have never been so affronted in my life, and what you have just told me does not improve my estimation of him."

She fell silent again and he continued, "I agree, Hastings can be a blackguard—he is indulged by Lady Ashton and believes he can do or say anything he pleases. I am here, however, to assure you, Miss Lilian, that he will be brought to book this time. I am determined that he will never again embarrass you or any other young lady of my acquaintance. I have spoken very severely to him and I intend to see Lady Ashton…"

Lilian interrupted him, more gently this time, thanking him for his apology and concern; however, she asked that nothing be said to Lady Ashton about the matter.

"Mr Armstrong, while I appreciate your apology, there is no need to involve Lady Ashton in this situation. It does not concern her, and as I expect to return home to Kent very soon, I have no desire to cause Her Ladyship any embarrassment over this incident. I know she is a friend of my aunt Mrs Tate, who would also be seriously distressed were these matters to become public. I do not wish her to be so mortified, either. So far, I have said nothing of this to her. So, if you wish to do me a service, please say nothing to Her Ladyship, except that I have become unwell and must return home immediately."

Then, looking very directly at him, she added, "How you deal with Captain Hastings is for you to decide. He is your friend and a member of your family. His conduct is certainly not what I would have expected to endure in the company of a gentleman. Suffice it to say that his behaviour is the worst I have encountered in my life, which though it has not been long, has allowed me the opportunity to meet people in many walks of life, from distinguished gentlemen like Mr Darcy of Pemberley to those ordinary working men who live and work on the Rosings estate. No doubt, you may not acknowledge some of them as gentlemen, but I can say to you quite truthfully that none of them has ever behaved in such an ungentlemanly manner as your cousin has done, nor has any other man given such deep offence."

Lilian could see Armstrong was deeply shocked and disturbed by her words. Yet she was unsure how much he knew of the incident involving Captain Hastings. Since she had decided not to complain of his conduct to her aunt, she was not now going to tell Mr Armstrong the details, either. Clearly, he had obtained some intelligence from his friend Percival St John, who may have been privy to the bet Captain Hastings had made, but not his subsequent conduct, after he had led her into the study.

Perhaps, she thought, Hastings may have boasted of his "conquest" to friends… she had no way of knowing and feared that anything she may say would only add to the rumour and gossip that would surely follow. She had been so mortified, she wished to forget the incident altogether and return to the safety and peace of her home.

When Josh Armstrong tried again to persuade her that she need not leave London; she would be quite safe from any further embarrassment, he would personally guarantee it, Lilian was gentler in her response. She thanked him for his concern but said firmly, "That is kind of you, Mr Armstrong, but I have decided that I must go home. I do not believe that I could ever feel at ease again in Lady Ashton's house. If Captain Hastings were present, there would be inevitable awkwardness and discomposure on both sides, and even if he were not, who is to say some other person in the party may not attempt the same? Someone who feels it is his right to harass a young woman only because he is a person of wealth and standing and she is a nobody in his eyes? It would be insupportable. Besides, were I not to tell my aunt and she should discover from some other source what took place last night, how should I explain my silence?"

Josh looked quite put out and tried once more to reassure her, but had to admit he had failed, when she declared that she had already told her aunt she wished to return to Kent and had written to advise her mother that very day.

"My letter is already sent to the post, I shall not change my mind," she said.

Lilian was genuinely touched by Josh Armstrong's words; the sincerity with which he had apologised for and berated his cousin's behaviour was unarguable. She had accepted his apology and indicated that she did not blame him for what had occurred, but there was little more to be said between them. When he left, having assured her of his own high regard for her and expressed again his regret at her departure, he was plainly downcast at having failed.

Lilian went upstairs to pack her trunk. She knew not how she would spend the rest of her time in London until her departure, but her spirits lifted at the very thought of going home.

Chapter Nine

C ATHERINE HAD SPENT THE morning debating with herself whether she should tell Frank Burnett about the letter she had received from John Adams and the proposal it contained.

Some days had elapsed since the arrival of the letter, and she had begun to feel the need to respond, yet was reluctant to do so. It was the first time she had faced an important decision with neither her husband nor her daughter at hand; it was not a comfortable situation. How should she decide without consulting anyone at all, she wondered.

Yet the question remained—who was she to consult? Not her sister Rebecca, whose mind seemed to be set against young John Adams. It would have been easier had Lilian confided in her mother, but she had not. Nor had Mr Adams mentioned in his own letter to her if he had already secured Lilian's affections and consent.

If that were the case, thought Catherine, what was there to say? And what would be the purpose of consulting other members of her family, who knew little or nothing of Mr Adams? Catherine's mind returned to Frank Burnett. He, at least, knew both Mr Adams and Lilian, albeit only for a comparatively short period of time. Her own mind was in confusion.

On the previous night, she had returned to the entries in her notebooks recounting her own experiences. She had read with renewed interest the record she had made of her conversations with Lady Catherine de Bourgh, after Her Ladyship had been made aware, probably by Mrs Jenkinson, that a friendship appeared to be developing between young Miss Collins and the librarian. It had brought everything that had been quite forgotten over the years very vividly to mind.

Lady Catherine had been nothing if not forthright.

Having first subjected her to an interrogation in order to ascertain the truth of what she had heard, she had made her disapproval perfectly plain. Catherine recalled the innumerable questions, probing and personal, demanding answers, laying bare her youthful feelings.

"And tell me, do you suppose yourself to be in love with Mr Burnett?" she had asked in a voice that suggested that such a supposition would be folly indeed.

Unsure if an answer in the negative would suffice to placate Her Ladyship and fearing that a positive reply would bring down more than her fair share of opprobrium upon her, Catherine had chosen to say, rather lamely, "I am sure I do not know, your Ladyship. I have not given the matter much thought."

But this admission had only brought more scorn and censure, with Lady Catherine expressing complete consternation.

"Not sure? My dear girl, do you mean to say that you have been trifling with the feelings of Mr Burnett? For I have been reliably informed that he appears to believe that your feelings are engaged. Have you not given him reason to assume this is the case?"

When Catherine, not knowing how to answer, had remained silent, she had said sternly, "Catherine, do not try to deceive me, for I surely will discover the truth. I wish you to understand that for as long as you are resident at Rosings, you are in my care. Indeed, I have said to your mother that I believe I am *in loco parentis* as far as your well-being is concerned, and she has agreed to that arrangement."

Catherine had said nothing, but had looked meek and submissive, knowing that to do otherwise would unleash upon her another sermon on gratitude and loyalty.

"Well, in the circumstances, and especially in view of your very young age, I believe it is my duty to advise you against the sorts of hazards that young ladies may often find in their path. Do you accept that, child?"

Catherine had said yes, she did accept. It would have been of no use to say otherwise.

As her notebook recorded, there had followed a conversation—or rather a long, uninterrupted monologue from Lady Catherine—in which she had been advised against letting her heart run away with her head and allowing her feelings to get the better of her good sense.

"Your mother was a woman of great good sense, who always heeded my advice, and I would expect that you, of all her daughters, would likewise place the interest of family and duty above some silly romantic notion of love. I do not mean to suggest that one must abjure the notion of love, but it is a flimsy foundation upon which to build a marriage. Besides, you are far too young to be thinking of marrying, and a wise young woman should not let it be thought that she is too keen; it diminishes her in the eyes of potential suitors."

Following this dissertation on love and marriage, Lady Catherine had said, "Now, I do not wish to hear any more of this nonsense. I am exceedingly particular that any young lady who remains under my protection keeps most meticulously to the rules I lay down for her own well-being, and I hope I will not have to speak to you of this matter again."

Thereafter she had abruptly changed the subject, as was her wont, and proceeded to ask Catherine about her drawing lessons.

"Are they coming on well? I should like to see you learn to draw and paint; it is an excellent accomplishment for a young lady and well worth the effort. I know you are working hard at your embroidery, but I should be very happy to hear that you have mastered the art of painting as well. I wish I had had time to study it myself; had I done so, I should have been truly proficient," she declared, with conviction.

And that, it had seemed, was to be the end of it.

But, like most things in life, it had not been that simple.

Catherine recalled that what she had said to Lady Catherine de Bourgh had been substantially true at the time. She had never acknowledged, even to herself, that she was in love with Mr Burnett, nor had she given him any encouragement to believe this was the case.

Their friendship had been both enjoyable and important to her. Through him, she had been introduced to a world of serious knowledge as well as a variety of entertaining literary materials, such as she would never have discovered for herself. She had learned to use the collection in the library at Rosings, to read and follow her interests, discovering more information, and she credited him with teaching her how to do so.

While in their discussions she had often found agreement with Mr Burnett, there had been times when she had contested him and, to her delight, found him quite untroubled by it. Indeed, he had encouraged her to develop and expound her point of view, so long as she produced the evidence to support it. When, for instance, she had declared a preference for the novels of Mr Dickens above those of Miss Austen, because she enjoyed the great variety of characters in them, Mr Burnett had smiled and said, "Indeed, that is as good a reason as any, but I trust in time you will learn to love Miss Austen, too, for hers is a rare and subtle talent."

This liberality had been refreshing indeed, after the general subservience of her opinions to those of Her Ladyship to which she had long become accustomed.

Undoubtedly, it had seemed to her that he enjoyed their association as much as she did and yet, despite the many occasions on which they had been together, often without another person in the room with them, he had not made any approach that she could have interpreted as romantic.

Catherine had been too young and far too inexperienced in such matters to even consider the reason for this behaviour, believing that Mr Burnett, who was some years her senior, regarded her merely as a young person whose company he enjoyed and nothing more. She was certainly neither vain nor devious enough to imagine that he could have fallen in love with her and was concealing his feelings in order to avoid displeasing his employer.

However, Lady Catherine had by her probing unsettled young Catherine's mind and excited ideas and feelings of which she had not been completely cognisant before. Lying in bed that night, Catherine had run through all of her recent meetings and dealings with Mr Burnett and there had begun to form in her mind a small kernel of awareness that lent itself to interpretation.

Perhaps, she had written in her notebook on the morrow, *perhaps, I do love him a little and maybe if I continue along this path, I may well love him some more and then, if he were to discover that he felt some affection for me, it may even be possible to conclude that we were in love with one another.*

But, very soon afterwards, common sense had prevailed.

It is quite possible, though not very probable, since Mr Burnett is a man of the world and I am sure does not regard me any more seriously than he would a schoolgirl. But, I must confess, since my conversation with Lady Catherine, I have, upon contemplating my own feelings, come to the conclusion that I greatly admire and esteem Mr Burnett, which Mama used to say is a very good foundation for a marriage.

Reading this again, after all those years, Catherine had blushed at her naiveté. She could not help wondering whether Mr Burnett had become aware of her feelings at the time or of Lady Catherine's involvement in their suppression. She wondered if Her Ladyship had similarly counselled her librarian. She thought not.

Despite Lady Catherine's expressed wish that their friendship should end, it had not been easy to do her bidding, for Mr Burnett had made no change whatsoever in his dealings with her. There had been no alteration in his manner, nor any diminution in his enthusiastic encouragement of her desire to read and learn.

On one or two occasions, Catherine had tried to make an excuse for not completing a book she had borrowed or failing to collect one he had found for her in the library, only to be scolded gently for her recalcitrance.

"Miss Collins," he had said reprovingly, in what she used to call his "schoolmaster's voice," "Miss Collins, I am surprised indeed. This is not like you. I had expected you would have quite finished that volume by now."

And when she had tried to explain that she had not been able to find the time to take up Mr Dickens's latest novel because of having to read a ladies' journal to Lady Catherine, he had been most censorious.

"Really, Miss Collins, so much exciting work awaits you on the road ahead, you will never come to it at all if you loiter in the alleys and lane ways of such paltry works. You must learn to read good literature with discernment and understanding."

Mrs Jenkinson, coming out of the schoolroom, had seen them talking earnestly together and Catherine had no doubt that Her Ladyship would hear of it before sundown. Her next encounter with Lady Catherine had been more solemn. It had begun with Her Ladyship appearing to rebuke her more in sorrow than in anger and concluded with a thinly veiled threat.

I knew Lady C was angry with me the moment I entered her private sitting room, Catherine had written subsequently, in a somewhat shaky hand.

Coming directly to the point, she said, "I am sorry, Catherine, that you have chosen not to heed my advice. If you will insist upon disobeying me, I shall have to send Mr Burnett away. It will not be possible for me to have in my employ a man who may put at risk your future at Rosings Park."
She looked very annoyed and clearly meant it and added, "He will have to go, unless you promise me that you will not become involved in some silly flirtation with him, which is bound to end in tears."
So horrified was I at the prospect of Mr Burnett losing his employment because of me, I gave my word instantly. I assured Her Ladyship that as far as I was concerned, there had never been any thought of "flirtation" with the gentleman and was astonished when she interrupted me to say, "There, you see, you do not know of what you speak, Catherine. Mr Burnett is not a gentleman."
And seeing the expression of disbelief upon my face, she added, "I do not deny he is an efficient and hardworking man, a good librarian whom I pay well for the work he does for Rosings. He is also a respectable and educated man, but his father is a tradesman and his family have no estate. Now, were he a barrister or a clergyman, even a junior one, it would be quite different, because there would be prospects of preferment and status in the community. But in his present position, with no inheritance and no estate, his income dependent upon employment alone, he can have no claims to being a gentleman. Which, my dear Catherine, is why he cannot be considered a suitable match for you."

As she read the words, Catherine's face burned with embarrassment.

How could she have accepted such a judgment, distorted as it was by the prejudice and conceit of Lady Catherine de Bourgh? Deeply distressed, even after so many years, it was plain to her that it had been both unfair and untrue. Frank Burnett, regardless of his antecedents and the humble occupations of his forebears, had become by education and his own efforts a man of skill and integrity, with the ability to practice an erudite and respected occupation, whose worth was never in question, even by Lady Catherine.

Quite clearly, he had not been impeded in his career by the disabilities attributed to him by Her Ladyship. Indeed, it could almost be said that the wheel had come full circle and the salvation of Her Ladyship's legacy at Rosings now lay in his capable hands.

Smiling as she pondered the quirk of Fate that had brought this about, Catherine turned once more to the present question of Mr Adams's letter.

Recalling her sister Rebecca's reservations, which seemed in a strange way to reflect the views of Lady Catherine de Bourgh, she read again Mr Adams's ardent declaration of love for Lilian and his simply stated wish to have her mother's consent to his proposal. Catherine could see nothing in his letter which gave her any cause for concern. It would be ironic indeed, she thought, if her own daughter were to be denied the chance to marry the man of her choice, for reasons similar to those that had been used by Lady Catherine to separate her from Frank Burnett many years ago.

The arrival of the post brought another, more urgent letter from London that claimed her immediate attention. It was brief, and in it, Lilian pleaded to be allowed to return home to Kent.

Dearest Mama, she wrote, *Forgive me for troubling you in this way, but I can remain in London no longer.*

Despite Aunt Becky's best efforts, I have no wish to spend the rest of the season here and am determined to return home. I cannot say more, but when we meet, I promise to tell you all about it. For now, all I wish is to return home.

It is unlikely that my aunt will agree to this, but if no one will come to fetch me home, I intend to leave and find my own way back to Kent. I have most of the money I brought with me to London and am sure it will suffice to purchase a seat on the train.

Shocked by the intensity of Lilian's single-minded determination, Catherine realised she would have to confide in Mr Burnett. There was no one else to whom she could turn. She was surprised by the ease with which she had decided to trust him.

When he arrived as arranged, later in the day, she showed him both letters. Having waited until he had read them, she said, "I intend to go to London myself to fetch Lilian home. I fear I shall have to take the train and my maid will come, too. I wonder, Mr Burnett, if you would be so kind as to accompany us on the journey?"

He said, without any hesitation, "Of course," and inquired when she intended to leave.

Having detailed the plan she proposed, Catherine asked Mr Burnett, "Do you think I am doing the right thing?"

His answer was unequivocal. "I most certainly do. Who could ignore such an appeal? Clearly, Miss Lilian is unhappy in London, and while I am sure your sister Mrs Tate may not be entirely aware of the reason for her distress, it is nevertheless unfair to expect Miss Lilian to remain in a place that she finds so uncongenial, when she clearly wishes to return home."

"I am relieved that you are in agreement with me on this; I do not wish to upset my sister, and I should have found it difficult to proceed without some support. But what of Mr Adams's letter? Have you no advice for me there?"

Mr Burnett was silent for a few moments, then said quietly, "That is a more difficult question for me to answer. As Miss Lilian's mother and in the absence of her father, it is right that Mr Adams should seek your permission to approach her with an offer of marriage. The answer you give must be yours alone."

Catherine shook her head, her uncertainty obvious.

"But do you not agree that it is Lilian's happiness that matters?"

"Indeed it is; I am certain that in responding to Mr Adams, you will do nothing that will be inimical to your daughter's happiness," he said.

Catherine nodded and thanked him for his confidence in her. Then she said, "Perhaps I could make it simpler for you; if I were to say that I have already written a letter, which I have not as yet sent to the post, informing Mr Adams that if Lilian's feelings were also engaged and she were to accept him, I would have no objection, what would you say?"

Mr Burnett appeared a little surprised, but answered without ambivalence.

"If you were indeed to say so, I would applaud your judgment, Mrs Harrison. From my knowledge of Mr Adams, which I grant is the result of only a brief association, I regard him as a fine young man with a promising future. In addition to his excellent character and disposition, his recent inheritance should make him a most eligible suitor. But—and in this I beg you not to misunderstand my reservations—it is in the end a deeply personal family matter, which only you and Miss Lilian should decide."

Catherine smiled; she was certainly not dissatisfied with his answer. Indeed, it was exactly what she had hoped to hear.

"I do understand and appreciate your meaning, Mr Burnett, but it is not the kind of decision I am accustomed to making, which is why I value your opinion and I thank you."

"Mrs Harrison, I have every confidence in your capacity to reach the right decision. I know how very much you love your daughter, and that alone would suffice to ensure that you will do only that which will ensure her happiness," he said and she could not doubt his sincerity.

"I thank you very much for that confidence, Mr Burnett," she replied. "For my part, I am not always so certain of my own judgment."

Even as she spoke, Catherine could not help speculating whether Mr Burnett could have had any intimation of her feelings for him in the past. He had shown commendable sensibility in his response to her and had seemed truly keen not to impinge upon what were matters for her family alone. Yet she had sensed a desire to reassure and give comfort, which she found quite touching. Could there have been some residual feeling, she wondered. But it had been a long time ago and she would not pry, lest she should embarrass him.

Their present situation, friendly and open as it was, uncomplicated by emotion, seemed to suit them both well, and Catherine was reluctant to do or say anything that might disrupt such an agreeable association.

Chapter Ten

THE ARRIVAL IN LONDON, at the house of Mrs Tate, of Mrs
Harrison and her maid, accompanied by Mr Frank Burnett, caused
both consternation and delight.

Delight was a word inadequate to describe Lilian's feelings when she saw
her mother alight from a hired vehicle at the entrance to her aunt's house. She
had been awaiting either a letter or a message, depending upon its contents to
determine what she would do next. That her mother would arrive without fuss
or fanfare to take her home was so completely unexpected, Mrs Harrison was
taken aback by her daughter's excessive expressions of joy.

The consternation of her aunt Mrs Tate, who had never believed that
Lilian was unhappy enough to run away and return to Kent, was more
difficult to deal with. Becky appeared affronted by the fact that her sister had
decided to travel to London to take Lilian home merely on the basis of the
girl's letter.

"I cannot comprehend it, Cathy," she cried. "Did you not believe that I am
sufficiently concerned about my niece's welfare and happiness?"

Try as she might, Catherine did not succeed in convincing Rebecca that
Lilian's desire to return home was no reflection upon her.

"My dear Becky, what can I say to persuade you that Lilian's letter is not a
criticism of you? Nor is it the sole reason for my being here—indeed, there is

a reason why I am keen to have Lilian home, which I cannot reveal now, but which will become clear to you very soon."

Becky's suspicions were immediately aroused. She was aware that Mr Adams, having concluded the business arising from his mother's death, might soon be returning to England and supposed that his arrival might well be the reason for Lilian's desire to be back in Kent. She did not, however, voice her misgivings directly but decided to wait until she could get her sister alone.

Mr Burnett, meanwhile, having taken leave of the ladies, had proceeded to his lodgings in a modest hotel where he usually stayed when in London. It was not very far from the Tates' residence, and after taking tea, he had decided to enjoy the freshness of the air by taking a walk in the park opposite. There, to his surprise, he met Mr Jonathan Bingley with another gentleman, who was introduced to him as Mr Colin Elliott MP.

"Mr Elliott is also my son-in-law," said Mr Bingley and added, by way of explanation, "I am here at his invitation to hear him speak in the Commons tomorrow, on the importance of a national plan for public education."

Frank Burnett was very impressed with Mr Elliott, who declared that his interest in the promotion of public education was one of the reasons why he had left the Tory party and supported Mr Gladstone at the election. His enthusiasm was undisguised; so also his disappointment at the inaction of the government, since coming to office.

"I had hoped to see a greater degree of keenness for my cause among members of the government," he said. "Sadly, they have become mired in a range of arcane constitutional issues concerning the Irish church, among other things, and have paid only lip service to the vital issue of public education. It has been a cause I have supported for many years now, ever since the late Prince Consort made it one of his own. This time, I have a chance to bring it to the attention of the parliament and the people through my support for a private member's bill, and I intend to use it."

When Mr Burnett explained his own presence in London and informed them that Mrs Catherine Harrison was staying at her sister's house, a few streets away, Jonathan Bingley appeared very pleased.

"That is most fortunate indeed, Mr Burnett. I have some good news for Mrs Harrison concerning her application to the Rosings Trust to start a school for girls in the parish. Mr Darcy has instructed me to support the project on his behalf at the meeting of the Trust. Perhaps I should call on her this evening and give her the news."

"Mrs Harrison will be very happy to hear it, Mr Bingley; Mr Darcy's word must carry considerable weight with the Trust," said Burnett.

"Indeed it does, and I understand his cousin Colonel Fitzwilliam does not oppose the project, either. With two of Her Ladyship's nephews supporting it, there is an excellent chance that Mrs Harrison will get her school."

Before they parted, Mr Elliott invited Mr Burnett to join Mr Bingley's party in the visitor's gallery at the Commons to hear him speak on the following afternoon, which invitation he was very happy to accept.

"I have never been in the gallery during a debate, sir; it will be a great pleasure, I thank you," he said as they parted.

That evening Jonathan Bingley called on Catherine Harrison at the Tates' residence and was made very welcome.

Jonathan, like his father Charles Bingley, was well liked. Through his close friendship with Mr and Mrs Darcy of Pemberley and his former position as manager of the estates of Lady Catherine de Bourgh, he commanded a good deal of influence in the family. Respected for his integrity and loved for his generous, amiable disposition, Jonathan was always a favoured visitor; both Catherine and her sister greeted him warmly.

When it was revealed that his visit was more than a courtesy call, that he had some genuine good news to convey, the ladies were even keener. The revelation that Mr Darcy and Colonel Fitzwilliam, both nephews of Lady Catherine and trustees of the Rosings estate, would support her application for a school, rendered Catherine Harrison almost speechless with joy, while Becky applauded their judgment.

Presently, Catherine Harrison turned to Jonathan Bingley. "Mr Bingley, I cannot thank you enough for being the bearer of such splendid news," she said, "with the support of Mr Darcy and the Colonel, I do believe we should succeed. Oh Becky, I know you will understand now why I am so keen to have Lilian home. We need to start making preparations at once if we are to be ready for the Spring term, and I want very much to have Lilian involved, helping me with the school; she has not been herself since her father's death. I believe it will engage her interest and concentrate her mind. Do you not agree, Mr Bingley?"

Jonathan, though unaware of the tension between the women, was in complete agreement with Catherine.

"I certainly do, Mrs Harrison; you may recall that my own daughter Anne-Marie was similarly afflicted after the death of Dr Bradshaw; her involvement in establishing and running the children's hospital at Bell's Field transformed her life. I am quite certain that the concentration of the mind upon activities outside of oneself has a salutary effect on us all. I am sure you are quite right about young Miss Lilian, too."

As he was about to leave, he remembered his engagement at the House of Commons on the morrow and asked if the ladies would like to attend. Both Mrs Tate and Mrs Harrison were delighted to accept, and the invitation was extended to Miss Lilian, too.

"Unless you think she may be bored by the speeches," he said and left shortly afterwards.

If Catherine was delighted with the news, Rebecca seemed quite genuinely pleased. It did seem as though her fears had been in vain. Perhaps, she thought, she had been mistaken after all in believing that Lilian's desire to return with haste to Rosings Park was based on hopes of seeing Mr Adams again soon.

Fortunately for Lilian and her mother, Mrs Tate was unaware of a recent communication that had arrived for her niece a day or two ago, in which Mr Adams had revealed that he expected to conclude his business in France and travel to England within the fortnight.

He wrote:

I hope by then to have received a response to a letter I have sent to your mother, Mrs Harrison. I venture to say that my future happiness will depend entirely upon her answer and—if I am permitted to place before you my proposal—your response, dear Miss Lilian.

I trust I shall see you again soon, when we are both returned to Kent, within the fortnight.

Lilian, upon receiving his letter, was in two minds. Should she or should she not apprise her mother of its contents? After two days of anxiety and contemplation, she decided to wait until they were back at home.

Convinced it would only lead to more acrimonious debate, she had no wish to risk alerting her aunt Becky to the imminent return of Mr Adams.

～ｾ～

On the day appointed for the introduction of the private member's bill on public education, the ladies, accompanied by Mr Burnett and Jonathan Bingley, went to the House of Commons to hear Mr Elliott speak.

There they met Mrs Colin Elliott, Jonathan Bingley's charming daughter Anne-Marie, who made no secret of her pride in her husband and her support for his cause.

"Mr Elliott has consistently supported the proposal that the British government should adopt a national public education policy," she explained. "It is mortifying that France and Germany spend considerably more on educating their children and have enunciated proper education standards, while English children are left to struggle on in ignorance—unless their parents are wealthy enough to have them taught by tutors or governesses."

Mr Burnett, who had just been introduced to Mrs Elliott, responded, "Indeed, there are few who would not agree with your husband, Mrs Elliott. Those children whose families are either too poor or too ignorant to educate them have nowhere to go but the Ragged Schools, and the quality of teaching there is so deficient as to be worthless. So much so, that parents of these children often prefer to send them out to clean boots on street corners or sweep chimneys and earn a penny or two, rather than spend unprofitable time at school."

Anne-Marie rejoiced that she had found yet another supporter for her husband's campaign and immediately suggested that Mr Burnett should meet with Mr Elliott afterwards. "I have no doubt he will welcome your support, Mr Burnett," she said, inviting him to join them for supper at Mr Elliott's townhouse in Knightsbridge that evening.

For Frank Burnett, the activities of Mr and Mrs Colin Elliott were a revelation. In his experience, he had met few men and women of the landed gentry who used their influence in the community to promote the improvement of children of the working classes. Many landowners and their stewards seemed indifferent to the plight of the poor, believing that educating them would only reduce their availability and compliance as labourers on their farms and orchards or as domestic servants in their mansions. Others, like Lady Catherine de Bourgh, feared the education of the poor would give them ideas above their station and erode the power of patronage. Only a few landlords and some hardworking clergymen, believing that education could only improve their communities, had supported and in some cases instituted and financed village and parish schools for the children of the poor.

Pleasantly surprised by the genuine passion of both Mr and Mrs Elliott, he expressed his own support for Mrs Harrison's project at Rosings Park.

In Parliament, Colin Elliott had spoken eloquently and from the heart.

"England," he said, "needs education above all things, to progress and regain her place in Europe, yet English children have too little of it," and everyone in their little party applauded him, which pleased Catherine very much indeed.

When they met that evening, Catherine was eager to congratulate Mr Elliott upon his speech and his courage in making it.

"I most sincerely hope and pray, Mr Elliott, that your wise words will convince the government and Mr Gladstone to implement a policy of compulsory education for all children. It is what our country needs above anything," she said.

Mr Elliott was touched by her praise.

"My dear Mrs Harrison, if I thought that my words would achieve such an object, I would rise in the Parliament on every sitting day and make a similar speech. We are all agreed that England needs at least as effective a system of public education as many less wealthy nations have today, but a variety of obstructions, based upon privilege, prejudice, and plain stupidity, stand in the way of progress."

"But can they not be made to see that, without a national system of education, Britain will fall behind these other nations, as more children in other parts of the world are taught to read and write, while our political and religious leaders dither and procrastinate?" asked Catherine, her usually gentle voice rising as she spoke.

"I could not have put it better myself, ma'am, and I can promise you I shall continue to campaign. I am absolutely committed to it," replied Mr Elliott. "Since we have granted more men the franchise, it is vital that we ensure those who vote receive an education, so they understand their rights and responsibilities and make proper choices when they do vote."

Catherine persevered, "And meanwhile, may we count on your support for our endeavour to establish a school for girls on the Rosings estate?"

"Most assuredly," said Colin Elliott, pledging his support unambiguously and wholeheartedly and, drawing his wife into their circle, added, "And, should you need help with lobbying anyone from the Lord Chancellor to the parish priest, my wife will assist you. She is the best lobbyist in the country!" he declared with complete assurance.

Concluding a particularly satisfying evening, the ladies returned to the Tate residence, but not before Catherine had arranged to meet with Jonathan Bingley and his wife Anna at their townhouse on Grosvenor Street for morning tea on the following day. It was one visit she intended to make on her own, leaving both her sister and her daughter at home. They were due to leave for Kent in two days' time, and Catherine wished to have a private conversation with Mr and Mrs Bingley on matters that neither Rebecca nor Lilian needed to know of at this time. Instructing Lilian to complete her packing, Catherine took a hansom cab to Grosvenor Street.

Jonathan and Anna were happy to welcome her; she had been in the past helpful and understanding at a time of crisis in their lives and they had not forgotten it.

Anna Bingley, who was Catherine's cousin, had always regarded her with respect, while Jonathan had had reason to be grateful for her steadfast, generous spirit at a time when he had been driven close to despair. His first marriage to her youngest sister Amelia-Jane had ended tragically, but Catherine, unlike some others, had never blamed him nor closed the door upon their familial relationship. He had the utmost regard for her, especially seeing her continuing efforts to contribute to the improvement of the people of the parish at Hunsford, even after the death of her husband.

Both Mr and Mrs Bingley were keen to discover how she was coping with life at the Dower House and what changes were in train at Hunsford. Having satisfied their interest on these and other family matters, Catherine proceeded to the main reason for her visit to Grosvenor Street.

She began by revealing Mr John Adams's proposal of marriage to Lilian.

"I hope, my dear Jonathan and Anna, that I do not presume too much upon our family connections by asking you to read this letter and to let me have the benefit of your thoughts on the subject. I am now placed in a situation where my youngest child Lilian is growing up without the advantage of her father's guiding hand, and in matters such as this, I am wary of making decisions entirely on my own. I should value very much any information or opinion you may wish to share with me, which will enable me to make the right decision for Lilian's sake."

Jonathan and his wife looked at one another, a little surprised but not at all discomposed by Catherine's appeal.

Anna had supposed, when her husband had told her of Catherine's desire to visit them and speak in private, that it was a matter concerning her sister Mrs Tate. She had known for some time that Catherine did not always share Rebecca's views, nor was she comfortable with some of her sister's society friends. Tales of Rebecca's friend Lady Ashton had filtered down to Hertfordshire and thence to Netherfield through letters received by her aunt Charlotte Collins, and they had enjoyed many an anecdote together. While Anna had some sympathy for Becky Tate, she had little in common with her.

Catherine Harrison was not the type of person who would seek to spread gossip or rumour, however, and Anna was not very surprised that her visit concerned not Rebecca—at least not directly—but Lilian and Mr Adams.

"I am not so ingenuous as to seek your intervention in Lilian's affairs, indeed I find it difficult enough to do so myself; yet as her only living parent, I have to decide how to respond to Mr Adams," she said, then appealed for their help. "And to do so, I ask only that you tell me honestly and without prejudice of any information, favourable or otherwise, which may reflect upon his character and his capacity to make my daughter a good husband. I ask no more and I give you my word that neither Lilian nor Mr Adams will ever know of this conversation. Anything you may choose to tell me will remain completely confidential."

After a short silence, it was Jonathan Bingley who spoke first.

"Mrs Harrison, I am sure I speak for Anna as well as myself when I say we are genuinely touched by your trust and the confidence you have placed in us. We are both aware of the onerous responsibility you bear since the death of Mr Harrison, more particularly for Lilian's welfare and happiness, and we would not hesitate to assist you in any way we can.

"As to the matter of Mr Adams's proposal, I think it is a fair letter; he places before you all of the facts regarding his circumstances, openly and without any equivocation. Would you not agree, my dear?" he asked, turning to his wife, who agreed immediately, adding, "Indeed, it is simple, unpretentious, and to the point," she said.

"But is he the right man for my Lilian?" asked Catherine. "Can he make her happy? What do we know of his character and family?"

This time Jonathan Bingley was more cautious.

"My dear Mrs Harrison, on that score, we none of us can say with any certainty that John Adams or any other eligible young man is right for Lilian. That is a matter which ultimately only Lilian can decide."

Seeing her face tauten as with disappointment, he added swiftly, "However, I am able to say, from my knowledge of Mr Adams and on the basis of his excellent references, that he has a fine reputation for hard work and honesty and has conducted himself in an exemplary fashion during the time he has been employed by the Rosings Trust. I can find no flaw in his character or his conduct so far. Both Anna and I conversed with him at length when he first applied for the position and were convinced of his suitability for the job. He has proved us right by performing all his duties and, on occasion, more than his duties, exceedingly well," said Jonathan.

"Did not his previous employer say anything concerning the situation of his family?" asked Catherine. "I understand that his mother has lived all her life in France…"

She seemed puzzled and on this matter, it was Anna who responded. "I have learned that his father was the youngest of three sons of a wealthy family of landowners in the north; but he left England to live in France following a bitter quarrel with his father and brothers," she said, adding, "I know also, and I had this from Mr Adams himself, that his mother was a Frenchwoman, the daughter of an émigré family who settled in England following the revolution. She was, he told me, an accomplished musician and teacher of the French language and he credits her with teaching him to appreciate the fine arts."

Catherine listened intently, appearing to take in everything Anna had said, and when Jonathan intervened to ask, "Have you answered his letter?" she nodded slowly and said, "I have, but only to thank him and say that if he succeeded in securing my daughter's affections, I would consider giving my consent. I know it is old-fashioned, but Lilian is not yet eighteen and I felt constrained to let him know that I need to satisfy myself that he would make her a good husband.

"You see, my dear Jonathan and Anna, I cannot forget the misery that my sister's daughter, Josie, God rest her soul, brought upon herself, poor Julian Darcy, Mr and Mrs Darcy, and all of their family, by making a hasty and unsuitable marriage. Indeed, Becky still blames herself for encouraging Josie to accept Julian, when the girl herself appeared to have reservations about the match. Josie was unsure that she wanted to be Mistress of Pemberley, but the prospect of seeing her daughter in that role at some future date must have been too tempting for Becky to resist. Clearly Josie and Julian were unsuited to marry and made one another miserable. To promote the marriage in the face of her doubts was a serious error of judgment.

"I do not wish to see Lilian make a similar mistake, and while I do not intend to interfere or forbid her to marry whomever she pleases, I would very much like to feel that if she accepts Mr Adams, she does so with the best chance of happiness and with full knowledge of his circumstances."

Both Jonathan and his wife understood Catherine's predicament and sympathised with her. Yet neither could entirely satisfy her quest for certainty regarding Mr John Adams. Catherine spoke softly, almost to herself, "I suppose I shall have to ask him directly if there is anything in his background or character of which I should be told. If he is the frank, honest young man we think he is, he will tell me and I think I shall be able to judge if he is speaking the truth."

Although Anna Bingley felt Catherine's approach might prove rather confronting, she agreed that it was certainly one way of putting Mr Adams's candour to the test.

Her husband was more circumspect. "Catherine, to my mind, John Adams is a personable young man of talent and integrity, who has proved he is capable of doing a difficult job well. If you must ask him such a deeply personal question, it would be best to put it to him as gently as possible. It is my belief that it would be neither fair nor useful to make him feel as though he were on trial."

Catherine smiled, nodded, and thanked him for his good advice. She rose to leave and embraced her cousin Anna warmly and thanked them both again.

"Coming to see you has helped me immensely. Mama always said you had a wiser head on your shoulders than many an older man, Jonathan, and I agree with her. Thank you both for letting me share my problem with you; I am quite clear in my mind now about what I must do."

Jonathan had sent for his curricle to convey Catherine to the Tate residence. As they accompanied her to the door, she asked, "Shall we see you at Rosings Park in the near future, Jonathan?"

To which he replied, "Indeed you shall, for I am due to attend the meeting of the Trust next month, and we hope there to reach agreement on your application for the school."

"And can we expect that you will have time to dine with Lilian and me at the Dower House whilst you are at Rosings?"

"Of course, I should be most happy to do so—I dislike dining alone; it will be a pleasure and I shall look forward to it," he answered.

This put Catherine in an especially good mood as she returned to her sister's house, there to find Lilian packed and ready for their journey to Kent on the morrow.

Chapter Eleven

THE JOURNEY FROM LONDON to Kent was accomplished with remarkable speed and in considerable comfort, since they had secured, through the good offices of Mr Burnett, excellent seats in a first-class carriage on the train.

On reaching their destination, they took a hired vehicle that transported the four of them comfortably to Rosings Park, where the early signs of Spring were everywhere and served to cheer them up after the grey skies and fogs of London.

Alighting at the Dower House, they were welcomed home by Mrs Giles the housekeeper, and Mr Burnett was invited in to partake of a much-longed-for cup of tea. Looking out on the garden in which some impatient daffodils were pushing up their heads already and drifts of tiny snowdrops lay under the trees, Catherine sighed, "I am glad indeed to be home, though I must not let myself become too attached to this place."

Mr Burnett looked concerned, "Why not, Mrs Harrison? You have no plans to move away, surely?"

She laughed, "No indeed, but my plans must always be subject to the wishes of the Rosings Trust. We live here, Lilian and I, at their pleasure. It was arranged by Mr Darcy and Jonathan Bingley, following the death of Mr Harrison, to allow me time to make some more permanent arrangement. I have to confess that I have not given that matter much thought, but I shall need to do so fairly soon."

"But should the Trust agree to your parish school, will that not mean you can continue to occupy this house?"

"Not necessarily; that would be a different matter altogether," she replied. "If it were to be extended, I would have to pay something on the lease. I could not impose upon their generosity any further."

"And how long does your present arrangement have to run?" asked Mr Burnett, and then as if realising that he was asking too many questions, he coloured and said, "Forgive me, I know it is none of my business… I did not mean to pry."

Catherine laughed. "There is no secret about it—the lease was paid for one year by Mr Darcy and will expire at the end of Autumn. So there is still plenty of time."

At that, Lilian, who had said nothing during their conversation, rose, and saying she was rather tired, asked to be excused and went upstairs.

Mr Burnett, who had risen to his feet, was about to take his leave, when Catherine asked if he would take another cup of tea. The question was clearly an invitation to him to stay on a little longer, and since it was still light outside, he thanked her and returned to his seat.

Catherine took her time, waiting for a fresh pot of tea to be brought in; when the maid had left the room, she poured out a cup and as she handed it to him, said in a somewhat guarded voice, "Mr Burnett, regarding the subject we discussed last week, before leaving for London, I think you will be happy to learn that having consulted with Mr and Mrs Bingley, who know Mr Adams well, I have decided to let the matter proceed to its conclusion between the two persons involved."

Frank Burnett, amazed at the coolness of her voice and manner, responded with some interest.

"Indeed? I am very glad to hear it. Does that mean you have given your consent?"

"There are one or two matters on which I am unclear. But, if the gentleman secures the lady's acceptance and comes to me, he shall have my consent on condition he gives me certain information, which only he can provide. If he does this to my satisfaction, I shall have no objection at all."

Mr Burnett knew that he could not expect her to tell him upon what matters she intended to question Mr Adams and discreetly took the subject no further, except to say, "I do most sincerely hope he will be able to satisfy you. I have found him to be an exceptional young man."

Catherine smiled and said, "I am happy to hear you say so. That is Mr Bingley's opinion, too."

Not long afterwards, Mr Burnett left to return to his lodgings and Catherine retired to her room, to rest awhile before dinner.

Later that night, after they had dined, mother and daughter were alone in the parlour, before the embers of a dying fire. As the last flames flickered out and the room grew cold, Lilian rose and, pulling her shawl around her, asked, "Shall I stoke it up, Mama? It needs more coal, I think."

Catherine rose too. "No, my dear, put it out and let us go upstairs. I have something I wish to show you before you go to bed."

Looking up at her mother, Lilian was at first confused, for it was already late, but realised soon enough that Catherine was quite serious.

When the fire had been carefully dowsed, they picked up their candles and went upstairs and into Catherine's bedroom, where Lilian sat on the edge of her mother's bed. Her eyes were bright with anticipation, although a little frown creased her forehead. She was uncertain what her mother was about to reveal, although she had a notion it might concern Mr Adams.

Going to her bureau, Catherine brought out Mr Adams's letter.

"I received this letter a few days before I left for London to fetch you home," she said, handing it to her daughter. "I should like you to read it."

Lilian, recognising the hand at once, took it eagerly. As she read it, a warm blush suffused her face. This was the letter John Adams had mentioned in his note to her in London. In it, he had so sincerely declared his love for her and so honestly acknowledged what he saw as his own shortcomings that her eyes filled with tears.

He wrote:

I must confess that I have no great estate to boast of, no title and no fine family mansion to offer Miss Lilian. However, thanks mainly to the generosity and kindness of my mother as evidenced by her will, I have some hope of a good income in the future and may look forward to the day when

I might acquire a modest property of my own in England, where I expect, if Miss Lilian will accept me, we would settle permanently.

Besides these undoubtedly important material considerations, I offer my deepest respect and love, promising solemnly to do everything in my power to secure her happiness and comfort.

The letter ended with his heartfelt wishes for Mrs Harrison's own health and happiness and the hope that she would not find it too difficult to give her consent to his proposal.

Catherine, seated at some distance from her daughter, had watched Lilian as she read the letter and knew from her attitude and countenance that her feelings were certainly engaged; how deeply, she was yet to discover.

"Well?" she said, as Lilian looked across at her; but she was silent for a while, as though lost for words.

Then, taking from the pocket of her gown a folded sheet of notepaper, similar to that used by Mr Adams in his letter to Catherine, she placed it in her mother's hands. It was the note she had received from him while in London.

When Catherine had read it, she looked directly at Lilian and asked, "Have you answered this letter?"

Lilian shook her head. "No, Mama, I did not wish to tell him how I felt until I had spoken with you. I wished to find out first how you had responded to his offer."

"And if I had forbidden it?"

Lilian looked aghast. "Oh Mama, you could not have, surely?"

Seeing her stricken expression, Catherine was immediately remorseful. Putting her arms around her, she said, "No, no of course not, I was only teasing you. There, do not be upset, I have written to Mr Adams and told him that if you accept him, I shall consider giving you my blessing."

"Consider it?"

"Yes indeed, for I shall need to speak with him first and ascertain that he is entirely suitable and right for you, my dear. It is my duty, especially now we have no papa to advise us. I could not part with you unless I knew you were going to marry the right man, one who will look after you and make you truly happy. I needed also to discover if you feel that you know and love him well enough to marry him."

At this, Lilian embraced her mother and told her she was completely certain that he was indeed the right man for her and she would be very happy being married to Mr Adams.

"He loves me, Mama, and I think I have loved him for many months, even before Papa's death, but I was afraid to let it show, lest Aunt Becky should discover it. She was forever making supercilious remarks about Mr Adams; I felt she disapproved of him and I feared she would persuade you to put an end to it."

Catherine frowned. "Lilian, whatever made you think that I would be so easily persuaded by Aunt Becky to do such a thing?"

"Oh, I do not know, Mama; Mr Adams was also rather diffident. At first I thought it was because he was shy and afraid of rejection, but then it seemed he was unsure whether he had enough to offer me. I think he felt that the income from his position at Rosings alone would not suffice. But, after he went to France, he wrote me this letter in which he told me how deeply he loved me and wished to ask your permission to propose to me. I understand now, having seen his letter to you, the reason for his earlier diffidence; clearly he felt he had little to offer, materially speaking, as though his love and regard were not sufficient, the silly man!"

Catherine defended Mr Adams. "My dear child, he is indeed *not* a silly young man at all—rather, I would say, he is a wise and sensible one, to have understood that in marriage, one needs must have both love and means, however modest, in order to succeed. Love alone cannot survive long under conditions of privation and suffering, while money without affection will bring only misery. But cheer up, there is no cause to worry on that score now; quite clearly, he will be well able to support you, and with the modest allowance you will receive from your papa's legacy, I think you will manage very well."

As Lilian smiled, feeling more confident now, her mother added, "There is, however, one matter on which I must speak with young Mr Adams before I can finally give you my blessing. If I am satisfied on that score, you need have no more concerns."

Lilian tried very hard to discover what her mother had in mind, but Catherine was determined that it was a matter to be settled between herself and the gentleman alone.

"Have patience, my love, he will soon be here and everything will be settled then," she said, and with that Lilian had to be satisfied.

John Adams arrived a few days later, on a fine morning, when the woods around Rosings were so full of the sounds and scents of Spring that Lilian had been unable to resist their allure. She had been gone but a few minutes, on one of her favourite walks into the village of Hunsford, when Catherine, sitting in the parlour, saw Mr Adams alight from his horse at the gate.

When he was admitted, she greeted him cordially and invited him to partake of tea or a glass of sherry, both of which he politely refused.

Clearly, he was nervous and had hoped for an expeditious interview. On learning that Lilian was out walking in the woods, he looked disappointed, but Catherine, feeling some sympathy for him, urged him to be seated. After the usual courtesies of condolence and inquiries about his journey from France, she told him also of their own visit to London.

He revealed then that he had already met Mr Burnett that morning and had learned from him of their visit to Westminster and their meeting with Mr and Mrs Jonathan Bingley and the Elliotts.

"I understand Mr Elliott is strongly in favour of the establishment of a national system of education, as is Mr Bingley. This must augur well for your plans for a parish school, Mrs Harrison," he said and Catherine agreed that it certainly did.

Though he spoke politely and answered every enquiry courteously, it was quite plain to Catherine that he was eager to get to the point of their meeting and she finally obliged. Noting that he was sitting somewhat stiffly in a very straight chair, she invited him to move closer to the fire and indicated a more comfortable armchair, placed to the left of the sofa on which she was seated.

The sunlight coming in at the bay windows played upon his hair, which was of a deep chestnut brown. It was, Catherine thought, a handsome, strong face, with a degree of sensitivity that was quite pleasing.

She spoke, slowly at first, choosing her words carefully.

"Mr Adams, I have no wish to harass you with a number of exasperating questions about your family, nor do I wish to offend you by my enquiries, but I must ask you, please, to understand that as Lilian's only living parent, I have to be satisfied on certain matters before I can confidently accept your proposal. Will you be so kind, then, to bear with me in this?'

John Adams looked directly at her and responded without the slightest embarrassment. "Mrs Harrison, please do not feel you must apologise or explain; it is no more than I would have expected you to do as Miss Lilian's mother. It would be unthinkable that you would consent to her engagement to me without satisfying yourself on every particular. I will attempt to answer any question you put to me."

Catherine smiled, pleased that he had taken no offence. "That is very good of you, Mr Adams, and I can say that on most matters that concern me as a mother, I am entirely satisfied. You have told me of your deep love for my daughter, and Lilian assures me she returns your affections in full measure. On that score I have no further concerns. As to your character, both Mr Jonathan Bingley and your friend and colleague Mr Burnett have spoken very highly of your industry, honesty, and good nature. I am inclined to trust their judgment in this, especially since it accords with my own observation."

By now Mr Adams was clearly pleased but a little anxious as well. With all these favourable reports, he wondered, what further questions did she have for him?

Catherine continued, "My only reservations arise from a circumstance that only you can explain. I have little information about your family and cannot work out how it is that you were settled and brought up in France and yet your father was an Englishman. I have heard that your father moved to France following a falling-out with his family; I should very much wish to understand the reason for this unhappy breach in your family. Surely, it cannot have been occasioned by a simple misunderstanding; such squabbles, though they may cause temporary discord, rarely result in a permanent rupture. Is it true that your father never returned to England?"

Mr Adams had sat very still while she spoke and when he answered her, did so without hesitation. "It is, with one exception—he returned uninvited to attend his mother's funeral. Indeed, ma'am, I should tell you that he never corresponded with his family at all, save for a single letter to my grandmother, informing her of his marriage to my mother."

"And did you ever discuss the cause of this terrible rift?" her voice was softer now. She could tell that it pained him to speak of it, but she had to know the truth.

Mr Adams shook his head and looked rather distressed. "My father never spoke of it; he was very bitter about the manner in which he had been treated by his family. But after his death, my mother told me everything."

"And would you be willing to reveal some of it to me—only that I might understand your situation and defend you when others with less knowledge of the facts revile you to me? I can assure you that it will be a matter of the strictest confidence, no one will ever hear any of it from me, not even Lilian."

John Adams stood up and walked to the bay window. The sunlight slanting into the room fell full upon his face, and Catherine could see the hurt etched upon his countenance as he spoke.

"Mrs Harrison, whether you had asked me about these matters or not, if Miss Lilian accepts my offer of marriage, it is inconceivable that I would become engaged to her while concealing from her the truth about my family. It is therefore without any reservation, and indeed with some relief, that I am prepared to reveal it all to you."

The tale he told was related simply, without undue histrionics or resort to melodrama. It was told as though he were detailing the story of some person wholly unconnected with himself.

"My own beloved father was the youngest son of Sir Samuel Adams, whose properties and business interests in the north of England are both extensive and valuable. My father's two elder brothers were more inclined to work on the family estate, while my father preferred the study of literature and music. Encouraged and funded by his mother, who was herself an accomplished and artistic lady, he moved to London, where he found lodgings in the house of a wealthy gentleman, a patron of the arts, who shall here remain nameless. He spent much of his time in study and attending concerts and galleries and in this received encouragement from his host, who treated him almost as a member of his own family.

"The children of the household had a governess, a young Frenchwoman, who was the daughter of an émigré family who had fled France when she was only a child, giving up everything to save their lives. Beautiful and very accomplished, she soon attracted the attention of my father, who was then a very young man. I need not go into too many details, but suffice it to say the two fell in love and subsequently became lovers.

"When it was discovered, the young woman was dismissed from her position and had to leave the house. My father followed her, for she had by now nowhere to go and no one to turn to. They moved into a small apartment in a much less salubrious part of town, where they lived together for several months.

It was, my dear mother told me, a difficult, hand-to-mouth existence, during which time he worked as a private tutor to foreign students."

Catherine could see now why he had seemed so strained as he spoke. She felt great sympathy for him.

"Later, my father gave up his artistic studies altogether and took work as a clerk in the warehouse of a trading firm, while my mother took in sewing and mending and other domestic chores for fine ladies. It was, she has told me, a very hard life and, if not for their deep devotion to one another, could have ended tragically."

Already shocked by his tale, Catherine asked, "How do you mean?"

"Because, ma'am, many young women in similar circumstances have been deserted by gentlemen who, when the truth was revealed, could not face the opprobrium of their families and friends and abandoned the women; but my father did not. He loved my mother and after I was born, arranged to marry her and wrote to his mother to tell her so. It was the only time he communicated with any member of his family."

The matter-of-fact way in which he had revealed the circumstances of his birth, with no attempt at concealment whatsoever, surprised Catherine; yet, she knew the manner of his telling it concealed the grief he must feel at having to speak of such intimate family matters.

Adams was silent for a few moments, then continued, "Thereafter, fortuitously, circumstances in France had changed, allowing them to return, and my mother was able to reclaim a small portion of her family's properties, chiefly a farm and a vineyard. There they lived for the rest of their lives, and my father built a thriving wine merchandising business, which brings in good money to this day.

"My two sisters were born later—they did not share my unhappy fate of being born out of wedlock, but it made little difference. My father and mother loved us all and indeed, if anything, I must confess, I was spoilt and petted and made much of, being the eldest and their only son. They also gave me the best education they could afford, insisting that I, being born in England, should pursue my studies in this country.

"At the age of ten, I was sent to school in London and encouraged to acquire a good knowledge of the English language, culture, and manners. No doubt they hoped it would stand me in good stead in the future."

Catherine intervened, "Which of course it has done, for here you are, for all the world an English gentleman. You have done well, Mr Adams, I am sure your parents were proud of you."

He bowed briefly to acknowledge her remarks and said, "When my father died, I returned to France, intending to stay there and assist my mother and sisters on the family farm, but my mother persuaded me to return to England once more and continue my studies for a further year. She was most insistent and I did so, for I was loathe to disappoint her."

After a moment's silence, he asked, "May I ask, ma'am, if I have answered your enquiries to your satisfaction?"

Catherine had said little during his narration. Now, she found it difficult to respond immediately, not because she had not been satisfied but because she had begun to experience feelings of guilt at having subjected him to such an ordeal.

When she spoke, her voice was very gentle. "Mr Adams, indeed you have. I should have spoken earlier—I did not need to hear all of your story—yet I thank you for your frankness and honesty. You have been more open with me than anyone could have asked of you. I am sorry to have caused you such pain as might have resulted from recounting these matters to a stranger. I hope you will forgive me."

Mr Adams's countenance revealed that he felt no such forgiveness was needed, as Catherine continued, "As for my concerns, such as they were, I can see now that they are of no account at all. They no longer signify, because nothing that your father and mother did in their early youth can be held against you, especially considering that they, in raising you, appear to have done everything possible to instil in you the best standards of conduct and decorum and provide you with a good education. Whatever their youthful mistakes, quite clearly, in their subsequent marriage they made amends for them and it has left no scars upon you."

He bowed, acknowledging the generosity of her words. Then, keen to be reassured, asked, "Then, you do not see these circumstances as an impediment to a marriage between Miss Lilian and myself?"

"I do not; if anything, I imagine it has made you more circumspect, more sensible of your responsibilities and the demands of decorum in your general behaviour. Am I right?"

"Indeed you are, ma'am; seeing the extent of suffering caused to so many persons by a single misdemeanour, I vowed never to place myself in such a situation, however innocently. I have been very particular in my general conduct towards all ladies," he said.

Catherine smiled and nodded. She had noticed his exceedingly correct behaviour towards Lilian whenever they were together.

"And you say you love my daughter?"

"Devotedly and passionately, ma'am, and I give you my word that I shall not spare myself to secure her happiness. I cannot find words to express my joy, I have often dreamed of this happy day."

"Well then, I can do no more than wish you success when you search for words to address Lilian herself. Should you walk through the woods towards Hunsford, it is very likely you will meet her returning from the village. When you do, you may tell her that you have my blessing."

He rose and thanked her from the bottom of his heart, kissed her hand, and was gone in a trice, leaving his horse tethered at the gate, striding away towards the woods to find the lady of his dreams.

Chapter Twelve

THAT NIGHT, AFTER MR Adams had finally departed and Lilian had told her mother for the tenth time how very happy they were and thanked her effusively for "being such a wonderful mother," Catherine retired to her room.

It had been a rather emotional and exhausting day, for when she had set out to test Mr Adams's frankness regarding his family, she had not dreamed that such a tale as he had told her would be revealed.

It was not that she was shocked by the circumstances of his birth; she knew that such things happened, especially when young men lived away from home, and most often they were hushed up by their families. The prevailing attitude in society was that a man should extricate himself from the situation with as little inconvenience as possible, whilst the girl was, more often than not, left to fend for herself. She would suffer the consequences of their indiscretion, with, if she was lucky, some small sum of money provided chiefly to purchase her silence, and the child, if it survived, would be taken into an orphanage.

That John Adams's father had voluntarily turned his back on his artistic ambitions and his family, to care for and marry the young woman he had loved and raise their child, had touched Catherine deeply. Clearly, she thought, his young son had drawn strength from the example, and though she had promised never to divulge their conversation to anyone, what she had learned would invest Mr Adams with a particular integrity in her mind. Consequently, it coloured her account of him when she wrote to her family of Lilian's engagement.

Two letters had priority.

The first to Jonathan Bingley and his wife, to whom she felt she owed a debt of gratitude for their kindness in helping her cope with her new responsibilities. The letter was written speedily and easily, since she knew that the news would cause no unhappiness at Netherfield; quite the contrary.

She wrote:

> *My dear Jonathan,*
>
> *Regarding the matter of Mr Adams's offer, which we have previously discussed, I am sure Anna and you will be happy to hear that he has called on me and has, in his conversations with me, completely satisfied all the concerns I had and is consequently now engaged to be married to Lilian with my blessing.*
>
> *While I am not at liberty to discuss the details of it, having given him my word that our conversation would remain confidential, I can say quite assuredly that there is nothing in his background that would cause me to have any further anxiety about my daughter's future security or happiness.*
>
> *They are both exceedingly happy and keen to be wed, but, being sensible of my feelings and the demands of decorum, will wait to be married until a few more months have elapsed since Mr Harrison's death.*
>
> *Because Mr Adams will continue in his work as curator of the Rosings estate, they plan to settle in the district when they are wed, which, as I am sure you will understand, is a source of great satisfaction to me.*

The second letter, addressed to her sister, presented some difficulty.

Catherine knew that Rebecca had not seemed to approve of Mr Adams; she was anxious, therefore, not to exacerbate her prejudice by saying anything that she might seize upon and use against him.

Mr Adams had called early that morning, and Lilian and he had gone out to take a turn about the grounds. Seeing them together, Catherine was quite convinced she had been right; they were clearly and unashamedly in love and having been apart for several weeks, were eager to talk about anything and everything, in the way that lovers often do.

Catherine decided to tell her sister how things stood between the pair, emphasising their love for one another, his greatly improved prospects, and Lilian's unalloyed joy, as well as her own pleasure in having made the right decision for her daughter by giving her consent to the engagement.

Having broken the news, she continued:

It is too easy, when considering such matters, to get trammeled up in questions of prospects and income and forget that we are talking of two young people who love each other. I am sure, Becky, when you see how very happy my Lilian is and consider that Mr Adams's prospects and income have improved vastly since inheriting his family's wine merchandising business, you will share my confidence in their future.

I find Mr Adams to be not only a man of openness and integrity, I also know him to be deeply devoted to Lilian and I believe he will do all he can to ensure her happiness. Dear Becky, I know how fond you are of Lilian and how keen you are to see her happily settled, and I am confident that you will be happy to receive this news.

The following day, the post brought two letters—one from her mother, Mrs Charlotte Collins, and another from her sister. Becky Tate's letter clearly pre-dated her own, which had been dispatched the day before, and Catherine opened it up first.

A curious communication, hastily composed, it was immediately apparent that Rebecca was, as yet, ignorant of Lilian's engagement to Mr Adams. She made no mention of any other matter, either, leaping without any of the customary courtesies into an extraordinary tale about Mr John Adams and a rumour she claimed to have heard about his parents.

She wrote:

Is it possible, dear Catherine, that Lilian has been misled into believing that Mr Adams is an eligible suitor from a respectable family, domiciled in France for reasons of business alone?

Is it likely that he has allowed her to think that his parents were respectable people, worthy of her regard? If this were the case, then poor Lilian appears to have been cruelly deceived and is likely sooner or later to be sadly disillusioned in Mr Adams and his family.

Dear Cathy, a most alarming piece of news has reached me from a close friend of Lady Ashton, who travels regularly to France and moves widely in society there. I am writing at once to apprise you of her information, in the hope that you may enlighten my niece and preserve her from the humiliation and hurt that must surely follow, were she to accept Mr Adams and learn the truth later.

By this time, Catherine's bewilderment was complete. Who was this friend of Lady Ashton and what information could she have that would cause such consternation, she wondered, as she read on:

Indeed, far from being the son of a respectable gentleman, it is being said that John Adams is the illegitimate son of one Mr James Adams and a French mistress!

The boy, it is said, was born out of wedlock in England, and the couple departed for France thereafter, to hide their shame, no doubt, which caused Sir Samuel Adams, father of James and a wealthy landowner in the north of England, to summarily cut his youngest son out of his will and forbid him ever to return to this country.

Considering the encumbrance he carries and the inferiority of his connections, it is no wonder Mr John Adams has attained only a lowly position at Rosings in spite of his education. Seen in this light, surely it is not appropriate that Lilian should become engaged to him and I am confident that if she is made aware of the truth, she will not do so. I do beg you, my dear sister, to inform her of these matters and persuade her with every means at your command that she can do much better than marry an ineligible and impecunious young man with little more than his good looks and pleasing manners to recommend him.

Do tell her also, that there are others, far more worthy than Mr Adams, who will be quite desolated if she accepts him!

This last cryptic sentence left Catherine quite bemused.

Who did Becky mean? It was a complete mystery to her. Presumably, Rebecca expected Lilian to know the identity of the person or persons involved, but Catherine had already decided that she would certainly not show her sister's letter to Lilian. It would serve no purpose at all, except perhaps to inflame Lilian's hostility towards her aunt.

She determined, therefore, to write again to her sister, a brief note, pointing out that Mr Adams had revealed all of the facts regarding his parents and his own birth to her before receiving her consent.

Dear Becky, she wrote:

> *While I do appreciate your concern for Lilian's welfare, I cannot agree that Mr Adams is an unsuitable person to marry my daughter.*
>
> *Indeed, he is now neither "ineligible nor impecunious" as you describe him.*
>
> *He has inherited a third of his mother's estate and all of his father's wine merchandising business. He expects thereby to receive a reasonable and regular income, which, taken together with the salary he is paid by the Rosings Trust, should enable him to support Lilian quite comfortably.*
>
> *I might add also that Mr Adams has received generous praise from Jonathan and Anna Bingley, who assure me that he came to the position at Rosings with excellent references.*
>
> *I do beg you, Becky, to try to understand the feelings of these two young people. I cannot begin to tell you how much pleasure it has given me to see my daughter so happy in her choice of a husband. Lilian is not a fool, nor has she made her decision in ignorance; she is aware of as much of the facts as I am and has accordingly made her choice.*

As she wrote, Catherine could not help recalling her own, very different experience. Unlike Lilian, she had been too compliant and impressionable to withstand the arguments put by Lady Catherine de Bourgh against her friendship with Mr Burnett. She had feared that by seeming to defy Her Ladyship, she would be offending her and would also consequently upset her dear mother, since Lady Catherine, having taken her mother's place, had demanded the same respect and obedience as a parent.

Catherine had been not much older than Lilian at the time. She could remember well how she had felt all those years ago, and an uncomfortable lump rose in her throat at the memory.

The arrival, at that very moment, of Mr Frank Burnett himself threw her into confusion, and she had to make some hurried excuse to retreat upstairs for a while, leaving him alone in the parlour.

When she returned, Mr Adams and Lilian had come indoors and joined Mr Burnett, who was congratulating them both upon their engagement. As Catherine entered, they turned to her and looked so cheerful together, she was glad of the time she had taken to splash her face with cold water and tidy her hair before returning.

Impulsively, she invited them to take a glass of sherry and seeing that John Adams had already been asked to dine with them, extended the invitation to Frank Burnett as well. It seemed the most natural and polite thing to do, she thought, rationalising her impulse. It would have been churlish to ask one of the two gentlemen to dinner and let the other go away to dine alone. Mr Burnett had accepted the invitation with pleasure, and she was sure Lilian and Mr Adams would not mind.

Lilian, engrossed in her conversation with John Adams, noticed nothing odd or curious about her mother's invitation to Mr Burnett. Indeed she and Mr Adams seemed to welcome his presence; it meant they could be talking privately, knowing her mother did not lack for congenial company.

The evening passed pleasantly during dinner and afterwards.

Both Catherine and Mr Burnett, left to themselves, found several subjects to talk about together. There was much they enjoyed in common and very little upon which they disagreed. Even when they did, each appeared so ready to listen to and accommodate the other's point of view, that harmony and concord were guaranteed.

There would be many such occasions in the weeks that followed, and Frank Burnett seemed appreciative of the invitations, making no secret of the fact that he enjoyed the company and preferred it greatly to dining alone at his lodgings.

※

Meanwhile, news of the engagement reached Mr and Mrs Darcy at Pemberley, from two sources.

Charlotte Collins, writing to her dear friend Elizabeth, was first with the news.

> My dear Eliza,
>
> Catherine has written informing me of young Lilian's engagement to a Mr John Adams, who is the curator at Rosings. She appears to like the young man and writes that he is a fine young gentleman, educated, cultured, and very much in love with Lilian. She mentions also that both Jonathan Bingley and Mr Darcy are acquainted with and approve of him, which fact, she believes, should reassure me of his suitability.
>
> But I have quite a different report of this young man from Becky, who has written me a most disturbing account of a tale told her by her friend Lady Ashton. It claims that Mr Adams is the illegitimate son of one James Adams and a French woman who became his mistress. I am quite bewildered and very concerned to discover if this is true.
>
> Dear Eliza, is there some way by which either you or Mr Darcy may assist me in this? I am reluctant to broach the subject with Jonathan Bingley, and while I am not generally inclined to interfere in such matters, if there is any truth in Becky's story, I should feel it my duty to inform Catherine and advise her to counsel young Lilian against the match.

Elizabeth was both concerned and confused by her friend's letter and determined to discover the truth of the matter.

On this same day, Mr Darcy had received a letter from Jonathan Bingley pertaining mainly to business matters arising from the Rosings Trust. However, in a concluding paragraph, he had added:

> I am not aware, sir, if you and Mrs Darcy have been advised already by Mrs Harrison, but Anna and I have received a letter informing us that her daughter Lilian is recently engaged to Mr John Adams, the curator at Rosings.
>
> Both Anna and I are convinced that Miss Lilian has made a happy choice. To our knowledge, Mr Adams appears to be a man of intelligence and integrity, with a most amiable disposition, and we are very pleased for both of them.

Mr Darcy, having read the letter through, took it upstairs to his wife.

"Lizzie, my dear, I am sure you will find the final page of Jonathan's letter of great interest," he said, handing it to her. When she had read it, Elizabeth put it down, rose, and walked about the room as if in exasperation.

"Really, Darcy, I am quite mystified! I cannot make it out at all! They cannot both be right."

"What is it? Who do you mean?" he asked and she replied by holding up Charlotte Collins's letter and saying, "If Mr Adams is so well thought of by Jonathan and Anna and Catherine is sufficiently satisfied to consent to his engagement to Lilian, how is it that Charlotte has had this dreadful story from Becky Tate about his family?"

Mr Darcy took Charlotte's letter from his wife and, going over to the window, perused it carefully. When he returned it to her, he looked very angry indeed.

"Lizzie, what you have here is a nasty piece of mischief! I cannot believe that Jonathan Bingley is mistaken in his judgment of Mr Adams, nor do I think Catherine Harrison will have agreed to let her daughter marry a man without making the most scrupulous enquiries about him, his family, and background. It is inconceivable that Mrs Tate's story is true."

Elizabeth merely shrugged her shoulders. "Why should anyone fabricate such a tale?"

Darcy, still looking quite shocked, replied, "I cannot imagine, but I am prepared to believe that Mrs Tate's friend Lady Ashton is in some way involved. I understand from Anthony Tate, who is most unhappy with his wife's association with Lady Ashton and her circle, that these people have little to do except play cards, go to balls and parties, and gossip, indulging themselves in the silliest way by destroying the reputations of others who are not of their group. I suspect this information comes from within her circle. Now, it may be that Mr Adams has in some way offended one of them. I think I would much rather trust Jonathan's opinion than theirs, my dear, do you not agree?"

Elizabeth agreed completely with her husband and expressed her determination to seek Jonathan Bingley's opinion herself. This she did subsequently, writing him a short note, which was despatched to the post immediately. She would wait for his reply before responding to Charlotte's letter, she thought.

Her husband, whose own mind was already made up, agreed that this was the best course of action.

"You are right to wait, Lizzie, there is nothing to be gained by distressing poor Mrs Collins to any greater degree than she has been by Mrs Tate's rather thoughtless retelling of rumour and gossip," he said.

❧

It did not take Jonathan Bingley long to realise the purpose of Elizabeth's note. Rising abruptly from the breakfast table, he laid it before his wife.

"Anna, my dear, something quite extraordinary is afoot. My aunt Lizzie has heard a curious tale about Mr Adams…"

"About Mr Adams? Who from?" asked his wife, puzzled by the intensity with which her usually calm husband had reacted.

"From Mrs Charlotte Collins, who has had it from Becky Tate, who has had it from a friend of Lady Ashton!"

"What? And what does she say?"

"Read it and judge for yourself. It beggars belief that people should stoop to put such stories about. John Adams, it seems, is to be pilloried for something his parents are supposed to have done in their youth."

Anna read Elizabeth's note and was as astonished as her husband had been by its contents.

"I find it difficult to believe that Becky would even take such a rumour seriously. Clearly, it is an attempt to damage Mr Adams's character and must be the work of some person of malicious intent. Yet, why do you suppose anyone would wish to do this?" she asked.

Jonathan admitted he had no explanation. "I cannot imagine, yet I suppose I shall have to find out—if only to set my aunt Lizzie's mind at rest. I suppose I could write to my sister Emma, she has many contacts in London… but I can hardly expect her to be impartial in the matter, for she has no regard for Lady Ashton, who Emma believes is a woman of very little sense and no scruples at all…"

He was interrupted by the maid, who brought in a letter which had just been delivered by express. It had come overnight from Rosings and contained a message sent in confidence to Jonathan by Mrs Catherine Harrison.

On opening it, Jonathan found therein the answer to the question posed for him by Mrs Darcy. Catherine, having received Rebecca's letter, had responded to her sister and then proceeded to write to Jonathan, fearing the rumour may have reached his ears, too.

In the clearest possible terms, she explained that in his answers to her questions about his father's estrangement from his family in England, Mr Adams had given her a full and frank account of the circumstances as told to him by his mother, including the fact of his own birth out of wedlock and the subsequent marriage of his parents, before their departure for France.

Catherine wrote:

He has provided me with all the facts—names, dates, places, every particular related openly and plainly, without any hint of equivocation. I believe him, Jonathan, I have no reason not to do so.

Besides, there is nothing in his conduct or character which one can point to as a pernicious consequence of the unfortunate indiscretion of his parents.

I should feel most un-Christian, indeed, were I to follow my sister's advice and forbid Lilian to marry him on such implausible grounds.

I beg you, Jonathan, to reassure my mother, and anyone else who may enquire, of my decision on this matter.

Jonathan was relieved indeed. Handing the note to his wife, he said, "I hope, my love, that this will be the final word on this unfortunate subject. I intend to see Mrs Collins first and then respond to my aunt Lizzie. Catherine's letter should suffice to set their minds at rest."

Anna agreed and shortly afterwards, Jonathan called for his horse to be saddled up and set off to ride over to Longbourn to reassure Mrs Collins.

Chapter Thirteen

WHILE JONATHAN'S WORDS DID reassure Charlotte Collins and
to an even greater degree Mrs Darcy, Becky Tate was not similarly
comforted by her sister's letter.

She could not believe that Catherine could be quite so sanguine about the
matter of her daughter's engagement. Urged on by Lady Ashton and her friend
and confidante Madame du Valle, who had been the original source of their
information, Becky decided to travel to Kent and confront Catherine with the
story. Convinced that Mr Adams was not the right man for her niece, she took
with her also another piece of information, which she hoped would assist her to
change Lilian's mind on the subject of matrimony.

Prior to her departure for Kent, she took morning tea with Lady Ashton.

"It seems almost as if my sister, still grieving for her husband, has temporarily abandoned her sense of responsibility," she complained, "else she could
not have countenanced such an engagement."

Lady Ashton agreed it was a most unsuitable match and had to be stopped,
for all their sakes.

"No one of any standing in society would recognise your niece and her
husband," she warned, intoning it as though it were a sentence of death.

Presently, they were joined by Mr Joshua Armstrong, Her Ladyship's
cousin. Rebecca had developed a great admiration for this gentleman and

regarded him as a most appropriate suitor for her niece, although she had made no mention of her hopes to Lady Ashton. He had appeared to show a keen interest in Lilian when she was in London, and Becky had sensed that he was attracted to her, although there was no evidence of any serious intention on his part. If only Lilian could be worked on, to give up Mr Adams and return with her to London, she thought, there was no knowing what might transpire when the two met again.

Becky was impatient to be gone and rather than wait for a hansom cab, Mr Armstrong drove her to the railway station in his gig. Helping her out of the vehicle and accompanying her to the train, he was courtesy itself and asked to be remembered to Miss Harrison and sent his compliments to her mother, by this gesture entrenching even deeper in Becky's mind his credentials as a most acceptable prospect for her niece.

Becky's unheralded arrival at the Dower House disconcerted her sister and annoyed Lilian intensely. Seeing her aunt alight at the gate, Lilian, who was looking out from the bedroom window, rushed into her mother's room to announce the news.

"Mama, you will not believe this, Aunt Becky is here; look, she is just getting her luggage out of the cab. What could she want now?" she cried, clearly unhappy with this turn of events.

Catherine looked and hurried downstairs, urging her daughter to be polite and conceal her irritation. She well knew that Lilian was aware that her aunt Becky had reservations about Mr Adams.

"Do be nice to her, my love, she is probably here to wish you and Mr Adams well and ask about your wedding plans," she said, but not with much conviction, for Catherine knew in her heart that Becky's sudden arrival did not bode well. Nevertheless, she welcomed her sister and asked Mrs Giles to make all necessary arrangements for her stay. Lilian, having greeted her aunt somewhat less warmly, returned to her room, claiming she had a headache.

The sisters were in the parlour, taking tea, when Rebecca explained the purpose of her sudden visit.

"I had to come, Cathy my dear, I could not have lived with my conscience if I had not. I knew, if I could only see you and advise you of what I have heard, you would see it differently. My friend Lady Ashton agreed. 'Do go to your sister, Becky,' she said, 'tell her how truly horrified we all were to learn about this Mr Adams's family scandal. I am sure she will not permit her daughter to make such an unfortunate marriage.'"

Catherine, unwilling to let her continue in this vein, interrupted her. "Becky, if this is to do with Lilian and Mr Adams, it is of no use at all to try to change her mind. Lilian knows all of the facts, which you detailed in your letter. Mr Adams told her himself, as he told me, before he proposed to her and she, having considered them, has accepted him and I have given them my blessing. I agree that the circumstances you speak of seem shocking, but they are none of them a reflection upon Mr Adams, of whom we have had only good reports. I cannot agree that he should be reviled for the actions of his parents when they were younger than he is today. Besides, they love each other, Becky," she said, with such quiet deliberation that Becky was temporarily silenced.

But not for long.

"I cannot accept this, Cathy," she said, recovering fast. "I used to believe all that too, but look where it got poor Julian and Josie. He loved her too, and I thought that was all that mattered and did everything I could to encourage them; indeed I blame myself, for my Josie was miserable. If only I had not persuaded her to marry him..."

Catherine interrupted her again, "But Becky, is that not what you want me to do with Lilian, except you would have me persuade her to give up Mr Adams, whom she loves and who loves her in return? You would like her to give him up. What benefit is there in such an exercise, which will only leave everyone miserable? I can see none."

Rebecca was unwilling to give up so easily.

"Catherine, what would you say if I told you that there was a much better prospect for Lilian: a Mr Joshua Armstrong, a cousin of Lady Ashton and a very eligible young gentleman indeed? His connections are excellent and he has well over five thousand a year, even before he inherits his father's estate. Now he, I know, is very fond of Lilian and has asked most particularly to be remembered to her and to you, Cathy. Would that not be a much better proposition for Lilian?"

This proposal was met with such incredulity by Catherine, as to make Mrs Tate doubt whether her sister was listening at all. Demonstrating her indifference, Catherine stated that she could not speak for her daughter, but she did not think Lilian would have any interest in the intentions of Mr Joshua Armstrong at all. For herself, Catherine declared that she hardly knew Mr Armstrong and could not see any value in the proposition.

"Lilian has hardly mentioned his name at all since her return," she said.

Undaunted, Rebecca persisted. "Do you not think I should speak to Lilian about it? He was excessively keen that I should give her his warmest regards…"

"My dear Becky, speak to Lilian if you wish, I shall not discourage you, and do give her Mr Armstrong's regards, but let me warn you, you will be wasting your breath for she will not listen," said Catherine, and even as she did so, the door opened and Lilian walked into the room.

She was dressed for driving out, and Rebecca was quite struck by the unusual lightness of her countenance and manner as she greeted her. This was indeed a very different Lilian to the unhappy young girl who had left London with her mother some weeks ago. Lilian reminded her mother that Mr Adams was to call for her at eleven; it was now not quite half past ten. Her enhanced confidence was difficult to miss.

Seeing an opportunity, which might not be repeated, Rebecca greeted her niece and launched directly into a description of a most entertaining ball given by Lady Ashton, to which all of the ladies and gentlemen had been instructed to wear medieval costumes.

"I confess I was quite astonished at the numbers of gallant knights and their ladies who arrived at the ball, including some of those with whom you might wish to claim an acquaintance, Lilian."

When Lilian showed little interest, she went on, "Mr Vanstone was there and Mr Josh Armstrong, of course—they looked splendid as two of King Arthur's knights! Mr Armstrong is a very fine-looking gentleman, as you will recall, I am sure. I was sorry that you had returned home just the week before the ball; I am sure you would have found it excessively enjoyable. Mr Armstrong certainly remarked that you would have enjoyed it, and I do believe he missed you and particularly asked to be remembered to you, Lilian, and your mama."

Lilian, who had been looking out of the window during this recital, apparently awaiting the arrival of Mr Adams, turned to face her aunt and to Catherine's astonishment, said in a voice tinged with sarcasm, "Please thank Mr Armstrong when you return to London, Aunt Becky, and would you oblige me by reminding him that on the last occasion on which we met, at your house as

I recall, I thought I had made it quite plain that I had no wish to meet him or any of his friends again."

Ignoring her aunt's gasps of shock and bewilderment, she went on—

"Their behaviour towards me at Lady Ashton's house was so dishonourable, so wanting in good manners and decency, that I could never meet any of them without suffering the strongest feelings of revulsion. While I will grant that Mr Armstrong did not actively participate in humiliating me, he did nothing at all to discourage his friends in their appalling behaviour. He did come the following day to apologise for their bad behaviour, but in my estimation, he is not a gentleman at all but, like all his fine friends at Lady Ashton's ball, merely masquerades as one."

Catherine could not believe what she was hearing. She had known Lilian had been bored and not very happy in London, but she had said nothing of humiliation, nor anything of the behaviour she spoke of, on the part of the men she had met there. Catherine was shocked into silence as Lilian spoke. Never before had she seen her daughter in such a passion.

But, even as she listened, unable for a while to say anything at all, she could not help feeling a tinge of envy mixed with profound admiration at her daughter's courage and honesty. She had not thought young Lilian, gentle and demure at all times, capable of such vehement frankness.

At last finding her voice, Catherine intervened gently. "Lilian, my dear, I do not think it is fair to speak so severely of all the young gentlemen you met; there may have been one or two..."

But Lilian would not be stifled; she had held it within her for weeks, now it would all pour out.

"No, Mama, I have hitherto said nothing of this to you, out of concern for Aunt Becky, because these men are the relations and close friends of her confidante Lady Ashton, but I will be silent no longer. They are not the honourable gentlemen you believe them to be. They waste their time and money on the silliest of pastimes and spend their hours devising ways to belittle and deride those they dislike. Their greatest delight comes from the discomfiture of others, like myself, whom they believe to be their inferiors and so fair game for their cruel sport."

As Becky tried in vain to protest, Lilian ignored her and went on.

"To them, I was an object of ridicule, because I was not one of their wealthy ladies of fashion, ready and willing to flirt with all of them. As for Lady Ashton, she gains no credit as a hostess when she permits her men friends to tease and torment young women who are her guests. I am not sorry to have missed her ball; I cannot imagine that I should ever wish to attend one. Indeed, I have no wish to see any of them and will thank you, Aunt Becky, not to commend them to me or me to any of them."

So saying, she begged her mother's pardon and asked to be excused, before leaving the room and retiring to watch for Mr Adams's arrival from a window in her bedroom.

Meanwhile, her aunt, stunned by the intensity of Lilian's attack upon Lady Ashton and her friends, did not speak for fully five minutes.

Equally astounded, but with a greater understanding of her daughter's views and feelings, Catherine tried to make amends.

"Becky, I am sorry, I had no idea Lilian felt so strongly about this. As you can see, there is nothing to be gained by trying to interest her in Lady Ashton's cousin. I fear Mr Armstrong will have to address his compliments to some other young lady. I hope he will not be too put out, but I daresay, for such an eligible gentleman, it will present no difficulty at all."

Rebecca was shaking her head in confusion.

"My dear sister, I am sorry, too. I was not aware that Lilian had felt so badly treated by any of the young men at the parties which she attended at Lady Ashton's house. I cannot think how it came about. They are all young men from prominent county families, men of wealth and fashion; besides, Lilian said not a word to me about any of this."

Her complete confusion was plain. She had known nothing of Lilian's unhappy experiences.

"It is possible, of course, that a few of them may indulge in flirtation—you know how it is with young men about town—but most of them are Lady Ashton's relations and close friends, they will not do anything too outrageous under her roof! Is it possible poor Lilian may have been mistaken? Could it have been some dreadful misunderstanding?" She was trying hard to explain away what may have looked to her sister as dereliction of her duty to her young niece while she was in her care.

But Catherine was not anxious to rub salt in her sister's wounds; it was sufficient that Lilian had so spectacularly exploded the sham of Lady Ashton's rich and fashionable friends, whose worth her sister had been eager to promote. No further mortification was needed.

"It matters not now, Becky," she said charitably. "It is very unlikely that Lilian will ever meet either Lady Ashton or any of her relatives and friends again; we move in very different circles here, and when they are married, so will Lilian and Mr Adams. You need not concern yourself about it anymore; whatever occurred to upset her so is in the past and what with all the excitement of preparing for the wedding, it will soon be forgotten."

"Will Lilian ever forgive me? Can you?" Becky asked, abject in her misery.

Catherine was magnanimous. "Forgive you? Oh Becky, what is there to forgive? You thought you were doing your best for her, no doubt. I know that well. But Lilian is stronger and more determined than either of us; as you see, she has made up her mind to marry Mr Adams and will do so," adding with a curious smile, "I confess I envy her, Becky. I wish that at her age I had had such strength of will. If that were the case, my own life may well have been very different."

Rebecca looked up and caught the fleeting expression of regret that had crossed her sister's countenance and, turning to her, asked, "What do you mean, Cathy? Why do you say that?"

Catherine sighed. "It's a long story, Becky, it goes back many years to a time when we were not as close as sisters should be, and so you never knew how I lived, nor I you. But, perhaps if you have time to listen, it will help you understand why I have refused to do as you asked and persuade my daughter to abandon Mr Adams, because some people think he is not good enough for her, especially people like your friend Lady Ashton."

Rebecca was eager to hear Catherine's story. She had had little intimate contact with her elder sister since Catherine had accepted Lady Catherine de Bourgh's invitation to live at Rosings and their mother had moved with her two younger daughters to Mansfield. They were very young then, and Rebecca had always thought her sister had enjoyed life under the patronage and care of Her Ladyship. Her own youthful recollections of Rosings had been of a life of ease and luxury compared to hers.

This was the first time she had become aware that Catherine had had any misgivings or regrets.

END OF PART THREE

RECOLLECTIONS OF ROSINGS

Part Four

Chapter Fourteen

T HE ARRIVAL AT THE house of Mr Adams—who had arranged to
take Lilian to visit the new rector at Hunsford Church, where they
planned to be married later that year—gave Catherine and Rebecca an
opportunity to spend some time together, undisturbed.

The sisters retired upstairs and there, in the privacy of her room, Catherine
related the story that had remained her secret for over twenty-five years. She
had told no one, not even her mother.

It was the story of a young girl, gentle, modest, and not fifteen years old,
who had been overwhelmed by the kindness and great honour bestowed upon
her after her father's sudden death by his wealthy, influential patron Lady
Catherine de Bourgh.

"I had always regarded Lady Catherine as a person of great consequence;
both Papa and Mama had made it appear so. Naturally I was grateful for the
way she drew me into her circle, as though I were a niece or another daughter
for whose welfare and happiness she had the greatest concern. She was kind and
generous to me, which is probably why it never occurred to me to question Her
Ladyship's judgment on most matters.

"I travelled with her wherever she went, I wore the expensive clothes and
hats which she decided I should have, I learned to draw and paint and play the
pianoforte just as she thought I should. None of these tasks imposed any strain

upon me; it was easy to oblige her by doing or not doing things as she wished, and there were not too many prohibitions placed upon me at Rosings. Indeed, I had more freedom to enjoy myself than I had had at the parsonage, where, as you know, Papa made the rules. I had no real complaints."

Rebecca could well believe it; her elder sister had always been compliant and easygoing, unlike herself or their rebellious younger sister Amelia-Jane.

"Was there nothing at all you wished you could do differently? No single occasion on which you wanted to defy Her Ladyship?" she asked.

Catherine smiled and shook her head. "Strange as it might seem, there was none during those first years, when my life at Rosings was freer and more full of interesting things and people than I had ever known at Hunsford," she replied. "You may recall, Becky, that we did not go out much except to Rosings or to the village or on rare occasions to London or Hertfordshire with Papa?"

Rebecca remembered it well; it had been stifling and dull for the most part and she had wondered how her mother endured it.

"Well, at Rosings, it was very different," Catherine continued. "Lady Catherine had many relations and acquaintances who would call on her. And she insisted that I should be included on all those occasions, so I would learn how to conduct myself in society. I was often placed alongside of one of her guests at dinner, to engage them in conversation. To Lady Catherine, I was never just a paid companion like Mrs Jenkinson; she treated me as favourite god-daughter, always presenting me to her visitors as such. Mama was rather surprised, because Lady Catherine had always stood on ceremony with others, but I do believe she had decided that I would be treated as a member of her family and it was her way of having me learn the essential arts and graces.

"I have to admit that I enjoyed it—even though some of the guests were dull, it was at least possible to observe and study them and I liked that very much. I was participating in a social world of which I knew little and to which I never would have had entry as the daughter of a country parson, were it not for Lady Catherine's intervention."

"Did you not miss your own family, Mama or me or Amelia-Jane?" asked Rebecca, to which Catherine said with an apologetic smile, "Dear Becky, you must think me exceedingly selfish, but truly I did not. There was always so much to do—I spent much of my time reading and learning to draw and play the pianoforte. I enjoyed the walks and drives; Miss de Bourgh was never well enough to go out much, so Lady Catherine took me everywhere with her. I accompanied her on visits to London or when she visited her tenants, and she was a most active and energetic landlord, telling everybody on the estate what to do and how to do it! I found it all quite fascinating.

"There were many interesting occasions, especially after Mr and Mrs Darcy were re-admitted to Lady Catherine's circle following Georgiana Darcy's wedding and Colonel Fitzwilliam's return from India. He was a great favourite of hers and later, when he was married, he brought his wife with him. Caroline, whom her Ladyship liked, despite her father being in trade, was wonderful fun. I think we all agreed that Caroline's charm was quite irresistible, and it was clear that the colonel was deeply in love with her. I believe I did learn a great deal from both Mrs Darcy and Caroline."

She stopped awhile to pour out more tea before continuing.

"It was on one of those visits that Mr Darcy, whose advice Lady Catherine sought often on matters relating to her estate, urged Her Ladyship to employ a librarian. He had visited the library, which was in the East Wing of the house where Lady Catherine rarely went. Everything was locked away in cabinets and no one used the library at all. Mr Darcy declared that its great collection, which had been put together by Sir Lewis de Bourgh and his father before him, was in danger of deterioration through neglect and the lack of professional care. 'It would be a great pity to let that occur. A good librarian will enhance and preserve the value of the collection,' he advised and Her Ladyship acquiesced and set about hiring one. Which is how I first met Mr Frank Burnett."

Becky raised an eyebrow, "The same Mr Burnett I met on my last visit? The gentleman who now works for the Rosings Trust?" she asked.

"The same. That was so long ago, that even I am surprised that I recall so clearly all the details of our association," said Catherine.

Sensing a story, the writer in Rebecca was agog. She asked eagerly, "And did he fall in love with you, Cathy?"

Catherine laughed. "No, Becky, he did not. But over the years of our acquaintance, I grew to like him very much indeed. He was so different to any of the other men I had met; well read, yet modest, his demeanour was cheerful and friendly, yet never brash or boastful, and his manners were naturally pleasing, with no trace of pretension. He was for me the very epitome of what a gentleman should be. And, though I did not suppose him to be in love with me, I will admit I had reason occasionally to think that he seemed somewhat partial to me in a friendly sort of way; I cannot claim that he ever showed by word or gesture that he was more deeply attached to me than a good friend would be."

"But, surely, Cathy, it was possible that with time, as you became more intimately acquainted, he may have done so?" Becky persisted.

Catherine shrugged her shoulders. "I don't know what he might or might not have felt, had there been time enough for us to pursue what I thought was a most pleasant and rewarding friendship. Yet, it was not to be."

"But why ever not?" asked Rebecca, her eyes wide with astonishment. "What was it prevented you from continuing what must surely have been a most agreeable association?"

Catherine looked at her sister directly and said in a voice that left Rebecca in no doubt at all of her sister's opinion, "It was the intervention, albeit with the best of intentions, of others; those who had no right to interfere in my life at all. One in particular may have believed she had a responsibility to do so, having given me a home and an income of my own when Papa died and so taken the place of a parent in my young life."

"Do you mean Lady Catherine de Bourgh?"

"I do. Having been told of my friendship with Mr Burnett by Mrs Jenkinson, who was in truth her spy, I think, she strongly advised me against the association and later, when I appeared not to heed her advice, she forbade me to continue the friendship," Catherine said.

"But on what grounds? Did she give you sound reasons? Were there any impediments, obstacles that could not be overcome?"

Catherine's countenance reflected her feelings. "Obstacles? Impediments? You ask what they were? There were none bigger and more immovable than the will of Lady Catherine herself. She insisted that no good would come of it. Mr Burnett, she declared, was not of a suitable background. While he did the job he was paid to do with exemplary diligence and attended to all other duties exceedingly well, his father, she said, was a tradesman and to Lady Catherine that was an unacceptable connection."

Seeing Rebecca's expression of disbelief, Catherine continued, allowing herself a little ironic smile as she did so.

"Now, had his father been a clergyman or even an attorney, it might have been a little less painful to Her Ladyship. It was, in her eyes, imprudent and unlikely to lead to happiness. She left me in no doubt that a continuation of the friendship would result in his dismissal from his position and my complete estrangement from her and Rosings. And because I was too young and unable to withstand her persuasive powers, I confess I gave in and complied with her wishes."

Rebecca had listened, more amazed by each new revelation. "And what of Mr Burnett? Did Lady Catherine forbid him too?" she asked.

"I do not know, I have never asked him and he has never said anything to me. But there was an end to it. Consequently she removed from my life perhaps the happiest, most engaging association I have ever known."

Rebecca felt deeply for her sister. "And tell me, Cathy, do you still regret the loss of it?"

"If I am to be honest, I must confess that while I was quite bereft at first, I did not give it much thought for many years, especially since Mr Burnett left his position at Rosings some months later and went away to Europe; but having met him again last year, I would be less than truthful if I did not admit that I do regret the loss, Becky, I regret it very much indeed."

It was now quite clear to Rebecca what had transpired in her sister's life.

Catherine had been persuaded by Lady Catherine de Bourgh to relinquish the one deeply felt attachment she had had in all her young life. She could not know that her sister had suffered much pain as a result, and for many months the sadness had hung over her like a fog, shrouding everything else around her. Visits to London and Bath had done nothing to improve her outlook, and Lady Catherine had become impatient with her lack of interest in all prospects of matrimony. But Catherine had persisted, claiming she had no interest in it, having accepted the inevitability of remaining a spinster.

It had been many years later that she had changed her mind.

The new rector of Hunsford, a Mr Harrison, whose admiration for her performance upon the church organ and with the choir had preceded his appreciation of her character and disposition, had approached first his patron and then the lady herself to ask for her hand in marriage. Lady Catherine had approved, and Catherine, then almost twenty-nine, had accepted and married him, much to the relief of her mother. Mrs Collins had almost given up hope of seeing her eldest girl married, and the news was very welcome indeed.

"Becky, I do not wish you to believe that I spent nine years of my life pining for Mr Burnett, because I did not. But, having known how very agreeable such an association could be, I did not find it easy to form an attachment for anyone else; for to tell you the truth, Becky, there was not another gentleman of my acquaintance who had half the attraction," said Catherine, with a degree of frankness her sister had not known before.

"And Mr Harrison?" Becky probed.

"Ah, my dear Mr Harrison, well that was nine years later, and when one is almost twenty-nine, the affections and attachments of nineteen seem a rather distant if sweet memory. Mr Harrison was kind, good-natured, eminently respectable, and loved me dearly, he said. Lady Catherine, on hearing of his proposal, declared him to be an excellent choice, Mama agreed, and so, my dear Becky, I accepted him and we were married."

"And were you happy, truly happy together?" Becky asked.

"Of course," replied Catherine.

"But Cathy, forgive me for asking this, have you ever thought that you may have been much happier with Mr Burnett?" Becky persisted.

Catherine's answer came without any hesitation. "I have not, because the question did not arise. Thanks to Lady Catherine, the possibility did not exist. Mr Burnett neither declared his feelings for me nor made me any offer of marriage. It would only have been speculation, and one cannot build a dream of happiness upon that alone."

Rebecca could not resist asking the question that had leapt into her mind no sooner had she discovered the identity of the gentleman concerned.

"And Cathy, now that Mr Burnett is back at Rosings, do you meet often?"

"Indeed and when we do, we meet as friends."

"Have you spoken of the past?" she persisted.

"If you mean do we recall our past friendship, no, not at all. But we do speak often of what Rosings used to be, before this terrible fire. Mr Burnett is desolated by the loss of so many treasures; he remembers them well and it is his hope that everything that can be saved will be preserved for posterity. But we do not dwell on the past, Becky, there are sufficient matters of today to engage our interest and much work to be done."

"And has he given you no indication at all of what his feelings might have been all those years ago?" asked Rebecca, still unsatisfied.

"He has not," replied Catherine, "and why should he? It is so long ago. Besides, who is to know whether he has had other attachments in the intervening years?"

"Have you no idea at all?"

"None, nor do I wish to know. We meet now as mature adults, friends with many shared interests. I do not hanker after the past, nor, I think, does he. Becky, I did not tell you this story to gain your sympathy because of an unhappy relinquishment over twenty years ago; rather, it was in order that I might draw your attention to the lessons we might take from the experience that interference in another's life is rarely beneficial and not recommended.

"We, Mr Burnett and I, were neither of us given the opportunity of ever discovering how much or how little we cared—how well we may have come to love each other and how happy we might have been together—only because of the gratuitous interference of Lady Catherine de Bourgh. That her intentions may have been honourable is of little matter; her intrusion into my life brought me only great sadness at the time. I cannot say how it affected Mr Burnett, but judging from the manner in which he responded at the time, he was, at the very least, disappointed."

Taking her sister's hand, she added gently, "Dear Becky, it is from this painful experience that I have learned the lesson which I ask you to understand too: that I will never permit anyone, not even you, to do likewise to my daughter and deny her the right to make her own choice in life."

Rebecca nodded, comprehending at last the depth of feeling that had caused her sister to resist all her attempts to thwart Lilian's engagement to Mr Adams.

"This may not be the best match Lilian can make, but it is the one she has chosen to make, because they love each other, and having examined all the circumstances, I can see no good reason to oppose it."

Once more, Rebecca nodded her acceptance and she could not hide the tears that filled her eyes as she rose and embraced her sister.

Shortly afterwards, the maid came to say that Miss Lilian and Mr Adams had returned and were in the parlour, at which the sisters went downstairs.

Making a deliberate attempt to remedy the situation after that morning's contretemps, Rebecca greeted the couple and made much of wishing them every happiness. She was, she said, happy to have met them together to convey her congratulations, for she was leaving on the morrow for London and intended thereafter to return home to Derbyshire, where she would spend the rest of the Summer.

Chapter Fifteen

CATHERINE COULD NOT EXPLAIN why she had set out to walk through the woods to Rosings instead of taking the path that led from the main gate to the house.

It was not that she had made a deliberate decision; indeed she had not given it any thought at all. After Rebecca had left for the station, she had found herself feeling nostalgic and unaccountably dejected. A walk in the woods always did her good and it being a particularly fine day, she had set off alone.

Reaching the main gateway to Rosings, she had stood for some time gazing at the gutted remains of the West Wing of the great mansion—blackened walls and smoke-stained windows hung perilously above what had been the grandest rose garden in the south of England. Not even at Pemberley, whose grounds were among the finest in the country, had she seen such a variety of blooms, with such hues and scents that delighted the eye and filled the air at Rosings Park with their fragrance. Ironically, many of the roses had survived the fire and, with the Spring rains and the Summer sun, were in bloom again. Catherine found them irresistible.

Even as she gazed upon the display they made below the stone steps leading from the house, she remembered how often she had come out there to collect the blooms to fill the bowls and vases for Lady Catherine. It had been her special task for many years and it was one she had loved.

Reaching into the pocket of her gown, she found a small pair of scissors; not very suitable for the job but they would have to do, she thought, and without further ado, she crossed the paved courtyard and entered the rose garden. There, with the scent of the roses all around her, she reached up to pick some. As she pulled down one of the tall canes, there were footsteps behind her and before she could look round, Frank Burnett said, "They were always your favourite, were they not?"

Startled, Catherine leapt away from the bush, letting go of the branch, which sprang back and he, stepping up, pulled it down again.

"Here, let me," he said and taking out a pocket knife, neatly sliced through the woody stems. Working quickly, he gathered a dozen or so of the best blooms, shearing away the thorns as he did so, and handed them to her.

She thanked him as she accepted them, but took them awkwardly for she wore no gloves, nor had she a basket to carry them in. Seeing her difficulty, he said, "Wait here, I shall be back in a moment," and raced swiftly up the steps into the house, returning with an old cane basket that had clearly seen better days.

"This one escaped the fire—it was stored in a cupboard under the service stairs together with a bag of gardening tools," he said, holding it out to her.

Catherine, who had hitherto been standing still as if petrified, suddenly smiled, delighted by his find.

"I cannot believe it, why it is the very same basket I used whenever I came out to pick the roses for Her Ladyship," she cried. "How could it have survived all this time? It must be all of twenty-five years or more."

He smiled and expressed surprise. "I cannot believe it is so long ago, it seems only yesterday that I found you here, in the rain, searching for a pair of missing secateurs! You had been gathering roses for Her Ladyship, I think?"

Catherine was so astonished at his recollection, she could not say a word for a few minutes.

"Have you forgotten?" he asked and then as if to jog her memory, added, "I recall it was the day on which Lady Catherine first invited me to dine at Rosings."

By this time, Catherine had recovered her composure sufficiently to say, "I have not forgotten, indeed I remember your kindness in returning despite the rain to retrieve the secateurs for me."

Matching his recollection with hers, she added, "And yes, I do recall that you dined with us that evening—Dr Halliday was visiting from Oxford, to plead the cause of one of his theology students, who was an applicant for a minor living on the Rosings estate. You were invited because Lady Catherine was keen to have someone who could converse confidently with him."

At that, Frank Burnett laughed. "I do not recall conversing confidently at all—I was very much daunted by the great man's reputation. He was an eminent dean, as I recall. But I do remember that it was a very pleasant evening altogether; the dinner was excellent and afterwards, you played the pianoforte to entertain us."

Catherine could not believe he had such a detailed recollection of the occasion after so many years had passed. She was still standing in the middle of the rose garden, looking rather confused and wondering what to do next, when he interrupted her thoughts.

"You look tired, will you not sit down?" he said and, taking the basket from her, led her to a stone seat beside a spreading elm. She was grateful for the respite and relaxed awhile.

"Were you on your way to Hunsford?" he asked, by way of making conversation.

She said no, she had been out walking and had come this way almost without knowing it.

"I did not mean to go into the rose garden at all. It was such a pleasant day, I thought after my sister had left to catch her train that I would enjoy the walk through the grounds. When I passed the entrance and saw the house, I stopped... it had been my home for so many years... it was hard not to stop and recall how it had been and then, I saw the roses all in bloom and could not resist them."

They laughed together then and he said, "Well, I am glad you came by and that I found you here."

She looked up at him, surprised as much by his tone as his words.

"I have been through these gardens many times and they hold memories for me too—though, I am sure, not as many nor as poignant as yours, considering the relatively short period I spent at Rosings," he said and as he looked at her, Catherine could not help thinking there was more feeling in his voice than she might have expected.

The sun was warmer and she rose and said it was time to return to the house, because Mrs Giles would begin to worry if she were late.

"I did not tell anyone where I was going, they will be anxious," she explained and he offered her his arm, which, because she was genuinely tired, she accepted gratefully as they walked back to the Dower House.

They did not speak much, except of trifling matters; Catherine was still a little shaken by the unexpected encounter. When they reached the house, she invited him in to take tea with them, but he thanked her and said he had pressing business to attend to.

He did, however, ask permission to call on her on the morrow.

"If I may, there are a few things I have retrieved from the West Wing, which may interest you. I should like to show them to you," he said.

Catherine agreed and asked him to stay to dinner afterwards.

"Mr Adams will be joining us too," she added, almost as an afterthought, and he accepted the invitation with pleasure.

"I shall look forward to it," he said and smiled, she surmised, as though his thoughts were very far away.

With that he was gone, leaving her thinking of their meeting in the rose garden and turning it over in her mind.

The fact that he had a clear recollection of their previous encounter there, so many years ago, had surprised her. Yet now, as she thought about it again, she was pleased he had not forgotten.

"At least it proves that I had made some significant impression and was not forgotten as some tiresome young girl who insisted on retrieving a pair of secateurs in the pouring rain!" she thought, with a little smile of satisfaction.

Catherine arranged the roses in a bowl and placed them in the centre of a table in the parlour. Their fragrance filled the room.

Thinking back over the years, she could recall many subsequent occasions on which they'd met, more pleasing and certainly more memorable. He must surely remember them, she assumed, if he had such a clear recollection of this one.

Yet when he had left Lady Catherine's employ, giving as his reason a desire to travel to Europe, Catherine had had no further news of him. Lady Catherine had never mentioned him, nor had anyone else, until he had returned to Rosings after the fire, employed now by the Trust to advise upon the restoration and preservation of that part of the estate that had survived the catastrophe.

A happy coincidence, perhaps, she supposed, allowing herself the luxury of speculation, something she very rarely indulged in. Her reputation for sound common sense and practicality was generally well based; her family never guessed that in a small corner of her nature, there remained a vestige of youthful romanticism, kept alive by her taste for the novels of Mr Dickens and Mrs Gaskell.

That night, Catherine returned to her notebooks and read again her accounts of her friendly association with Frank Burnett, this time with renewed interest, since she knew that he must surely have his own memories of many of these occasions. She could not help wondering how they might differ from hers.

It was a mind-teasing exercise that absorbed her thoughts until the early hours of the morning, when she finally fell into a deep sleep.

Frank Burnett came the following evening about half an hour before the hour usually appointed for dinner guests to arrive.

Lilian was still upstairs enjoying a long bath, but Catherine had been expecting him and was waiting in the parlour when he was admitted. He had brought with him a satchel containing several small items salvaged from the fire, a folder of documents, and a roll of drawing paper, tied up with string.

Catherine was intrigued when he, having seated himself beside her, drew out the roll of papers and spread them out on the table in front of them. He proceeded, then, to explain.

"I received last week a letter from Mr Jonathan Bingley, instructing me to seek out any material available in the archives at Rosings, which might be used to assist your application to start a parish school. On going through Dr Harrison's papers, I had found some notes and two letters pertaining to the school, one of which referred to a set of plans, which he had commissioned. I searched everywhere but could find none, until it struck me that they may still be at the church in Hunsford.

"I took the liberty, then, of approaching Mr Jamison, the new rector of Hunsford, and to my relief he was exceedingly obliging. He urged me to search the parish files and even his own office. I did as he suggested and lo and behold, there they were. You see them here—a complete set of plans for a parish school to be built on a piece of common land behind the church hall."

Catherine had been listening in silence, her eyes bright with excitement.

"Mr Burnett, that is excellent news," she said in a whisper.

"Indeed it is, and even better is the news that Mr Jamison the rector is just as enthusiastic about the project as you are."

"Is he?" She could not believe this good fortune.

"He has long been, he admitted to me, a convert to the idea of educating the children of the parish and in fact undertook such a venture in Southampton, where he used to serve prior to his transfer to Hunsford. I believe you will find him a most useful ally."

"I cannot tell you how happy I am to hear this. I must thank you for the work you have done, I do appreciate it very much." She was eager to make him understand that his efforts on her behalf were not taken for granted.

But he was equally keen to assure her that it had all been done willingly and with pleasure, for as he said, "I am entirely in sympathy with your desire to set up a parish school and educate the children of this estate. Mr Bingley has mentioned to me that such a project was once thwarted, and he hopes very much that this time the Trust will accept it. He believes that the lack of a decent education will deprive many British children of their birthright in what is an increasingly competitive society. I agree—in Europe, particularly in Germany, the state spends large sums of money on educating their young, yet we in England seem content to leave it to charity."

To Catherine's ears, this was sweet music. "Then, if you were called upon to advise the Trust on our scheme for a parish school, may I assume your advice will favour us?" she asked and his answer was unequivocal, "Certainly, I could not do otherwise."

The arrival of Mr Adams, while it did not necessarily end the conversation, changed its direction somewhat; but for Catherine the evening was perfection itself. Nothing could dull her pleasure. If only the Trust would now approve her project and allow her to implement the late Dr Harrison's plans, she thought, she could not ask for more.

As for Mr Burnett, she saw him now in a new light; not just as the man whose amiable nature and genuine erudition had brought her much to enjoy but as a valuable ally in the most important cause she had adopted in all her life.

Chapter Sixteen

As Summer waned into Autumn, Lilian and Mr Adams became increasingly preoccupied with their wedding plans, spending every available hour together, leaving Catherine to organise her campaign for the parish school with the assistance of the rector Mr Jamison and Frank Burnett.

The week preceding the meeting of the Rosings Trust was a busy one. While Mr Darcy was being represented by Jonathan Bingley, who would occupy a room in the surviving wing of the great house as he did on all his visits to the estate, Colonel Fitzwilliam was sending his wife Caroline to attend the meeting on his behalf, and she had written to ask if she might stay at the Dower House with Catherine.

Delighted to agree, for Caroline was loved and welcomed everywhere, Catherine nevertheless found herself overwhelmed with a myriad of tasks. Unwilling to appear inhospitable, she had instructed her housekeeper Mrs Giles on every particular of their guest's accommodation and comfort, but found she still had her hands full with paperwork for her presentation to the Trust. There was no one she could appeal to for assistance save Mr Burnett and, having collected together all her material and scribbled down a plethora of notes, she summoned up the courage to go over to Rosings and approach him in his office there.

As she walked, she ran through in her mind what she would say to him when she got there. It was quite a straightforward appeal; she decided to say simply, "Mr Burnett, all I need is to have someone who is conversant with the procedure of meetings of this nature advise me on the presentation of the facts and figures pertaining to my project. I am not at liberty to appeal to Jonathan Bingley because he represents a trustee himself. Mr Adams, apart from being preoccupied with his wedding plans, is not sufficiently familiar with all of the matters relating to the parish school, nor is Mr Jamison, who is new to the parish. If you could help me..."

As she pondered her words, and his probable response, Catherine found she had reached the house and, going directly up the stairs to the floor where his work-rooms were situated, she knocked twice and entered the room. Mr Burnett was not in the room, but since the door had been left unlocked, she assumed he could not have been far, probably somewhere in the building attending to a matter of some importance and no doubt he would return soon, she thought. The urgency of her own cause allowed her to believe that it would be best if she remained in the room to await his return rather than go out to seek him.

Catherine had only ever visited this part of the house since the fire with Lilian and Mr Adams. She had never been in this room before.

At first glance, she was struck by the tidiness of the room and the orderly manner in which were arranged rows of files and books on shelves along one wall of the room. Beside a large desk stood a glass-fronted bookcase well stocked with volumes of various sizes.

Seating herself at some distance from the desk, she waited, but he did not come. Restless and a little anxious, she rose and looked out of the window, then wandered over to the bookcase, hoping to see some title with which she was familiar. She saw none; they were all books relating to his work—the conservation and preservation of rare books, artworks, and antiquities in many parts of the world.

She was about to return to the window when a picture on one of the shelves caught her eye and, on closer examination, made her catch her breath, as she recognised a framed drawing of herself.

It was one of the drawings from her late husband's collection, that Mr Burnett had brought to her attention and from which they had together selected a few to be framed for her family. Yet, here was one of herself alone, framed in silver and placed in his book case, in such a position that only a person standing directly in front of the cabinet or seated at the desk could see it clearly enough to recognise the subject.

There was only one possible conclusion. Mr Burnett must have taken one of the drawings himself and had it framed.

Confused, Catherine did not know what she should do. If she stayed in the room until he returned, he would have no doubt that she had seen it and that being the case, would probably expect her to question him about it.

If she did not, he might assume the need for some explanation on his part, there would be embarrassment and awkwardness—she had no doubt of it—and just at this time, when she needed his help so badly, it would be the very worst thing!

It would not do.

Deciding quickly that retreat would be the best strategy, Catherine left the room and hurried downstairs to find one of the servants. She found a young boy working in one of the rooms and asked if he could find Mr Burnett and give him a message.

"He is in the West Wing, ma'am, with the restorers. Shall I tell him you're here, ma'am?" the boy asked.

"No, no, don't do that. He is probably busy. I don't wish to disturb him. I'll give you a note. Take it to him and say it is urgent. That will do."

So saying, she extracted a sheet of paper from her folder and hastily scribbled a short note, requesting his help in a matter relating to the school. If he was free to call at the house that afternoon, it would be much appreciated, she wrote.

The boy took it, and as he made his way towards the West Wing, Catherine slipped quickly out of the building and hurried home.

As she walked through the grounds, her mind was beset with a new conundrum. She wondered what was about to happen to her hitherto tranquil existence. The sight of her picture framed in silver, sitting in his cabinet, had thrown her into a state of confusion, for which she was singularly unprepared. She could not decide if she was flattered, pleased, or angry. She was certainly perplexed and discomfited.

After the initial shock, however, the more she thought about it, the more it seemed that pleasure rather than annoyance dominated her sensations.

Catherine had not experienced such feelings in many years and was scarcely able to recognise them for what they were.

In this perturbed state of mind, she spent the afternoon trying to put in order all the information she had gathered together for the meeting of the trustees, but her thoughts would not settle on anything, wandering over and over again to the same topic. It was deeply frustrating, for she knew not how it could be resolved. She had questions for which she could see no way of obtaining answers without admitting to having been to Mr Burnett's room at Rosings that morning. It was not the kind of situation in which she usually found herself.

She was further discomposed by the fact that he did not appear to have received her note, for he neither came, nor sent any message of explanation. Catherine was not happy and spent the afternoon in a state of turmoil, a condition that was quite unfamiliar to her.

Later that evening, soon after they had risen from the dinner table, the door bell rang and the maid admitted Mr Burnett into the parlour. Lilian was tired and begged to be excused, leaving her mother to greet their visitor.

Asking for coffee to be served in the parlour, Catherine went to meet him.

Rising from his chair, he apologised for the lateness of the hour. "Mrs Harrison, I am truly sorry I could not come earlier, but we have had a minor crisis in the West Wing; a crumbling piece of masonry was dislodged by a workman and fell onto one of the lads working below," he explained.

Catherine looked alarmed. "He is not badly hurt, I hope?" she asked.

"No, just a little bruised and sore and rather shaken. But I had to take him into the village and have the apothecary look at him. I did receive your note earlier in the day and I am sorry I could not respond sooner."

Catherine brushed aside his apologies. "Pray do not apologise, Mr Burnett, I am very sorry about the boy. I hope your prompt action has helped lessen the pain of any injury he may have suffered."

Reassuring her very quickly on that score, he went on to ask how he might be of assistance. "I assumed it must be urgent else you would not have come to Rosings in search of me. How can I help?"

When Catherine explained, he was most obliging; listened carefully to her request, perused her notes, and offered to take them away and prepare for her a brief but cogent summary, which she could use to convince the members of the Trust of the rightness of her cause.

"I need do no more than list all the facts and figures for you; your own commitment and personal enthusiasm for the project will do the rest. Mr Bingley will be here in a day or two to take a tour of the estate before the meeting of the trustees; he is firmly on your side," he said encouragingly.

"And so is Caroline Fitzwilliam, who will represent Colonel Fitzwilliam. I doubt she will need persuading," said Catherine in response. "Caroline and her sister Emily have done much good work supporting the parish schools at Kympton and Pemberley. Their efforts over the last decade have achieved admirable results for the children of those villages. I am aware that Mr Darcy is very appreciative of their work and he supports my plans for a school at Hunsford. If he had had his way, we should have had one already."

Mr Burnett agreed and added that he hoped the Trust would be persuaded.

❧

When Mr Burnett left that night, promising to return with her material in time for the meeting, Catherine was confident that he had no indication that she had been in his office earlier that day. There had been no trace of awkwardness in his manner and she was relieved, indeed, at not having to confront the matters that might have arisen from such a discovery. It may have caused embarrassment and constrained their efforts to achieve what was a most valuable goal.

She turned her mind to preparations for Caroline Fitzwilliam's visit. Jonathan Bingley had already accepted an invitation to dine with them, as had Mr Adams. She had sent a note to the rector Mr Jamison and had just that evening extended the invitation to Mr Burnett as well.

Consulting Mrs Giles, she planned the meal, which she hoped would be a pleasant prelude to a successful meeting with the Trust on the following day. Mrs Giles had assured her that a meal for seven would present no problems for the cook and her staff; they were fortunate to have a wide variety of fresh produce readily available from the garden and the village.

Catherine looked forward to the day, determined to enjoy it. Yet, one thing disturbed her equanimity. She could not rest for wondering why, if Mr Burnett had taken the drawing for himself and had it framed, he had not mentioned it to her?

Could it be that he harboured some affection for her, which he did not wish to reveal? If this was the case, what could his intentions be? Did he expect never to speak to her of his feelings?

Or was it possible that she was making too much of it?

Perhaps he had taken the drawing because it had struck him as an elegant piece of work—she recalled how he had praised Dr Harrison's sketches and he was well versed in the appreciation of the arts. The picture of her, seen through her husband's eyes in the early years of their marriage, was quite an appealing work in itself, accentuating her best features—the brow, eyes, and mouth all skilfully drawn. Perhaps, she thought, Mr Burnett may have liked the portrait, quite apart from the identity of its subject.

Why then did he fail to tell her of it? He had pointed out the qualities of others in the folio—drawings of the children and one particularly sweet grouping of her with two of the children, whose composition and character he had openly admired; there had been no awkwardness there.

Catherine could not comprehend it at all.

Sleep did not come to relieve her wandering mind till the very early hours, and when she awoke, it was well past her usual breakfast time. Though she had arisen with the same nagging thoughts that had occupied her mind the night before, she was determined not to let them overwhelm her.

Dressing quickly, she went downstairs to find a letter waiting for her from Mrs Darcy. She opened it hurriedly and read it through even before sitting down to breakfast. Letters from Lizzie were always welcome. But, apart from the customary courtesies and reports of family matters, this one brought some unwelcome news.

Elizabeth was writing specifically to inform her that the third trustee, Sir James Fitzwilliam—Lady Catherine's eldest nephew and brother of the Colonel—was unwell and was sending his daughter Mrs Rose Gardiner to attend the meeting in his place.

I think you will not mind my cautioning you, dear Catherine, wrote Elizabeth, *to beware of this lady.*

> *She is intelligent and artistic enough, but is self-willed and inclined to be stubborn, easily offended, and not given to compromise.*
> *My dear Mr Darcy believes that James Fitzwilliam is unlikely to*

support the parish school project, and if Rose represents her father to the letter, you may have a battle on your hands.

I write mainly to urge you to be well prepared with all the facts and figures you need to convince not only the trustees but the attorneys as well, since their support is likely to make the difference. Should Rose prove recalcitrant, Mr Darcy advises you to ask the chairman, who will be Jonathan Bingley, to put the matter to a vote, after you have placed all the evidence before the meeting.

On no account, says Mr Darcy, should you agree to a postponement, for that will set back your plans by several months and allow the nay-sayers a chance to regroup and move against you.

It was clear to Catherine that Mr Darcy and Elizabeth expected Mrs Rose Gardiner to oppose the school, while Jonathan and Caroline would support it—hence the need for a vote. However, it was also important that all the relevant facts should be presented to enable those voting to do so with confidence. Catherine was quite determined that she would, to the very best of her ability, argue the case before the meeting.

The arrival of Caroline Fitzwilliam and her maid lightened considerably the somewhat tense atmosphere and that evening, as the guests gathered for dinner, Catherine's confidence grew.

Caroline was especially supportive. "I believe you need have no fears, Catherine," she said, exuding the kind of assurance she had gained over years of working with and for her husband in the promotion of a range of worthy causes. "I am aware that Sir James is unlikely to support you, but with the rest of the trustees on your side, I believe you need only convince the attorneys that your cause is not only just and good but also practical. Lawyers are not renowned for their altruism and it would be futile to appeal to their generosity or charitable instincts, for I am willing to say they have none. However, put before them a practical proposition with the prospect of a successful enterprise and they will listen."

Catherine thanked her for her sage advice and prayed that the material she had to put before them would suffice to convince them.

Frank Burnett arrived, bringing with him the notes he had prepared for her, and Catherine, on reading them, was greatly encouraged. His well-planned paper was couched in clear, simple language, eschewing all verbosity and placing the facts directly forward for consideration.

She was very pleased and did not conceal her appreciation. "I cannot tell you how grateful I am, Mr Burnett. With this to assist me and Caroline's support, I am now a good deal more confident of success."

Jonathan Bingley arrived almost together with the rector, and they went in to dinner by eight. It was a most satisfying party and Catherine's pleasure increased as she saw how easily her guests mingled together and made conversation, even those who were but recently acquainted, as though they were all lifelong friends. Especially pleasing to her, as it was to Lilian, was Caroline's attention to Mr Adams, who had charmed her during the meal with his stories of life in France, while Jonathan was quite clearly enjoying the company of Frank Burnett.

It mattered not to Catherine that she was left to entertain Mr Jamison the rector, so pleased was she that everything had proceeded so well.

By the time the gentlemen had joined the ladies in the drawing room for coffee, it was clear to Catherine that both Caroline and Jonathan would support her at the meeting and Caroline intended to go further. She proposed to approach one of the attorneys—a Mr Parker, who had recently done some work for Colonel Fitzwilliam.

"Mr Parker is a decent sort of gentleman, I am sure he can be persuaded, and if possible I shall try to sound him out discreetly before the meeting," she promised.

When Jonathan and Mr Burnett joined them around the coffee table, Caroline returned to the topic. "Jonathan, do you believe Rose Gardiner will stand against the school project, in spite of the support of the other trustees?"

Jonathan confessed he knew little of Mrs Gardiner's intentions, but added, "My aunt Lizzie certainly believes that to be the case. I have received a cautionary letter from her on the subject."

"And I," volunteered Catherine. "Lizzie is convinced, as is Mr Darcy, that Rose will, on the instructions of her father, obstruct our plans for a school. It is difficult to believe that a woman of intelligence, widely travelled and well read, can be set against the very idea of a school for girls less fortunate than herself."

At that, Caroline laughed, a light sardonic laugh.

"Ah Catherine, you are mistaken in believing that they would wish to see all young women educated and helped to improve their lot in life."

"Why would they not? What can they possibly have to lose?" asked Catherine, shocked by the prospect.

"Why, who then would cook and clean for them all day long? Rose, like her mother Lady Rosamund Fitzwilliam, must fear that educating poor country girls will result in a dearth of chambermaids and skivvies!"

While Catherine did not contest this, Mr Burnett spoke up to agree with Caroline, pointing out that where he grew up, education for the poor was generally regarded as dangerous.

"There was a genuine fear that educated men and women would forget their place in society and seek to usurp the roles of their superiors," he explained.

"Sounds very much like high Tory philosophy!" quipped Jonathan, but Catherine had to ask, "Yet, many enlightened landowners have established schools for the children on their estates—Mr Darcy and my own brother-in-law Anthony Tate, for example."

"Indeed, Mrs Harrison, if only more of them could be persuaded that it is in their own interest to do so," said Mr Burnett, and Jonathan, seeing the anxiety on her face, urged her to have confidence.

"I am very confident of success tomorrow, Catherine; your keenness and the excellent plans drawn up for the late Dr Harrison as well as fine work done by Mr Burnett in discovering them will surely help us win the day," he said, and she was grateful indeed for his reassuring presence.

C ATHERINE CAME DOWNSTAIRS TO breakfast quite early the
following morning to find Caroline there already. Always an early
riser, she had been reading the newspapers. She put them away when
Catherine joined her at the table and poured out more tea.

"I do like your Lilian's young man, Cathy," she said. "Mr Adams is such an
amiable gentleman, with the most charming manners; if I did not know better,
I would have said he was French. He puts me very much in mind of my sister
Emily's late first husband, Paul Antoine."

Catherine agreed. "Yes indeed, he is a very likeable young man and you are
right to some extent, Caroline, for his mother was French and he spent all of
his childhood in France," she explained.

Caroline's eyes sparkled. "I knew it; he has that very particular manner,
a natural charm without effort or pretension, that is quite irresistible. And
he is educated and well spoken, with a good income. Your Lilian is a very
fortunate girl."

Catherine had to agree once more, saying without wishing to sound
boastful that she believed Lilian had made a good match and she knew it would
be a happy one, too, because Mr Adams loved her dearly.

Before she could continue, Caroline added in a softer voice, so as not to be
overheard by the servants, "And so is your Mr Burnett."

When Catherine looked to see if she was teasing, she added, "Such a distinguished-looking man, so knowledgeable, yet so modest in his general manner. I was quite astonished when Jonathan told me Mr Burnett has worked for the British Museum and is an authority on the preservation of artworks and antiquities."

Once again, Catherine could not but agree. "Yes indeed, Mr Burnett is an eminent scholar in his field and is dedicated to his work," she said.

"And clearly devoted to you, I think, Cathy," said Caroline artlessly.

"I beg your pardon?" Shocked, Catherine put down her cup with a clatter.

Caroline seemed unmoved. "Why, have I surprised you?" she asked. "Come, Catherine, you are far too modest yourself, else you could not have failed to notice how he looks at you and speaks to you with a distinct partiality; the tone of his voice is quite unmistakable." Then seeing the look of complete incredulity with which Catherine regarded her, she added, "You are not aware of this? Ah well, I suppose it is understandable, one does not at this time of life expect to notice these things. But mark my words, my dear, Mr Burnett, if he is not already in love, is in grave danger of being so and unless you wish to break the poor man's heart, you had better give some thought to the matter and decide what you intend to do about it."

Catherine was left speechless with astonishment. This was something completely unexpected. She had had no idea that Mr Burnett's regard for her could have attracted the notice of anyone else. Indeed, she had scarcely paid any attention to it herself, and except for the chance sighting of the framed picture in his office room, the question would not have crossed her mind.

It surprised her to discover that Caroline had noticed anything significant at all. She was aware that Caroline had a reputation in the family as an incurable romantic and she wished she had been able to provide an immediate denial of her suspicions. But their conversation ceased abruptly when the door opened and Lilian came in to join them at the table. Lilian was delighted to hear Caroline say how very highly she thought of Mr Adams, and Catherine was glad indeed of an excuse to leave them together to finish their breakfast and retire upstairs to prepare for the meeting of the Rosings Trust later that day.

James Fitzwilliam had never been a particularly strong character; indeed it might have been said that, apart from the one occasion on which he had defied his aunt and married Miss Rosamund Camden, he had never made a stand on anything at all. His aunt, Lady Catherine de Bourgh, had never liked her nephew very much and had liked him even less when he had failed to oblige her by falling in love with a lady of means and fashion whom she had selected for him. Instead, he had chosen to marry the daughter of a north country farming family, a young woman who had never been out in London society and was distinctly beneath Her Ladyship's notice.

For some years, whilst they were plain Mr and Mrs Fitzwilliam, the couple had been very much out of favour and not included in the Rosings circle. However, when it became clear James would succeed to the family title, his rehabilitation had begun and his wife, understanding the value of Lady Catherine's patronage, had set out to please her in every way possible, which is how Sir James had come to be one of the members of the Rosings Trust, together with his younger brother Colonel Fitzwilliam and Mr Darcy.

So accustomed had the Fitzwilliams become to the ways and views of Her Ladyship, they adopted them as their own and became increasingly distant from the rest of their family and friends. Their daughter Rose, who was married to Caroline's brother, Robert Gardiner, had been deeply influenced by the same outmoded ideas espoused by her mother and nothing, it seemed, could move her to abandon them. Mother and daughter were invariably of one mind on most matters and equally unshakable in their opinions.

It was this implacable opposition that Catherine faced when she appeared that morning before the trustees, or in this case, their representatives, to put the case for her parish school.

The matter was taken up after sundry administrative tasks had been speedily attended to. No other item of importance remained, and those around the table seemed to think a decision would not take long to achieve. Once the proposal for the school had been introduced and Catherine had presented her information, laying before them the facts—the numbers of girls who could benefit, the type of useful education they would receive, learning initially to read and write and then proceeding to other practical lessons which would stand them in good stead in life—the chairman, Jonathan Bingley, asked for the views of the trustees and their attorneys.

There were general expressions of approval and interest around the table; even Mr Parker, one of the two attorneys present, seemed convinced of its value. His conversation with Caroline Fitzwilliam had clearly proved enlightening.

But it was Rose Gardiner who expressed the strongest reservations, pointing out the objections of her father and then reminding them of Lady Catherine's original rejection of a parish school as unnecessary. Refusing to agree even to have the matter voted on, because she had no instruction from her father on how to vote in such a case, she made as if to leave the meeting. Not even the gentle intervention of Mr Jamison, the new rector, who spoke in glowing terms of the potential for good that would follow the establishment of a parish school, could alter her determination.

After much argument, Rose was persuaded to return on the morrow, when it was hoped they would have received their instructions by telegraph. The chairman obligingly agreed to request from Mr Darcy and Sir James clear directions to their representatives in the event of a vote on the matter.

When the meeting broke up, Caroline expressed her annoyance—she had no doubt about how she would vote—Jonathan was all discretion and patience, but poor Catherine was desolated.

"I never imagined it would be easy to persuade Mrs Gardiner," she said, fighting to hold back her tears, "but I must confess I did not think it would be so difficult, either! I cannot believe that a woman in her privileged position can be so intractable, so unwilling to acknowledge the needs of other young women less fortunate than herself. How does she have the heart to deny them what she has benefitted from herself?"

Mr Burnett, who had arrived hoping to hear good news, had to help Caroline comfort Catherine and urge her not to give up hope, because Jonathan Bingley, who had immediately despatched messages by electric telegraph to Mr Darcy and Sir James Fitzwilliam, was confident of receiving their responses before the meeting next morning.

Catherine was not easily comforted. Having invested so much time and effort in her plan, she was loathe to admit defeat, yet could not see a way through, unless Rose could be persuaded to agree to a vote, which she could clearly lose.

The following morning was unseasonably warm, presaging a return to late Summer weather. Cloudless blue skies and a light prevailing breeze suggested a day more suited to a picnic in the park, rather than another meeting of the Trust. But there was nothing for it, Mr Bingley had insisted, the issue had to be settled.

Almost as soon as they arrived at the meeting room, Catherine and Caroline could see that something had changed. Jonathan was walking around quite jauntily, while Rose stood to one side talking earnestly with her attorney, who had come specifically from London to advise her.

"If I were to make a judgment on the basis of her countenance alone, I would have to say, Cathy, that Mrs Gardiner is not very pleased," said Caroline quietly and she was soon to be proved right.

As the meeting opened, Mr Bingley produced not one but two messages received by electric telegraph overnight, which he laid on the table.

One came from Mr Darcy and, as his representative, Jonathan read it to the meeting. Addressing the trustees and their representatives, Mr Darcy stated in the clearest possible terms his support for the Parish School project proposed by Mrs Harrison; he wrote:

I have no doubt whatsoever of the value of this school for the people of the parish and of the Rosings estate, and I believe quite firmly that Lady Catherine de Bourgh, had she been alive today and in possession of all the salient facts, would have concurred.

I strongly support the scheme and propose that Mrs Harrison be permitted to list such items and moneys as may be required for the work to begin. I have instructed Mr Bingley as my representative to vote in favour, and I wish Mrs Harrison success in her most worthy enterprise.

I might add that I have already arranged to have the rent on the Dower House paid for a further year, so she might continue to reside there while proceeding with plans for the school.

Catherine's eyes filled with tears as she listened to the message. There was hardly any need for further discussion, but Jonathan proceeded to hand the second message, this from Sir James Fitzwilliam, to Rose Gardiner's attorney.

It was short and to the point. It instructed his daughter as his representative to vote as she thought fit, according to the strength of the arguments put forward at the meeting for and against a parish school. It did not tell her how to vote, simply to settle the issue by agreeing to vote on it.

And there was an end to it. Rose voted against, but with the support of both attorneys—the other had confessed to have been persuaded by Mr Darcy's eloquent letter—the matter was finally settled.

Rose Gardiner, having cast the only vote against the school, left with her attorney, leaving the meeting in no doubt that she considered the entire project a waste of money. The ill grace with which she had responded to her loss did little to recommend her to the rest, who were far more concerned with congratulating Catherine on her success and assuring her of their support.

Not long afterwards, relieved at having done their duty, they went their separate ways—Jonathan to visit his sister Emma Wilson at Standish Park in the same county and Caroline, who had expressed a wish to meet with a friend in Hunsford, went with Mr Jamison the rector, promising to return to the Dower House in time for dinner. This left Catherine to return home alone, this time in a much better frame of mind than she had been in on the previous day.

It was not a great distance to the Dower House if she took the path through the grounds of Rosings Park and it being a fine, warm day, Catherine decided to walk rather than accept a ride in Mr Parker's gig.

She had not gone very far, however, when the sun, which had been shining all morning, seemed to disappear behind heavy grey clouds, which had blown in out of nowhere. What had been glorious early Autumn weather threatened suddenly to bring down upon her a late Summer thunderstorm.

Catherine hurried on, but having no umbrella and wearing only a light coat over her gown, she felt the heavy drops fall faster and, conscious of the documents she carried in her case, which may well be damaged by the rain, she decided to take shelter at Rosings.

Leaving the path, she made for the East Wing, where most of the staff would by now be engaged in their chores. Rushing to avoid being drenched as the rain began to fall more heavily, she almost ran into Mr Burnett. Clearly taken aback by her appearance, he stopped, irresolute and not a little confused, then said, "Mrs Harrison, I was coming over to ask if the meeting had gone well this morning. I had just reached the vestibule when the storm broke and I turned back to fetch an umbrella from my room."

Unable to hide her excitement and heedless of the discomfort of her damp shoes, Catherine blurted out the news.

"It has all been agreed, thanks to dear Mr Darcy and Jonathan Bingley; Mrs Rose Gardiner was well stymied. We are to proceed with plans for the school with a view to opening next Spring and I am to continue at the Dower House for another year!" she said, openly enjoying her delayed moment of success.

His delight was plain to see, and as they shared the pleasure of the moment, they almost forgot the rain that was still pouring down outside. Then, as if suddenly aware of the problem, Catherine said, "I must get home and change my shoes, I'm afraid they are wet through. Would you be so kind as to let me borrow that umbrella of yours?"

With such a direct request, there was no possible way for Frank Burnett to refuse. He seemed startled but recovered quickly and said, "Yes, of course. Are you quite sure you do not wish to wait until the rain has ceased completely? I could take you down to the dining room and the housekeeper would get you some tea, while they dried out your shoes."

It had been his last hope, but she shook her head.

"No, I should not delay; were I to catch cold, that would be a dreadful way to celebrate our success. Thank you, but an umbrella will be quite enough to get me home; the rain seems to have eased already. However, there is another favour I must ask of you. I should be much obliged if you would keep these documents safe for me in your office. They include records of the meetings and decisions of the Trust. I should hate to have them ruined by carrying them around in this weather."

This time he said, "Certainly," and led the way, as she walked with him towards the room in which he had left his umbrella; the very room she had been in just a few days ago. As they entered, he moved to the window to open the curtains and the room filled with light. Catherine's eyes were drawn instantly to the glass-fronted cabinet beside the desk and to her amazement, the framed picture was no longer there. She looked again, unable to believe her eyes, and her mind raced as she wondered how and why it might have disappeared.

Meanwhile, Mr Burnett proceeded to light the fire, fanning it to a warm blaze, hoping perhaps to distract her with his attentions to her comfort. He then went to fetch the umbrella from the stand in the far corner of the room.

As he did so, Catherine moved towards the desk upon which she sought to place the folder of documents she carried, saying, "This folder holds all our plans, calculations, and proposals—it is very precious indeed. I hope it will not be too much trouble for you to keep them here. You do have a secure cabinet, do you not?"

"Of course, they will be quite safe with me," he said as he came towards her on the other side of the desk and, taking a key from his pocket, turned to open the glass-fronted cabinet in which had stood her picture.

At that very moment, as he stood with his back to her, she saw it lying face up on the desk. Quite clearly, he had taken it out of the cabinet himself. Catherine imagined him holding it as he sat at his desk and placing it flat on the desk before leaving the room. Perhaps, she thought, he had intended to put it back and was interrupted.

Even as her mind wandered over the possible explanations, Frank Burnett turned and stood directly facing her; the picture lay between them.

There was no avoiding it now.

It took Catherine a few moments and some deliberate effort to look up at his face. Their eyes met instantly, and as they both looked down at the picture, their mutual discomposure was palpable. Though he said nothing at first, she could sense from his stance and the expression of absolute dismay that had suffused his countenance that this was an encounter for which he was utterly unprepared.

Her face reddened as she realised the implications of this moment, yet because she felt cold and drew her scarf more closely around her, he was able to use the time to ameliorate the awkwardness of the moment with some practicality.

"Forgive me, I am forgetting your wet shoes!" he said and, disappearing momentarily behind a screen at the back of the room, returned with a towel. Moving a chair closer to the fireplace, he invited her to be seated and said, "Please remove your shoes and dry your feet or you *will* catch cold. Your shoes will dry out quickly if we place them by the fire."

He had produced also a long blue wool scarf, obviously a gentleman's—his own perhaps—which he placed around her shoulders, taking away her damp shawl and laying it over a chair to dry in front of the fire. Then, as she began to dry her feet, grateful indeed for the warmth and comfort of the fire, he drew up a chair and sat opposite her.

He spoke slowly, with great deliberation.

"Mrs Harrison, I can explain everything, about the picture, I mean. I took it from Dr Harrison's collection and had it framed in town last year along with all the others. I am sorry I did not ask your permission, as I should have, only because I was embarrassed—I did not know how to ask and what reason to give, nor did I wish to give offence or compromise you in any way. I am truly sorry if I have offended you. Of course I will put it away directly, though may I say in my defence, I have been very discreet. No one has seen it but myself, until today."

His words did not come easily at all, and Catherine, who had been drying her feet with meticulous care, looked up at him and smiled.

"Mr Burnett, I have a confession to make, too," she said quietly. "I was here in this room only a few days ago, when I called to see you and you were out. I saw it then in your cabinet over there. I too was unwilling to cause you embarrassment; I left the room, found the servant downstairs, and sent you a note. So you see, I have seen the picture here before."

He stood up, shaking his head, as if in disbelief. "I would never have guessed; you did not question or reprimand me when we met. Were you not outraged, as you had every right to be?" he asked, amazed at her admission.

"Should I be?" she asked. "Surely my outrage would depend upon your reason for taking the picture in the first place, would it not?"

He looked very miserable indeed, conscious of his own culpability and unable to make any plausible defence of his actions.

"I fear I have no excuses to offer. When I first saw the drawings, I thought they were charming. I wanted very much to have a picture of you but did not dare ask your permission—"

"Why ever not?" she asked, interrupting him.

"Because I was afraid, not just that you would refuse me but because it might have led you to accuse me of disrespect and withdraw your friendship, which I have cherished these many months."

Catherine's voice was a little gentler; she could see his discomfiture and had no desire to torment him. "Why should I have done such a thing? Surely, you know how much I have appreciated your advice and assistance? Why would I be so outraged by such a request as to withdraw my friendship simply because of a picture? Did you think I valued our association so little?"

Frank Burnett was astonished at the coolness of her response. He had expected her to be affronted, at the very least, sufficiently annoyed to demand some explanation for what might be considered a most high-handed and impertinent action on his part. To have secretly taken a drawing of herself, had it framed, and then displayed it in his rooms could well be cause for a lady's indignation. He would not have blamed her.

Catherine's calmness also worried him somewhat. Did it, he wondered, signify indifference? He wanted an opportunity to explain, perhaps even to admit the true reason for his conduct, but she gave him none. When, soon afterwards, she put her shoes back on and rose to leave, he tried once more to apologise, but she was ahead of him again. Speaking quite casually, as if nothing untoward had occurred, she said, "Jonathan Bingley is unable to dine with us tonight—he is expected at the Wilsons in Standish Park and has already left, but Caroline will be there. She leaves for Derbyshire tomorrow. Would you care to join us? I think we deserve a celebration, do you not agree?"

He did agree and accepted with pleasure. Her graciousness should have pleased him, but it did not; for he assumed that it signalled only her indifference to him. She was neither outraged by his conduct nor did she mean to avoid him in future. Clearly, he thought, she intended to continue as before—dealing with him as a useful employee of the Rosings Trust—no more—and he had only himself to blame. It was a wretched situation indeed.

When Catherine had left with the borrowed umbrella, he returned to his room and, sitting at his desk with her picture before him, put his head in his hands. It was of no use to pretend; he knew now that he had to tell her of his true feelings and hope for her understanding and perhaps her forgiveness; he dared not hope she would reciprocate them.

It was therefore with a very great deal of trepidation that Mr Burnett made his way to the Dower House later that day.

The evening, following the afternoon's thunderstorm, was soft, with fresh scents in the air and a clear sky above. As he approached the house, he met Mr Adams who was just leaving. They greeted one another and stopped to exchange a few words.

He had just left Lilian at home, he said; they had been into town all afternoon to look at wedding rings and other gifts and she was tired and wished to retire early.

"I have some work to complete as well, so although I was invited to stay to dinner, I have most reluctantly declined," he explained.

For some unaccountable reason, this information pleased Mr Burnett a great deal. Much as he liked John Adams and Lilian, it would be good to enjoy an evening at the Dower House free of their company, he thought.

Caroline Fitzwilliam was in the parlour when Frank Burnett arrived at the house. He had heard a great deal about her remarkable life and indefatigable zest for work, but had been surprised on meeting her to find she was still a very handsome woman of remarkably youthful appearance.

In earlier years, when the Colonel and his young wife had been regular and welcome visitors to Rosings, he had heard of their great love story and the amazing way in which Caroline had thrown her energy and enthusiasm behind the causes that had drawn her husband into politics.

Lady Catherine may not always have agreed with her nephew's wife, but Mr Burnett had heard her say of Caroline, "She is the most determined young woman I have met; she has been the making of my nephew, who used to be a rather indecisive young man. He is a most fortunate fellow to have found her."

Frank Burnett could see Caroline had not changed in the intervening years.

Caroline greeted him graciously and, having invited him to help himself to a glass of wine, had informed him that Lilian was too tired after a day in town to join them and Catherine would be a little late coming down to dinner.

"She had been caught in a heavy shower this afternoon and reached home quite sodden. I have instructed her maid to prepare a warm bath with camomile and lavender and let her rest awhile afterwards, so as to avoid catching a chill. So I am afraid you will have to put up with me for a while," she said.

Mr Burnett indicated politely and quite sincerely that he would have no difficulty doing so, he was confident they would have much to discuss as they waited for Mrs Harrison to join them.

"Indeed we do, because I dare say you are eager to hear what took place at the meeting of the Trust?"

This indicated to him quite clearly that Catherine had not spoken to Mrs Fitzwilliam of their encounter at Rosings that afternoon. Relieved, he agreed immediately.

"Yes, I most certainly am. I assume the matter of the school has been settled satisfactorily?" he asked.

"It has indeed, thanks to the foresight of Jonathan Bingley and Catherine's absolute determination," said she and proceeded to give him a most entertaining and colourful commentary upon the events of the meeting.

"You should have seen Rose Gardiner's face when Jonathan produced the message from Sir James, her father, sent by telegraph, urging her to vote as she saw fit to settle the matter once and for all. Consternation all round!"

She laughed, clearly enjoying the discomfiture of her sister-in-law, in whom Caroline had been very disappointed.

"Truly, Mr Burnett, Rose is married to my youngest brother, Robert, but I can find no sympathy in my heart for her position. She and my brother have followed for many years a life of selfishness and shameful disregard for the interest of anyone but themselves. Now my brother Dr Richard Gardiner is quite different—the very opposite, in fact. I don't suppose you have met him?" she asked and Mr Burnett admitted he had not had the pleasure recently, but when he worked at Rosings many years ago, he recalled meeting Richard Gardiner and Cassy Darcy when they were engaged.

"I recall that they were a most handsome couple. I understand that he has since acquired a great reputation as a physician."

"He certainly has," said Caroline, who was justly proud of her distinguished brother. "He is Sir Richard Gardiner now. There is no greater contrast with the self-seeking ways of Robert and Rose than the lives of Richard and Cassy. It pains me greatly, Mr Burnett, to see how my young brother has strayed from the sound principles and generosity of our parents. My dear father was benevolent and charitable, and Mama—her kindness was at the heart of all her dealings with people, no matter who they were. Yet Robert seems to have turned his back on all of that. I have to say I mostly blame his wife and his mother-in-law Lady Fitzwilliam for the change in him. Although Mr Darcy is inclined to say that Robert must also accept some responsibility for it, and I daresay he is right, too. I am afraid I lay most of the blame on the two women."

At this moment, the door opened and Catherine entered the room.

Frank Burnett rose, noting how different was this elegantly dressed lady to the wet and windswept person of that afternoon. She held out her hand and he bowed politely over it.

"I am truly sorry, Mr Burnett, but I was tempted into indulging myself and taking my time, because I knew Caroline would keep you company."

"Indeed she has, Mrs Fitzwilliam has been telling me all about the meeting and how Mrs Gardiner was eventually vanquished. You must be very happy with the result," he said and Catherine knew from his remark that she need not have been anxious at all; clearly, he had said nothing to Caroline of their earlier meeting at Rosings that afternoon.

That they had both followed the path of discretion must signify something. She was able to smile and say with sincerity, "Happy? Oh yes, and very relieved. If we had not been permitted to proceed, all our plans and all that work would have been in vain and the girls of the parish would have faced another bleak year without any teaching at all."

He was amazed at her energy and interest. It was as though she had, with the approval for her school, received a burst of vitality; she absolutely glowed with enthusiasm for the project, which he knew was bound to be an arduous task.

"I hope I can count on your advice, Mr Burnett; Mr Adams has already promised to help and so will Lilian, but they are certain to be very busy with wedding plans until October," she said.

He agreed at once and said she could call on him whenever she required his assistance.

"My work at Rosings continues, but is far less demanding now, since I have completed the inventory of items that have been saved from the fire. It is now more a matter of supervising the demolition of the West Wing and the preservation of what remains," he said as they went in to dinner.

Her gratitude, expressed with a charming smile, cheered him up considerably.

The dinner, though no less delectable, was more informal than usual. Since there were only the three of them, Caroline was invited to occupy the seat at the head of the table, while Catherine and Mr Burnett sat facing one another on either side of her. Throughout the meal, he was acutely conscious of her presence, and she could not avoid meeting his eyes as he looked across at her. Both sent their compliments to the cook on the excellent meal, upon which neither had been able to concentrate.

When they returned together to the parlour for coffee and sweets, Caroline confessed to being weary after her busy day and retired to the chaise longue by the fire, content to let Catherine and Mr Burnett continue their conversation without her active participation.

"Do chat away, I shall listen. I've done my share of talking for today," she said.

Mr Burnett, being conscious of the lateness of the hour, did not stay long. However, before leaving, he begged to be allowed to return on the morrow.

Speaking urgently but in a low voice, so as not to be overheard, he asked, "Mrs Harrison, I must see you privately, so I may explain my conduct. I am so mortified at having done what I did, I must ask you to grant me a little time to redeem myself. Would you be so kind?"

Catherine knew she could not refuse. Besides, she wanted very much to discover what more he wished to say. Having apologised twice, she wondered what further explanation he wished to provide.

When she responded, it was with kindness. "Mr Burnett, of course you may see me. Lilian and Sally are taking Caroline to meet the train tomorrow; they leave at ten, will that suit?"

He indicated that it would and thanked her.

She then added, "But let me assure you there is no need for you to feel any mortification or embarrassment on my account; I am not offended, quite the contrary, in fact."

Before he could respond to this surprising statement, Caroline, who had dozed off in front of the fire, awoke suddenly and standing up, addressed the room.

"My goodness, it must be very late. I do believe I fell fast asleep. Cathy my dear, I think I shall go to bed, I have a long journey tomorrow," she said and turned to kiss her hostess and wish Mr Burnett good night.

"I trust we shall meet again, Mr Burnett, when we all return for Lilian's wedding."

"Indeed, ma'am," he replied cheerfully, "when I shall have the honour of being Mr Adams's best man." Taking her hand and bowing over it, he expressed his great pleasure at having met her.

After she had left the room, he prepared to take his leave of Catherine.

It was a still, cool night with not a trace of the earlier thunderstorm. As he moved into the vestibule, Catherine produced his umbrella. "You must not forget this, I was most grateful for its protection; you may need it tomorrow."

The remark and the recollection of the circumstances in which she had borrowed his umbrella lightened the atmosphere between them and they laughed together. Then he said good night, kissed her hand, and left.

It was late and the house was quiet.

Catherine waited but a few minutes before following Caroline upstairs. Proceeding to her own room, she undressed slowly and deliberately, putting away her clothes with meticulous care. Her mind was absorbed not by the success of the day but by her memory of the face of Frank Burnett as they had parted and her own feelings as he had kissed her hand.

She had not believed it possible that she could experience such profound pleasure at such a simple gesture. She recalled briefly how calmly she had entered into the engagement with Dr Harrison and wondered at her present state of emotional ferment. She could not deny the excitement she felt, without a trace of guilt or regret. It was like nothing she had known before.

Trying to quiet her racing heart, she slipped into her nightgown and curled up in an armchair, absorbed in delightful contemplation of what might be, before finally retiring to bed.

Chapter Eighteen

PRIOR TO THEIR MEETING, on the day following, Catherine and Frank Burnett had spent some time in contemplation, each of their own situation and feelings.

Catherine, until certain recent events, had regarded Mr Burnett chiefly as a valued friend, whom she had known, as if in another existence, at Rosings many years ago. Pleasantly surprised by his reappearance and gratified by his attention and regard, she had not given much thought to the feelings of the gentleman himself.

Viewed in a practical light, she saw that their association could only be beneficial to her, since his greater learning, information, and knowledge of the world would surely complement her own education and be a source of advice upon which she could depend. However, if she were honest with herself, she would have to admit that more recently, especially since telling her sister Becky of the youthful attachment she had once felt for him and reading again her own accounts of it, there had been a reawakening in her of certain feelings, which she had believed to be quite extinct!

As she prepared to see him that morning, these and other recollections made her nervous and rather shy, for she was uncertain of his thoughts on the matter.

As for Frank Burnett, he had long acknowledged to himself that the feelings Catherine had inspired in him as a young man had not merely lain dormant over the years to be awakened upon his meeting her again; they had in truth been enhanced and deepened in the last six months. As he had come to know her and appreciate the qualities of the woman, in ways that had never been possible with the girl, surrounded as she had been by the carapace of Lady Catherine de Bourgh's protection, he had discovered in her someone for whom he could feel the very deepest love. He had yearned to tell her so, but for reasons of propriety, for she was only recently widowed, he had not spoken.

Of Catherine's emotions Mr Burnett knew very little.

Indeed, from her informal manner towards him, treating him always without ceremony or fuss, he had begun to wonder whether she'd ever had any attachment in youth, which might be transformed into a deeper affection, or if it had only been the ephemeral though sincere feelings of friendliness. If the latter were the case, then could she perhaps be persuaded, he wondered, or was it all too late? Would the gentle warmth he had recognised in her nature encompass him, or had too many years passed and were the tender feelings he had once thought she had for him, which he had hoped once more to arouse in her, gone forever?

These and other agonising prospects had tormented him while he had waited patiently for an opportune moment to speak. Her discovery of the framed portrait had brought that moment forward sooner than he had anticipated. Now the day was here, he had asked to see her and she had agreed. No postponement was possible.

❦

At approximately ten o'clock, Caroline Fitzwilliam and her maid set off for the railway station in a hired vehicle, accompanied by Lilian and her mother's maid, Sally. They expected to wait until noon, to see Caroline safely into her seat on the northbound express, before returning home in the early afternoon.

At precisely fifteen minutes past the hour, Frank Burnett arrived at the Dower House and was admitted into the parlour. Catherine, who had been waiting for him, rose to greet him, suddenly a little more formal in her manner than usual. She invited him to be seated and offered him some refreshment, which he politely declined. He seemed impatient, unable to settle into a chair, rising and walking restlessly about the room, then sitting down again.

They had both been seated only a few minutes when he stood up, walked across the room to look out of the window, and then returned to sit again, but this time, beside her on the chaise longue.

When Catherine looked at his face, it seemed to her that his expression was one which in all her life had never been turned upon her by any man. A little apprehensive, yet inexpressibly tender, it stirred feelings in her for which she was quite unprepared.

For all that she had been married, and contentedly so, for many years, Catherine had not known such emotional tumult as she felt then. It was too much for her to absorb and she wished she could have run from the room, but conscious of her situation in the household, she stayed. Yet, unable to meet his eyes, she looked away and down at her hands.

Moments later, he reached for her hand and when she did not withdraw it, said in a quiet voice, "Forgive me, Catherine, I had planned to make a fine speech explaining my feelings for you, telling you how long I have waited for this moment. I had it all in my head this morning but alas, it has quite deserted me, fled from my memory. Now, all I can do is to ask you to believe that I love you dearly and to understand that my action in taking your picture can only be pardoned if you accept that it was done out of the deepest and most sincere affection. If you will, tell me and I shall continue; if not, stop me now and I shall leave and never speak of it again."

Catherine did not have the words to answer him directly. No one had ever addressed her in such endearing terms before.

Her first proposal from Mr Harrison had been written, couched in serious terms, in which both love and marriage were clearly understood for what they were, important parts of a social convention and a sacred sacrament. There had been no extended courtship in their case; deep personal emotion, passionately felt and openly acknowledged, was quite new to her.

She was hard pressed to respond. Her silence, though not longer than a few minutes, must have seemed an eternity to him. Taking it to be a prelude to rejection, he rose and walked away towards the bay window at the far end of the room.

Catherine, realising this, could not bear to let him suffer. She spoke gently, "Mr Burnett, pray do not judge me by my silence... or my lack of appropriate words... I have not the proficiency to speak as easily on these matters as I might on other more commonplace subjects. Please do not suppose that, because

I seem tongue-tied, I am also indifferent to the feelings you have expressed. In truth, it is the very fact that I am deeply touched by them that makes it so difficult for me to find the right words to respond and say what I feel... Oh dear me, I am sorry... I am not doing too well, am I? I feel so foolish..." she knew she was stumbling, her words making little sense, and feeling inadequate and silly, she stopped abruptly.

He returned to her side then and, taking both her hands in his, said, "If it is only words you have difficulty with, Catherine, may I assist you? Will you tell me simply, with no attempt to spare my feelings, if the sentiments I have expressed please you, or if I have offended you by speaking of them?"

Catherine looked genuinely surprised that he should ask. "Mr Burnett, how could you ask such a question? Of course I am pleased, who would not be?"

"You are not affronted, then?"

"Not in the least. How could any woman be affronted by such a generous declaration of feeling?"

He looked immeasurably relieved and continued, "And were I to ask if there is a chance that you might feel some similar affection for me, what would you say?"

This time she was more forthcoming. "If you were to ask me and I was to answer truthfully, I should have to say, yes, there is."

The exclamation of pleasure that this simple answer provoked was such that Catherine, quite taken aback and afraid lest the servants might hear and presume upon his rejoicing, put up her hand to restrain him.

At which he held it, kissed it, and said, "And will you then, my dearest Catherine, agree to marry me?"

"Must I answer immediately? May we not for just a short while enjoy the pleasure of knowing we love one another and talk together of our feelings, before launching into matters of matrimony?" she asked. Then seeing the disconsolate expression this brought on, she added quickly, "I ask only because I fear it may not be seemly for us to be openly betrothed before Lilian is married. It is not yet a year since Mr Harrison's death; were I to agree to marry you and this became widely known, would it not seem rash—impetuous, even? Might it not draw adverse comment, even censure upon us?"

Frank Burnett looked less aggrieved on hearing her reasons, but he had his own case to argue and this he did with great feeling.

"Censure and adverse comment, Catherine, are these not the very things that kept us apart all those years ago? Were they not the paltry reasons Lady Catherine de Bourgh used to bring about an end to our friendship? I did not believe they were justified then, but in my position, could do nothing to contest or overthrow them, especially in view of your situation in her household. Today, as we are both free to decide our destiny, I cannot and will not accept them as reasons for not proclaiming my love for you."

Seeing the look of complete bewilderment upon her face, he asked, "Did you not know, Catherine, that Her Ladyship had made it very clear to me that I would not be acceptable as a suitor for you—that your family would not agree to it, indeed, that you were already spoken for?"

His voice was low, but there was no mistaking the depth of his feelings.

She was so shocked, she could say nothing at first and then spoke only to apologise. "I am sorry, I knew nothing of this. I had no idea that Lady Catherine had sought to discourage you as well. She certainly worked hard at persuading me we were not suited and warned me against anything more than a casual friendship. She even suggested that if I persisted, against her advice, your position at Rosings would be in jeopardy. I assured her that it was no more than friendship and suppressed all other hopes I might have had. Since I had no means of knowing what your feelings were, I assumed they were not seriously engaged either."

Seeing the look of disbelief that crossed his countenance, she added, "I had long ceased to blame Lady Catherine for her intervention in my life, but to have led you to believe that I was already committed to someone else... that was not true and if she did so, it was very wrong indeed. There was no one, not then and not for many years after you left Rosings," she said and her voice broke.

Catherine was clearly distressed and he would not let her continue, for he could sense there would soon be tears. He sought to draw her away from recriminations by pointing out that Lady Catherine had probably acted according to her own standards, by which a librarian, with no fine connections and no estate, was no match for a young lady she had condescended to accept into the privileged circle of her family.

In a lighter tone, he added, "Now a clergyman, especially one with prospects of preferment, would have been, in Her Ladyship's eyes, a much better match and certainly more socially acceptable at Rosings Park."

There was a slightly sardonic smile on his face, but Catherine would not be easily placated.

"How can you make light of her conduct and be so generous in your judgment of her, when she has wronged you so?" she cried. "I had thought my own grievance slight, but now I see how much her interference has cost us both, I cannot contain my resentment as I did before."

Sensitive to her distress, he intervened gently. "Dearest Catherine, these are matters of the past, of which we may speak later, if you wish. Let them not impinge upon our present happiness. Your wish that we might enjoy speaking of our love for one another is a much better suggestion; indeed, I cannot think of anything I should enjoy more. You may tell me as often as you please why you love me and with your permission, I shall do likewise. I believe it should prove a most agreeable occupation," he said, hoping to lighten her mood.

Then becoming serious again, he said, "My dear Catherine, if you can only say that you love me and agree to be my wife, I promise I will do everything in my power to ensure your happiness and nothing else will signify at all. As to the issue of propriety, I am quite prepared to wait for you until the twelvemonth is elapsed, and if you so desire, we shall keep our engagement a secret from our friends and families until after Miss Lilian's wedding, if that is more acceptable to your family."

She shook her head and said firmly, "No, Frank, I do not like concealment. There is nothing dishonourable in our feelings for one another; I am not ashamed of mine, and if we love each other, we should want to tell our friends and our families, knowing they will all share in our happiness."

"I agree, indeed, for my part, I love you dearly and do not care who knows it," he said, matching her openness.

Perhaps it was the strength of her own feelings or the passionate sincerity of his words; whichever it was, feelings she had not known before flooded through her and Catherine could hold out no longer. He reached for her hand and in the next instant, she was in his embrace, accepting his love and declaring hers, without reservation.

～❦～

Later, when they were both sufficiently composed, he suggested that they take a walk in Rosings Park, where many years ago they had often met as friends. "It is such a fine day, perhaps we might walk in the direction of the rose garden; I have a very clear and happy recollection of you there. It is quite deserted now; we will not be disturbed or overheard, so you may ask me anything you like," he said and she, taking him at his word, agreed, upon one condition.

"I know you said we must not dwell upon the past and I agree; but while there are some matters that are best left alone, I do not think I could be satisfied unless I knew the answers to certain questions."

He was quite amenable. "Certainly, ask away, and I will answer every one as best I can. However, I can only give an account of matters which lie within my personal knowledge. I cannot provide explanations, nor will it be right to speculate about the actions and motives of others," he cautioned.

Catherine agreed and soon, having fetched her bonnet and wrap and told Mrs Giles they intended to walk to Hunsford, she left the house with him and took the path that led through the grounds to the rose garden that had once been the pride of Rosings Park.

Catherine was eager to discover what Lady Catherine de Bourgh had told Frank Burnett in her most unjustifiable, but successful campaign to end their friendship.

"Tell me everything; only then will I understand it all. It is not because I wish to increase my vexation against Lady Catherine—I do not and it would be of no use to do so—but I wish to understand how it came about and what harm was done in the accomplishment of it. If you were deliberately misled about me, I want the opportunity to set it right."

Over the next hour or two, as they walked through the lovely groves and gardens of Rosings Park, he told her all she wished to know.

Ranging over a few years, he explained his increasing interest in her, which he suspected Mrs Jenkinson had noted and reported upon to his employer.

"I had only regarded you at first as I would a schoolgirl, a younger sister or cousin of Miss de Bourgh, whom I would meet but occasionally and forget soon afterwards. But over the months, it was not that easy to ignore you. I enjoyed our conversations and looked forward more and more to your visits to the library and our discussions about books. I began to believe, perhaps because I wished it were so, that you had some affection for me."

Catherine smiled. "I felt exactly the same, except I did not, even for one moment, believe you were partial to me in a romantic sense, but I did hope you liked me sufficiently to wish to continue our friendship," she said.

He did not deny this. "I did, but it soon became obvious to me that in addition to keeping Miss Anne de Bourgh company and providing Her Ladyship with a compliant and admiring audience, Mrs Jenkinson was a source of intelligence on the activities of other members of the staff at Rosings."

"No doubt she hoped to advantage herself by keeping Lady Catherine well informed," said Catherine, a supposition with which he was inclined to agree.

"She suspected my interest in you quite early, I think—perhaps even before I was aware of it myself," he said, with a wry smile.

"Yet, Lady Catherine continued to invite you to dinner and introduce you to her fine friends?" said Catherine, puzzled by this apparent anomaly, but he explained it quite candidly.

"I had no illusions on that score. I was useful to Her Ladyship—not all the guests who dined at Rosings were eager to hear her rattling on about her own family and their accomplishments; they were generally men of intellect and learning, from one of the universities or the church, and since she could not trouble herself to become acquainted with their interests, I was a convenient stopgap guest, who could carry a conversation. I was always glad of the dinner and the company, as well as the chance to see you there. It was a special pleasure, one that made the rest of the evening worthwhile. However, when Lady Catherine made it quite clear to me that I had no chance with you, I decided to move on elsewhere. It would have been too painful for me to continue at Rosings."

He had hitherto made few criticisms of his former employer, and this confused Catherine. "I cannot comprehend how you are so charitable towards her. You gave up your position and put your life's work and your happiness in jeopardy. May I ask, in all the years that followed, did you not wish to marry at all? Was there no one who could tempt you to settle down?"

He smiled, somewhat abashed, and confessed that some ten years ago, he had proposed marriage to a lady, a schoolteacher in whose parents' house he had been a lodger for a year.

"She was a good woman: kind, intelligent, and amiable. I had hoped we would be good companions together. But she changed her mind and married someone else instead."

"But why?" asked Catherine, astonished that he could be displaced by another.

"Because, she said, she believed that while I had offered her my hand, my heart was not altogether hers. I would have to admit that she was not entirely wrong in that judgment," he said. "As you now know, my heart had long been given to another, who was by then out of my reach."

This confession brought another moment of tenderness, which so concentrated their attention that they had to stop awhile to reassure each other, before proceeding even more slowly on their walk.

Still surprised by his acceptance of Lady Catherine's dictates, she asked, "Did you not think to speak to me of your feelings before you decided to leave Rosings and travel to Europe?"

"I dare say I could have, but I had given my word. Lady Catherine had extracted from me a promise not to approach you," he replied, adding, "She said, and quite correctly, that you were not yet nineteen, untutored in the ways of the world and likely to be tempted by the prospect of romance into making a mistake you would regret for the rest of your life. Besides, she declared that you had been spoken for already—a fine young clergyman, who was keen to apply for a living on the Rosings estate, was the fortunate man. Lady Catherine had approved his appointment and she was convinced he would be right for you."

Amazed by these revelations, Catherine asked, "Did she tell you who this clergyman was?"

He answered directly, "She did not, but when, on returning to England several years later, I met Mr Jonathan Bingley in London, I asked after you and was told you were recently married to a Dr Harrison, the rector at Hunsford, I naturally assumed that he was indeed the lucky man."

Realising how easily she had been manipulated and how cruelly Frank Burnett had been tricked into abandoning his interest in her, Catherine was so angry, she wept. Only his gentle persuasion and the reassurance of his continuing affection, as he put his arms around her and held her awhile, could comfort her.

In the end, because he was a man of sensibility and wisdom, he did succeed in convincing her that the deep and genuine feelings they now shared were even more worth having than the youthful affection they had been forbidden to declare, and while Lady Catherine had, by her devious machinations, denied them the pleasures of young love, she had probably contributed to the enhancement of their present happiness.

While Catherine was not yet ready to forgive Lady Catherine her arrogant interference in their lives, she could not fail to smile when he said, with just a hint of sarcasm, "If Lady Catherine could see us now and understand how very well suited we are and how dearly we love each other, I do not doubt that even she would suspend her disapproval. After all, wherever she may now be, it is unlikely that matters of rank and wealth will have the same importance as they had for her when she presided over Rosings Park. Am I not right?"

"Of course you are," said Catherine, smiling. "It is also quite clear to me that you do not intend to let me sink into an orgy of regret and recrimination. Am I right?"

"Indeed you are," he replied. "Do not believe, dearest Catherine, that I have not felt deeply the injustice I suffered, for indeed it was many years before I could accept that you were not for me. But what would be the benefit to us of spending more time in contemplating the past, excoriating Lady Catherine or nursing our resentment?"

Determined they should waste no more time bemoaning past grievances, he spoke from the heart. "So much time has been lost already, is it not far better to use what remains to celebrate our present felicity?"

This was said with such warmth and sincerity that she could offer no other response but agreement. In all her life, Catherine had not experienced such feelings as she did now and she knew intuitively that it would be foolish to waste the chance for happiness that life had so fortuitously offered her by indulging in futile recriminations.

Sitting in the rose garden, in the shadow of the ruins of the West Wing, they spent the best part of an hour in conversation, speaking of those things that lovers suddenly discover they must tell one another without delay. They talked of the future with confidence, anticipating keenly the delights of living and working together. She reminded him of her commitment to the parish school.

"You do know I shall have to spend a good portion of my day at the school. I shall have to work hard to make a success of it, I owe it to the children and the trustees," she cautioned and he promised her his wholehearted support for her work, making only one condition.

"Catherine, I know what this school means to you and will never begrudge the children of the parish your time. I have but one request—that when you return home to me each day, your attention will be mine alone."

It was a promise she gave without reservation and was rewarded with a warm embrace.

Enjoying the warmth of the sun and the pleasure of each other's company, the time slipped by without their noticing it at all, until Frank Burnett consulted his watch and announced that it was almost four o'clock, whereupon Catherine exclaimed that it was time she was home.

"Lilian will have returned; shall I tell her tonight, do you think?" she asked and he smiled at her eagerness.

"Certainly, if you so wish; do you think she will be pleased?" he asked and to his surprise, she said in a most determined voice, "She had better be, for I have decided that this time I shall please myself first and give my love where I choose."

He laughed then and congratulated her upon her wisdom; then to her astonishment and delight, he kissed her.

They decided that for the moment, only Lilian and Mr Adams would be told of their engagement. The rest would have to wait until she had written to inform her mother, Mrs Charlotte Collins, and her sister Becky.

"I shall inform Mama that we do not intend to marry until after Lilian and Mr Adams have left on their wedding journey to France. That should allay her fears of my being censured for undue haste," said Catherine, only to be assured that surely, no one would deny them the right to find happiness together after all these years.

Of this, Frank Burnett was quite certain. "Were you to tell your mother that, if not for the unwelcome meddling by Lady Catherine, we might have been a happily married couple these many years, I have no doubt she would raise no objection to our marrying tomorrow!"

Despite the lightness of his tone, the logic of his argument so convinced her, she was immediately and warmly appreciative. "Thank you for being such a comfort to me," she said, pressing his hand and looking up at his face to assure herself he was being serious as well. "You have a reasonable argument to support my every wish and allay all my fears. If we continue thus in future years, I am perfectly confident of our lasting felicity," said she, teasing him and provoking him to insist that he had already reached the very same conclusion.

They returned taking a shorter route through the groves, and Catherine, growing a little tired, was grateful for the support of his arm. She did not object when he drew her closer to his side as they walked, believing that their mutual pleasure in being together was sufficient reason and enjoying the secure warmth of his closeness to her.

Having been robbed in her youth of such simple joys as these—for Dr Harrison, being a very proper clergyman, had never walked alone with her in the woods before they were married, nor had he ever kissed her in the rose garden—Catherine enjoyed them with a special pleasure.

When they reached the boundary of the park, he helped her over the stile and they took the road leading to the Dower House, arriving at the gates by half past the hour. There was still plenty of light in the sky and some hours before dinner.

"You will come in and take some tea?" she asked and he was only too happy to accept.

However, as they reached the front door, it was not Lilian, but Mr Adams who met them, plainly in a state of some anxiety.

Behind him, in the vestibule, Mrs Giles appeared and Catherine could see instantly from her expression that something was wrong.

As she moved indoors, she asked, "Mrs Giles, what is it… is something…?" but before she could frame the inevitable question, the housekeeper blurted out her news.

"Oh ma'am, it's Miss Lilian and Sally, they are not home yet and we cannot discover what has become of them."

END OF PART FOUR

RECOLLECTIONS OF ROSINGS

Part Five

Chapter Nineteen

CATHERINE'S DISTRESS, ON HEARING Mrs Giles's words, came close to panic.

The clock showed it was a few minutes after half past four; Lilian and Sally had left the house to accompany Caroline to the railway station, which was situated some miles away, at approximately ten o'clock that morning. Caroline's train had been due to leave for the north of England by midday; by any reckoning, they should have been home an hour or more ago.

They had been gone over six hours. She could not imagine—indeed, if she could, it might have been much worse—but she could not reasonably imagine what could have happened to the two girls.

Mrs Giles hastened to explain. Mr Adams, she said, had arrived at four o'clock, and only then had Mrs Giles, who had earlier retired to her room, been alerted to the fact that Lilian and Sally had not yet returned. She had immediately despatched young Tom Higgs, the gardener's boy, to the village to discover whether the hired vehicle, in which they had set out, was back from the journey. The carter, a Mr Sparks, was well known to them. They were still waiting for Tom to return when Catherine and Mr Burnett had appeared at the door.

"What could possibly be keeping them?" asked Catherine for the fifth or sixth time. "I am so afraid; Mrs Giles, are you sure there has been no message of delays on the railway or an accident on the roads?"

"No, ma'am, we have heard nothing, which is why I sent Tom to find out if the vehicle was back," she replied. Mrs Giles had been with the family for almost all of Lilian's life and Sally was her niece; her anguish was palpable.

Mr Adams, equally distressed but with very little idea of what to do, was fretting too and it took all of Frank Burnett's powers of persuasion to keep him from racing off down the road on his horse.

"What good would it do for you to go off alone? How far shall you ride?" he asked, urging his friend to wait until more was known and then they would devise a plan to look for the missing girls.

When Tom Higgs finally arrived at the gate, half a dozen voices shouted questions at him, none of which he could answer. All he could tell them was the stable was empty where the horse was usually tethered, the vehicle was not in its place in the barn, and the carter Mr Sparks was nowhere to be seen.

Catherine went pale with fear as dreadful memories from the past assailed her.

"Good God, that must mean there has been an accident," she cried and turning to Frank Burnett, appealed for his advice. "Please, Mr Burnett, tell me, what should we do?"

In fact, Frank Burnett had already determined that he would go immediately with Mr Adams to Rosings and, having commandeered a carriage and driver, would travel the route which the vehicle bearing Lilian and her maid Sally would have taken, returning from the railway station to Rosings Park.

With great gentleness, he spoke first to Catherine.

"Mrs Harrison, pray do not make yourself ill with worry. It may well be a simple problem: a horse may have thrown a shoe or they may have damaged a wheel or an axle, which has required repair and so delayed them; it may well be nothing more than that, else we would have had news by now, from the county police or a passerby."

He urged Mrs Giles to attend closely upon her mistress, assuring them both that he would find the missing girls and bring them home.

"I am certain we shall find them safe and sound," he said, assuming for her sake a degree of confidence he did not altogether feel.

Catherine, wishing with all her heart that he was right, insisted that they take her manservant, George, with them.

"Let him ride with you. He could help, if help is needed, or bring us back a message, if necessary; please take him with you," she pleaded and they agreed.

It was still light and they set off, hoping to be on the road within the hour.

No sooner had they gone than Catherine went upstairs and, in the privacy of her room, wept. As the tears she had held back flowed, she was riven with illogical but understandable feelings of guilt, because she had not been home. The day that had brought her such promise of happiness had not concluded as auspiciously as it had begun.

"Had I been here, instead of in the rose garden at Rosings, I might have become aware much earlier of the lateness of the hour and I would have caused a search party to be sent out," she cried, yet now she was all too conscious of her own helplessness.

Immensely grateful for the presence of both Mr Adams and Mr Burnett, she knew that with no father or brother to go out in search of her, Lilian's safety depended upon these two men. With what gratitude did she think of Frank Burnett, seeing him offer himself without a moment's hesitation to undertake what she herself was quite powerless to do.

While poor dear John Adams had seemed bereft and despondent, Mr Burnett's determination and sound judgment would no doubt be a source of comfort to him as it had been to her, she mused.

Mrs Giles came upstairs with a tray of food, urging her mistress to partake of some refreshment. It could be a long and anxious night and she would need to be strong. Plagued by recollections of the accident at Maidenhead on the road to Bath, which had taken the life of her youngest sister, Amelia-Jane, Catherine could not easily be persuaded to hope that everything would turn out well. As the hours passed she would wait, longing for some word of them, yet dreading the arrival of a messenger bearing bad news.

Meanwhile, Frank Burnett, acting with expedition, making all the arrangements necessary and not losing a moment, had left with Mr Adams for Rosings. Sensitive to the tender feelings of both Catherine and his friend John Adams, he had tried to allay their fears with reassuring words, yet he had his own apprehensions.

They had set out from Rosings, Messrs Adams and Burnett in the carriage, while the manservant George and a stable hand from Rosings rode with them.

While it was still light on the open road, he was aware that as they passed through the woods and night fell, it would soon be much darker.

The coachman, a man familiar with the roads they were to travel, had insisted that at least one of the men should carry a pistol in case they encountered any of the villains who were seen from time to time and occasionally apprehended on country roads, especially at night.

Frank Burnett, though he thoroughly disliked carrying arms, had agreed. The safety of the ladies may well depend upon it. The stretch of road from the boundary of Rosings Park to the railway station at Redhill was a good one and not generally known to be frequented by footpads and thieves, but one could never be too careful. On one side of the road lay well-wooded country and on the other open pasture and farmland.

As they travelled, they passed not a single other vehicle going in the opposite direction towards either Rosings or the village of Hunsford, a circumstance that puzzled them greatly. Since it was not a private road, it was generally well used, especially in Summer, when there was a fair amount of traffic in the area. Yet, for the first seven or eight miles, they saw no sign of anyone.

Further on, there were signs that it had rained rather heavily and as it grew darker, visibility was limited. Though Mr Adams and Frank Burnett leaned out and strained their eyes, fixing their gaze upon the road ahead, it was the manservant riding alongside and a little to the fore of the carriage, who first caught sight of debris beside a culvert. Not much further up the road, a wrecked vehicle lay overturned in the ditch.

In the late evening light, it was difficult to make it out, but George recognised it as the vehicle from the village, the one in which Lilian and Sally had set out with Mrs Fitzwilliam that morning.

Calling out to the coachman to pull up, George immediately dismounted and somewhat warily approached the wreckage. No sooner did the carriage come to a standstill, the gentlemen leapt out and joined George, who by now had ascertained there was no one either in the wrecked vehicle, nor did there appear to be anyone lurking with evil intent in the vicinity.

But, there their relief ended. For while there was now no doubt that there had been an accident of some sort—there was no trace of the driver Mr Sparks, nor of his passengers. There were some traces left by the horse.

"It would seem, sir," said George, "that the horse has bolted for some reason—you can tell from the drag marks of the wheels up this way into the ditch."

It was quite clear the animal had pulled away from the road in alarm and probably pitched the vehicle into the ditch as it fled.

John Adams was pale and very agitated.

"My God, Frank, what has happened to Lilian? How on earth shall we find her? Where do we start to look?" he asked in a trembling voice that betrayed both his youth and his deep affection for her.

Frank Burnett was determined not to let him subside into panic. Adopting a tone calculated to bolster his friend's hopes, he replied, "Well, clearly there has been an accident, but equally clearly, it would seem to me that no one has been badly injured or killed, else there would have been a guard placed over this spot, the police or the county authorities would surely have been alerted, and they would have set off for Hunsford, being the nearest town. We have met no one going in the direction of Rosings Park or Hunsford, so I think we can hope that the driver and his passengers are alive, even though they may have suffered some injuries in the accident."

John Adams was not convinced. "We cannot be certain of that!" he cried and Mr Burnett replied, "No indeed, we cannot, but we can hope and when hope is all there is to be had, my friend, we must cling to it, must we not?"

Meanwhile, George and the stable hand had begun to comb the ground around the vehicle and the ditch in which it lay and had found a canvas bag, which George recognised as one Sally had been carrying that morning, and a man's boot, probably the carter's. Further along, they found bits of the harness and reins, which the horse had shed as it bolted.

Finding nothing else and certainly no blood at the scene, they were about to reenter their carriage and proceed to the village up ahead, where they could make enquiries, when two men appeared pushing a farm cart, laden with empty baskets. They were the first people they had seen that night. Seeing the horses and the carriage, one of the men stopped and peered at them. The other appeared to be too drunk to be aware of his surroundings and sat down in the dirt beside the road.

Approaching them, George, pointing to the wrecked vehicle, asked if they had seen anything of the people who had been in the accident. Was there a farmhouse or a cottage nearby, where they may be sheltering? he asked.

The younger, more sober of the two spoke, though not very clearly, and Frank Burnett could not comprehend a word of his rather rough and slurry dialect. He gave thanks that he had heeded Catherine's advice and brought George along. He was from the area and seemed well able to understand the man.

He returned to report that the man had claimed to know nothing of the accident—he had passed that way in the morning on his way to market and was only just returning home. But he had directed them to the house of a farmer, which was situated in the lee of a hill, over to the west. They looked in the direction in which he had pointed and could just make out signs of smoke rising from its chimneys, above the trees that crowned the hill.

"He says the farmer is a Mr Barnaby, sir, whose land lies to the west of the road, which runs past his estate; if anything had happened here, on his property, he would surely be the one to know."

Greatly relieved to have a clue at last, Mr Burnett and Mr Adams set off with George to walk across the paddock and over the long low hill, to locate the farmhouse and Mr Barnaby, leaving the stable boy with the carriage. They had no certainty of finding anyone, but at least it was a start. They kept a look out for any other pieces of evidence, signs that Lilian and Sally may have come this way, but found none.

The house was still some distance away and it had started to rain again. Neither John Adams nor Frank Burnett had much protection from the weather, apart from their hats and overcoats. Turning up their collars, they hurried on, until they reached a rough gravel and dirt road, which, when followed, led directly to a large country house, before which stood a carriage drawn by two horses.

As they approached, a man came around the back of the house; he was, they assumed, the driver of the same vehicle and seeing them, he called out to ask who they were.

John Adams rushed forward eagerly.

"Pardon me, sir, are you Mr Barnaby?" he asked in a voice so desperate the man hastily took a step back, as if in alarm. Holding up a lantern to get a look at his face, he replied, "No indeed, sir, I am not. Mr Barnaby is my master. But who might you be, sir?"

"My name is Adams. We are come from the Rosings estate and are looking for two young ladies who were travelling in a vehicle that was involved in an accident on the road about a mile from here. Have you seen or heard anything of them? Has there been any news—?"

The man interrupted him, "Well, sir, if that be the case, I think you had best see my master Mr Barnaby right away…"

"Does he know of the accident?" asked Mr Burnett, who had joined them.

"He does, sir, but hadn't you better get yourselves out of this rain first?"

"Oh thank God!" cried John Adams, then turning to Frank Burnett, asked, "Did you hear that, Frank? This man says Mr Barnaby knows about the accident. Are the ladies here then?" he asked, but before the man could answer, a window was thrown open above them and a man's voice called out, in some irritation, "What is going on down there, Thomas? Who is that with you?"

"Mr Barnaby, sir, there's two gentlemen here. They say they are from the Rosings estate, looking for the young ladies who were in the accident, sir," answered Thomas.

"Are they?" said the voice from above, this time a little less annoyed. "Well, they had better come indoors, then," and the window was pulled shut again.

Thomas went to the door and rang the bell and soon they were admitted into a spacious, comfortable parlour, warmed by a large log fire. The servant who had opened the door took their sodden coats and hats and, going into the kitchen, returned directly with clean towels so they could dry their faces and hands. While they were doing so, a maid brought them hot drinks, which were most gratefully accepted. Thomas meanwhile took George around the house to the kitchen, while the two gentlemen waited in the parlour for Mr Barnaby.

Frank Burnett was interested in the house, which had on its walls a variety of exotic souvenirs, but Mr Adams was most impatient, his anxiety for Lilian overwhelming for once his good manners.

"Frank, what do you think? Do you really believe Lilian and Sally are here in this house?"

A voice boomed behind them, "They certainly are and they are upstairs resting after their most dreadful ordeal." Descending the stairs was Mr Barnaby, a pleasant, cheerful-looking man and with him a kindly, middle-aged woman, who was clearly his wife. Both appeared eminently respectable and seemed rather bemused at what had happened that afternoon.

"The young ladies have been very anxious indeed. Miss Harrison was most insistent that we should inform her mother they were safe. I was preparing to send Thomas over to Rosings with a message, when you turned up."

Mr and Mrs Barnaby were keen at first to ascertain who the two men were before they agreed to bring the two young girls down to meet them, a fact that Mr Burnett thought did them great credit.

"After all," he said later, "they had no means of knowing who we were. We may well have been blackguards bent on kidnapping the two young ladies."

Mr Adams protested; he could not comprehend how anyone would think that he would do anything to harm one hair of Miss Lilian's head!

Once Mr Burnett and Mr Adams had introduced themselves and explained how the young ladies came to be in the carriage and Mr Barnaby had then issued dire warnings about the dangers of letting two young women travel along country roads unprotected, Mrs Barnaby went upstairs and brought the girls down to the parlour. It transpired also that Lilian, not wishing to be separated from her, had claimed that Sally was her cousin, a fiction they were now all obliged to maintain.

There was no mistaking their joy when Lilian and John Adams saw one another. It had already been explained to Mr and Mrs Barnaby that the pair were engaged to be married.

"The ladies will both need to keep warm on the journey and I recommend that they should be seen by the physician, who will probably have them tucked up in bed for a few days," warned Mrs Barnaby. "They were both very wet indeed when we found them. And all because Miss Harrison insisted on trying to save the life of the unfortunate carter."

Frank Burnett realised then that they had all been so concerned about Lilian and Sally, they had quite forgotten poor Sparks.

"Where is he? Was he badly hurt?" he asked, only to be told that the man had been thrown so hard when his horse bolted, he had suffered a broken leg as well as concussion. He had been removed to the infirmary in the nearest town.

"Miss Lilian insisted," said Sally, earning herself a black look from her erstwhile "cousin." "She said we could not leave him lying in the road. So we carried him over to the side and put him under some bushes, for shelter from the rain, but he groaned and moaned each time we touched him... it was terrible!" she said, with tears in her eyes.

By this time Lilian, who had been standing beside John Adams, pleaded that she wished to be taken home, and Mr Burnett asked Mr Barnaby if he would be so kind as to have Thomas convey them to the road, where their carriage waited.

Not only were the Barnabys happy to oblige, they supplied the travellers with scarves and rugs aplenty to keep them warm and insisted that they take blankets to wrap the two ladies in, before they sent them on their way, with many good wishes for their swift recovery.

They set off, having thanked Mr and Mrs Barnaby profusely for their great kindness. It had turned out they had once been tenants on the Rosings estate, in the days when Mr Jonathan Bingley had been Lady Catherine de Bourgh's manager. Mr Barnaby was very complimentary indeed about Jonathan Bingley's stewardship of the estate. Following the death of Lady Catherine, Mr Barnaby, who had come into some money, had purchased the farm and land where they now lived.

"When we said we were from Rosings, it was as though we had said the magic word," Lilian explained. "After that Mr and Mrs Barnaby could not do enough for us."

Lilian would have wished to tell them more, but she was beginning to feel the effects of her ordeal. As they reached the road and transferred to their carriage, they wrapped her up well, but she was too cold and weak to talk. Henceforth, they had to depend for most of their information upon Sally, who being younger and a good deal more resilient than her mistress, was able to tell the tale.

It had been an extraordinary sequence of events.

They had reached Redhill well in time, only to discover on arriving at the station that Mrs Fitzwilliam's train to Derby would not leave until one o'clock, due to a death on the railway line. A man had been killed; no one knew if he had committed suicide or had been accidentally run over by the train, but there had been officials and police everywhere, said Sally, explaining with her eyes wide with horror.

"It was dreadful, the dead man still on the platform, his face covered with a coat. Mrs Fitzwilliam was most upset and Miss Lilian was in tears!" she said, shuddering at the memory.

Despite that inauspicious beginning, they had settled Caroline in her seat and when the train was about to leave, said their farewells and returned to their vehicle to find the carter Mr Sparks complaining that his horse was out of sorts.

"The poor creature looked like he were having a fit," said Sally, "frothing at the mouth and tossing his head all restless like."

Mr Sparks had left them with the vehicle and gone to get the horse some medicine and when he returned some half an hour later, he had forcibly administered the concoction, pouring it down the horse's throat. Shortly afterwards, they had then set off for home, around two o'clock.

"We had not gone far when we heard noises; gunshots, like someone shooting rabbits in the woods. We thought it were poachers; it got louder and nearer and the horse took fright and bolted. Try as he might, Mr Sparks could not hold him; he pulled the cart this way and that, then the horse broke loose and fled up the road and into the woods." Sally's vivid and terrifying account conveyed to them how close they had come to disaster.

"Poor Mr Sparks, he tried to hang on but he were thrown onto the road and the cart pitched onto its side in the ditch. Miss Lilian and I, we clung to each other and screamed, I thought we would die, for sure. But then we fell upon each other, so we was not badly hurt. Miss Lilian has a bad bruise on her knee and my arms is all black and blue," she said, proceeding to tell how they had crawled out of the wrecked vehicle and tried to help Mr Sparks.

"Miss Lilian said we could not leave him in the road or he would die. We tried to move him but he groaned something terrible, so we left him under a bush and walked until we found a crofter's cottage. The woman there had no one who could help, but she told us to go to the big house over the crest of the hill, where they had a carriage and servants who could take the carter to the apothecary in the village."

"It was raining again and Miss Lilian and I had no umbrellas or anything; by the time we got to the house we must have looked real frights, because the housemaid who came to the door screamed and would not let us in. She ran away and then a man came and Miss Lilian pleaded with him and said we was from Rosings Park. I think Mrs Barnaby must have heard her through the open door, because she came at once and took us in. After that they was all very kind to us," she said, adding with a little giggle, "Miss Lilian told them we was cousins, so they would not send me off to the kitchen with the servants. She wanted me to stay with her. Mrs Barnaby was very kind; she had the maids bring up hot water and towels for us to wash and gave us hot soup and bread to eat.

"But Miss Lilian wanted them to send a man to look for Mr Sparks, she kept telling them he would die. When Mr Barnaby came in, he sent Thomas and another lad to find Mr Sparks and take him to the apothecary, but when they came back they was not very hopeful. He had a broken leg, too, they said and the apothecary could not say if he would live.

"Then Miss Lilian told them her mama would be sick with worry and she wanted to go home, but Mr Barnaby said no, he would not risk it in this weather, they might have another accident. He offered to send Thomas with a message to Rosings saying we'd be safe and Miss Lilian said she would write a note to her mama for Thomas to take. Mrs Barnaby got her some writing paper and a pen and ink, but just then, there was this great commotion in the yard and Mr Barnaby opened a window to look out and Miss Lilian recognised Mr Adams's voice. She cried out then in happiness like and we hugged each other, because we knew we was found at last!"

Sally's tale concluded on such a high note as to suggest that it seemed to her that it had all been a big adventure, something she would tell and re-tell to all her friends and family for years to come. Not much younger, but certainly sturdier than Lilian and better able to withstand the rigours of their perilous journey, she would recover more easily. She was cold and a little weary, but not injured or unwell.

Lilian, on the other hand, was clearly suffering from exposure and extreme fatigue. Despite the best efforts of Mrs Barnaby to keep her warm, she appeared to have caught a chill. She had begun to shiver and by the time they had reached the entrance to the Dower House, was too weak to walk and had to be carried from the carriage.

Catherine had been watching from the window of her room, which afforded her a clear view of the road, for what had seemed like interminable hours. Refusing all food, taking only a cup of tea, she kept vigil, until in the distance she saw a man on horseback approaching the house. It was George, who had ridden on ahead of the others to bring her the news.

Rushing downstairs, she flung open the door and demanded to know, "George, have they found them? Are they safe?"

"Yes, ma'am, Miss Lilian and Sally are in the carriage with Mr Burnett and Mr Adams; they should soon be here, ma'am."

"Thank God," was all she said, as she waited beside the open door until the carriage drew up at the gate. She watched then as Mr Burnett lifted Lilian out and carried her into the house.

≈

Everything had been made ready, because no one had known in what state the travellers would return. But when Catherine saw her daughter carried in, pale and quiet, while Sally had stepped out of the vehicle and walked in the door on her own two feet, she was afraid something dreadful had befallen her. Perhaps there had been an accident and Lilian had been badly hurt. Her mind raced ahead, anxious and afraid.

Having carried Lilian into her room and laid her on the bed, Frank Burnett turned to reassure Catherine.

"It is probably only a chill, they have been through a terrible ordeal, but there is no time to lose, I must get the doctor at once," he said.

He went immediately, taking Mr Adams with him, confident that Catherine did not need the added strain of John Adams's anxiety at this time. She understood the intention behind his actions and was grateful indeed for his thoughtfulness.

They returned from Hunsford with Dr Bannerman, who together with his partner Dr Whitelaw had attended upon the Harrison family for several years. He examined both girls and pronounced Sally to be un-injured save for some bruising for which he recommended treatment.

Lilian had been his patient since she was a child. Hers had never been a robust constitution, less likely to withstand colds and chills than Sally's. Despite the kind ministrations of the Barnabys, the excessive exposure to cold and rain which Lilian had endured had clearly combined to give her a heavy cold. He saw no sign of infection yet, but they must guard against pneumonia, he warned.

Dr Bannerman, reluctant to alarm Mrs Harrison, was nevertheless very insistent that Lilian must be kept warm, persuaded to take the medication he prescribed regularly throughout the night, and get as much rest as was possible. He left, promising to call again in the morning to check on her progress.

After Dr Bannerman departed, Catherine had thanked Mr Burnett with tears in her eyes. "Frank, what can I say? I cannot imagine what we would have done had you not been here… Please accept my thanks…" but he would not let her continue; gently and lovingly reassuring her that he wanted no expressions of gratitude, he was thankful that he had been there and able to do something to help find her daughter. Promising to return the following morning and urging her to get some rest as well, he left them.

When the gentlemen had gone, there followed for Lilian and her mother a disturbed and uneasy night, for Lilian became restless and feverish, muttering strange, incoherent scraps of sentences as she tossed and turned, unable to sleep. Her head and limbs ached and her breathing was laboured. Mrs Giles came to sit with her to let Catherine get some rest, but she could not bear to leave her daughter's bedside, even for a few minutes. She had an easy chair brought in from her sitting room and, placing it close by the bed, sat in it for the rest of the night.

Occasionally, out of sheer fatigue, she would nod off, but waking suddenly, she would anxiously feel her daughter's brow, which alternately became hot and fevered or cold and clammy as she would sweat out the fever. Catherine would moisten her lips with water, soothe her forehead with lavender, and pray as she had never done before, for her child's recovery.

When Dr Bannerman called early on the following day, he was disappointed not to see an improvement in Lilian and indeed, to find a worsening of her mother's condition. Having had no sleep all night, Catherine was exhausted but determined to remain at her daughter's side.

Dr Bannerman was sufficiently concerned to speak with Mrs Giles, who saw him to the door. Clearly, he said, the medication he had given her had not had the desired effect on Lilian; he prescribed more potions and would go into town to consult a colleague, who might recommend something stronger. Meanwhile, he urged Mrs Giles to ensure that her mistress was looked after, that she took some nourishment and rest during the day.

"We cannot have Mrs Harrison falling ill, too," he said. "She must not fret, I am confident Miss Lilian will recover, though it may take some time. She is healthy and young, though not as sturdy as some young women. I intend to return and if she has made no progress, I will call in a physician from London, who has much experience in treating this type of condition."

Reassured by his words, Mrs Giles went upstairs to Catherine, who, despite the doctor's counsel, had returned to her daughter's bedside. Her anxiety and grief would not let her leave the room, but when Mrs Giles brought in some soup, she partook of it gratefully and not long afterwards, seated in her chair beside the bed, fell asleep for the first time in two days.

That afternoon, Mrs Giles entered the room and whispered that the two gentlemen from Rosings—Messrs Adams and Burnett—had called and were in the parlour.

"Will you go down to them, ma'am?" she asked. "I will stay with Miss Lilian while you do."

But Catherine shook her head. "No, Mrs Giles, it is not me they want to see. Mr Adams must be desperate to know how Lilian is faring. He will not be content with seeing me."

When Mrs Giles looked confused, she added softly, "Tell them they can see her for a few minutes, if they are very quiet. She must not be disturbed. Then, bring them in."

When Mr Adams and Frank Burnett entered the room, which had been darkened by closing most of the drapes, they took a while to get accustomed to the partial light. John Adams moved towards the bed and when he saw Lilian, he gasped, his heart deeply grieved by the sight. It was too much; he could not hold back the tears. Catherine went to him at once, as he stood looking at Lilian, lying pale and languid, so utterly different to the lively young woman he knew.

Catherine tried to comfort him but she could not. His tears flowed down his cheeks and he ran from the room. It was then that Frank Burnett spoke softly to Catherine. He too had been shocked by the deterioration in Lilian's condition in so short a time. Not wishing to impose in any way upon her, yet wanting desperately to help, he asked, "Catherine, will you let me do something for you? May I send a message to your sister, Mrs Tate? I am quite certain she will wish to be with you and help you care for Lilian. I did consider sending a telegraphic message last night, but waited, not wishing to act without your consent. May I?"

The thought, which had not even occurred to her, seemed to express exactly that which Catherine needed at that moment. It summoned up images of sisterly affection and assistance, which Becky could always be counted on to provide. Catherine knew there was nothing her sister liked more than to be asked to help in a crisis.

She turned gratefully to him, "Oh Mr Burnett, if you would, please do. I cannot think of anything I would like better at this moment; Becky is very practical and kind. Thank you for your thoughtfulness, I have not yet had the time to say how very grateful I am for all you have done."

He spent no more than a few minutes longer, telling her she must not think he expected gratitude. "Who could have done otherwise in the circumstances? If you must thank me, Catherine, let it be by looking to your own health, for I can see how exhausted you are and I beg you, do not allow yourself to fall ill through lack of care. That is all I ask of you just now. Will you promise me this?"

Touched by his concern and remembering again the warmth of his affection for her, she nodded and promised to do as he asked. He was, for the moment, content, and taking one last look at Lilian, who was still asleep, he took Catherine's hand, kissed it, and left the room.

She heard him descend the stairs and returned to her chair, deeply grateful to him. With Lilian ill and the rest of her family thousands of miles away, his strong presence in her life was her only comfort.

Frank Burnett had found John Adams in the parlour, his face a picture of abject misery. He seemed convinced that his beloved Lilian was at death's door and could not be comforted. The inclement weather that had continued over the last two days seemed only to increase his despair.

"Please let me remain here, Frank, I must wait until the doctor calls so I may know what his prognosis is. If I went away now, I would not have a moment's peace," he begged and Frank Burnett was loathe to deny him his meagre consolation. Presently, he left the house and rode into Hunsford, from where he despatched an urgent telegram to Mrs Rebecca Tate, telling her, while giving few details, that Lilian was gravely ill and her sister needed her help.

It would be two days at least before Rebecca could be expected, and in the meantime they could only hope that Dr Bannerman's second application of medicines would be more successful than the first.

⁓ꝏ⁓

It was a long, anxious night.

Neither Catherine nor Mrs Giles could sleep for long; both women had watched Lilian grow from a somewhat delicate child into the most promising member of the family. Her looks, intelligence, and generally sweet disposition had endeared her to everyone, and there were many waiting with keen anticipation to see her happily wed.

To her mother, whose elder children had been closer to their father and each other than to her, Lilian was more than a daughter; she was almost a friend to whom she could speak with little reservation. This unfortunate accident had only served to underscore how precious she was and how easily she might be lost to her.

The following morning saw not only a return of warmer weather; it brought a renewal of hope, when Lilian at last showed some small signs of improvement in her condition.

Catherine awoke from a short sleep to hear much less laboured breathing, a gentle movement of her chest as she slept, and best of all, at least to the touch, no sign of the fever!

An hour later, Lilian opened her eyes, and asked for something to drink. It was the first time a coherent sentence had passed her lips and Catherine, having helped her take a few sips of water, raced down to ask Mrs Giles to have some weak tea prepared.

Returning to the room, she was delighted to find that Lilian was able to sit up in bed and actually asked for the curtains to be opened to let in the light. Quite clearly the headache that had tortured her for two days was gone.

As the day wore on, Lilian improved materially in every respect and by the time Dr Bannerman called, she was so much better he was able to interpret the symptoms and declare that she was out of danger. He did, however, take time to caution his young patient.

"You are indeed a very fortunate young lady; but I must warn you, Miss Lilian, your recovery will depend upon persevering with your medication regularly for a further week, continuing to rest, and taking all of the nutritious food your mama will have prepared for you. If you do not," he warned, "there is always a danger of relapse, and I should not think you would wish such a thing upon yourself, especially not with a wedding in the Autumn, eh?"

Lilian, who in her weakened state had no desire to argue with him, thanked him for his care and agreed to do everything Dr Bannerman and her mother asked. Indeed, so assiduously did she follow their instructions, by the time her aunt Becky arrived from Derbyshire she was well enough to come downstairs and sit for a few hours in the parlour each day.

Often during these times, Mr Adams would find himself in the area and arrive with flowers or fruit or sometimes a new book, which he would read to her. During these days, Catherine observed how his concern and affection were expressed in all the things he would do for Lilian. It was something she remarked on to Frank Burnett, and even as he knew and understood her anxiety, he was happy that his young friend's concern for Lilian had not gone unnoticed. As for his own efforts, she had told him again and again how deeply they were appreciated, thus ensuring that he felt amply rewarded with her affection.

With the terrifying ordeal of the accident and Lilian's subsequent illness behind them, she could proceed with plans for her daughter's wedding in the Autumn, with even more confidence in the certainty of her future happiness.

Chapter Twenty

BECKY TATE WAS NOT particularly disappointed to find, upon her arrival at the Dower House, that her niece had been declared to be out of danger.

In fact, while she had responded instantly to Mr Burnett's message, making immediate preparations to leave her home and travel down to Kent with all possible speed to be at her sister's side, there had been another, quite different reason why she wished to be there.

A letter had arrived from her husband, some days previously, causing her to take stock of her present circumstances, and she was exceedingly grateful to have the opportunity to confide in her elder sister and seek her counsel. It was therefore not at all incompatible with her intentions that with the immediate danger past and Lilian's recovery in progress, Rebecca should find that it suited her very well to be in her sister's house at this time.

Catherine was very pleased to have her. Since her last visit, when certain matters concerning Lilian and Mr Adams had been discussed in depth and an understanding reached between the sisters, Catherine felt a great deal more comfortable with Becky. Besides, there was much to be done and with Lilian compelled to rest a great deal, she welcomed another pair of hands and the agreeable presence of another woman with whom she could speak in confidence.

There was, however, one matter which she had as yet told neither Lilian nor Becky, and it would soon have to be done.

Despite her determination to tell Lilian of Frank Burnett's proposal and her response to it, the events of that afternoon and Lilian's subsequent illness had thwarted her plans. There had been neither the time nor the inclination to speak of it. And now that Lilian's condition was much improved and Becky was here, there had been other, more pressing matters that demanded her attention.

Most importantly, Catherine felt the urgent need to call on Mr and Mrs Barnaby and thank them for their attention to her daughter and Sally, as well as their assistance to Messrs Adams and Burnett on the night of the accident. Furthermore, some days later, Mr Barnaby had sent his man Thomas with a basket of fruit and farm produce and a note enquiring after the health of the young ladies. It was a generous and kindly gesture, which Catherine felt had to be acknowledged; she decided to visit them and take the good news of Lilian's recovery herself.

"It will not be sufficient to write a note, it will seem a cold and formal thing to do, when they by their actions have probably saved Lilian's life," she declared and asked Frank Burnett if he would organise the visit. "I think we should take Becky with us," she added, "it will do her good to meet the Barnabys, whose generosity and kindness must far outweigh their lack of rank and title, even in her estimation."

Frank Burnett could not agree more. He was happy to oblige and sent a note to Mr and Mrs Barnaby, advising of a short visit the following week, if that was convenient. Their speedy answer, inviting the party to afternoon tea, settled the matter.

They borrowed the smaller carriage from Rosings for the occasion and set off on a fine afternoon, reaching the Barnabys' farm a little before teatime on a perfect Summer's day. They had brought with them the blankets, rugs, and scarves provided to the stranded travellers by the Barnabys and a basket of the finest roses for the lady of the house, of whose kindness both Lilian and Sally could not say enough.

This time Mr Burnett, being the only member of the party who had met the family, went to the door and rang the bell.

Both Mr and Mrs Barnaby awaited them in the parlour and greeted their visitors with such friendliness and warmth as to surprise and delight them all. When Catherine and her sister had been introduced, they were invited to be seated and partake of a truly splendid afternoon tea. Plates and dishes laden with a variety of cakes and dainty pastries, together with a pyramid of fruit— grapes, peaches, and plums—were there for their enjoyment. Catherine, always a somewhat abstemious eater, had long given up, in her home at least, the tradition of serving such lavish afternoon teas.

Rebecca, who admitted to having a sweet tooth, did enjoy such excesses but had of late been too preoccupied by other matters to indulge. The Barnabys, however, seemed to enjoy it all and urged their visitors to do likewise, while the servants appeared ready to refill their plates and cups at a moment's notice. Excellent tea, which Mr Barnaby assured them came direct from the tea gardens of India and Ceylon, was available too and much enjoyed by Catherine, who confessed she was always partial to a good cup of tea.

In between partaking of this feast, she did succeed in telling their host and hostess how very grateful she was for the care and concern they had shown to the two young ladies.

"My daughter Lilian must surely owe her life to you and your wife, Mr Barnaby. She became quite ill afterwards; she is not very strong and Dr Bannerman assures me she would not have survived had she not been sheltered, cared for, and kept warm immediately following the accident. There was a real fear of pneumonia and we must be grateful that it did not eventuate, thanks mainly to your timely intervention. I cannot tell you how many times I have thanked you in my thoughts and prayers," said Catherine and clearly, the Barnabys appreciated her words, although they did their best to minimise their part in Lilian's rescue, pointing rather to the intrepid quality of the two girls and their insistence in the midst of great discomfort that the unfortunate carter Mr Sparks be found and treated, too.

Catherine acknowledged their remarks and said, "You will be pleased, I am sure, to hear that Mr Sparks has returned home and his leg is mending well. The doctor was afraid he would not walk again, so severe was the injury, but Mr Burnett has made some enquiries this very day and we are told he is much improved, although it will be a while before he can drive his cart again."

Mr Barnaby nodded and then asked, "And your niece has recovered well, too? She seemed a much sturdier girl than Miss Lilian."

This brought a look of astonishment from Rebecca, to whom they had omitted to relate the tale of Sally being Lilian's cousin for a day. It was Mr Burnett who interposed swiftly to answer cheerfully, "Miss Sally was up and about the very next day—she is indeed a very resilient young person and had suffered little from the experience."

An exchange of looks between Catherine and her sister was all that was required to silence Becky, while Catherine proceeded to regale them with news of Lilian's forthcoming nuptials.

"I would not be happy if I did not say that we hope very much that you, Mr and Mrs Barnaby, will be able to attend. I know that I speak for both Lilian and Mr Adams and we shall look forward to seeing you there," she said, adding that a formal invitation would be sent in due course.

The pleasure that this brought the Barbabys was plain to see, for both husband and wife beamed and rose to thank Mrs Harrison for her invitation. They would be honoured to accept and would take note of the day and ensure that they kept it free of any other engagements, they promised, and sent their best wishes and blessings to the young couple. Their own children had been married many years ago, they explained; it would be a very great pleasure to be present at Miss Lilian's wedding.

As they left the Barnabys' place to return home, it was with a feeling of immense pleasure and satisfaction that Catherine said her farewells, certain that in the kindly couple she had made good friends whose decency and generosity of heart was without question.

As the carriage drove out of the property and onto the main road, however, Becky turned to her sister, a quizzical look upon her face and asked, "Cathy, who is this sturdy young niece you have been hiding from me all these years?" and the sisters burst out laughing. It took awhile to tell the story and explain Lilian's reason for pretending her maid was her cousin. As Catherine told it, Becky enjoyed the tale immensely and said, "Ah well, I dare say there's no harm done, is there? Sally was a Miss Harrison for one day, that's all."

It was Frank Burnett who pointed out that it was not quite so simple.

"Of course, Sally will have to return to being Miss Lilian's cousin when the Barnabys attend the wedding. It will not do to have her in mob cap and apron, serving the guests, will it, Mrs Harrison?"

His remarks were lightly meant, but Catherine was so taken aback, she put her hand to her mouth, shocked at the prospect. "No indeed, oh dear, what have I done? We shall have to find a way to conceal Sally among the family at the wedding breakfast, so the Barnabys will not notice her. She certainly cannot be seen serving at tables."

But Catherine had not counted on Lilian, who on hearing of the difficulty, declared without a moment's hesitation, "Well, that's easily settled—Sally can be my bridesmaid. I did wonder whom to ask. Sally will do very nicely. After all, we almost died together, that should be sufficient reason, do you not think?" she asked and John Adams was the only one of the party who said at once, "Certainly my love, I am sure there can be no better reason."

No one else said a word; it was plain Lilian's mind was quite made up; it would have been futile to argue with her. As to how this was to be explained to the rest of the family, Becky was sure it would not be beyond their capacity to concoct an acceptable explanation.

⁓✥⁓

That evening, Mr Adams and Mr Burnett dined with them and Lilian came downstairs to dinner, looking very well and feeling so much better, that her aunt Becky declared it was worthy of a special celebration.

Afterwards, the two gentlemen did not stay long; Lilian retired early and Catherine was free to spend a couple of hours with her sister over tea in the sitting room.

"And how did you like the Barnabys, Becky?" she asked, to which her sister answered with surprising alacrity that she had liked them very well indeed.

"They are such kind, hospitable folk and I must say I was pleasantly surprised by the modest style of their home. Too often these new country houses display more of their owners' money than good taste."

"Oh, come now, Becky," said Catherine a little testily, "you are not going to judge them by the standards of your fine London friends like Lady Ashton and Mr Armstrong, are you? These are very genuine, hardworking farmers with their roots in the soil of Kent, not one of your absentee landlords, with an expensive house in town and several properties all over the country."

Taken aback by the vehemence of her sister's words, Becky protested.

"Pray do not misunderstand me, Cathy, I did not intend to denigrate the Barnabys at all; I thought they were very worthy, decent people. I would rather know them than many of those you call my fine London friends, though indeed, they are none of them very genuine friends, which fact I have learned of late. The Barnabys seem to be the very opposite, I think."

"Indeed they are," said Catherine, "and Becky, please forgive me if I appeared too ready to condemn your friends; I did not mean to do so." She had not meant to hurt her sister's feelings, but she continued, "However, when I think of the shabby way in which my Lilian was treated by those rich young men at Lady Ashton's ball, where she was a guest, and consider how different was the conduct of Mr and Mrs Barnaby, who were complete strangers to her, I cannot help but make such a judgment and I hope you will pardon me. I do not expect you to abandon your friends, Becky dear, but you must surely acknowledge their faults?"

"I certainly do, Cathy," Rebecca protested, "and indeed I see much less of them now than I did before. Lilian's unhappy experience has opened my eyes, and having seen her with Mr Adams, who seems an exemplary young man, I no longer feel the need to heed the opinions of Lady Ashton and her friends on any of these matters. In truth, I can no longer apologise for them and I doubt they will do as much for me in my present circumstances."

This extraordinary admission, rather sadly spoken, touched Catherine to the extent that she rose from her chair and went to sit beside her sister on the sofa.

"You must not feel like that, Becky; you certainly do not need to apologise for them, nor do you need them to speak up for you. You owe them nothing. Among your friends and family, you are known for your generosity and kindness. You need not depend upon their good opinion."

She noticed that Becky seemed unusually preoccupied and wished to ask the reason for it but was reluctant to pry. Instead, she decided she would lighten her sister's mood with some good news of her own. She said, "Becky dear, there is something I have to tell you—oh don't look so apprehensive, it is a piece of good news, which I am sure will make you very happy. But I am afraid I must ask you to keep it a secret for a while."

Rebecca was immediately interested. There was nothing she liked better than a little secret; her writer's instincts alerted her to a good story and she sat up facing her sister, eager for her news.

Catherine, having decided it was best to tell her the facts first, said quickly, "Becky, Mr Frank Burnett and I are engaged."

She had expected her sister to exclaim and perhaps express shock, even consternation. The news was unlikely to please her, she had thought.

To her complete amazement, however, Rebecca did none of these things. She did look a little surprised as she asked, "Engaged? Mr Burnett and you are going to be married?"

Catherine nodded, not able to believe how calmly she was taking the announcement.

"Not immediately, but yes, it is quite settled between us; we no longer need anyone's permission to marry. But we shall wait until after Lilian's wedding, though; we have not made any firm plans as to a date."

"Have you told Mama?" Rebecca asked.

"I have not, no one knows but you. I was going to tell Lilian on the very day I accepted him, but the accident and her subsequent illness intervened. So you, my dear sister, are the very first to know. I shall tell Lilian, of course, and then I will write to Mama. But tonight, I felt so very happy, I had to tell you. Becky, he loves me; he told me he has loved me for many years and I know now how very dearly I love him. Indeed, if it were not for the interference of Lady Catherine, we may well have been happily married these twenty years…" Her voice broke and Becky embraced her sister, saying, "Oh Cathy, I am so very happy for you and Mr Burnett. I wish you the greatest happiness, with all my heart."

Catherine held her close and felt tears on her face, Becky's tears. She tried then to tease her sister and make light of it.

"Becky, you must not cry; I absolutely forbid it, not when I am so happy. Why, I have not felt so lighthearted in years and you must share my happiness," she said, smiling, her face alight with pleasure.

Rebecca smiled too, but it was a different kind of smile. Then she sighed. "I do, I do, but, Cathy dear, I too have a story to tell and it must also remain a secret for a while. Sadly, it is not such a happy tale as yours, so you will have to forgive me if I shed a tear or two," she said.

Catherine was immediately attentive. "Why, Becky, what is it?" she asked.

She feared her sister had had some bad news; perhaps it concerned her son, Walter. He was, as he had always been, a rather self-willed, obstinate young man, who, having married the daughter of one of his father's business partners, lived a life somewhat apart from the rest of the family.

"Is it Walter?" she asked apprehensively.

Becky shook her head. "No, it is not Walter, it is my husband, Mr Tate. I have had a letter from him from America."

"What does he say? Is he unwell?"

Becky smiled a little wistfully. "Oh no, he is never unwell. No, Cathy, he has written to ask me to agree to a separation."

Catherine was so outraged, she sat silent, unable to say a word. This was appalling news, quite impossible to believe, and she knew not what to say. Finally she asked, "Why, Becky? What reason does he give?"

Rebecca reached into the pocket of her gown and produced a letter, two pages in a clear, strong hand, recognisably that of Anthony Tate. It explained in the plainest terms that he had decided to make his permanent home in America, where his newspaper and journal business was thriving and, since he had no reason to return to England, he asked for a separation.

He made no criticism of her, nor was there any suggestion of some other woman in his life; the letter stated simply and clearly that he felt he would prefer to live out his life separate from her, as he had done for almost a year, in the United States. He made no mention of a future divorce, but did promise to make a generous settlement upon her and let her have the house he owned in town and all of the assets associated with it. The business he had built up in the Midlands would be transferred to their son Walter, as would the family property at Matlock, with some conditions attached.

"He does suggest that I might wish to reach an arrangement with Walter and his wife, to occupy part of the house at Matlock, if I choose to continue in Derbyshire. But Cathy, I do not fancy that at all," said Rebecca, biting her lip.

Catherine was astounded. She could not comprehend it. Her brother-in-law had always been an upright and honourable man, much respected in the community. Becky and he had shared many interests and worked together on campaigns. How then could he do something so unfeeling?

There were tears in her eyes. "Oh Becky, I am so sorry, but I do not understand. I always thought you loved each other—you seemed to have such a good marriage. How did it ever come to this?" she asked.

She was to be even more astonished by Becky's response, as she explained that she had not been so shocked herself, because their marriage had long been little more than a partnership of convenience.

"It is many years now since we were anything more than partners in a successful enterprise. We worked well together and shared some interests, that is true, but since Josie's death, even that has not been as easy as it once was. My husband blamed me for Josie's problems. He always thought that Josie was too young to marry Julian Darcy and believes, with some justification, I must confess, that I was too eager to see her become the next Mistress of Pemberley. Josie was his life; losing her left him desolate and empty, and he has not forgiven me. It has not astonished me that he wishes us to live apart."

Catherine listened, shaking her head.

"But Becky, tell me truly, when you first read his letter, you cannot have been as sanguine as you are now. It must have saddened you?"

Becky did not meet her eyes and her voice was almost a whisper. "It did, I cannot deny it, it was unexpected and it hurt my feelings to have it so coldly expressed. We have had some good times and whatever our troubles, I did not think he would wish to leave me. I most certainly would not have done so myself. But, there it is, Cathy, it is what he wants and I am almost recovered now," she said, trying to sound cheerful.

Catherine, who had already moved to live at Rosings then, had not seen much of the courtship between her sister and the young Mr Anthony Tate. He was then a handsome and personable man of wealth and influence. He had inherited the Camden's newspaper and printing business and acquired a reputation in political circles as an active reformist. Catherine had always assumed they had loved each other; they had certainly worked very well together and supported several worthy causes with great enthusiasm.

The many friends and colleagues whom they had gathered around them over the years must surely have known had there been a hint of a rupture as bad as this. Yet she had heard nothing and suspected nothing.

"Did you not love him then, Becky?" she asked.

Rebecca did not answer her question directly. But she did confess that while Anthony Tate had courted her with some degree of ardour, her own ambition to be a writer and her desire to have her work published in his journals had overwhelmed all other personal considerations when she had agreed to be his wife.

"Indeed, you might say that, over a period of some weeks, realising that he was moving towards making me an offer of marriage, I had argued myself into a situation in which, when he proposed to me and I accepted him, it was his promise to let me write regularly for the *Review* that excited me more than his declaration of love. As I see it now, our marriage was more a consequence of youthful passion on his part and some reciprocal fondness on mine. He was attractive and eligible, certainly, but had he not been the heir to the Camden's publishing business, I doubt our friendship would have ended in matrimony."

Catherine was very shaken. It was useless to try to hide her dismay. She could not imagine that her sister could have contrived such a proposition. It went against everything she believed in.

But, surprisingly, Becky appeared somewhat less than desolated. She admitted that the early years of their marriage had been "fun"—sustained by the natural affection and desire of youth. Their two children had brought them much pleasure, especially Josie, who had soon become the very centre of her father's universe.

"She was so full of fun and vitality, I do believe he loved her more than he has ever loved anyone in all his life, and she adored him. He would have given her anything she asked for," she said.

Catherine was aware of this, and of the blow that Josie's death had been, but asked if they had not found sufficient reward in the good work they did together. Becky agreed that their dedication to the improvement of their community had provided opportunities to build a partnership, which had endured for many years; likewise, the excitement of their involvement in the politics of reform had afforded them much satisfaction.

"But as the years passed, and more especially since Josie's death, I think our lives were emptied of all feeling save despair," she said and Catherine could not hold back the tears. "My husband came to hate London; he sees it as the place where Josie fell prey to those who destroyed her life, which is probably why he has decided to live permanently in the United States. He cannot forget the pain of losing her, and I fear I have become a constant reminder of that agony."

There was such a profound sense of finality in her words, Catherine was deeply shocked. Taking her sister's hand in hers, she asked, "My dear Becky, what will you do?" It had never before occurred to her to feel this kind of protective concern for Rebecca, whose capacity to organise her own life and cope simultaneously with half a dozen other matters had never been in doubt. She was renowned for her hard work in pursuing successfully a number of causes, whether it was the extension of the franchise or the promotion of education for girls. Yet now, to Catherine, she seemed alone and vulnerable.

But Becky Tate was not about to surrender to helplessness.

She explained that she had already written to her husband to agree to the separation, on certain conditions.

"At least it will show that I bear him no ill will, which I do not. We may not have much love and very little happiness left between us, but we have always had some respect for one another. I should not wish to lose that. If he is prepared to let me have a reasonable income and the house in London, as he has suggested, I think I could manage very well."

"And will you live in London then?" asked Catherine.

"Good God, no! It would drive me quite mad," Becky replied. "Besides, just think what a fine thing it would be for Lady Ashton and her circle of busybodies; I would become a subject of gossip and hilarity at every party. No, Cathy, I do not think I would like to live in London. Indeed, one of the conditions I have set down in my letter to Mr Tate is that the title of the house in London be transferred to me, because I should like to sell it and acquire a modest little property, somewhere in Kent, perhaps? What would you say to that?"

Catherine, though delighted at the prospect of having her sister settled in the same county, was unprepared for such precipitate decisions. All her life she had given much thought to every situation before taking action.

"Have you really thought it all out, Becky? Will you not miss your friends? Life in these parts is pretty quiet, especially now Rosings is no longer occupied. We see very few people except those who live and work here."

"Cathy dear, I do believe I am ready for a quiet life. It would suit me very well to spend my days in writing and tending my garden and seeing you and my dear niece from time to time. If any of my friends miss me, they will be welcome to come and visit," Becky said cheerfully.

When her sister looked a little doubtful, she added, "My dear Cathy, pray do not worry about me. I shall manage very well. Whatever my troubles, they are largely of my own making. I have no grievance, no other person to blame. It is you who must grasp the chance for happiness that you have been offered and look forward to a truly felicitous future with your Mr Burnett."

Catherine blushed. "He is not my Mr Burnett yet, Becky," she cautioned.

"Oh but he is, Cathy, I am sure of it. He is devoted to you, I could see that quite plainly, and now you have explained all the circumstances, I can see that his feelings for you must surely have been particularly deep and enduring," said Becky rather wistfully.

Conscious of her sister's situation, Catherine tried in vain to suppress the pleasurable feelings of satisfaction that swept over her as Becky continued, "You are quite clearly well suited, and Lady Catherine had no right to interfere and keep you apart. It was hard-hearted and cruel, and she deserves to be censured most severely for it."

Catherine protested gently, "That is not fair, Becky, Lady Catherine was, in most matters, very kind and generous to me. She probably thought she was doing the right thing for me…"

"How? By forbidding you to enjoy his company? By precluding Mr Burnett's interest in you with threats and deception, pretending that you were already spoken for? You cannot believe that, Cathy; you are far too charitable to her. But we need not argue about it now. Destiny will not be denied, you know, and here you are, together at last, and I cannot tell you how pleased I am for you and how completely confident that yours will be a truly happy marriage."

Despite the sadness she felt for her sister, Catherine could not hide her contentment. Becky had accepted without question her estimation of Frank Burnett and, if she had needed it, provided a complete confirmation of her decision. While Catherine had not doubted her own judgment, it was comforting to have such enthusiastic endorsement of her hopes for the future.

Becky rose and embraced her sister. "Now, it really is time you were in bed. You've had a very long day, and remember, tomorrow we are to meet the rector and take a look at the plans for your school—it will be most exciting! So you must get some rest."

So saying, she left Catherine, a little tearful and confused, but more certain than ever of the warmth and generosity of her sister's heart.

Chapter Twenty-one

THE FOLLOWING MORNING BROUGHT an unusual number of visitors to the Dower House.

First, Mr Adams appeared at his usual early hour to take Lilian for a drive around the park. He had recently acquired a curricle and was very proud of being able to take her into the village or around the grounds until she was strong enough to walk long distances again.

Then, there was the steward from Rosings, who had brought over a box of documents that had arrived from Mr Jonathan Bingley, all of them pertaining to the business of the parish school and the piece of land on which it was proposed to build it. They were to assist Catherine and the rector Mr Jamison in making their plans for the construction of the school.

Finally, around mid-morning, Mr Frank Burnett arrived to accompany Catherine and Mrs Tate to Hunsford, where they were to meet with the rector and discuss the plans for the school, which had been prepared some years ago for Dr Harrison but sadly aborted by Lady Catherine de Bourgh.

Upon entering the house, Mr Burnett was greeted by Becky, who was eager to offer her felicitations. Having first informed him that Catherine had told her of their engagement, she expressed her most sincere pleasure at the prospect of their marriage. They shook hands warmly and then became immediately engaged in a discussion of the exceptional qualities and sweet disposition of her sister. By both word and manner, Mr Burnett demonstrated how pleased he was to have been accepted by Catherine, and Rebecca agreed with his belief, quite passionately expressed, that they would be very happy together.

"There has been no other woman of my acquaintance of whom I could have made such a claim with the same degree of confidence," he declared, and Becky had no doubt at all of his sincerity.

"Mr Burnett, may I say with equal confidence that with you, I am certain my sister's happiness is in the best possible hands," she replied.

Frank Burnett thanked her; he had been a little apprehensive of Mrs Tate's response to the news of his engagement to her sister. Aware of her previous association with some members of the London social set, he had wondered if she might not have objected to him on the grounds of his humble antecedents or perhaps his lack of any real estate or inheritance. He had thought she would regard this as a distinct disadvantage in a man in his fifties. He had wanted to speak of this possibility to Catherine, but there had been no opportunity to do so.

It was, therefore, with a great sense of relief that he accepted her congratulations and good wishes, realising as he did so that Catherine had probably revealed to her sister some salient details of the history of their relationship.

As they waited for Catherine to join them, Rebecca had added her own appreciation of his role in assisting her through what must surely have been a very trying period. Referring specifically to the business of convincing the trust to permit the establishment of a parish school for girls, she said, "My sister is something of an innocent at large when it comes to such matters, Mr Burnett. Catherine has not experienced, as I have, the excessive vexation and discouragement that accompanies the business of dealing with governments and councils. As for the duplicity and hypocrisy of certain individuals one may encounter, they are so far removed from her own standards of conduct that she is totally incapable of anticipating them. I am well aware of your role in helping her cope, and I thank you for it most sincerely."

Frank Burnett was sufficiently modest to point out that the intervention of Mr Darcy and Jonathan Bingley had eased considerably his own task, but wise enough to allow her to praise him for his part in it. With Mrs Tate on his side, he was confident of gaining the general approval of the rest of Catherine's family, including her mother Mrs Collins.

When Catherine came downstairs and saw them talking together, it was plain to her that she had been the subject of their conversation. It was an impression that was immediately confirmed when Frank Burnett greeted her with even more than usual affection and, taking her hand in his, raised it to his lips, thus openly acknowledging their relationship in a way he had not been able to do before. Then, as if to seal it with her blessing, Becky kissed her and wished them both every happiness.

Having ascertained that Mrs Giles had all the domestic arrangements for the day in hand, Catherine rejoined Mr Burnett and her sister and they set off together for Hunsford. It was a particularly fine day and the pleasant walk through the grounds did not take long. Mr Jamison the rector was waiting for them at the church and ushered them into the vestry. There on the table were laid the original plans for the parish school and some local maps and drawings of the land that was to be used for the building.

The rector was clearly delighted that the school was to go ahead. A man of some learning and with progressive views, he had welcomed the decision that had made it possible and was happy to become involved in carrying out the plans.

"There is just one problem," he said, pointing to the map, "as you see, the only access to this piece of land at present is through the churchyard, which while it may not be of any consequence at first, when the numbers of students are small, may well pose a more intractable problem were the school to grow and enroll many more children in the future."

Of this, Catherine had not even been aware; it had never exercised her mind. She had hoped the numbers of pupils *would* increase with time.

Mr Jamison explained further, "The boundary of the church property lies alongside a lane that divides the Rosings estate from a freehold farm, which used to belong to a former steward of the estate, a Mr George Gross, who has since passed on. It is a private road. While parishioners do use the lane to attend church, there is no certainty that the owner will agree to let it become a public thoroughfare leading to the school," he said.

Catherine was dismayed. To have everything else approved and then to be confronted with such a strange obstruction was so frustrating, she was ready to weep. It was Rebecca who asked, "Who does hold the title to the farm through which the lane runs?"

Mr Jamison, being new to the living, did not know.

"Could we find out?" she persisted and Catherine remembered the pile of documents that Jonathan Bingley had sent her. "Perhaps there will be some indication, a letter or an agreement that will tell us," she suggested.

"If we could discover who owns it now, we might be able to negotiate an arrangement with them," said Rebecca, who was becoming interested in the idea; it was this type of business that she had enjoyed dealing with over many years, when she, Caroline Fitzwilliam, and Cassy Darcy had used their combined wit, charm, and influence to obtain for the people and especially the children of their district a range of useful facilities, by persuading or cajoling landowners and councillors to cooperate with them.

Promising to return when they had the necessary information, they left the church and retraced their steps. Back at the Dower House, they sat down to examine the documents that had arrived that morning, a task that so engrossed them, they were still working when Mr Adams and Lilian returned from their drive.

Frank Burnett and Mr Adams left them then, and the ladies continued their search, this time with Lilian's assistance. Her sharp eyes found a vital clue in a letter from an attorney at law, referring to the will of Mr George Gross, formerly steward at Rosings Park. It seemed the freehold property of Edgewater, gifted to Mr Gross at his retirement, had been bequeathed at his death to his grandson Mr George Grahame, who was then only fourteen years old. A note attached many years later by Mr Jonathan Bingley stated that Mr George Grahame had since moved to live in South Africa; his interest in the property was being looked after by an attorney named Gunning in the neighbouring town of Hallam, which was but a short drive from Rosings Park.

This information caused much excitement as Rebecca pointed out that if the owner no longer occupied the property, his attorney would be able to negotiate with them on the matter of the lane way.

Lilian agreed but Catherine was much less optimistic. "What if he turns out to be a crusty old man who will not budge, who insists that every i is dotted and every t crossed by his client before a decision is made? It will take forever to find Mr George Grahame in South Africa; the Lord alone knows where he is. We may never be able to get his consent, which means we cannot start work on the school. I had hoped to have classes starting in the Spring," she complained.

"Come, Cathy, it is not like you to be a pessimist," Becky chided her sister, but Catherine had little knowledge of such dealings and was immediately dispirited by the discovery that after all their efforts, the lack of public access to the piece of land could disrupt her plans.

Undeterred, Rebecca with Lilian's help gathered together all the relevant material on the matter, and later that afternoon, they set off to find Mr Burnett and arrange an appointment with the attorney Mr Gunning. However, prior to making the journey into town, Rebecca decided that it would serve their purpose well if they took a look at the property themselves and she made plans to do so on the morrow.

～❧～

That night, Catherine waited until her sister had retired to her room and sought out Lilian in her bedroom. She found her sitting on her bed, reading some notes she had made in her diary, which she put aside as her mother entered the room.

The closeness of Catherine's relationship with her daughter should have made it easier to confide in her, but on this occasion, she became somewhat tongue tied and needed Lilian's help when she tried to tell her of Frank Burnett's proposal.

"Lilian, my dear, there is something I have to tell you… I would have spoken of it sooner, I do not wish you to think I was concealing it from you, but there have been many other matters which intervened… and I have been concerned about you after your accident, too… but now, I think the time has come for me to…"

"…Say that you and Mr Burnett are engaged to be married?" Lilian concluded the sentence for her and so startled her mother, she was speechless for a few minutes.

Seeing her discomposure, Lilian laughed merrily. "Oh Mama, did you think it was not apparent to us? Why, John and I have been speaking of the possibility for weeks now. It was so plain to both of us that Mr Burnett loved you, yet we did not know how you would respond to any approach from him. We talked of it; indeed we wished it were possible—"

Catherine interrupted her then. "Did you? Tell me, Lilian, truly, did you wish it? I know Mr Adams would, for they are good friends, but what about you? Would you be pleased if it were to be so? Tell me, my dear, I must know how you feel," she pleaded.

Lilian put her arms around her mother.

"Dearest Mama, of course I am pleased. John has known for some time that Mr Burnett, during his earlier time at Rosings, when you were under the protection of Lady Catherine de Bourgh, had an interest in you, which was cruelly suppressed by Her Ladyship, who ordered him not to pursue the matter. It was something they spoke of as intimate friends, when Mr Adams first confided in Mr Burnett about his feelings for me. Yet he said nothing to me, not wishing to compromise his friend, until very recently; indeed until after the accident, when we were speaking of the immense debt of gratitude we owed to Mr Burnett. Only then did I learn of Frank Burnett's feelings for you and how they had been renewed since his return to Rosings."

"Were you very shocked?" asked Catherine, still concerned that her daughter may have disapproved in some way of this association.

"By the revelation of Lady Catherine's interference, yes, I was, but not by the news that Mr Burnett loved you. Why should it surprise or shock me? Are you not the kindest person I know and most deserving of love in the world? Why should you not be happy? But tell me, Mama, do you love him as well as you did then? Are you certain that you *will* be happy together now, after all those years?"

Catherine looked into her daughter's serious eyes, understood her concern, and said, "Yes indeed, my darling Lilian, I am. I do love him now—far, far more than I could have when I was a young girl, for I can appreciate fully the extraordinary qualities that make him the fine man he is. He has helped me more than I can say and the depth of his feelings has given me a new under-standing of love. Yes, I am happy, and even more so, Lilian, that you are pleased too, for my own pleasure would have been greatly diminished had it not been shared with you."

Mother and daughter spent some time assuring each other that no such circumstance was even remotely possible, before they parted for the night.

On the following day, once again accompanied by Mr Burnett, Catherine and Rebecca walked through the grounds, met with the rector Mr Jamison, and crossed the Hunsford churchyard into the lane that marked the boundary of Rosings Park.

Approaching the old iron gates of the property known as Edgewater, it was clear to them that the property was unoccupied; the grounds, though not extensive, did not appear to have been cared for to any extent, as drifts of early Autumn leaves blowing across the lawn testified.

Attached to the locked gates was a notice, which announced that the property was available for lease. Interested parties were invited to inspect it by contacting the caretaker, and anyone who then wished to sign a lease was urged to see a Mr Gunning, attorney at law in the town of Hallam.

Becky Tate turned to her companions with a gleam in her eye.

"If the property is available for lease, it is surely unlikely that the owner will make much of the matter of schoolchildren using the lane way," she said.

"Ah," said Mr Jamison sagely, "that may be so, but whoever leases the property may very well object and refuse permission. Many people, especially those who are unfamiliar with the area, assume that children from the village are thieves and rascals; they may be accused of trespass."

Catherine was disappointed and Rebecca appeared exasperated, but only for a moment or two; then, turning to Frank Burnett, she said, "Mr Burnett, I do believe we need to see Mr Gunning sooner than next week. If you will be so kind as to drive us in tomorrow, I think I should like to lease the property myself."

"Becky!" Catherine was astonished. "You cannot possibly do that!" she protested.

"Why not? I shall need a place of my own when I move out of the house in London, and this is as good a place as any I am likely to find in the area."

"But you have not seen the house yet. It may well be too large or a complete ruin inside," said Catherine, betraying her rising anxiety about this sudden turn of events.

"Oh, I think not, Mrs Harrison," said the rector. "I understand the property is regularly inspected and is in good condition. My housekeeper knows the caretaker and his wife well, and if Mrs Tate wishes, we could apply to see the house, as this notice invites us to do."

"Of course," said Becky, "let us do so now, why delay any longer?"

She rang the rather rusty bell at the gate to summon the caretaker. The man arrived, a cheerful old fellow with a large bunch of keys, and having heard of their interest in the property, he admitted them and took them around the house to the front door.

It was quite a substantial house, but compact and well-built in early Georgian style, with a pair of bay windows, which must have been added some time later, looking out across the lawns towards the small natural lake that gave the property its name. Despite having been unoccupied for some time, it was generally in good order and Rebecca soon became convinced that it would suit her well.

"It is rather large for me, I will admit, but then, I shall bring some of my staff with me and I have no doubt we shall have visitors to stay," she said cheerfully.

The grounds left something to be desired, it was true, but the house, it was agreed by all, was far from neglected, being both solid and reasonably well appointed, though not extravagantly so. The traditional colour schemes were pleasing enough and though there was not a lot of good furniture, that did not trouble Rebecca, who had a house full of fine furniture in town.

With barns, outhouses, and stables screened from view by a shrubbery and a well-cultivated kitchen garden, it appeared to be a good proposition, and even Catherine's initial reservations began to abate as they walked around the property.

Becky grew more enthusiastic with every step.

Having thanked the caretaker and ascertained that there had been as yet no offers for the place, they determined to go into town on the morrow and meet with the attorney Mr Gunning.

⁂

That evening, Mr Burnett called to see the ladies and report that he had sent a message by telegraph to Mr Gunning indicating Mrs Tate's interest in the property and suggesting an appointment for half past ten.

Becky was most impressed. "Well done, Mr Burnett. I am keen to settle this business. If the lease price is reasonable, I intend to sign up immediately," she said, but Catherine still harboured some doubts.

After dinner, when Lilian and Becky had both simultaneously discovered how tired they were and retired upstairs, leaving them together in the parlour, she expressed her fears to Mr Burnett.

"I do wish I could be as certain as Becky is that this is the right way to proceed. I would hate to think she is doing this only to help me with the school. Should all our plans go awry, I fear she may lose a lot of money," she said anxiously.

Taking her hand in his, he spoke earnestly, trying to reassure her.

"My dear Catherine, it is quite clear to me that your sister is eager and anxious to do this for you, but it must be admitted there is also something in it for her. I do not wish to pry into her private affairs, but am I wrong in assuming that Mrs Tate's marriage is not entirely happy?"

Catherine had no alternative but to tell him of the letter her sister had received from her husband, and so he would understand the reasons for it, she explained also something of the history behind it.

"It was devastating to the entire family. Their paths have diverged ever since Josie's tragic death; my brother-in-law doted on her and has never been able to come to terms with his loss. Poor Becky has been very much alone for many years, which is probably why she wishes to become involved with the school at Hunsford—it will be a new interest," she said.

"Well then," said Mr Burnett reasonably, "though it may initially stem from her distress, it is possible that this may be exactly what Mrs Tate needs to help her cope with her situation. From a practical standpoint, she is possibly well placed to help you and herself. My impression of your sister is that she is both courageous and resilient and is determined not to be daunted by circumstances. Am I right?" he asked.

Catherine nodded, smiling as she realised how very right he was. "You are indeed, but is there not a danger that her intrepid nature will lead her into making decisions she may later regret and may well cause friction between us?"

"Catherine, my dear, I do not believe there is any danger of that. Your sister is as likely to regret assisting you to set up the parish school as I am to regret returning to Rosings Park and finding you again. If it gives her so much pleasure, why set your mind against it?"

This gentle hint was sufficient to change the direction of their conversation, which soon took a turn towards more personal matters.

Catherine had never wished to appear inquisitorial and so had resisted the temptation to ask too many questions about Mr Burnett's return to Rosings Park. However, now that the opportunity presented itself, she was less reluctant to do so. She had occasionally wondered at what point after his return Mr Burnett had rediscovered his interest in her. It was a matter of curiosity to which she addressed her first tentative question.

"Frank, would you consider me very unladylike and silly if I were to ask you to recall for me the moment, or even the day or the week after your return, when you discovered that your feelings for me were unchanged?"

Frank Burnett was genuinely surprised by her question, simply because she had never, until then, interrogated him in the way that younger women were wont to do with their lovers. However, he regained his equanimity very quickly and replied, "No, not at all, why would I? Catherine, you may ask me anything you wish and I would answer you without hesitation. There is nothing naïve or unladylike in your question and you are certainly entitled to ask it.

"As to my feelings, I did not have to rediscover them; they had remained with me. As I told you before, I had found it impossible to so much as feign an interest in anyone else. I will admit that I tried once or twice, quite deliberately, knowing my case was futile, to put you out of my mind altogether, but I was hopelessly unsuccessful."

"And when you returned to Rosings?" she prompted.

"I did so for professional reasons alone. The position offered was too good to turn down and my superior at the museum, who had recommended me to Mr Bingley, advised me to take it. I have no estate and not a great deal of money, except for some savings invested in the funds, which bring me a modest income. I must have employment and need to earn a reasonable salary. I had no other motive at the time. Besides, as far as I knew, you were married to Dr Harrison; I had no idea he was ill," he explained.

Catherine reassured him, "I did not mean to suggest that you had any other motives, but my question goes to the time after Dr Harrison's death, when Lilian and I moved to the Dower House. Did you then continue the association with a view to the future?"

He regarded her gravely as he answered, keen to have her understand the sincerity of his intentions. "I confess I did, and I make no apology for doing so. I am not unaware that many women in our society are left to fend for themselves when widowed. Some are fortunate enough to be well provided for, others are not. Most need some practical help. I had no knowledge of your situation, but I cared enough for you to wish to stay around and if the need arose, offer you my friendship and assistance at least," he explained and seeing her interest, continued.

"For my part, I had discovered soon enough after my return to Rosings that my feelings for you were unchanged—indeed they were if anything deeper than before—but I did not know if you would welcome an association that offered more than friendship. If you did need me, I intended to be there for you. Is that so reprehensible? Do you blame me for hoping?" he sounded somewhat anxious, but she soon set his mind at rest.

"Blame you? Of course not. Nor would I have, had you not done so. I would have assumed that you were occupied with matters of work and quite indifferent to me. I had no claim upon your time or your friendship. But, when they were offered, I will admit I was most grateful. Lilian and I, though we were fairly well provided for materially, had been left very much alone, and if not for the generosity of Mr Darcy and Jonathan Bingley, our lives may have been very different indeed. Mr Adams was eager to help, but being such a young man, I would have been reluctant to impose upon him in any way. Your kindness in offering both friendship and practical advice was deeply appreciated."

"And you suspected nothing of my feelings?" he asked.

"Not at first; indeed, not until I saw my framed picture in your work room at Rosings!" she replied, with a smile.

He threw back his head and laughed, as colour flooded over his face at the memory of his embarrassment. "Ah, that picture! How very badly I felt when you found me out; I had thought that my secret had been so well concealed!" he confessed, still a little awkward at having to admit to that deception.

But his discomfiture was soon replaced by a glow of pleasure when Catherine, in the kindest and most loving words, assured him that having found out his secret, she had discovered within her heart a reawakening of her own feelings for him. Indeed, she admitted, her feelings were far deeper and more intense than anything she had felt in her youth.

"I had not thought it possible for me ever to feel such love as I do now," she confessed and in so doing, provoked a response of such tenderness, as made their shared affection far more rewarding than any association she had known before and ensured that the delightful exercise of reminiscing would be repeated on many other occasions.

Chapter Twenty-two

Their meeting with the attorney Mr Gunning proved to be infinitely simpler than any of them had anticipated.

The gentleman into whose chambers they were ushered by a clerk of some considerable antiquity was Mr Gunning Jr., who had long succeeded his father. Far from being the crusty old lawyer Catherine had feared meeting, he turned out to be a most agreeable young man and a friend of Mr Jonathan Bingley, for whom he claimed he had done some work in the recent past. Having thus established a congenial basis for their business dealings, they were able to conduct their negotiations with a minimum of fuss and with considerable trust in each other.

Young Mr Gunning, conscious of his responsibilities to his client Mr George Grahame, was pleased to deal with Mrs Tate, for whose knowledge and clarity of purpose he soon developed a good deal of respect. When she offered to pay a year's lease in advance, he was absolutely delighted.

An efficient as well as affable fellow, Mr Gunning had the papers drawn up immediately and promised to have the property ready for her inspection and occupation by the first week of September.

Their business concluded, they repaired to a hotel for a light luncheon before returning home to break the good news to Lilian and Mr Adams.

Becky was most excited. To have the place at the beginning of September would mean she would be able to move her furniture and establish her staff there while the weather was still quite mild.

"I should not have liked the prospect of moving things down from town in Winter; besides, it will be nice to be settled in well before Lilian's wedding in October. I can be of some use to you in the preparations for the day, and some of the family can stay with me at Edgewater. Will that not be a good thing? Oh Cathy, I have to confess I am quite delighted with the way things have turned out and all accomplished so simply."

"Becky, are you quite sure about this? You have not jumped in too soon?" asked Catherine, still a little doubtful.

"No, indeed I have not. I have rarely been more certain of anything. Cathy dear, do you not realise that this means I shall be an independent woman at last? I need not depend upon my daughter-in-law's goodwill for a place to stay, I shall be near you and my dear Lilian, and best of all, I shall be here to help with your plans for the school. That is something I shall enjoy very much; indeed, I am reminded of the days when we were young girls, after Papa's death, when Mama moved to Mansfield and set up the school for young ladies there. I used to help her with the accounts and with some of the teaching, and I have never enjoyed anything as much. I was a good teacher, Cathy, would you believe?"

Catherine remembered well. "I certainly would. You were the best educated of us all, and I always said you should have been a teacher; you were very good at explaining things and could read poetry so well…"

"Oh, I can do more than that now; my work with Cassy Darcy and Caroline for the Kympton parish school and library taught me a great deal. Caroline is such a good businesswoman, she insisted that we keep accurate records and maintain the books in perfect order, so I am well able to help you with the accounts for your project. You will need someone to do that, will you not? I cannot imagine that poor Mr Jamison is much good at it, so I will look after the books, while you and Mr Burnett can get on with the plans for the school and whatever other happy arrangements you may have in prospect! Is that agreed?"

Catherine blushed, seeing the mischievous little smirk on her sister's face, but she was grateful for her generous offers of help and her understanding. Though she was still to be entirely convinced by her sister's enthusiasm, she appreciated very much the encouragement Becky gave her.

"Thank you, Becky dear, you are the most generous sister one could have. Of course I shall enjoy having you living in the neighbourhood. I know I shall miss Lilian when she is married—she and Mr Adams are already looking at houses to rent. They do want a place of their own and I hope it will not be too far from here."

Becky smiled. "And what about you, Cathy, have you written to Mama yet about Mr Burnett?" she asked.

"I have; my letter is written and will be in the post tomorrow morning," Catherine replied. "It is time I told Mama everything. I must confess to being a little anxious about her response. She knows so little of Mr Burnett, it may be too much of a shock."

Becky was untroubled. "You may add a postscript asking her to apply to me if she is concerned and I shall tell her what an excellent man he is."

Seeing a look of some surprise upon her sister's face, she added, "No, Cathy, I do not mean to tease you at all, I believe with all my heart that your Mr Burnett is one of the best men I have ever met. You are indeed fortunate to have his love, and I wish you both great happiness."

Catherine was deeply touched. While she had expected Rebecca's understanding of her association with Frank Burnett, she had not anticipated such praise as this. Her eyes, a little tearful, revealed her gratitude as she said, "It is very kind of you to say so, Becky, and I am sure Mama would not disagree, were she to meet him and understand his nature."

"Indeed, she would not. Furthermore, Jonathan Bingley will surely have convinced her of his merits, even if I cannot. You do know she trusts him implicitly," Becky replied.

⁂

When Charlotte Collins received her daughter's letter, she was quite unable to take it all in.

Catherine had written to say that she was engaged to marry a Mr Frank Burnett. Charlotte had heard the name mentioned in passing once or twice but knew nothing of the gentleman himself. It was awhile since she had spent any time at Rosings Park, and she knew little of what had occurred since the catastrophe of the fire. Her own recollections of Rosings dated back to her days at the parsonage at Hunsford with the late Mr Collins and visits to Rosings to accept with gratitude the hospitality and the regular admonitions of Lady Catherine de Bourgh.

Her independent and more active life at Mansfield following her husband's death and later at Longbourn had long subsumed those earlier, less agreeable memories.

Reading the letter through a second time, she noted that Catherine had mentioned that Mr Burnett was known and well liked by Jonathan Bingley, who had been instrumental in appointing him to the position at Rosings Park.

Charlotte decided that she needed to discover more about this Mr Burnett, and it seemed Jonathan Bingley was the man to ask. She sent a servant to Netherfield, with a message for Jonathan, requesting him to call on her at his convenience, as she had a matter of some importance to discuss.

Jonathan Bingley, who had also received a letter from Catherine Harrison, had a shrewd idea why Mrs Collins wished to see him in such a hurry. Taking the note into his wife's sitting room, he read it to her.

"Anna, my love, I do believe Mrs Collins has finally discovered that your cousin Catherine is to wed again."

Anna, who knew her aunt well, was a little concerned at her husband's rather light-hearted remark. "Oh dear, do you suppose Catherine has written to her, too? I do hope my aunt has not learnt of this through some gossiping busybody like Lydia Wickham. That would surely upset her and greatly reduce her enjoyment of Catherine's news."

Anna was genuinely concerned, but her husband was more sanguine.

"I very much doubt that is the case," he said. "Catherine is a very proper person and I cannot believe she would write to tell us of her engagement to Frank Burnett if she had not already informed her mother. But, I think she has told Mrs Collins that I am well acquainted with him, hence this invitation to visit her. Do you not agree?"

On reflection, Anna did agree. She was pleased for her cousin Catherine. She had always had a great deal of admiration for her and though she had regarded the Reverend Dr Harrison with awe, for he was a learned clergyman, Anna had sometimes wished her cousin had married a more lively and interesting man than the eminently respectable, but rather dull, incumbent of Hunsford parish.

That Frank Burnett had proposed to Catherine and been accepted was, to Anna, unarguably good news and she was not reluctant to say so.

"Do you suppose Aunt Charlotte is displeased?" she asked. "Because if she is, I intend to tell her that I think it is a very good match and I am exceedingly happy for Catherine."

Jonathan laughed; he knew his wife well enough to know that she meant it. She would be completely forthright, of that he was certain.

"I cannot think why she should be displeased. Dr Harrison, though he had Lady Catherine's patronage and approval, had neither money nor property and Mrs Collins approved of him. Mr Burnett is no different, except he is an authority on antiquities instead of the scriptures," he said.

His wife went further, "At the very least, he is a man with an interest in art and literature as well; he has a sense of humour and does not suffer from the disadvantage of a narrowness of intellectual attainment, which for me, made conversation with Dr Harrison a great effort," said Anna. "I make no claim to know a great deal about his character, but I have found Mr Burnett to be both amiable and interesting and am prepared to say so. Doubtless, Catherine herself will have vouched for his disposition and character."

Jonathan smiled, "And I have no doubt at all, my love, that with such a fine recommendation, your aunt will need little convincing that Catherine has indeed made the right decision in accepting him."

"And what will you say?" she asked.

Her husband, who had turned away to look out of the window, spoke lightly, "Oh, I am afraid I shall have to tell the truth; the man's an absolute bounder and not to be trusted!"

Anna, even though she knew from his voice that he was teasing, turned round so swiftly to face him and looked so appalled, he was compelled to reassure her immediately.

"Anna, my dear, you know I am joking! Of course I shall say he is a man of excellent education and understanding, who came highly recommended by one of the most distinguished scholars in the land—a curator at the British Museum. I have found him to be thoroughly likeable. He is straightforward and unpretentious in his dealings with me. With both of us so determined to praise him, I do not doubt that your aunt will be well satisfied."

Charlotte Collins lived at Longbourn with Jonathan's daughter Anne-Marie and her husband Mr Colin Elliot, MP. The couple were away in London for the Autumn session of Parliament when Jonathan and his wife called to see Mrs Collins that afternoon. She greeted them cordially and immediately asked for tea to be served.

Charlotte had a very special affection for Jonathan Bingley and his wife, who were always welcome at Longbourn. Harriet, her companion and house-keeper, had set the table for tea in the library, where the fire had been lit and they could talk in private. It was a pretty Autumn afternoon, and Charlotte had asked that the curtains not be closed for a while; she did not go out a great deal now and was glad of the view of the rose garden from the windows. Charlotte had been responsible for planting and tending the roses for many years and still took a great interest in them.

Jonathan and Anna pleased her by admiring her roses, before they sat down to tea and some of Harriet's excellent cake, when Mrs Collins asked, "I suppose you have been wondering why I asked you to call—not that I need a reason to do so, you are always welcome—but I did have a particular question to put to you..."

Jonathan and Anna looked at one another and then Anna put down her cup and said, "Indeed, Aunt, we guessed it might have something to do with the good news we have had from cousin Catherine."

Mrs Collins looked at her and then across the table to Jonathan before saying quietly, "It is exactly because I wished to be certain that it *is* good news that I wished to speak with you. You seem surprised, Anna, but in truth, I have long stopped believing that the mere fact of a woman being married is to be regarded as good news. It was certainly considered to be so, in times past, when I was a young woman and a girl had little else to look forward to if she did not marry. Today, we know different. While I am pleased to hear that Catherine hopes to be happily married to Mr Burnett—her letter certainly assures me that she has no doubt at all of this—I need to be reassured that this is indeed the case."

She sighed and went on, "I have seen too many unfortunate and unhappy marriages—even in our own family we have known much sorrow. There was poor little Josie whose life ended so tragically, and now Becky too has her share of problems; I need not speak of them all, but you will understand my concern, I think. I wish to be reassured that if my dear Catherine is to marry again, it is to a good man, with whom she can hope for a truly happy life."

Jonathan and Anna had remained silent, realising the depth of Charlotte's disquiet. Their own light-hearted conversation earlier that day had failed to take account of her genuine fears. Born and raised in an era when a woman who did not marry was the most unfortunate of creatures and any marriage was likely to be regarded as better than no marriage at all, Charlotte's present concern for her daughters had been forged in the fires of experience. It was no longer enough that a woman should find a respectable man who would marry her and give her a comfortable home. She had at first been content with such a situation herself, but for her own daughter, for Catherine, the child to whom she had bequeathed most of her goodness of heart, her sensible, kind disposition, Charlotte wanted more.

It was with a much greater sense of responsibility that Jonathan now undertook to assure her that to his knowledge, Mr Frank Burnett was in every way a good and honourable man, who had loved her daughter for nigh on twenty-five years and was deeply and sincerely devoted to making her happy.

Charlotte Collins seemed startled. "What do you mean he has loved her for all these years? Were they acquainted before he came to Rosings last year?" she asked, and Jonathan knew then that Catherine had not revealed to her mother the entire story of their relationship, as she had told it to him and Anna. It became then his task to enlighten her, gently and honestly.

Charlotte listened as he spoke and asked a few questions. "Am I to understand that he had this strong affection for her but for some reason was not able to speak of it? Why was this? Was there some impediment?"

Jonathan nodded, "Yes, and if you will permit me, Mrs Collins, I will explain. The reason that Frank Burnett never approached Catherine directly was that Lady Catherine de Bourgh, who was then his employer and under whose protection Catherine lived at Rosings, decided that it was not to be. She expressly forbade the continuation of their friendship, which as far as Catherine knew was all it was at the time, for Mr Burnett had said not a word to her of love or marriage. Her Ladyship threatened to dismiss Mr Burnett from his position as librarian if he pursued the matter and told him that Catherine was already spoken for, which was, of course, clearly not true. Mr Harrison had not even taken up the position at Hunsford at that time, and it was many years later that he made an offer for Catherine's hand. Lady Catherine was the only impediment."

The expression on Charlotte's countenance and the tears that welled in her eyes said it all. She could not speak for several minutes, and when she did, her voice was soft and sad.

"It was not right. Lady Catherine has been very good to our family and particularly generous to Catherine, but I have to say she had no right to interfere. She should have referred Mr Burnett to me. I am Cathy's mother and I should have been told of his feelings for her. Poor Catherine, she has never told me any of this."

Both Jonathan and Anna indicated as best they could that Catherine had not suffered very greatly at the time, because there had been no romance, no broken engagement, for no such words had ever been spoken between them. Anna said gently that Catherine had revealed that there had been only a warm friendship, which might have developed into love.

But Charlotte shook her head. "That may be so, and yet, do you not see, that were it not for Lady Catherine's unjustifiable intervention, he may have told her he loved her, and asked her to marry him and she may or may not have accepted him; whatever the outcome, it would have been Catherine's choice to make. Catherine should have had the chance to make that choice. I do not mean to cast any aspersions upon Dr Harrison, but she may never have married him had she known earlier of Mr Burnett's intentions. Indeed, they may well have been happily married long before Dr Harrison appeared on the scene at Rosings."

Charlotte appeared to be both tired and unhappy as she spoke. "So many years have been spent—I shall not say wasted, for there have clearly been blessings—but spent apart, without the affection and comfort they may have given each other. It is most unfair and a cruel thing to have done," she said and there was no doubting the sadness in her voice.

Unromantic she may have been, but Charlotte was far from lacking in sensibility, and it was clear she was keenly aware of Catherine's loss.

Turning once more to Jonathan Bingley, she said, more seriously, "Thank you, Jonathan, for being open with me. No doubt Catherine did not wish to dwell upon the past and bring sadness where there should be only joy, but I appreciate your telling me the truth. I shall write to Catherine and tell her I have spoken with you and, having done so, wish her every happiness. If, as you say, Mr Frank Burnett is a good man, educated and cultured as well, and has loved her for so long, I am confident they will be happy together. Catherine certainly deserves it."

Charlotte's letter arrived at the Dower House, bringing much happiness to her daughter, who had harboured a few doubts as to her mother's willingness to accept Frank Burnett without having known him at all. It was a great relief to her to learn that she was pleased to do so, and Catherine knew she must owe some part of that comfort to Jonathan Bingley and his wife.

When she showed Frank Burnett her mother's letter, he was elated. While modesty prevented him from accepting all that was implied in it of his goodness of character and conduct, he too acknowledged the role of Mr Bingley. "We do owe him a considerable debt of gratitude, my love, not only for his kindness in convincing your mother of my suitability, but in having brought us together in the first place. Were it not for his good offices, we may never have met again. I would have continued my work at the museum in London, while you remained here alone," he said, and Catherine, to whom even the contemplation of such a melancholy prospect was anathema, realised that with every day his affection grew more important to her. She smiled and agreed that Jonathan Bingley certainly held a very special place in their hearts.

"He is one of the best men I have known; I am happy indeed that you and he are good friends already," she said.

❧

Some days later, two letters were received at Pemberley for Mrs Darcy.

Although they came from different counties, one from Hertfordshire and the other from Kent, Elizabeth found them to be remarkably similar in content.

She opened first the letter from her dear friend Charlotte Collins, who, having first asked after the health of herself and Mr Darcy, proceeded to break the news that her eldest daughter Catherine, who had been widowed last year, had become engaged to a Mr Frank Burnett.

Considering that Charlotte had had no knowledge at all of this Mr Burnett and had never before mentioned the prospect of Catherine marrying again, Elizabeth was somewhat surprised at the very matter-of-fact manner in which she had written.

I know, my dear Eliza, she wrote, *that you will share my joy at Catherine's decision to marry again, for she is too young and active to live alone for the rest of her days, especially now that Lilian is about to leave the nest.*

Elizabeth could not but agree as she read on:

I am assured by Jonathan Bingley that Mr Frank Burnett is a man of excellent character, who I understand has loved Catherine for many years, but was prevented from making her an offer in the most extraordinary circumstances.

And so, in summary, Mrs Collins proceeded to tell her friend the tale of thwarted love that Jonathan and Anna Bingley had revealed to her. Clearly, it had affected her deeply, for in writing to Elizabeth, she expressed not only her appreciation of Mr Burnett's conduct but did not omit to censure in the strongest terms her late husband's patron, Lady Catherine de Bourgh.

It is surely a very cruel thing to deliberately set out to thwart the course of such an attachment and to deny two young people (as they then were) the pleasure of one another's love, for no good reason. Yet, to judge by her conduct towards you and Mr Darcy on an earlier occasion, conduct of which we have often spoken in a lighter vein, it would seem to me that Lady Catherine had no scruples on that score and had learned nothing from the failure of her previous schemes.

Though Elizabeth was surprised at the vehemence of her words, she could not resist a chuckle at the memory of Lady Catherine's crude attempt to separate Mr Darcy from her and the totally unintended but delightful consequences that had flowed from it. Indeed, the result had been the very reverse of her expectations. Quite clearly, as a matchmaker, or even a match breaker, Her Ladyship could not lay claim to a high rate of success, she thought with a smile. Still, there was the matter of her plans for Catherine, and the hurt she may well have caused.

Elizabeth picked up the letter from Catherine Harrison, knowing even before she had opened it what news it would contain.

Catherine wrote more delicately, seeking chiefly to acquaint Mr and Mrs

Darcy, for whom she had the highest regard and warmest affection, with the news of her recent engagement and to invite them to meet Mr Frank Burnett when they attended Lilian's wedding. She was confident they would find him a man of excellent character and of their hopes for marital happiness, she declared, she had no doubt at all.

We have too may interests in common ever to be bored with one another's company and have no reason to believe that the deep affection we share will not deliver lasting happiness.

In a touching tribute to her mother, she added:

I am truly delighted that Mama has given us her blessing; it will greatly enhance our pleasure and bring a measure of comfort to her as well. I am aware that she has been concerned for my future welfare since Dr Harrison's death last year.

I know that you and Mr Darcy will wish us joy; your own felicitous union has been an example to us all these many years. I am aware from what Mama has told me in the past that Lady Catherine strenuously disapproved of your marriage and strove fiercely to prevent it. She did likewise when she forbade Mr Burnett to propose to me those many years ago and did succeed in separating us, for a time. It would seem that her disapproval only served to guarantee your happiness, and I pray it will have a similar effect upon ours.

Mr Burnett and I look forward very much to seeing you when you attend Lilian's wedding next month.

Taking both letters, Elizabeth went downstairs and out across the lawn to find her husband, who had left her after breakfast to fulfill a promise to take his two grandsons fishing.

She found them by the lake. The boys were concentrating so well upon their sport, they hardly noticed her arrival, but Mr Darcy beckoned to her to join them. Sitting down beside him, Elizabeth handed him her letters one by one and watched for his response.

As he read Charlotte's letter, his face remained calm, though he did express some exasperation on reaching the paragraph in which she wrote of the manner in which his aunt had interfered in Catherine's life.

"My aunt was truly incorrigible! This is most high-handed," he said in a voice that suggested suppressed anger. "Mrs Collins is absolutely right. It was to her that Frank Burnett should have been referred; Lady Catherine, by inviting Miss Collins to stay at Rosings, had not acquired the right to usurp the place of her mother."

Elizabeth nodded in agreement but said nothing, handing him Catherine's note. She could not fail to see how her words moved him. Twice he stopped and shook his head, as if unable to believe what he had just read. When he read the lines about her separation from Mr Burnett for many years, he put down the letter, his face dark and melancholy.

"Elizabeth, I must confess I had not thought Lady Catherine could be as cruel as this. I was well aware of her fixed and often prejudiced views on matters pertaining to marriage, and I have heard her express them frankly and in a way that often embarrassed me. But, that she should have used her influence over a young person living as a guest under her roof, to detach her from a perfectly reasonable young man, who wished to make her an offer of marriage, is unconscionable," he continued in a grave voice. "There was clearly no objective reason to reject Mr Burnett—he was respectable and well educated, worthy in every way, except he did not meet with my aunt's approval. It was an appalling error of judgment.

"It puts me in mind of Lady Catherine's stubborn attitude towards her own daughter. On realising that her plans for Miss de Bourgh could not be fulfilled, my aunt determined to keep her to herself, a hostage to wealth and prestige, living subject to her mother's will, in a palatial mansion that might well have been her prison. Bereft of real friends and unable even to choose her own companions, hers was a lonely life, from which there was no relief, until her mother's death.

"In the case of Miss Collins and Mr Burnett, the fault is compounded by her misrepresentation of Catherine's situation to Mr Burnett, falsely claiming that she had been spoken for. Doubtless she intended by this deception to keep Catherine at Rosings at her convenience. It is quite outrageous!

"Lizzie my dear, I wish there was something I could do, even at this late stage, to make amends for the grievous wrong they have both suffered at the hands of my aunt."

Elizabeth listened, understanding his anger but not wishing to exacerbate his indignation by further censure of his aunt's conduct. She did, however, make it quite clear that she did not believe he should feel any guilt on Lady Catherine's account.

"Pray do not blame yourself, dearest, you are in no way culpable, and while I understand your sense of outrage, it is not a matter for which anyone other than Lady Catherine was responsible. Neither Catherine nor Charlotte would ever say otherwise, I am certain of it."

He was grateful for her understanding, but Elizabeth knew him well enough to realise that it would not satisfy him.

※

Later, after they had returned to the house and the boys had gone upstairs, Mr Darcy retired to the library for the rest of the afternoon.

His wife had decided to rest awhile before dressing for dinner; their daughter Cassandra and her husband Dr Richard Gardiner were to dine at Pemberley that evening, and Elizabeth looked forward to breaking the news about Catherine's engagement. She knew Cassy shared her affection for Catherine. She was about to rise and ring for her maid when Mr Darcy entered the room.

"Elizabeth my dear," he said, "I should like your opinion on a matter of some importance."

His wife knew both from the tone of his voice and the fact that he had called her Elizabeth, that something serious was afoot.

In his hand was a letter, which he held out to her.

"I am writing to Mr Burnett to offer him the position of manager of the Rosings Trust."

Ignoring the look of astonishment that crossed her face, he continued, "It's a matter I have been considering for some time. I have raised the subject with Jonathan and he has agreed that it would be useful for the Trust to have a permanent manager on the estate, but we had not begun to consider whom to appoint to the position. I believe Mr Burnett would do very well; he is well qualified and has a thorough knowledge of the place. In addition to an appropriate income, it will entitle him to a residence within the estate. I shall propose that when they are married, Catherine and her husband continue to live at the

Dower House. With Catherine's interest in the parish school, it will be, I think, an ideal solution. It will mean they will have a place of their own for as long as they stay on at Rosings Park."

Looking directly at his wife, he asked, "What do you think, Lizzie?"

He was clearly eager to have her approval and approval he received in full measure, for Elizabeth understood how keenly her husband had felt the callousness of his aunt's actions. This was his way of ameliorating, in some practical manner, the hurt she had caused all those years ago.

Elizabeth spared no words in warmly supporting his generous impulse, for she more than anyone knew his feelings and understood his true nature. Yet he continued to surprise her with the extent of his generosity.

"I intend to write to Jonathan, too, and tell him what I propose. He will need to make the formal arrangements and have the necessary documents drawn up. I am certain he will concede that it is both fitting and fair; do you not agree, my dear?" he asked and once again, she agreed completely.

"Indeed I do, I know that you will not rest until you are satisfied that enough has been done to make amends for Lady Catherine's cruel interference in their lives. You are being very generous, and I would not have expected you to be otherwise. I have no doubt that Jonathan will be of the same mind, and if I may say so, my dear, both Catherine and Mr Burnett should be absolutely delighted with your proposition."

❧

On the following day, the mail carried two letters from Mr Darcy and one from Elizabeth. The former, directed to Frank Burnett and Jonathan Bingley, set in train Mr Darcy's proposal, while the latter conveyed Elizabeth's thoughts to her friend Charlotte Collins.

Amidst the many happy sentiments expressed regarding the news of Catherine's engagement and the forthcoming marriage of Lilian Harrison to Mr Adams, Elizabeth wrote also of the feelings of outrage that she and Mr Darcy had experienced on learning of the duplicity of Lady Catherine de Bourgh's dealings with Frank Burnett and young Catherine Collins.

Dear Charlotte, she wrote, *how I wish you had been with us today to see for yourself how deeply and grievously wounded Mr Darcy feels on learning of the utterly intolerable conduct of his aunt towards Catherine and Mr Burnett.*

I too was shocked, but thanks to my previous experience with Her Ladyship, not as much as my dear husband, whose sense of decency and family honour seem to have been outraged by this news.

So keenly does he feel it, he is determined to recompense the couple in some way and has proposed a scheme which will, I am sure, please them and meet with your approval as well.

Having explained, in confidence, the proposition that Mr Darcy had put to Mr Burnett, Elizabeth expressed her belief that both Catherine and Frank Burnett would welcome the prospect of continuing their valuable work at Rosings.

I am quite convinced that it will afford them the opportunity to achieve what they have both set their hearts on: a new and happy life together.

Nor could she resist one final derisive comment:

It will not be without some degree of irony, dear Charlotte, that we can look forward to seeing the couple agreeably established at the Dower House in Rosings Park in the future; a circumstance, I think you will agree, that would surely have left Lady Catherine de Bourgh "seriously displeased"!

Chapter Twenty-three

WHO CAN BE IN any doubt of what was to follow?

Preparations for Lilian's wedding were well advanced when Mr Darcy's letter was received by Mr Burnett, and upon his arriving with it in hand at the Dower House, both he and Catherine were thrown into such a state of confusion, a mixture of surprise and gratification, they were quite unable to concentrate upon the tasks at hand.

Catherine had long known of Mr Darcy's generosity of spirit; her mother had spoken of it often when they were children, she said.

"When Mr Darcy was first introduced to the community around Meryton in Hertfordshire, where my mother lived, he was widely regarded as proud and arrogant, with few virtues save for his considerable wealth. But he then fell in love with Mama's dearest friend, Elizabeth Bennet, and the transformation of his character that followed their marriage was, Mama says, quite remarkable. She now deems him to be one of the most generous and thoughtful men she has had the good fortune to meet," she explained.

"And does she credit Miss Elizabeth Bennet with effecting this remarkable change in his nature?" asked Mr Burnett, with some degree of amusement, to which Catherine replied cautiously, "Not entirely, I think. In spite of the general opinion amongst people in Meryton, who deemed Mr Darcy to be haughty and ill natured, Mama believes he was much misunderstood; she says he was, in reality, exceedingly shy and often gave offence without meaning to do so. Miss Bennet certainly influenced that aspect of his character, making him more open and amiable, but in most essentials I believe he remained as he had always been—a generous and honourable gentleman. Mama certainly thinks so."

Seeing Mr Burnett's interest, she added, "It is a view I am able to confirm from my own experience of his consideration and kindness to us, since the fire at Rosings and the ill health and death of Dr Harrison. No one could have done more, and in this offer to you, we have proof of it once again."

Frank Burnett had little knowledge of this side of Mr Darcy's character, knowing him only as a respected member of the Rosings Trust, whose knowledge and authority on matters pertaining to the estate were always well regarded. Jonathan Bingley clearly held him in high esteem. That Mr Darcy should choose to offer him a position of such responsibility was an unexpected honour, one Mr Burnett was delighted to accept.

Catherine was quite certain it was an indication that Mr Darcy trusted Frank Burnett and endorsed her own opinion of him.

"It is his way of indicating that he approves of you," she said and he teased her, declaring that surely she did not need Mr Darcy's blessing to marry him.

"Certainly not," she retorted with a smile, "but it does please me to have it and I am very proud of you, for it is not often that Mr Darcy bestows such wholehearted approval upon any person. It proves how well he regards you and how much he values your work at Rosings. He is a gentleman for whose character and judgment I have the greatest respect, and his good opinion is therefore doubly valuable."

While this interpretation pleased Mr Burnett well enough, he was far too sensible to be flattered by it and in his response, argued that it was chiefly the warm affection that Mr and Mrs Darcy felt for Catherine that must have prompted the generous offer to him. But she would have none of this and was determined to establish her point.

"No, Frank, I cannot accept that. While I know that Mr and Mrs Darcy, as dear friends of Mama's, would have some affection for me and for Lilian, it is not believable that such feelings alone would persuade Mr Darcy to offer you such an important position at Rosings. He is imbued with a very strong sense of responsibility as the chief trustee and would not have appointed you unless in his judgment, you were the right person for the job. I am convinced that Mr Darcy's decision was based upon a good deal more than affection for myself," she said decisively, unwittingly expressing the truth of the matter.

Even mature and sensible lovers are sometimes inclined to spend time in trivial controversy, and since this pair were no exception, they became engaged in several minutes of debate, before they could settle upon an explanation that pleased them both. When they did, it was done with an agreeable degree of humour and fondness.

Frank Burnett was willing to be amenable. He asked, "Then, will you have me accept that, not only is Mr Darcy a benevolent gentleman, who wishes to ensure your continuing comfort, but he is also a shrewd man of business, who has decided to offer me this position believing that it will ultimately prove beneficial to the Rosings estate?"

"Certainly, I do believe that to be the case; he would not do otherwise," replied Catherine confidently.

"And do you also contend that Mr Darcy, being a good judge of character, is confident that I will carry out all the duties of the position to his entire satisfaction?" he persisted.

"Indeed I do, else he is unlikely to have made you the offer," she concluded, with a clear assumption of winning the point.

But she was generous in victory. "I must add, my dear Frank, that I am exceedingly happy that you have understood my argument exactly. That with so little disputation we have reached agreement on this matter augurs well for our future, I think. I pray we shall always be able to resolve our differences so amicably," she said, unable to conceal a playful smile, which immediately put him in mind of the bright young person he had met at Rosings many years ago.

Frank Burnett, who had waited a very long time for the felicitous relationship he now enjoyed with Catherine, found no difficulty in convincing her of his complete confidence that their marriage would bring them both harmony and happiness in good measure.

"Dearest Catherine, how could it be otherwise? In all the years of our separation from one another, I confess I have striven to suppress my feelings for you, when I thought you were out of my reach, but never was I able to forget you nor did I wish you were different in any way. Every aspect of you that I could recall, your sincerity, your clear-eyed honesty, your complete lack of affectation,

I recalled them all with the greatest affection. On returning to Rosings, I found that my memory of you was in every way commensurate with what you now were, only more so. The young girl I had fallen in love with and had tried to forget was now a woman I could never leave.

"Now, on the verge of having what I have longed for, I know I am truly blessed with such happiness as I had never hoped to find. No trivial disputation will ever erode its value. All this, my dearest, I owe to you."

Such a heartfelt declaration brought Catherine close to tears, and abandoning her teasing, she was able instead to indulge in a warm and affectionate exchange of promises that confirmed their hopes for future happiness.

Lilian's wedding brought many members of the families together at Rosings Park.

Jonathan Bingley and his family, arriving from Hertfordshire, brought with them Lilian's grandmother, Mrs Charlotte Collins, while Mr and Mrs Darcy were accompanied by their son-in-law Sir Richard Gardiner and their daughter Cassandra, for whom both Lilian and her mother had the highest admiration. They were deeply honoured that they had all accepted their invitations and travelled down to Kent for the occasion.

But perhaps the most welcome of all their guests was Lilian's elder brother Matthew. His unexpected arrival, on account of his ship having to return to England following the sudden death at sea of her captain, brought both joy and tears. Lilian was overwhelmed to have her brother home to see her wed.

For Catherine too, the return of her son, to whom she had been trying to write without success, brought relief. Now, he could meet Frank Burnett before being told that his mother was to marry the gentleman.

With both her older children away overseas for many years, Catherine had grown particularly close to her youngest daughter. With Matthew home on leave, it was possible to feel again the pleasure of having most of her family around her. Catherine's happiness was almost complete.

On Lilian's wedding day, it was clear to her mother that she was entering the marital state with more than the simple optimism of youth. In the year since her father's death, Lilian had grown in maturity; combining both good sense and sensibility, she had been a source of much comfort to Catherine. Yet, she had a degree of independence and had demonstrated clearly an intelligent awareness of her own circumstances.

Young and eager for romance, she had accepted the proposal of marriage from John Adams in good faith, looking to the future with confidence, while giving every indication of understanding all the practical implications of her situation. Catherine enjoyed seeing her daughter's graduation to young woman-hood and wished she'd had some of Lilian's self-assurance in her youth.

She confessed as much to her sister as they stood a little apart from the guests, who crowded around the young couple.

"Becky, had I possessed even half her confidence, I should never have been intimidated by Lady Catherine. I would have been less easily persuaded that she knew what was best for me... I may even have ignored her advice, when she declared it would be most imprudent to let Mr Burnett believe that I may welcome his attentions. Indeed, had I done as I felt inclined to do at the time, he may well have proposed and I may have accepted him all those years ago... all those wasted years..."

As her sister turned to regard her, she added quietly, "He loved me then, Becky, and has ever since. Think how very different my life would have been had matters been permitted to run their course. But I was too young and compliant, never self-assured or strong enough to contest Her Ladyship's injunctions. I can blame no one but myself for my loss."

Becky knew well the dangers of encouraging such dismal thoughts on the morning of Lilian's wedding; her sister could easily lapse into melancholy and that would never do. Tightening her fingers around Catherine's, she said quietly, "And if you had done, have you considered that you would not have been here, on this perfect morning, watching your lovely young daughter arrive at the church on the arm of her handsome brother? Have you thought of that, Catherine? Looking at your children, would you really have it different?"

Startled by the thought, Catherine wrenched her mind away from contem-plating the past to confront the present, saying with some vigour, "Certainly not, Becky, my children have been my entire world for many years. I have no regrets on that score, and though I dearly love Frank, it is my belief that I could not have loved him then, as well or as deeply as I do now, as he deserves to be loved. I was too callow and inexperienced in the ways of the world and whilst I may have been happy and enjoyed the romance of it, as a young girl would, I seriously doubt if I could have appreciated his true worth, for he is an exceptional man, Becky."

Becky listened with interest; Catherine had never spoken so openly of her feelings before. She recalled the calm, almost matter-of-fact manner in which her sister had announced the news of her engagement to Dr Harrison. It had surprised both Becky and their younger sister, Amelia-Jane, that Catherine was not more excited by the prospect of marriage and she had said as much at the time to her friend Emily Gardiner.

"I cannot believe she is so unmoved by it, Emily; yet she says she loves him. Is it possible?" Becky had said, but Emily had supposed that Catherine, who was almost twenty-nine at the time, may have been too sedate and proper to show her true feelings.

"I do not think she would have agreed to marry him if she did not love him, Becky," she had said, reassuring her young friend.

Yet, here she was, twenty years older, genteel, wise, and unquestionably much more serene in every way, but confessing her deep love for Frank Burnett and clearly exhilarated by the thought of marrying him.

It was a remarkable conversion and Becky could not but marvel at the change in her sister.

"He has profoundly transformed my life, Becky," Catherine admitted. "I do not mean in matters of art and literature alone, to which he has certainly opened my eyes; he has taught me also to look beyond the here and now, not to regard everything and everyone so seriously. I have learnt to laugh at others and at myself; he even lets me laugh at him! I could never have laughed at Dr Harrison, I was far too much in awe of him," she confessed and continued more softly, "Perhaps most particularly, he has taught me to enjoy the warmth and joy of loving, as I never have before. I was unaware of it, but I have never known what it is to love someone deeply, apart from my children, of course, and receive all of their love in return. It is quite a revelation to me. In past times, when my life seemed dull, I would hope for a better day on the morrow; with Frank, that day is a reality today. I owe him all this and whilst I still deplore Lady Catherine's deviousness in separating us, now that we are so delightfully reunited, I have no recriminations."

Becky was astonished by her magnanimity.

As the sisters turned to one another and smiled, the newly wedded couple moved out into the sunlit garden, surrounded by their guests, all wishing them well, and Becky saw Catherine's eyes fill with tears.

Frank Burnett, who, having carried out his duties as best man, had chosen to remain discreetly in the background, seeing Catherine and Rebecca, moved to join them.

As he approached, suddenly Catherine reached for her handkerchief.

He saw her tears; unaware that they were other than the customary and predictable tears of the mother of the bride, he smiled and offered her his arm. "Shall we join the throng around the happy pair?" he asked, to which she replied, "Indeed, and share some of their joy."

Becky smiled and watched them go, confident that her sister's future happiness was secure.

∼❦∼

Her own prospects for contentment were looking somewhat brighter, too.

On the previous evening, Elizabeth and Mr Darcy, together with Jonathan Bingley and his wife Anna, had visited her at Edgewater.

It had been an unexpected pleasure to show them around the property and hear both Mr Darcy and Jonathan comment favourably upon her decision to lease it. Lizzie too had seemed more amiable and friendly towards her; a rare circumstance indeed, for they had barely spoken since the dread-filled days of Josie's illness and death.

Having admired the house and seen something of the grounds, which they all agreed needed further work, they had repaired to the sitting room and taken tea together as they talked of the plans for the parish school. Jonathan and Mr Darcy had been interested as Becky had explained, with enthusiasm, her desire to help her sister with the project.

"I believe I could be of assistance with keeping the accounts, leaving Cathy with more time to organise the teaching," said Rebecca and Mr Darcy had expressed his appreciation, commending her on her decision.

Elizabeth had made mention of her previous work at Mansfield, reminding everyone that Becky had been a very successful and popular teacher at her mother's school for young ladies.

"I can see no reason why you should not teach the girls, too, Becky," she had said. "Your mama always believed that you were her best teacher."

Becky had coloured at such praise, especially coming from Elizabeth; yet she was clearly pleased to be so complimented. Perhaps, she thought hopefully, Lizzie had decided to regard her with a friendlier eye than before.

As the wedding celebrations drew to a close, the Darcys and their party prepared to leave for London, where they would stay overnight prior to returning to Derbyshire. Their carriage waited for them, but before they left the house, Mr and Mrs Darcy invited the rest of the family to join them at Pemberley for Christmas.

"It is quite some time since we have all been together at Christmas," said Elizabeth. "Georgiana and Dr Grantley will be with us, too, and we are looking forward to it very much. You are all welcome to join us at Pemberley on Christmas Eve."

Catherine noted that Mrs Darcy had turned especially to Becky as she spoke, particular to include her in the general invitation. She was delighted, knowing the hurt that her sister had suffered.

In happier times, Becky Tate had been a particular friend of Cassy Darcy's; both young women being about the same age, they had also shared many common interests. But this had ended when, contrary to Elizabeth's hopes, young Julian Darcy had married Becky's daughter, Josie. As their marriage had crumbled, the entire family, except perhaps their mother Charlotte, who was Elizabeth's special friend, had felt the coldness that had come between Lizzie and Rebecca. The terrible circumstances of Josie's death had only exacerbated the situation to the point where they had hardly spoken except in formal terms.

Now, it seemed as if Elizabeth had decided to end their prolonged estrangement. It was especially pleasing to Catherine that she had chosen to do so on Lilian's wedding day.

Catherine's own happiness at the courtesy shown to Frank Burnett by both Mr and Mrs Darcy was enhanced by the hope of a rapprochement between Becky and Elizabeth. She loved her sister and had the highest regard for Elizabeth; that they could be friends again was a source of great satisfaction to her. Looking across at her sister, she caught her eye and smiled; clearly Becky was pleased, too.

When the wedded couple had departed on their honeymoon and the last of the guests had left, the two sisters retired upstairs to Catherine's room.

Weary from the long day, they kicked off their shoes, shed their fine gowns for loose robes, and lay on the bed, as they had done when they were young girls, returning from a formal function at Rosings or a boring afternoon in church, attended dutifully but with reluctance.

Becky could recall clearly the intimacy they had shared, when more often than not, she would confide and Catherine would counsel caution. Often they would indulge in girlish gossip and laughter until their mother came to urge them to be quiet. This time, there would be no one to reprimand them.

Becky announced that she had brought her sister a "wedding present purchased in Paris"!

"A present from Paris?" Catherine exclaimed and was urged to open it. When she did, she found within a pretty confection of silk and lace, embellished with ribbons, and as she held it up and looked at it, she glanced at her sister in some bewilderment and asked, "Becky, are you sure you have not made a mistake? Is this not a gown for Lilian?"

At which Becky broke into peals of laughter, further confusing her sister, until she said, "Oh no, Cathy, it is not a gown for Lilian, it is a *nightgown* for *you!*"

The depth and extent of the blush that suffused Catherine's countenance and flowed down her neck and shoulders was proof enough that no such thought had even entered her head.

"A nightgown?" she cried and Becky replied, "Indeed, a nightgown for your honeymoon. You cannot go away to Europe on your wedding journey and wear the white cotton homemade things you wore at the rectory at Hunsford, Cathy—it will not do."

There followed protestations from Catherine and much teasing and laughter about the nightwear she was accustomed to wearing and warnings that she must remember that Mr Burnett is not a clergyman, after which they subsided gradually into a more subdued mood.

The sounds of the servants downstairs, clearing away the debris from the wedding breakfast, receded as they lay there, cocooned in a comfortable silence, each deep in her own thoughts.

After some time, Catherine, turning over to regard her sister with serious eyes, asked in a quiet, tentative voice, "Becky, am I right... is it better now between you and Lizzie after all this time?"

Her sister spoke, lying flat on her back, her eyes closed.

"Yes, it has been a long time; I felt that she never understood my pain at losing Josie, she could think only of Julian. But I do believe Lizzie means us to be friends again. Perhaps, now that Julian is married again happily, she no longer blames me for his sorrow as she used to do. I am glad and I shall certainly behave as though this is the case. I bear her no grudge."

"I am glad, too; Mama would like that, too," said Catherine. "Shall you go to Pemberley at Christmas then?" she asked, hoping Becky would say yes.

She was not disappointed.

"I probably shall. I cannot imagine that it will serve any useful purpose to refuse. Besides, what would I do alone down here? I might as well enjoy the hospitality of Pemberley and let Lizzie see that as far as I am concerned, the past is over and forgotten," said Becky, opening her eyes and regarding her sister. Then, raising herself on an elbow to look at Catherine, she asked, "And you, Cathy? Tell me, are you going to be very happy with your dear Mr Burnett?"

Looking directly up into her sister's eyes, Catherine replied, "Oh yes, I am. I intend to be very happy with my dear Mr Burnett, that at least I can promise you, Becky. I have never been more certain of anything in my life."

This time, there were no tears, only the blessed laughter that comes from deeply felt affection and contentment.

END OF PART FIVE

An Epilogue . . .

TWO WEEKS LATER, WITH Lilian and Mr Adams still away on their wedding journey and young Matthew Harrison having returned to his ship, Catherine and Rebecca travelled to Hertfordshire to join their mother at Longbourn.

Frank Burnett had already arrived at Netherfield House, at the invitation of Mr and Mrs Bingley. Enjoying there the comfortable elegance of their home, he could not fail to contrast the gracious life at Netherfield Park with the stiff formality that had been imposed upon everyone in the domain of Lady Catherine de Bourgh.

An informal reception had been arranged, hosted by Jonathan and Anna Bingley, to celebrate the wedding of Catherine and Frank in the presence of a small gathering of close family and friends. Catherine's mother, aunt, and cousins, the Faulkners and Elliots, attended, while Frank Burnett's sister travelled down from Newcastle for the occasion and was so delighted with Catherine that she could not cease telling her brother what a fortunate man he was to be marrying such a lovely woman.

"We had quite given up hope that Frank would ever marry," she declared. "We thought he'd decided to remain a bachelor for the rest of his life," as Frank and Catherine smiled and said nothing.

The day turned out exactly as the couple had wished it to be.

Catherine's marriage to Dr Harrison had been celebrated at Rosings, with

Lady Catherine generously hosting the impressive function, presiding imperiously over the wedding breakfast attended by guests from around the county and beyond, many of whom were quite unknown to the bride or her immediate family.

Apart from the scent of hundreds of roses, Catherine's recollections were of a long day with many formalities, meeting and greeting dozens of Lady Catherine's distinguished guests, which had left her quite exhausted. There had been no time for a honeymoon; Dr Harrison had an important report to write for the bishop, who was visiting the diocese. Consequently, they had gone directly to the parsonage at Hunsford and on the following morning, being Sunday, she had accompanied her husband to morning service. The solemn faces of the congregation had matched her own mood of serious sobriety, as she had contemplated her future as the wife of the parson of Hunsford parish. Later they had travelled to Bath for a week's stay with Dr Harrison's family.

This time, it was quite different.

On awakening, Catherine had felt an unusual degree of elation, for which she could find no logical explanation except it was the day she was to marry Frank Burnett. Looking out across the unfamiliar lawns, the small park at Longbourn, pretty but quite unlike the grand grounds at Rosings, she wondered at her own excitement. She had to remind herself that she was not a young bride going to her groom. She had been married before and had three children, yet she could neither deny nor explain the tumult that assailed her as she thought what the day would bring.

Catherine had no recollection of any similar feelings experienced before her marriage to Dr Harrison. In fact, she recalled, she had been calm, astonishingly so, as she had prepared for the wedding.

Catching sight of her reflection in the long mirror, she stopped to look critically at herself. Unlike her sisters Rebecca and Amelia-Jane, Catherine had not been in the habit of paying much attention to her looks, yet she had been fortunate enough to be blessed with a clear complexion and fine features, which together contributed to the impression of a handsome, slender woman, whose appearance belied her years. On that particular morning, the impression was enhanced by a gentle flush upon her cheeks and eyes bright with the anticipation of happiness.

Catherine was quite content with her appearance, yet could not help wondering how the man who would soon be her husband might see her. For a brief moment, she worried that he might still retain an image of the fresh young girl he had loved many years ago, occasioning inevitable disappointment, but the thought passed quickly as she recalled his recent ardent expressions of affection. He had arranged that they would travel to Europe after the wedding, and Catherine smiled, recalling Becky's gift, which her sister had ensured was packed into her case for the journey.

The arrival of her maid Sally with breakfast interrupted Catherine's reverie and returned her to the practicalities of the moment.

"There is a message from Mr Bingley, ma'am," the girl said as she drew back the curtains and prepared to pour out tea for her mistress. "He will be here with the carriage at half past ten to accompany you to the church."

Catherine thanked her; she had been awake early, there was plenty of time. The girl left the room, promising to return to help Catherine dress and put up her hair. Her pleasure at seeing her mistress in her wedding gown, a simple, elegant garment of cream silk, brought tears to her eyes as she said, "You look lovely, ma'am—I hope you will be very happy."

When Jonathan Bingley called at Longbourn in his carriage to escort her to church, Catherine came downstairs. She felt a quick rush of blood to her cheeks as she strove to calm her racing heart, hoping to conceal from Jonathan her excitement.

Arriving at the small parish church at Netherfield, a more intimate, less awesome setting than the grand chapel at Rosings had been, she was more composed, but Jonathan was clearly aware of her agitation. Helping her from the vehicle, he took her hand and pressed it, as if to reassure her. Meeting his eyes, wordlessly she expressed her gratitude as she took his arm and prepared to enter the church.

Waiting for her at the church, Frank Burnett endeavoured to subdue his feelings. Since realising that he was in love with young Catherine Collins, in vain, as it turned out, he had spent many years with no hope at all of making her his wife.

More recently, on finding her again, first married to Dr Harrison and then widowed, there had been months of uncertainty and trepidation, during which he had feared he would betray his feelings and lose both her friendship and regard. When she had discovered his secret, forgiven his impertinence in purloining her picture, and later agreed to marry him, delight had been followed by months of longing for this day.

Now she was here, his emotions threatened to overwhelm him.

He watched as she walked up the aisle towards him, if anything, more desirable a woman than she had been a girl. Her serene countenance and warm smile he had never forgotten in all their years apart.

He turned to her and she smiled.

The rector Mr Griffin approached; they had been warned by Anna Bingley that he was a solemn, almost doleful fellow, prone to making long, portentous sermons.

"Be warned, Cathy, he will not let you off with a few words of wisdom; Mr Griffin takes weddings very seriously. Prepare yourselves for a weighty homily," she'd said as they dined at Netherfield on the previous evening.

Mr Burnett and Catherine made an effort to maintain appropriate expressions of gravity as Mr Griffin droned on, reminding them of the duties of married couples to one another, warning them that Love, "while it conquers all, must be supported by those trusty lieutenants Faith and Respect." All this they knew yet, as was his wont, Mr Griffin reiterated with much seriousness these and other familiar sentiments for their benefit.

Plainly hearing little of the homily, Frank Burnett stared straight ahead at the stained-glass window behind the altar. Beside him, Catherine could sense his restlessness and in a moment of innocent mischief, her hand, concealed within the folds of her sleeve, crept surreptitiously into his. Very soon, she seemed to say, it will be over. His fingers curled around hers, confirming her impression that he had waited for a gesture from her and was grateful for her understanding. As they stood thus together, it was as though they had already been joined together in love, oblivious of Mr Griffin and the congregation around them, feeling only the joy of this day that had been so long in coming.

Then it was done. Mr Griffin led the way to the vestry, the organ played, bells pealed, and friends and relations milled around them, wishing them happiness; but they knew only the relief and joy of being at last together, man and wife, as they had always wished to be.

~❧~

In the days that followed, they spent but a day in London before travelling by train to Dover and crossing the channel to France, where Frank Burnett had lived and worked for many years. They had planned to stay a week in Paris and travel thence to Italy. If Paris was where Frank had learned his craft, it was in Italy that he had lost his heart to the fine arts. He had long wished to share his enthusiasm with Catherine, whose burgeoning interest he had encouraged from the earliest days of their association.

While they were not in time to witness the entire festival of the Grand Carnivale, which Frank had described to her in minute detail, Catherine did have the opportunity to view from the balcony of their hotel the amazing antics of persons young and old, as they danced and paraded up and down the Corso on foot, in carriages, or on horseback, exchanging volleys of confetti, sweets, and flowers as they passed.

The music, the colours, and the enormous energy of the scene below them brought a kind of high excitement such as she had never experienced before in her life. Never had she been in the midst of such bewitching entertainment. It absolutely assailed her senses. Turning to her husband, she saw him watching her, clearly pleased by her response.

"Is it as enjoyable as you thought it would be?" he asked.

Her eyes shone and she nodded. "Oh yes, indeed it is, and much more besides. All these people, so much vitality and high spirits, had you not told me of it, I should never have imagined it. I have seen nothing like it in all my life."

"Then you are glad we came to Italy?" he asked.

Her answer left him in no doubt. "Of course. I would not have missed it for the world."

These were by far the most delightful and enlightening days of Catherine's life. Not since childhood, certainly not since she had entered the gilded cage of Rosings, had she known such freedom to feel, think, and speak as she wished. Untramelled by the constraints imposed upon her by Lady Catherine's patronage and years of watchful compliance at Hunsford parsonage, where Dr Harrison's reputation took precedence over all else, she could now seek and respond to new experiences and emotions without reservation. Freed of her inhibitions and customary reticence, she could, with her husband's help, enjoy all that life offered them, delighting with him in their easy intimacy and close understanding.

Catherine had never been to France or Italy, nor even ventured outside the home counties, except to visit Pemberley or Bath. There were a myriad things Frank had told her of, which she was eager to see and learn, and since he was a most conscientious teacher, keen to show her all his favourite sights and places, their days were filled with the pleasures of stimulating and agreeable companionship. At the end of each day, her mind was brimming with images and ideas, all new and exhilarating. Catherine had never known such freedom, nor such fun.

Even sweeter was the joy of loving one another, secure in the knowledge that they had been emancipated from the tedium of conformity and were accountable to no one but each other. The openness and freshness of Italy and the liberality it afforded them was blessedly sweet. It enhanced every new experience, filling each day with new pleasures and each night with the hope of something more to look forward to on the morrow.

They travelled through several towns and picturesque little villages, until at last on a fine, clear day, they reached that most seductive of Italian cities— Florence. Frank had promised her she would be enchanted and she was.

For Catherine, everything about Florence was astonishing, and though she knew little of its complex history, her husband took special pleasure in introducing her to all that he had learned and loved there, delighting in the depth of her response. The splendid bridges over the river Arno, the palaces of the Medici with their works of art, of a scale and magnificence to take one's breath away, all set in a landscape of such exquisite loveliness, left Catherine filled with wonder and bereft of words.

Nothing at Rosings, with its grand collections of art and artifacts, had moved her as these did.

"I do not think I could ever absorb completely what I have seen here," she confessed one afternoon as they sat watching the sunlight retreat from the river into the hills, leaving smudges of indigo and smoky blue shadow across the landscape. "There is so much loveliness, I feel privileged to be here," and reaching for his hand, she thanked him, "especially with you to tell me all about it. I owe all this pleasure to you; without your guidance, I should not have known such beauty existed. Dear Frank, thank you."

He was deeply moved by her appreciation.

"Dearest Catherine, it has been the fulfilment of my fondest wish to have you here with me, to share my enjoyment of places and works of art which have obsessed and absorbed me for years. To recall our enjoyment of them in future years will be my special pleasure."

"I understand," she said softly, "it will be mine also."

～✥～

Even as she accepted Frank Burnett's love, Catherine had not imagined that at her age, she could feel as she did now.

The discovery that the passage of time had not dulled her capacity to feel passionately and enjoy being deeply loved brought profound and singular satisfaction. It was something entirely novel in Catherine's experience. Nothing in her life so far, or in her previous marriage, had prepared her it.

Writing to her sister, she spoke briefly of their travels in France and Italy, but more intensely of their shared happiness. Becky was struck by her candour.

> *How can I describe, dear Becky, the change in my life?*
>
> *So much has happened, we have shared so many wonderful days, there is too much to tell. Perhaps if I were to choose just one thing to illustrate what marriage to Frank has meant to me, it may help you understand. It is the difference between waking up alone in a cold bed, from which my husband has already risen to go about his parish duties, leaving me to get on with mine, and awakening to the warm presence of a man who has utterly transformed my life with his love. Need I say more?*

...she wrote, leaving Becky in no doubt of her meaning. Becky, more than any other person, could understand exactly how her sister felt.

As the days passed and the year slipped deeper into Winter, these shared experiences so engaged them, they were reluctant to acknowledge that it was time to return to England. But there were just two weeks to Christmas and they had an invitation to Pemberley. Catherine had not forgotten their obligations.

"Much as I have loved it, we have been away too long. Poor Becky must be tired of her own company; besides, we are expected at Pemberley on Christmas Eve," said she one morning, when a bitter wind sweeping down from the Alps had kept them indoors in their room, where a lively fire added comfort to inclination.

Turning away from the window, where he stood watching two little boys playing in the snow, her husband feigned astonishment. Why, he declared, only last night she had confessed to him as they lay in bed that her love for Italy was increasing with every day they spent in the country. She had professed she never wanted to leave.

"Am I to understand, my love, that you wish to leave Italy with all this beauty and return to a damp English Winter?" he asked and she, smiling, replied without dissembling, "Only because we must, Frank, we have some promises to keep; else I think I would happily stay here with you all Winter, for never have I been so thoroughly contented."

"Nor I, my dearest Catherine," was his heartfelt response, as he held her in his arms, unwilling at that moment to admit the need to depart. "If my only obligation was to our mutual happiness, I would not be able to give you a single reason to leave this lovely place. I should beg you to stay here with me all Winter and into Spring. But, I fear you are right, duty calls and it is probably time to return to England."

Plainly neither wished to end the pleasures they had enjoyed, yet both were well aware of their responsibilities.

Two days later, with the weather threatening to worsen as the Alpine winds stripped the last of the Autumn leaves from the oak trees and swirled them around the fountain in the piazza, they left Italy to return to England.

Taking a hired vehicle from Victoria Station, they drove to a hotel, where they spent the last night of their honeymoon, before journeying to Rosings Park on the morrow.

They found John Adams and Lilian settled comfortably into the house they had taken a few miles outside the boundaries of Rosings Park, while Becky had spent the final days of fine weather having more of her furniture moved down from London and installed at Edgewater.

Arriving at the Dower House, Catherine's newfound sense of freedom was renewed as the realisation dawned that for the first time she had a home of her own to share with a husband, one who had declared unashamedly that his chief preoccupation in life was ensuring her happiness.

It was the type of situation she had believed existed only in the romantic imaginations of young women whose wits had been addled by reading too many cheap novellas! No sensible woman of any intelligence would credit it. Indeed, a year ago she would have laughed to scorn anyone who had suggested such a possibility for herself. Yet, here she was, unable to contain her joy.

The house itself had been transformed in their absence.

Mrs Giles and her staff had cleaned, aired, and readied the rooms upstairs for them. Becky had generously provided new drapes and fine linen for their bedroom and filled the vases with sweet-scented lavender and Winter roses from the conservatory at Edgewater.

Every aspect combined to create for them a welcoming atmosphere of warmth and comfort, where for the foreseeable future, they would have only one another to please.

It was a prospect that could not fail to delight their hearts.

Postscript

ARRIVING AT PEMBERLEY ON Christmas Eve, they found a large party gathered there already. Pemberley looked splendid, as usual, while their host and hostess seemed in excellent spirits.

An excellent evening's entertainment of music followed a delectable meal provided in the best traditions of Pemberley House as Mr and Mrs Darcy welcomed their many guests.

That night, as the family and their guests retired to their rooms, Catherine began a letter to her mother, who had been prevented by ill health from making the journey to Derbyshire.

Giving her all the news, she wrote:

> *The Bingleys from Ashford Park and Netherfield, the Grantleys, Fitzwilliams, Wilsons, and Gardiners are all here.*
>
> *It is surely the biggest family gathering in many years. It seems such a pity Julian and Jessica could not be here, too.*

However, on Christmas Day, to almost everyone's surprise, a carriage arrived towards midday, bringing Julian Darcy and his wife. Mr and Mrs Darcy had kept their secret well; only they had known, because the rest of the party had believed the pair were not expected back in England before Easter. As they were overwhelmed with exclamations of pleasure and welcomed by all their relations, Jane Bingley had whispered to Catherine that Jessica was expecting a child early in the new year, "Which is why they have returned to England earlier than expected," she had said. "Julian insisted she must come home."

That I can well believe, wrote Catherine, continuing her letter that night, *and Mrs Darcy, too, must have wished that Jessica should return to Pemberley for her confinement.*

> *Mama, this must be the best news Mr and Mrs Darcy have had in years. I could see how very pleased they were, although nothing was said to the rest of the party. I daresay they will all discover it soon enough; there is no possibility of keeping such happy news secret for very long!*
>
> *Clearly Jessica's maid must be in her confidence; very soon the rest of the staff will know it, too. They looked remarkably well, especially Jessica, who is quite beautiful now and not at all weary, considering they have come directly from Southern Africa where, Frank informs me, it is still high Summer.*
>
> *Mama, I know you will be as pleased as I am for Jessica's mother, Mrs Courtney. I understand from Jane Bingley that poor Reverend Courtney is weaker now than he was a year ago and is not expected to last more than a few months. Sadly, he was too ill to come to Pemberley on Christmas Eve; Julian and Jessica have gone today to Kympton to call on him. It says much for their kindness and loyalty that they should do so, almost immediately after their long journey from South Africa.*
>
> *I am told, again by Jane Bingley, that since his marriage to Jessica, Julian Darcy is a changed man, far more thoughtful and concerned for others, she says, and his mother is said to be delighted. I do not doubt it.*

Catherine had no intimate knowledge of either Jessica Courtney or Julian Darcy, at least not since the days of their childhood, when Julian had visited Rosings with his parents. She had known little of the young man who had married her niece Josie Tate, and even less of the distinguished scientist who was now the husband of Jessica Courtney.

Too enmeshed in the matters of Hunsford parsonage and Lady Catherine's concerns, she had been appalled by Josie's marital problems and her tragic death, but had little knowledge of Julian's situation. Characteristically, she refused to make adverse judgments or apportion blame upon either of them, without sufficient information.

Distressed and guilt-ridden following her daughter's death, her sister Rebecca had confessed that Josie had at first been reluctant to accept young Julian Darcy's proposal, but had been persuaded by her mother to do so. Shocked by the revelation, Catherine had realised the sheer foolhardiness of such action, bringing happiness to neither partner and certain misery to both in due course.

Now, seeing Julian and Jessica together, she recognised in them a couple whose mutual affection seemed to sustain them completely.

Continuing her letter to her mother, Catherine wrote:

> *Julian and Jessica seem exceedingly happy. On occasions such as this, I cannot help thinking of poor Josie. Becky feels it, too. She blames herself for much of Josie's troubles and so, it would seem, does Mr Tate.*
>
> *Becky is still unhappy about Mr Tate going off to America; he seems unlikely to return to England. I do pray that she will find contentment again.*
>
> *Emily Courtney sends you her love. She looks tired and much older than her elder sister Caroline, yet Becky says she never complains. I have always thought she had the kindest heart, yet she appears to have had the hardest life of all.*
>
> *And now to some really good news!*
>
> *Tomorrow is Boxing Day and a big day at Pemberley. Young Anthony Darcy is to accompany his grandfather to the function at which the household staff and farm labourers receive their Christmas boxes. Cassy says he is very excited indeed.*
>
> *He is a handsome little fellow and devoted to his grandparents. Quite obviously, Mr Darcy is very proud of him.*

Catherine's letter did not fully convey her feelings at seeing young Anthony Darcy, bereft not only of his unhappy mother but deprived also of the benefit of a father's influence in his life. A fine-looking, tall, intelligent lad, he was a credit to his aunt Cassandra, who had raised him with love and care to fulfil his destiny as the next master of Pemberley. Yet, to Catherine he seemed an unusually grave child. She could not help wondering how much he knew of his parents' predicament and to what extent this knowledge would colour his own life.

It was a question to which she could find no answer.

It was late and Catherine had almost concluded her letter, when the door opened and her husband entered the room. Seeing her still at the bureau, he hesitated, not wishing to disturb her, but she held out her hand to him and he came to her.

"I am almost done, dearest, will you let me conclude my letter to Mama? I shall not be much longer," she said gently.

"Of course," he said, staying with her while she completed her letter.

She let him read over her shoulder as she wrote, knowing he would take pleasure from the last few sentences.

> *Frank sends his love and together with mine and Becky's, I hope it will help keep you warm and happy this Christmas season. We expect to travel down with Jonathan and Anna early in January and hope to spend a few days with you before returning to Kent, to prepare for the opening of our parish school. We are all very excited about it.*
>
> *Dear Mama, you are much missed. I should have liked to tell you all about our time in Italy, and I do so wish you could have been here with us to see how deeply happy I am. Frank and I, though we are far from being rich, want for nothing more than what we have now, for we have each other at last.*
>
> *One thing I do know; we are on the threshold of a wonderful year! Do take care, Mama, and mind that you avoid cold rooms and draughts, which you know will make you ill.*
>
> *God bless you,*
> *Your loving daughter*
> *Catherine Burnett.*

"There, it is done," she said, rising from her chair and turning to her husband, who had waited patiently for her.

"Good, your mother will surely enjoy the news from Pemberley," he said, drawing her into his arms. "But I, too, have some news which I am quite certain will please you."

When she seemed surprised, he added in a quiet, matter-of-fact way, "Mr Darcy wishes to make a donation towards the Parish school at Hunsford, in memory of his father-in-law, Mr Bennet."

Catherine could not believe her ears; this was better news than she could ever have hoped for. Fixing him with a quizzical expression, she demanded to know, "Frank, is this your doing?"

He smiled. "No—well, not entirely. I believe Jonathan Bingley has done a great deal more than I have. He has taken your cause very much to heart and of course, Mr Darcy values his opinion greatly. Indeed, I have only mentioned the matter of the school to Mr Darcy once, tonight before dinner, when he was showing me the treasures of the Pemberley library."

"Did you say we needed money for the school library?" she asked.

"I did not... at least not in so many words. I did mention the fact that you intended to use some part of your legacy from Lady Catherine to establish a library for the school, to which he responded that it would not be right that you should do so. Mr Darcy said no more at the time, but when we spoke again after dinner, he informed me that he had discussed the matter with Mrs Darcy and they had decided to make a significant donation to the school in memory of her late father Mr Bennet, particularly for the provision of a library."

Catherine had no words to express her joy as she tightened her arms around him.

"Oh Frank, I did tell you Mr Darcy was a most generous man, did I not?"

"You certainly did," he said, smiling, "and it appears that like Mr Darcy, Mr Bennet also believed in the value of education and the importance of reading. Mr Darcy wishes very much to encourage you in your endeavour. He suggested also that I should break the news to you tonight, as a sort of late Christmas present."

Her loving response was predictable and greatly appreciated. "He was right," she said, "I could not have asked for a better gift."

As they prepared for bed, he asked, as though it were an afterthought, "Catherine, do you really believe this is going to be a wonderful year?"

She replied without hesitation, "Indeed I do; what's more, I intend to enjoy every moment of it and you, my dear husband, are invited to join me."

It was an invitation he could not possibly refuse.

Appendix

A list of the main characters in *Recollections of Rosings*:

Mrs Catherine Harrison—daughter of Charlotte Lucas and Mr Collins.
Dr Harrison—her husband and parson of the parish of Hunsford.
Miss Lilian Harrison—their youngest daughter.
Rebecca Tate (Becky)—Catherine's sister.
Mr Anthony Tate—her husband, a publisher.
Mr John Adams—curator at Rosings Park.
Mr Frank Burnett—a former librarian at Rosings, who returns some years later to assist with the conservation of the treasures of Rosings Park.
Mr Jonathan Bingley—son of Jane Bennet and Mr Bingley; nephew of the Darcys, and a former manager of the Rosings Estate.
Anna Bingley—his second wife (his first wife, Amelia-Jane Collins, was killed in an accident).
Anne-Marie Elliott—Jonathan Bingley's daughter.
Colin Elliott MP—her husband, a member of Parliament.
Mrs Caroline Fitzwilliam (née Gardiner)—Elizabeth's cousin and wife of Colonel Fitzwilliam of Matlock.
Lady Isabel Ashton—a London socialite and friend of Becky Tate.
Mr Joshua Armstrong—her cousin.

And from the pages of *Pride and Prejudice*:

Mr and Mrs Darcy of Pemberley

Mr and Mrs Bingley of Ashford Park

Lady Catherine de Bourgh of Rosings Park

Colonel Fitzwilliam—Mr Darcy's cousin

Mrs Charlotte Collins (née Lucas) of Longbourn—Elizabeth's friend

Acknowledgements

The author acknowledges her debt to Miss Jane Austen, whose genius has been her inspiration.

Special thanks to Ms Claudia Taylor for her invaluable research and advice, to Marissa O'Donnell for her artwork and to Robert and Anthony for technical help.

To all those from Alaska to New Zealand, who read The Pemberley Chronicles series and write to say how much they love them, many, many thanks.

—Rebecca Ann Collins
www.geocities.com/shadesofpemberley
www.rebeccaanncollins.com

About the Author

A lifelong fan of Jane Austen, Rebecca Ann Collins first read *Pride and Prejudice* at the tender age of twelve. She fell in love with the characters and since then has devoted years of research and study to the life and works of her favorite author. As a teacher of literature and a librarian, she has gathered a wealth of information about Miss Austen and the period in which she lived and wrote, which became the basis of her books about the Pemberley families. The popularity of The Pemberley Chronicles series with Jane Austen fans has been her reward.

With a love of reading, music, art, and gardening, Ms Collins claims she is very comfortable in the period about which she writes, and feels great empathy with the characters she portrays. While she enjoys the convenience of modern life, she finds much to admire in the values and world view of Jane Austen.

The Pemberley Chronicles

A Companion Volume to Jane Austen's Pride and Prejudice
The Pemberley Chronicles: Book 1
Rebecca Ann Collins

"A lovely complementary novel to Jane Austen's *Pride and Prejudice.*
Austen would surely give her smile of approval."
—Beverly Wong, author of *Pride & Prejudice Prudence*

The weddings are over, the saga begins

The guests (including millions of readers and viewers) wish the two happy couples health and happiness. As the music swells and the credits roll, two things are certain: Jane and Bingley will want for nothing, while Elizabeth and Darcy are to be the happiest couple in the world!

Elizabeth and Darcy's personal stories of love, marriage, money, and children are woven together with the threads of social and political history of England in the nineteenth century. As changes in industry and agriculture affect the people of Pemberley and the surrounding countryside, the Darcys strive to be progressive and forward-looking while upholding beloved traditions.

"Those with a taste for the balance and humour of Austen will find a worthy companion volume."
—*Book News*

978-1-4022-1153-9 • $14.96 US/ $17.95 CAN/ £7.99 UK

The Women of Pemberley

The acclaimed Pride and Prejudice *sequel series*
The Pemberley Chronicles: Book 2
REBECCA ANN COLLINS

"Yet another wonderful work by Ms. Collins."
—BEVERLY WONG, AUTHOR OF *Pride & Prejudice Prudence*

A new age is dawning

Five women—strong, intelligent, independent of mind, and in the tradition of many Jane Austen heroines—continue the legacy of Pemberley into a dynamic new era at the start of the Victorian Age. Events unfold as the real and fictional worlds intertwine, linked by the relationship of the characters to each other and to the great estate of Pemberley, the heart of their community.

With some characters from the beloved works of Jane Austen, and some new from the author's imagination, the central themes of love, friendship, marriage, and a sense of social obligation remain, showcased in the context of the sweeping political and social changes of the age.

"The stories are so well told one would enjoy them even if they were not sequels to any other novel."
—*Book News*

9/8-1-4022-1154-6 • $14.96 US/ $17.95 CAN/ £7.99 UK

Netherfield Park Revisited

The acclaimed **Pride and Prejudice** *sequel series*

The Pemberley Chronicles: Book 3

REBECCA ANN COLLINS

"A very readable and believable tale for readers
who like their romance with a historical flavor." —*Book News*

Love, betrayal, and changing times for the Darcys and the Bingleys

Three generations of the Darcy and the Bingley families evolve against a backdrop of the political ideals and social reforms of the mid-Victorian era.

Jonathan Bingley, the handsome, distinguished son of Charles and Jane Bingley, takes center stage, returning to Hertfordshire as master of Netherfield Park. A deeply passionate and committed man, Jonathan is immersed in the joys and heartbreaks of his friends and family and his own challenging marriage. At the same time, he is swept up in the changes of the world around him.

Netherfield Park Revisited combines captivating details of life in mid-Victorian England with the ongoing saga of Jane Austen's beloved *Pride and Prejudice* characters.

"Ms. Collins has done it again!" —BEVERLY WONG, AUTHOR OF *Pride & Prejudice Prudence*

978-1-4022-1155-3 • $14.95 US/ $15.99 CAN/ £7.99 UK

The Ladies of Longbourn

The acclaimed Pride and Prejudice *sequel series*

The Pemberley Chronicles: Book 4

REBECCA ANN COLLINS

"Interesting stories, enduring themes, gentle humour,
and lively dialogue." —*Book News*

*A complex and charming young woman of the Victorian age, tested to
the limits of her endurance*

The bestselling *Pemberley Chronicles* series continues the saga of the Darcys and
Bingleys from Jane Austen's *Pride and Prejudice* and introduces imaginative new
characters.

Anne-Marie Bradshaw is the granddaughter of Charles and Jane Bingley. Her father
now owns Longbourn, the Bennet's estate in Hertfordshire. A young widow after
a loveless marriage, Anne-Marie and her stepmother
Anna, together with Charlotte Collins, widow of the
unctuous Mr. Collins, are the Ladies of Longbourn.
These smart, independent women challenge the
conventional roles of women in the Victorian era,
while they search for ways to build their own lasting
legacies in an ever-changing world.

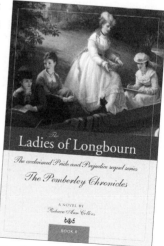

Jane Austen's original characters—Darcy, Elizabeth,
Bingley, and Jane—anchor a dramatic story full of
wit and compassion.

"A masterpiece that reaches the heart."
—BEVERLEY WONG, AUTHOR OF *Pride & Prejudice Prudence*

978-1-4022-1219-2 • $14.95 US/ $15.99 CAN/ £7.99 UK

Mr. Darcy's Diary
AMANDA GRANGE

"A gift to a new generation of Darcy fans
and a treat for existing fans as well." —AUSTENBLOG

The only place Darcy could share his innermost feelings...

...was in the private pages of his diary. Torn between his sense of duty to his family name and his growing passion for Elizabeth Bennet, all he can do is struggle not to fall in love. A skillful and graceful imagining of the hero's point of view in one of the most beloved and enduring love stories of all time.

What readers are saying:

"A delicious treat for all Austen addicts."

"Amanda Grange knows her subject...I ended up reading the entire book in one sitting."

"Brilliant, you could almost hear Darcy's voice...I was so sad when it came to an end. I loved the visions she gave us of their married life."

"Amanda Grange has perfectly captured all of Jane Austen's clever wit and social observations to make *Mr. Darcy's Diary* a must read for any fan."

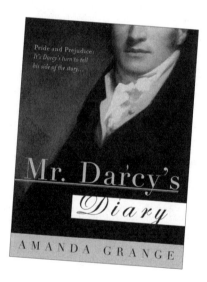

978-1-4022-0876-8 • $14.95 US/ $19.95 CAN/ £7.99 UK

Mr. and Mrs. Fitzwilliam Darcy: Two Shall Become One
SHARON LATHAN

"Highly entertaining... I felt fully immersed in the time period. Well done!" —*Romance Reader at Heart*

A fascinating portrait of a timeless, consuming love

It's Darcy and Elizabeth's wedding day, and the journey is just beginning as Jane Austen's beloved *Pride and Prejudice* characters embark on the greatest adventure of all: marriage and a life together filled with surprising passion, tender self-discovery, and the simple joys of every day.

As their love story unfolds in this most romantic of Jane Austen sequels, Darcy and Elizabeth each reveal to the other how their relationship blossomed from misunderstanding to perfect understanding and harmony, and a marriage filled with romance, sensuality and the beauty of a deep, abiding love.

What readers are saying:

"This journey is truly amazing."

"What a wonderful beginning to this truly beautiful marriage."

"Could not stop reading."

"So beautifully written...making me feel as though I was in the room with Lizzy and Darcy...and sharing in all of the touching moments between."

978-1-4022-1523-0 • $14.99 US/ $15.99 CAN/ £7.99 UK

Loving Mr. Darcy: Journeys Beyond Pemberley
SHARON LATHAN

"A romance that transcends time." —*The Romance Studio*

Darcy and Elizabeth embark on the journey of a lifetime

Six months into his marriage to Elizabeth Bennet, Darcy is still head over heels in love, and each day offers more opportunities to surprise and delight his beloved bride. Elizabeth has adapted to being the Mistress of Pemberley, charming everyone she meets and handling her duties with grace and poise. Just when it seems life can't get any better, Elizabeth gets the most wonderful news. The lovers leave the serenity of Pemberley, traveling through the sumptuous landscape of Regency England, experiencing the lavish sights, sounds, and tastes around them. With each day come new discoveries as they become further entwined, body and soul.

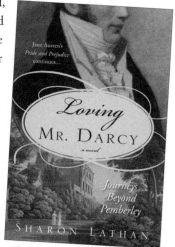

What readers are saying:

"Darcy's passion for love and life with Lizzy is brought to the forefront and captured beautifully."

"Sharon Lathan is a wonderful writer… I believe that Jane Austen herself would love this story as much as I did."

"The historical backdrop of the book is unbelievable—I actually felt like I could see all the places where the Darcys traveled."

"Truly captures the heart of Darcy & Elizabeth! Very well written and totally hot!"

978-1-4022-1741-8 • $14.99 US/ $18.99 CAN/ £7.99 UK